Xima

Rich Blecher

Ordering Information: Rich.Blecher@yahoo.com

Print ISBN: 978-1-7348861-0-8
eBook ISBN: 978-1-7348861-1-5

Printed in the United States of America.

First Edition

This is a work of fiction. Any resemblance to actual events or persons, living or dead, is entirely coincidental.

Acknowledgment

When writing your first book, you may have no idea what you are doing or even if it's an exciting story. I owe much of this book to my friends and family who read through the initial draft, provided guidance and critical feedback, opened my mind to write better, then proofread the final draft to ensure I hit the mark. They offered help with character names and some of the storylines. Their support was critical to keep me going and influencing me to complete my first novel. Thank you so much to Tonya K., Stephanie S., Sarah H., and Nik H.

I could not have done this without you.

Table of Contents

Part I - Earth

Chapter 1

2140 AD, Earth

"Don't step on that mine!" Colonel Jenkins yelled.

I fearfully leaped to the side and saw the small patch of dirt he was pointing at, then sighed in relief.

"That was close," he added, nodding his head and looking expectantly for me to thank him for saving my life.

He continued his whittling where he usually sat, in the far corner of the compound where no one bothered him

Colonel Jenkins was an odd man. Some said he went crazy in the war, others claimed the faction had poisoned him, but in reality, he was a kind man who told us stories—the type of stories that weren't told in school and the type our parents didn't want us listening to. But we would meet with him from time to time, hoping to listen to a new adventure or history lesson we hadn't heard before.

"What are you making, Colonel Jenkins?" one of the other boys asked.

"Always face the Griff," he whispered. "Always face the Griff." He said that every time we met with him, but we never knew what he meant.

One time, I asked my father what a Griff was. He knew right away that I'd been talking with Colonel Jenkins and said there was no such thing, that it was just something in the old man's imagination.

We lived in what was left of a suburb of New York City. My father worked for the American Defense Services (ADS) as a scientist. ADS was initially founded as an organization made up of police and military to protect and defend the people from the ever growing faction. The faction called themselves Friends of Green or FOG. They started as a peaceful protesting organization, but over time, they grew into a militant organization creating a civil war like the world has never seen.

For as long as I could remember, my father, mother, and I lived safely in a fortified housing compound. A coarse brick wall as tall as my father surrounded hundreds of houses in our community.

Everyone who lived inside had some affiliation with the ADS. Those who didn't were on their own in the cities and were fed via the local synthetic food distribution centers. It was not unlike how food was given out at the homeless shelters of the distant past. The one exception was Colonel Jenkins. We had no idea why he lived inside our walls—he was just a retired hermit with no family to speak of.

Growing up in a walled compound was frustrating. My parents said it was for our protection, but I never knew what I was being protected from. I'd heard stories about what happened outside, but, for the most part, none of the adults talked about it around the kids. My friends and I would discuss ways we could escape and build our own city or even travel through space and live on the planet Xima.

The synthetic foods had various flavors, and the pasty jell it came in was something we all grew used to. Occasionally, we'd get real, natural food like bread, some type of vegetable, or meat on very rare occasions. We never knew what kind of meat it was. Sometimes, it was reddish in color, other times, white or gray. The flavors and textures were quite diverse, too, ranging from savory and moist to sour and chewy. We would imagine what type of animal it came from based on those clues. We heard that, despite the ADS's protection, extremist members of FOG attacked nearby farms from time to time.

As we grew older, we kids would climb on the wall and look out beyond the compound. We lived on a large hill and could see tall buildings, some old vehicles, and piles of rubble in the distance. There was a large river and a forest nearby, but there wasn't much else to see. Sometimes, we could hear dull booming noises that sounded like explosions. I was told it was simply construction work or thunder, but we knew it was another FOG bombing.

We went to school during the day to learn the basics of math, science, English, and, of course, world history. We were also taught about the history of space exploration over the past two hundred years—from the first people to set foot on the moon, to cameras that could see deep into space, to the first people on Mars.

Some of the better lessons came from Colonel Jenkins. He was always whittling something while he sat near a part of the lower wall where we could see for miles—the forest and rivers and some old fields that once grew bountiful crops of beans, corn, and grains for bread.

He told us the history of how FOG grew and would burn entire croplands. Thousands of acres were reduced to ash, and if anyone challenged them, they would be killed. He told us little parts of history like that with long pauses as he sculpted his tiny characters. He told us that FOG would do the same to farm animals; they would kill all the livestock to reduce the amount of carbon dioxide in the air and save oxygen.

We would ask our teacher about these stories. Every time, she knew we'd gotten the stories from Colonel Jenkins, and each time, she confirmed they were true but were a dark part of our history that she didn't want to teach.

* * *

In school, we were taught about the alarming studies many years ago, which convinced the world that the output of carbon dioxide nearly exceeded the output of oxygen in the world.

Since the earth is mostly nitrogen, oxygen, and carbon dioxide, animal life, including humans, has always relied on oxygen over carbon dioxide to survive. As man began to burn fossil fuels, deplete forests worldwide, and increase oxygen-breathing animal life, carbon dioxide levels—measured in parts per million (ppm)—increased as well. Once carbon dioxide levels surpassed oxygen, scientists warned, oxygen-breathing life would begin to struggle to survive.

Estimates of when Earth's carbon dioxide ppm would exceed oxygen ranged from fifty to five hundred years. The consensus was that something needed to be done or else all oxygen-breathing life would suffer. They differed, however, in their proposed solutions.

One day, I asked our teacher if what Colonel Jenkins said about burning crops and killing livestock was true.

She hesitated, walked to the window for a moment, then turned back to us. "Yes, it's true." She went on to tell us that at first, the conflict was limited to political parties feuding in heated debates on stages. It later became something far more dangerous. Protest movements grew around the world. Calls for political action turned into violence. Small, organized groups formed and tried to take matters into their own hands. The cattle farmers were easy targets. The protesters thought that killing all the beef cattle would start to resolve the oxygen depletion crisis. In their attempts to protect their livelihood, farm families found themselves embroiled in a battle that would eventually cost them their homes and, for some, their lives.

Motivated by the fear spread by politicians and the media, chaos was everywhere, and it was festering like an infection throughout the world.

When we asked our teacher what leaders of the world were doing to solve the crisis, she explained that there had been mining camps on the moon and Mars for many years.

At one point, there was an effort to colonize Mars and send large groups of people there. It would take time, but it was a peace offering of sorts to initiate off-world population growth.

The ADS's plan to save Earth and appease FOG had been to build a large underground city on Mars for people to move to.

Scientists had found a way to extract oxygen from the vast amount of carbon dioxide on Mars and refine it. Relocating to Mars would help to reduce the population on Earth, allowing it time to grow more trees and produce more oxygen than it had in centuries. The ADS had planned to create large cities within Mars over time and, eventually, grow its own vegetation.

For over ten years, engineers built tunnels deep within Mars. Large ice pockets were found within the planet's surface, which were used to create the organic water needed to sustain life. The ice pockets, consisting of hydrogen and oxygen, covered many square miles—similar to the glaciers on Earth.

The carbon dioxide on Mars made up over 90 percent of the atmosphere, and with sufficient Mars oxygen ISRU experiments, or MOXIEs, it was estimated that millions of people could breathe oxygen for thousands of years underneath the planet's surface, which wasn't feasible on Earth due to either the heat or water impacting the amount of deep underground tunneling required.

Hundreds of workers had built a fantastic infrastructure, with shipments from Earth continuously bringing supplies to expand the work underground.

* * *

By the time I was thirteen years old, I knew every part of our compound—from the nearly dead apple trees Mr. Jackson kept trying to grow near the wall to the aromatic smell of our backup generator at the rear of the compound.

One time, we found Colonel Jenkins sitting by the fence that housed the generator. He was nearly done with one of his figures and showed us. It fit in the palm of his hand and resembled a dog with wings. He said, "The Griff. Never turn your back on the Griff." He showed off some of his other work too. There was a bird, something that resembled a deer, and several versions of the Griff. None of us ever read about any such animal in our books—not even the ones about Xima—so we weren't sure what a Griff was or even *where* it was. We only knew it was something Colonel Jenkins had on his mind a lot.

Aside from academics and watching Colonel Jenkins, we also played on the playgrounds and in our friends' yards—whether it was soccer, kickball, or even role-playing "FOG vs. ADS," which was more of a game of tag than anything else.

Within the compound, there were narrow concrete holes in the ground covered with locked round metal plates. When we pretended to be Fog, we found a few holes with broken locks on the covers and hid in them. We soon memorized all of those hiding places. So, whoever used them would lose, which may not have been so bad, as it smelled quite horrid in those little hiding places and no one knew where the holes led. Some of the kids thought it was a secret bunker, and others said it was where dead people went. I leaned toward the latter, as the rank and pungent smell, mixed with a tinge of sickening sweetness, was enough to make me vomit.

There were also many old gas-powered cars on the compound we would play in, pretending to drive to places we learned about in history class.

Sharp, rusted springs and toxic fumes made those husks of vehicles a hazardous playground, but as kids, we played with anything we could get our hands on.

Electric cars were the only ones still in use. Solar power charged the car batteries, and wind turbines met the compound's energy needs. In addition, there was a fenced-off area where a large gasoline-powered generator was housed. The generator was supposed to power the compound in an emergency, but I'd never seen it used—perhaps because gasoline was so rare.

We were taught to use electricity sparingly to avoid the risk of an outage, which would switch on the precious generator.

My mom would often meet with other mothers in the compound. I rarely knew what they did, but she would bring me along and tell me to hang out with the kids while they had their meetings. Sometimes, I'd listen to their conversations by hiding under the window of the room they were in. They spoke about the conditions in the cities outside of our compound and wondered how people survived. They'd also talk about small cities that had been pillaged by FOG and the people who were forced to pledge their allegiance to it.

They talked about the many children in the orphanages and would always try to figure out how they could help, but the ADS forbade any residents from going outside our walls unescorted, which made that sort of activism difficult.

I heard terrifying rumors of gangs that roamed outside the walls of our compound, who wouldn't hesitate to mercilessly ambush travelers for food or clothing.

Everyone was given a food and clothing allowance, but the production of clothing was slow, which created a mob-like atmosphere whenever it was available. People would fight their way in to get their hands on a scrap of cloth, even if it didn't fit them. There were always conflicts. In the cities, starving people fought and died for the most basic necessities for survival in a deprived population.

Fortunately, in our compound, interactions were much more civil, and everyone supported each other.

We had family gatherings on occasion. The moms would help set up and take care of the kids, but the fathers would stand out of hearing range and talk. Anytime one of us kids would approach, they'd tell us to go away. Despite his best efforts to hide his work from me, I learned what my father did for the ADS—somewhat. I only knew he did something with medicine.

We never really knew what other parents did to support the ADS, but it was clear they were all involved somehow.

During one family gathering, we kids played soccer when we saw Colonel Jenkins sitting in his normal corner of the wall, but he wasn't carving anything. Instead, he was drawing something in the dirt along the wall. We walked up to him, and I asked, "What are you doing, Colonel Jenkins?"

"Always face the Griff," was his usual response, and then he told us more about FOG and why they became so destructive.

He told us that nearly half a million square miles of farmland were covered in wind generators or solar panels. Many billions of dollars were funneled into programs that attempted to improve Earth's future. The use of fossil fuels gradually reduced until, eventually, they provided only 10 percent of the world's energy. Almost all available land—land which was previously used for crops or cattle grazing—was converted to natural energy generators with the hope that other green vegetation would grow around it to enhance greater oxygen-to-carbon-dioxide ratio.

He went into a whisper and motioned us to get closer as though what he was saying was highly classified.

Around the year 2080, Colonel Jenkins explained, a group of world leaders met in a secret location in Switzerland. They discussed the economic impact of green energy and how it wasn't cost-effective, especially in comparison to nuclear or fossil fuels. They also reached the conclusion that they couldn't afford to subsidize the new harvesting techniques being employed by farmers, which produced very little yield.

The solar panels and windmill blades couldn't be recycled, and rebuilding them was more expensive than manufacturing new ones. The governments were in a no-win situation. They knew that an uprising would be even more costly than it had been in the past if they converted back to the old ways. The price of repairing millions of systems across the planet couldn't be sustained indefinitely without the governments taking over the countries and regulating everything to include the people themselves. An authoritarian system was exactly what governments had tried to avoid, but appeared to be the only way to control the people and stop the violence.

Collectively, at the Switzerland Accord, the world leaders engineered a solution that betrayed the ideals of FOG. They would no longer sustain the natural-energy-producing generators and would instead secretly supply new fossil fuel plants. They also agreed to shift their focus away from Mars to pursue the newly discovered planet, Xima.

Then, Colonel Jenkins said, "I was part of the first ADS squad on Xima, and that's when I encountered… never turn your back on the Griff!"

* * *

When I was fourteen, I finally managed to confront my father about the nature of his work for the ADS—a topic of much curiosity and speculation among the kids in the compound. All of my friends concocted wild explanations for their fathers' secrecy. When I finally got the truth out of him, I was, frankly, disappointed…

He developed medicines and technologies that were intended to make everyone stronger and healthier. He would give me a shot occasionally, telling me it would ward off some disease, but I'd never actually seen anyone get sick in our compound. I hated getting shots, but he said it was to keep me healthy.

He was always very stressed and worked late hours. Whenever he did come home, he would sleep, eat, and then leave again. He rarely had time to spend with me.

One afternoon, he came home earlier than usual and sat me down at the kitchen table. He locked the doors and pulled down the shades.

A worried look crossed his face. For an instant, he looked like a man on the run—chased by something I could not see or understand. It made me nervous.

"Zack, I need to give you another shot, but this time it might hurt a little more than usual—and it'll leave a lump under your skin." He opened a small case, which contained a syringe with the thickest needle I'd ever seen. It looked like some tool used to fix the wind turbines, not something that belonged lodged beneath my skin. It made my heart sink to my gut.

"Please, Dad. I don't want to," I said, moving to stand.

My father placed his hand on my leg.

"Trust me, Zack. It's important—and no matter what anyone asks, never tell a single person about this. Not even your mother."

He pulled the large syringe out of its case. I tried to escape and run out of the room, but he grabbed my arm and held me down again.

"Zack, this is necessary. One day, you'll understand."

I saw a small, black, ball-like object floating in the liquid inside the syringe.

My heart raced as I strained against the back of the chair and braced myself. I didn't want that thing inside of me.

"What is it?" I asked, staring at the tiny object floating in the liquid. I shuddered at the thought of what it might do to me.

"It's something that will help you grow stronger. Now, please, I need to do this. Grip the chair with your other hand and turn your head. I'll try to make it quick."

I did as I was told and grimaced in agony when he punctured my skin with the needle.

I cried out, "It hurts, Dad!"

"Hold still… almost finished," he said. "There, all done." He placed a bandage on my arm. "Now remember, never tell anyone. Your life will be in danger if you do."

I grabbed my arm and felt a lump under the skin. The pain was excruciating. Tears rolled down my cheeks as I looked up at him.

He smiled in the same way my mother would when she was concerned and said, "It's a medicine that could cure millions, and you'll notice it working in time." He pulled me in close to give me a hug. He never hugged me, but he held me close for a long time. "Don't worry, Zack. You won't even notice it after a while." He stared at me, and I saw tears form in his eyes.

"What's the matter, Dad?"

He hugged me again. "I love you, son. So very much. Promise me you won't tell anyone of this. If FOG ever found out you had this…" He never finished, but I knew whatever it was couldn't be good.

I nodded and embraced him in return. "I won't tell anyone, Dad."

The next few days went on like normal. The lump in my arm wasn't all that painful, but it remained noticeable—at least to me. I didn't know if I actually felt the device under my skin, or if it was just in my mind. But I knew it was in there—doing what, I didn't know.

Chapter 2

A few more weeks went by. My father seemed anxious. He was always looking out the window, checking to make sure the doors were locked—and he stopped going to work completely. Any sudden noises would cause him to leap up from wherever he sat. He had stayed home every day since he'd given me the shot, which wasn't like him.

I'd wanted to ask my father about his plans for my fourteenth birthday, but I decided to ask my mother instead. As I entered my parents' bedroom, her pallid face told me that she was concerned about him too. "Leave your father alone," she said. "There are more important things than your birthday right now. We'll celebrate it soon."

He would stay awake long after I went to bed each night—his dark, baggy eyes gave him away. I couldn't help but think he was in some type of trouble.

* * *

An explosion ripped through the house, waking me up from a sound sleep. I had no idea what time it was, but I heard a commotion toward the front of the house. I jumped out of bed in a panic and walked to my bedroom door when my father breathlessly rushed into my room. He grabbed my arm and pulled me quickly to the back door of our home.

"Zack, you need to run and hide—hide somewhere no one will find you. Quick, run!"

A gunshot echoed through the house, and I heard the sound of my mother crying out. I ran away as fast as I could. Barefoot and wearing only my pajamas, I fled swiftly in the direction of my friend's house.

I made it a couple hundred feet away before I was stopped by the sound of more gunfire back at the house. I turned around to see my father lying on the ground. ADS men in military uniforms with lights and guns swarmed from the back door of the house. I was blinded by a dozen flashlights pointed at me.

"There he is. Get him!"

I turned and ran as they charged toward me. My fright made my legs move faster than they ever had before. I heard a gunshot and the sound of something whizzing by me. I remembered one of the drain holes near my friend's house that didn't have a lock on it, but I didn't want them following me there.

I had a head start, so I ran around the corner of my friend's house and stopped suddenly in front of Colonel Jenkins.

"Quick, under the car," he said, pointing to an old car in the yard that we played in. I dove to the ground, scrambling to wedge myself beneath the hunk of metal that had been there for decades. The sound of fabric tearing made me stop for a moment, as I realized my pajamas were snagged on a piece of metal, but I was soon able to move into position and hide.

My heart and mind raced. *Did the ADS kill my parents? They can't just kill people in the compound.* I tried to remain quiet, but I was breathing erratically. Lights of houses came on around the neighborhood as people were awakened by the explosion and gunfire. I knew one of the cement holes in the ground was only about twenty feet from me, but if the house next to me turned on their light, I'd probably be seen.

"I saw him run this way!" Colonel Jenkins yelled out in the distance, distracting them from me.

The ADS men ran by the car and kept running. When I could no longer hear them, I crawled out to run toward the hole in the ground. Prying the heavy cover off was always difficult, and it proved an even greater challenge while I panicked. I finally got my fingers underneath the lid and slid it aside. I saw the men with their flashlights coming my way.

As I eased the heavy metal cover back over the entrance, I saw the men looking over the car I had just been hiding under only moments ago. *They would have found me for sure.* I slowly lowered the cover back into place, making as little sound as possible, then descended the iron bars of the ladder on the wall of the narrow concrete tube. I could still hear the men's footsteps as they raced by overhead.

Whew! Thankfully, only us kids know about the broken locks on these holes.

It was completely dark in the tunnel. I couldn't see my hands, which were mere inches from my face, yet I carefully reached for the next rung of the ladder and climbed down. *But down to where?* We would hide in here when we played, but no one actually went down to the bottom.

It smelled like a bathroom that had been used by someone with the runs. The scent already made me want to throw up, but I had to continue going down. I found my entire body shaking as though I was freezing, yet the temperature was warm.

Each step I took was hesitant as my feet and hands shivered with fear. I reached down each time, hoping for another step, not knowing how far down the tunnel went. Soon, I moved my foot around in the dark for a rung below the one I was on, but I didn't feel anything except the wall. The sound of trickling water below confused me, and the stench somehow worsened. I didn't know how far down the next rung was, so I lowered myself a little more, trying to feel for the bottom, when my hands suddenly slipped from the metal rungs.

I gasped as I fell what, fortunately, turned out to be only a few feet into the dark, rank water below. The smell was unbearable, and I felt like throwing up. But I held it back. I could see nothing but darkness. It was as though I had suddenly gone blind. I reached around, only to find walls on either side of the water. I was in some type of drainage system. I stood there, confused and unsure of what to do next as the water ran around my legs.

Why would the ADS come after me and my family? Will they find the broken lock to this tunnel?

I thought about waiting for a little while and doubling back to see what had happened. I reached up for where I thought the ladder may have been but could no longer find it. Only darkness surrounded me as I stood completely still, trying not to cry—but my knees suddenly buckled, sending me to kneel in the revolting smell of sewage. Everything that had played out over the past several minutes flashed through my mind, and I began to sob.

Why would they shoot at me or my parents? Will my neighbors turn me in if I go back? I didn't know how long I was there but realized I couldn't stay where I was. *Perhaps following this waterway will lead me out? Then I can find help. But who will help me if the ADS wants to kill me?* I didn't understand anything that was happening around me.

I spent what seemed like hours walking barefoot through the wet stench before I noticed some light ahead of me. I could begin to make out the concrete lining of the tunnel and the water current running in front of me. My legs carried me faster, and as I rounded a bend, the orange glow of early morning appeared through some vertical metal bars that seemed to be intended to prevent anyone from coming in—and which, unfortunately, prevented me from getting out. As I approached and looked out through the bars, I saw the tunnel's filthy water pouring out into a pond below.

Peering out of the grate, I noticed a forest on one side of the pond, and on the other, an open field scattered with what looked like burnt cars. The charred frames looked like rusted, metal rocks protruding out of the majestic bending grass. I gripped the bars and scanned the area for any sign of human life – I saw no one.

I was outside of the compound. Memories of my mother talking to other mothers about the horrors outside of the compound flooded my mind. But I was blocked from going forward, so I sat along the edge of the tunnel above the water line. I broke down and cried. That was where it would all end.

The bump on my arm was still sore where that *thing* was injected. I thought about my father and how he wouldn't have taken the risk to give me something if it wasn't important, and then I realized that I couldn't give up on him.

The bars were too close together for me to fit between. If I was just a little thinner, I might have slipped between them. Unfortunately, my chest and head couldn't quite squeeze through. I saw a crack in some of the cement on the side where the shorter bars went in. Then I noticed a small metal rod, perhaps six inches long, at the bottom of the grate with water flowing over it.

I grabbed the slimy piece of metal and tried to pry at some of the cracks in the cement. I picked at it with my fingers and tried to wedge the rod into the crevice. My fingers were soon bleeding from my attempts, but I had managed to chip away a little more. It was getting brighter outside, and soon people would be moving around. I wanted to get out of there before anyone saw me.

The pain in my fingers was excruciating. The blood began to look like finger painting on the cement from the cuts on my fingertips, but

I kept scraping away at the crack. Finally, I was able to get the piece of metal into a small crevice and pry the concrete apart. The metal rod was bowing, but finally, the old concrete gave way. I had a better grip, so I pulled off some of the leftover fragments, letting them fall into the water below.

The metal bar was loose but still in the concrete. It wouldn't come out. I kept wiggling it until it was finally far enough away from the other bar to squeeze through. I fit my head past the bars, which was promising, and the rest of my body soon followed.

Standing on a small ledge and hanging onto the remaining bars, I looked for a place to climb down but saw nothing. *Whoever built this did a good job of ensuring that no one could get to the compound,* I thought.

I looked all over for options. Nothing. Would I have to jump into the pool of water below? How deep was it? But I knew it didn't matter—I had no other choice. I took a moment to peek over the ledge, and a wave of vertigo washed over me. It was so far down. But what else could I do?

I looked all around me while holding one of the metal bars in the grate. Nothing but flat stone all around, and I was standing on only a sliver of concrete outside of the grate.

"Hey, what are you doing up there?" a voice shouted.

Startled, I let go of the bars and tumbled to the pool below.

All around me was dark water, and I didn't know which way was up. I twisted and spun, trying to find my way to the surface. All I knew for sure was that I needed to get to the forest to hide—*fast.*

I felt the impact of the falling water behind me and guessed that the woods must be to my right. There was a small pool in the compound where my mother forced me to learn to swim. I hadn't seen a need for it at the time, as no one was allowed to play in the pool, but she always told me that someday I would be thankful I'd learned.

I swam underwater as far as I could until I reached mud. My hands pulled at the muck as I popped my head out of the water to see where I was.

"Go home! You don't belong here," the voice said again.

I turned to see a man on the other side of the water. He wasn't in an ADS uniform and didn't have a gun, so I assumed he was a local. I quickly looked away and climbed up onto the muddy shore, out of the hellacious water. As I ran into the woods, I could hear the man in the distance yell, "You don't want to run in there by yourself!"

I ran for a few minutes and stopped by a large tree, which I leaned on to catch my breath. I heard about mentally ill people living in the woods from stories my mother would talk about with her friends. My entire body trembled as I scanned the forest like a bird on the ground wondering what to do next or what predator would soon come at me. I fled in the direction opposite of the compound, hoping to find someone for help.

The ground was unforgiving on my feet as I occasionally stepped on sharp sticks and branches, but my fear and desperation distracted me from my bleeding soles—all I could think was, *I have to get through the woods, I have to get through the woods.*

I had no idea where I was going, and I kept looking behind me to see if anyone was following. But no one was there—I was completely lost, scared, and alone.

Exhausted, I stopped at the edge of the woods and slowly peered around a tree while heavily panting. The compound I came from was in the distance to my left.

All I could see were the walls and the tops of some of the houses, but I recognized my home, my safe place. At least, it was, until my father started acting so nervous, making my home feel less safe than before. I thought back to the night it all began, when he put that thing in my arm.

I remembered how he didn't return to work after that day and his paranoia as he constantly peered out the windows, obviously searching for what would inevitably arrive.

The last words my father said to me rang in my ears: "run and hide." Then I saw him on the ground after the ringing of gunshots. My mother's cry after a loud bang. And they were shooting at me! I rubbed my arm. *What could it all mean?* I wondered as I stared in the direction of the compound again, the morning sunlight on my back. Despite how much I wanted to make sure everyone was okay, I knew it was too risky to go back to my home.

I cast my gaze around and saw only devastation along the horizon. In the distance were large piles of debris that appeared to have been buildings at one time, and burned-out cars littered the land as far as the eye could see. I didn't know how far the woods went, but I decided that my best bet was to follow them away from the compound, in case the ADS were still looking for me.

I looked down at the bottoms of my feet and saw several cuts, and there was a trail of blood on the ground behind me. *They could track me*, I thought. I had to keep moving.

I weaved my way through the trees for what felt like hours. The strange scents and sounds of the forest combined with the clammy sensation of damp leaves underfoot only amplified my fear. I hid from time to time, waiting to make sure I hadn't been followed, and then continued. When I came to the end of the woods, I slowly approached the edge of an open field.

Standing behind a tree, I looked beyond the open space to see what was left of a city. Many buildings lay in ruin, some standing without walls, others reduced to piles of rubble. I tried to imagine what my surroundings must have looked like in the time before FOG. The dilapidated buildings were so large, and people walked peacefully through the streets.

My stomach rumbled. I was hungry and scared. I could feel my heart pounding in my chest as though it wanted to burst out, but I didn't know what to do or who I could trust. I desperately wanted to wake up from my nightmare, but I realized I never would.

I saw some kids playing by one of the buildings and a couple of ADS vehicles in the distance driving down a street as though they were on patrol. I couldn't go out by myself and risk getting caught, but I knew I couldn't stay where I was much longer.

I longed to get out of my wet clothes, fill my stomach with hot food, and give my aching feet a rest.

I sat down between two large tree roots that were like big, gnarled armrests. The moss on the roots was soft and damp. I ran my finger along the soft, green surface and thought about the possibility of my parents being dead—but no, that wasn't possible. How could it have been?

I thought everyone in the compound was under the protection of the ADS, but it was the ADS who broke into our house. It was the ADS who shot my parents. I recalled again the high-pitched sound of the bullets whizzing by me.

Why did they kill my family? I wondered. *And why do they want to kill me?* I buried my face in my hands and cried, not knowing what to do next.

"Why are you crying?"

The voice made my heart jump. I attempted to stand as my head snapped up to look in the direction of the voice, but I slipped back between the tree roots. A girl stood next to the tree a few feet away.

"W-what are you doing here?" I asked, eyes darting as I searched to see if anyone else was around.

"I saw a rabbit, and when I chased it over here, I heard you. Why are you crying?"

"Leave me alone." I buried my face back in my hands.

"Where did you come from?" she asked.

My eyes met hers in fear. "Why?"

"I live over there." She pointed to the buildings I saw with the kids playing around. "I've never seen you before."

My heart raced as I looked at her and collected my thoughts. She was perhaps a year younger than me, with olive skin and black curly hair down to her shoulders. Her face was dirty. She had tattered shoes and wore a blue flowered dress. I didn't know what to say to her or even what to ask.

Finally, I said, "Do you have a family?"

She looked down. "My parents died when I was younger. I live with the other kids." She pointed to a spot in the distance. "Miss Linda takes care of us. My name is Katia. What's yours?"

I looked at her and tried to read her face, but she looked kind and unthreatening, not to mention very pretty. Still, if others found out my real name, it might lead ADS right to me. I needed to stay hidden. "My name is Zan. I woke up in the woods and don't remember anything else." I realized it was a lame answer, but I didn't dare say where I was really from. I couldn't trust anyone.

"Hi, Zan," she said. "Would you like to come with me? Maybe Miss Linda can take care of you, too."

It was like I was about to jump from the ledge into the pool below again—I had no other options. If I was being pursued, it would only be a matter of time before the ADS found me in my dirty, wet pajamas. But the girl before me looked happy, well fed. I wondered what kinds of food awaited me if I were to follow her. I thought of the soft, warm bed I could rest in. Food and shelter were tempting, but I needed to hide among other kids my age and get out of the woods even without them.

"Okay, I'll go with you."

Katia smiled. "Good. There are a lot of kids living there. Some are kind of mean, but most are very nice."

I walked with her across the small field to the building. The grass was long, and I reached down to hit the seeded tops while I looked around and tried not to be suspicious. My heart raced as I saw the ADS guards walking around the perimeter of the buildings in the distance. I wanted to hurry. In my head, I thought, *The faster we get inside, the lower my chances of getting caught,* but I knew I'd attract even more attention by running.

We walked to the building, which was on the outskirts of the city. I followed Katia up the stairs to the second floor and to what looked like an office. We walked inside, and an older woman met us with a scowl.

"Katia, I saw you run toward the woods. I told you to stay away from there—it's not safe!" she scolded.

Katia replied, "Yes, Miss Linda. But I met this boy, Zan, over there by the woods. He was hiding behind a tree."

Miss Linda looked at me, and I quickly saw fear grow in her eyes. It was as though she had seen a ghost. She quickly ran around her desk, past us, and closed the door. Kneeling before me, she held my arms to look me over more closely.

"Is your name… Zack?"

Fright ran through my body, my eyes opened wide, and my arms trembled. *How does she know?* Questions overwhelmed me, and my vision began to blur. The rapidly forming tears ran down my cheeks.

"They killed my mom and dad," I murmured.

She covered her mouth, and her watery eyes widened. Then she removed her hand, and her gaze softened. She smiled as my mother would when I cried.

"Come this way, and let's get you washed up," she said, holding out her hand. "You smell like a sewer."

I looked around at the cracked walls, paint peeling from the ceiling, and thoughts ran through my mind that I'd met my end—surely she would lock me in a room until ADS came to get me. She reached into the small stall and turned on a shower.

"Here's some soap. The water is cold, but you need to clean up. I'll bring some clothes, so don't go anywhere."

She walked off, leaving the door to the shower cracked slightly. I was alone, and she knew who I was. She was probably on her way to tell the ADS. I tried to open a small frosted window on the wall, but it wouldn't budge. *I'm on the second floor, so I would get hurt if I jumped, anyhow.* I had no choice but to trust Miss Linda, so I took off my filthy clothes—I was almost used to the smell—and stepped into the shower to wash up.

The cold water felt like needles as it hit my skin. Shivering, I quickly washed my body with the soap. I heard the creak of the door open. *This is it,* I thought. *They're going to shoot me.* I stood there waiting for the loud report of a gun, but it didn't come.

I peered around the flimsy, torn shower curtain. I had nowhere to run. This was the end.

"Here are some clothes that should fit you, and a towel. Get dressed and come out when you're done." *It's Miss Linda. Thank God!* My breathing slowed as I calmed down. I began to think that I might be able to trust her.

When I finished washing up, I stayed in the icy shower a little longer trying to figure out what my next move would be. I couldn't run without being seen and followed. The window wasn't an option either. I was trapped.

Miss Linda could have notified the ADS while I showered, but instead, she brought me clothes. She was my best chance at not getting caught, and I needed to trust her. I thought of Katia and how kindhearted she was to help me. She seemed innocent, and I hoped to see her again soon.

I turned the loud squeaky knob to the water off, dried myself, and put the clothes on. They were a little baggy, but they would work for the moment. I walked barefoot to Miss Linda's office. She had the door closed, and I realized Katia was no longer in the room.

I slowly, bashfully approached Miss Linda while looking down at my feet. Only when I glanced up at her eyes did she ask, "You're the boy from the compound, aren't you? I want to help you, but I need to know the truth. Are you Zack Bates?"

I wasn't supposed to tell anyone. But there was no one else in the room, and having someone I could trust would be helpful in my situation. She seemed sincere. My father told me not to tell strangers about myself, but he probably never expected me to be in such a situation. I decided that I could trust Miss Linda, so I nodded.

But I didn't need to say a word—my face gave me away. Miss Linda said, "I knew it. I don't know what happened, but the ADS is looking everywhere for you. They were here just earlier, before Katia brought you. They said your family was attacked and you ran off before they could rescue you. What happened?"

A hoarse whisper came from my throat at first. She waited patiently, then I cleared my throat and told her about the explosion, the sound of my mother's cries, and the gunfire. I told her about my father's final words and how I saw him lying on the ground. I told her how scared I was of the high-pitched sound of bullets flying overhead and how I got through the sewer and the woods.

"And then I saw Katia in the forest," I said, reaching the end of my tale. "And even though I was afraid of the ADS finding me, I thought I'd be safer following her than staying in there alone."

She had her hand on her mouth, and tears filled her eyes again. That time, they ran down her cheek as I told the story. "Where did you come up with the name Zan?" she asked.

"When Katia asked me my name, I didn't know what to say. So I just made up one."

She nodded and said, "Well, your name is Zan while you're here, and never tell anyone else what you just told me. No one. Do you understand?"

I nodded. "Thank you for helping me."

I saw that her eyes were still watery and she had a faint smile as she looked at me. She gave me a hug.

"The ADS was supposed to protect us, but it seems like you never know who you can rely on. We need to be suspicious of everyone until we're sure they're trustworthy." Her emotional words brought tears to my eyes. "You do trust me, don't you, Zack?"

I sighed and nodded. At that point, I had to have faith in someone; so far, she seemed honest.

We walked down a hallway while she talked. "This was an old school at one time, but since it was one of the few buildings around that hadn't been blown up, the ADS turned it into an orphanage for children who lost their parents."

She took me to a large room with several beds and small lockers next to each one. The walls went up high, and windows outlined the top portion of the walls. It looked like old army pictures I saw in school where many men slept in one room.

"This will be your bed and locker. The other boys should be back soon to get ready to eat. I'll find you some additional clothes and, of course, shoes. Remember to introduce yourself as Zan, and say you were sent here from the North Province because they didn't have any beds available. If anyone asks about your parents, tell them you don't remember them." She knelt and looked into my eyes.

"You must do as I say. You are in a lot of danger. Do you understand?"

I swallowed hard and nodded. She pulled me against her chest, gave me a hug, and whispered, "We are both in a lot of danger if you are ever found here." Standing up, she wiped tears from her eyes and said, "The other kids will be here soon. Remember what I said, and follow them to lunch." She walked off, stopping to look back at me one more time before she went out the door. The old door closed with a metal on metal thud which echoed throughout the large bare room.

I sat on the edge of my bed and looked around. Despite how much I was looking forward to sleep, I was way too nervous to take a nap. The room was large, with a hard tile floor. There was a larger table on either end of the room. One end had a deep metal sink that looked like it was built into the brick wall, and there was a long yellow line that ran the length of the room between the two rows of beds, which were against opposite walls. Windows lined the top portion of the walls allowing light in, but they were too high to see out of.

I mulled over everything I'd seen since the explosion. It already seemed like ages ago. I still couldn't believe it—just a day earlier, I had been part of a happy family, and then suddenly I wasn't and the people I'd been raised to trust were looking to kill me.

I lay down on the bed and cried. I remembered that little black ball from the shot my father had given me. I rubbed the lump on my arm with my hand, reminiscing about my time with him and lamenting all the time we had lost.

Chapter 3

"Hey, look! We have a newbie!" I popped my head up, wiping the tears from my eyes and trying to focus on the boys coming into the room. "Oh, and he's a crybaby, too."

I sat up and looked at the five boys walking in. The one who had called me a crybaby was the biggest, and he was carrying an old soccer ball.

"Does the crybaby have a name?" he asked, and they all stopped at the foot of my bed.

I quickly scanned the boys, trying to get a feel for how trustworthy they were. They were all dirty, wearing worn and tattered clothes. "My name's Zan."

"I'm Bram. Why are you crying, and where are you from?"

He was a little taller than I was, perhaps fifteen years old. The other boys were about my age. I replied, remembering Miss Linda's instructions, "I was moved here from the North Province, and I don't know anyone here."

"I don't know about any North Province," the older boy said, "but if you're going to stay here, you'll have to follow my rules. Understand?"

The other boys' nods and looks of admiration indicated their acceptance of his leadership role. For the time being, I'd follow suit, so I nodded as well. I couldn't afford to make any waves.

A bell rang, and the boys ran toward the sink. Bram said, "Come on, Zan! That's the pre-lunch bell. We need to get cleaned up, or we won't get any food."

Having just taken a shower, I figured I was clean enough. I sat on my bed and waited for the other boys. Once they were ready, they stood on the yellow line. Bram was first.

"Well, don't just sit there," he said. "Get on the line. We get inspected before we go to lunch."

I climbed down from the bed and walked to the end of the line. An elderly man walked through the door and asked in a barely audible raspy voice, "Bram, has everyone cleaned up for lunch?"

"Yes, Mr. Adams."

Mr. Adams looked every boy over and then came to me. "You're new. What's your name?" His breath reeked, and the presence of no more than two and a half teeth made for a sight I couldn't stop staring at.

"I'm Zan. Miss Linda brought me here."

"Miss Linda didn't tell me of any new boy," he said, squinting at me. "I'll have to see about this. All right, follow the others and go eat some lunch."

In the cafeteria, we walked in single file with our plates. Processed food was scooped from a pot and put on our trays, along with bread rolls. I'd had synthetic food for as long as I could remember, but it looked like nothing I'd seen before. There were three different colored scoops of what looked like gelatin on every plate, and we were each given a glass of water. It was fascinating to watch the brown, blue, and orange scoops of food jiggle next to each other as I walked to where the other boys were going.

We sat down at the table together. Staring at my indescribable meal, I looked up to see the other boys devouring their food. I leaned down close to smell it and noticed a scent similar to the one I had smelled as I ran through the woods earlier, but I couldn't put a name to it. Since I hadn't eaten in almost two days, my hunger got the best of me, and I took a bite.

"Wow! This is good," I said, too hungry to contain my excitement. I ate faster as my appetite grew, stimulated by the delicious taste.

Bram said, "Yeah, it looks like something from the toilet. We don't know what it is, but it tastes good."

I understood his toilet analogy, but he was right. I watched the other kids wipe their plates with dinner rolls to add a little flavor to the bread, so I followed suit. It did make the bread taste much better.

After we were done, we took our plates to a window near the kitchen to drop them off, then went back to our room.

A woman was waiting for us there. Bram said, "That's Miss Stacy, our teacher. We have class in the morning and then again after lunch."

"We aren't all the same age, but we have one teacher?" I asked curiously. "What grade is this?"

Bram replied, "It's not really a grade, but they teach us at a middle-school level in the hopes that we'll remember something."

I remembered my school at the compound, which was more similar to a standardized education. There, we were placed in different grades according to our age and then passed on to the next grade every year as we got older. The orphanage's system seemed a little strange in comparison.

We learned some math that afternoon. I'd already studied the same level of math at the compound a couple years earlier, but I went along with it anyhow, especially since I hadn't done very well last time. She taught several other subjects as well, including history, which I was especially fascinated with.

Most of what I learned that day confirmed the stories Colonel Jenkins had told us—perhaps he wasn't so crazy after all.

In the early twenty-first century, scientists determined that the production of carbon dioxide would exceed the production of oxygen. Many concepts were proposed—and fought over—to resolve the crisis and save mankind. Genetically-engineered plants were created, which maximized the production of oxygen. Large herds of livestock were euthanized. FOG was formed around an ideology that justified the elimination of livestock, and even people, in order to reduce oxygen consumption. Recommendations were made to establish a maximum lifespan of sixty-five. The theory was that after that age, people consumed resources but wouldn't be able to contribute to society. The US government put a stop to the age restriction, but some countries did not.

The most technically advanced countries combined efforts to populate Proxima Centauri with the goal of emigrating people away from Earth.

Ms. Stacy asked, "Zan, were you taught how Proxima Centauri was found in your previous school?"

The kids turned to me, as I was sitting behind all of them.

"That's Xima, right?" I asked, and the kids laughed.

Ms. Stacy smiled and said, "Yes, it is." Then she continued to give us a history lesson about the planet's discovery, much of which I hadn't been aware of.

She taught us that in 2030, a discovery was made that shocked the scientific world. The *Voyager 1* spacecraft was launched in 1977 on an exploration mission to send back images of other planets in our solar system. In 2012, *Voyager 1* left our solar system for deep space, reducing the rate of its transmissions to once a month in order to preserve its power supply. In 2025, the last transmission was sent to Earth, and having provided thousands of brilliant photos of our solar system, the successful program was shut down.

On July 21, 2030, a retired *Voyager 1* scientist who kept some monitoring equipment operational, hoping for a miracle transmission, received a signal from *Voyager 1*. What shocked everyone was that the image it sent was of a solar system almost twenty-five trillion miles away: Proxima Centauri.

The *Voyager 1* mission was reopened as the scientific community searched for an explanation of the phenomenon. Their calculations indicated it would take over four years for a transmission to reach Earth, which confirmed the location of *Voyager 1*. But how did it get there so quickly?

All countries pooled their resources to send another craft into space, that time with decades of advanced technology far exceeding what was available in 1977.

The goal of the project was to create a nuclear fusion pulse propulsion ship, which could provide continuous thrust. It would allow the vessel to fly much faster through space while also carrying high and low gain transmission systems, which were designed to enhance the data and speed of transmissions to Earth.

A ship large enough to contain all those advanced functions would be too massive to leave Earth's atmosphere, so it was decided that it would be built on the moon.

The project took almost twenty years, but in March of 2051, the ship *Destiny* was launched along the same flight path as *Voyager 1*.

Destiny transmitted data daily until late June 2051, when it became silent. The craft reached its hypothesized goal in approximately three months: a wormhole.

Scientists around the world were on the edge of their seats as they waited for the proof they'd always hoped for—proof that wouldn't arrive for nearly four more years. During that time, the primary focus of interplanetary expeditions was to make Mars habitable, with the ultimate goal of colonization. That collaboration maintained peace with FOG for many years.

Finally, on March 27, 2055, the world cheered as NASA's Deep Space Network received *Destiny*'s image of a solar system in Proxima Centauri. Perhaps more importantly, Earth received an image of Proxima B, the theorized habitable planet that researchers had studied for decades.

Destiny was equipped with a small landing pod, which was designed to disconnect from the main ship, land on Proxima B, and relay environmental readings through *Destiny* and back to Earth.

Coordinating the operation over transmissions from Earth would take years, so *Destiny* was programmed to accomplish the task autonomously upon reaching the planet's orbit.

Daily messages arrived to Earth from *Destiny* as programmed, but the next important message arrived almost a month later. It was confirmation that Proxima B was indeed habitable, with a very similar atmospheric makeup to that of Earth.

All the governments of Earth put the Mars project on hold while they explored the revelation. That went against the will of FOG, which had already waged war on the world after the Switzerland Accord.

With the success of *Destiny*, another ship was built, that time equipped to carry passengers. A shuttle system was developed to carry people between the planet and the mother ship. Thousands of engineers signed up for the mission, but only twelve were selected—their descriptions of traveling through a "window in space" validated centuries of theories about wormholes.

Over the next several years, transport ships took people and supplies to facilitate further research on what came to be known as the planet Xima.

Researchers soon noted that life existed on the new planet, which the people of Earth were quick to marvel over. There were large four-legged birds, hairless dogs, and horse-like creatures, which were called kohls. Visually, kohls looked like a mix between an ox and a horse, with ram-like horns on their heads and long, droopy ears.

Early on in the exploration, the ADS and a team of engineers went to Xima to assess habitable locations and decide where to create the first city. They also evaluated the planet's resources and developed the ability to extract fuel for future shuttle flights between the mother ship, which remained in Xima's orbit, and landing sites on the surface.

After almost two years, the first city on Xima was constructed: Lauri.

Larger ships continued to be built on the moon, as they remained the primary mode of transportation from Earth's orbit to Xima's. A smaller transport shuttle was created to transfer people and supplies from the planet to the ship. It landed in a storage bay on the mother ship, where it was fueled for its next destination. Several of these transportation ships were built and operated on each continent to support operations on Xima.

Each day in the orphanage, we were taught more and more about the history of Earth and, more importantly, Xima. My fascination with Xima grew every day as I learned more. The thought of no bullets flying by my head made my interest even greater… and eventually turned into an interest to perhaps live there one day.

Earth sent farming and construction tools to help the people grow and sustain themselves, but guns were outlawed. Each shuttle flight was strictly inspected to ensure no weapons were smuggled to the planet.

Collectively, the leadership of the world decided to use Xima as a penal planet, where all the criminals and other undesirables of Earth would be transported. The policy was supposed to reduce the consumption of oxygen and resources, but it also served as a crime deterrent. Family members of the prisoners were sent away with them to help populate the new planet.

People from all walks of life were encouraged to go to Xima, but most initial colonists were criminals or political outcasts. However, governments still tried to send a variety of people to begin the colonization of the new planet.

Lauri was the only city on the planet, but other villages and camps were scattered across the land for miles around Lauri. Some villages and encampments produced foods and goods to sell, not unlike villages in the ancient times on Earth.

A journey to Xima took several months and required huge reserves of food, water, and an even more precious resource: oxygen. A sedation system was developed, which reduced the temperature of the pods that held the colonists, as well as a concentrated sustainment liquid that was injected via a needle in the arm.

A communication network was set up, connecting relay stations through the wormhole and allowing transmissions to travel over the course of days instead of years.

A vast amount of what Ms. Stacy taught us was different from what I'd learned at the ADS compound. There, I was taught that the colonists were volunteers who wanted to move to Xima to start a new life, so the fact that Xima was populated by mostly criminals was alarming to me. Rather than a planet of peace and prosperity, Xima was actually a place where the ADS sent the criminals that they were hired as mercenaries to round up and eliminate. When I was living on the compound, I'd heard some stories of how Xima was a great place to live, but my life with my parents was good. I had no real desire to live there.

Even though I knew the truth that criminals lived there, since that fateful night when my parents were killed and I was hunted, it still sounded like a fantastic place to live compared to Earth.

After our lesson ended for the day, I sat in my bed thinking about Xima until it got dark and Mr. Adams yelled, "Lights out!"

* * *

Day after day was made up of the same routine at the orphanage: wake up, breakfast, school, lunch, play, school, free time, dinner, and sleep. Fortunately, I got along with the boys well. We all had a common bond of no longer having parents and having to figure out what to do after we grew up.

We became a close group of friends over the next several months. Since it was based out of an old school building, the orphanage was one of the few large buildings left standing in the area. Many other buildings had been completely leveled, and some were emptied with sections missing and windows broken. Burned-out cars littered the streets. Our building was on the outskirts of the city, which was probably why FOG left it alone.

The children who lived in the orphanage were sent there by the ADS, who usually found them in the aftermath of FOG attacks that took their parents' lives. Bram, for example, was orphaned after a raid on the town he grew up in. He told me how trucks of armed people came into the city one day. None of the intruders wore a uniform, but they all carried guns. His parents hid him in a small crawl space under the house and told him not to come out until they came to get him. He heard gunfire for many hours in all directions.

He stayed in that small spot under the house for two days, but his parents never came for him. Starving and thirsty, he crawled out into the house for water. He called out for his parents, but they didn't answer. He walked outside and saw the dead bodies of his friends and neighbors. He found his mother and father next to each other, lying on the road in front of their house, dead. He cried next to them for almost a day before the ADS found him and brought him, along with other newly-orphaned children, to the orphanage.

I struggled to believe such a thing could happen, but then I remembered the explosions and gunshots in my own home, and I knew it was all true.

Once in a while, I'd see Katia outside during our playtime. She would smile at me occasionally—a smile that would warm me every time. I'd smile back and wave. I couldn't help but notice how pretty she was and think about how she'd saved my life. I was eager to find out more about her, but most of the time, I played sports with the boys and wouldn't make the effort to go by her.

One day, Bram was ill, so we didn't play our usual game of soccer outside. Some of the boys kicked the ball around while others played in an old car. I just walked around. The rumble of a shuttle taking off from a launch site not far away made everyone pause. The small object perched atop a long, bright trail of glowing fire was always magical to watch.

A shuttle took off every month, bound for Xima. Each launch was incredible to watch, but we could only see them for a few moments before the shuttles were out of sight. Most landings took place at night, but we saw a few during the day. Many times, we didn't even notice landings, as they weren't as loud as takeoffs.

"Hi, Zan." I turned around and saw Katia. Just seeing her next to me made my heart race. Her silky hair was dark and curly, and her soft eyes, with their long lashes, made me melt. I quickly became too nervous to talk properly.

"Hi, Katia. You're looking pretty! I mean, you look good. Ummm..." I panicked because I didn't know what to say. I liked her, and I didn't want to say anything stupid. "I mean—*hi*!" My face got warm. *How could I be too scared to say hi to her like this?* She was wearing the same flowered dress I saw her in when we first met, but she was cleaner. She looked fabulously beautiful—like artwork you could stare at all day.

Katia smiled at my inability to speak coherently. Then she asked, "How do you like living here?"

"I like it a lot. The boys are good friends."

She smiled up at me and said, "So, you've been here for a while, and I keep wanting to ask you something. Where did you come from, and why were you in the forest in wet pajamas when I found you that day?"

Fear immediately consumed me, and I looked around to see if anyone else had heard her. My heart lurched against my ribs as I remembered what Miss Linda had told me.

"Well, I was taken from my parents in my hometown and driven around for a long time. When the men stopped, they thought I was sleeping, so I snuck out of the car. I ran for the forest and kept running until I got here."

She looked frightened for me, "Oh my. Something terrible could have happened to you." She then placed her hand on mine. My heart raced again—no longer out of fear of being caught or fear of the device in my arm. Her holding my hand sent shivers through my body, and I noticed a feeling I'd never felt before.

"I'm so sorry, Zan," she said. "Maybe you'll find your parents again someday."

I didn't like lying to Katia, but I didn't know what else to tell her. I was usually an honest person, so I was impressed with how easily I'd made up a story on the spot.

We walked around for a little while and found ourselves at the ruins of a building next door. There were large chunks of concrete and metal bars sticking out in every direction. Remnants of furniture were strewn throughout the debris, along with the occasional smashed car under a pile of rubble.

Katia said, "Those were some of the old offices that FOG blew up many years ago. We're not supposed to be playing around here, but I like to see all of the strange things lying around in the rubble."

An ADS vehicle turned a corner and headed toward us.

We sat down on some pieces of concrete that were just large enough to serve as a bench and turned to look at the rubble to avoid them seeing my face—close call.

We spent a couple minutes scanning through the debris to find something intriguing. Katia seemed to have the place memorized.

Katia told me about her past. She grew up in a compound, just like me. Her parents were ADS guards who protected corporations and other organizations that required security. She looked down as she told me about the day FOG blew up a building they were guarding. Everyone inside was killed instantly, including her parents. The ADS went to her home and brought her here.

"I see you're hanging out with Bram and the other boys a lot," she said, a smile forming on her lips as her eyes brightened. I could feel her disposition instantly become cheerier. She continued, "I've wanted to come by you and talk, but I didn't want to interrupt your fun."

I nodded. "It's okay. You can come by anytime. Yeah, there are six of us who like to hang out together." I didn't want to talk about my background and hoped she wouldn't pry. I plucked a long blade of grass from the ground and ran it through my fingers. I placed it between my thumbs, cupped my hands the way my father once showed me, and blew into it. The blade of grass made a whistling sound as it vibrated. Katia giggled, and her contagious laughter immediately spread to me as well.

"That's a pretty cool trick. Where did you learn that?"

I dropped the grass, thinking of my father, and stared at the ground. "I don't remember."

Katia excitedly stood up and reached for my hand. "Oh, I remembered. Come with me. I want to show you something."

She led me around the building to a burned-out car, which had a large hole where the driver's door would have been and small holes scattered randomly throughout the body. There were traces of blue paint in some of the crevices, but it was mostly a rusty-brown color with a charred interior.

"Look underneath," she said.

I lay down and saw a hole in the ground under the car. She said, "It's supposed to go to some other building, but I don't know of anyone who's gone down there."

I crawled under the car to take a look. It was dark, and I saw the top couple rungs of a ladder on the sides of the hole. Memories flashed through my mind. It was exactly like the tunnel I'd used to escape the compound.

Crawling back out from under the car, I sat up and stared at the hunk of metal, remembering the fateful night when I lost my parents.

"Where do you think it goes?" Katia asked, bringing me out of my bad memories.

"Maybe it's a secret portal to Xima." I chuckled.

Katia laughed, which made me laugh even harder, but part of me hoped I was right and we could both have a fresh start on a new planet.

I looked from the old wreckage of a car to the rubble in the distance. I thought of my parents and rubbed my arm, feeling the black orb. Although they hadn't spent a lot of time with me, my mom and dad were both as loving and caring as any son could want. I couldn't imagine why anyone would want to kill them—or me, for that matter. What could I have done that made them want to kill me?

I couldn't help but think about my future at the orphanage. *Am I destined to be an orphan forever? And what happens when I grow up? Will I be forced to work for the ADS too? The very people who killed my parents? There's got to be a better place than this.*

The pre-lunch bell rang. We stood and began our walk back to the school building. The boys needed to wash up before Mr. Adams came in to inspect us, and I knew he would be grouchy if I wasn't ready.

"Going somewhere?" a gruff voice called out.

Suddenly, a man stepped from behind an old car near a mound of rubble, startling us. I didn't know how we hadn't seen him earlier. He looked dirty and old, and ripped clothing hung from his body like rags. Much of his hair was missing, and his teeth were brown and broken. A stench emanated from him as he walked closer—almost putrid enough to make the sewer drain smell good. That was it. He must have come from that drainage hole.

"Excuse me, sir, but we need to get back," I said as I nudged Katia toward the orphanage.

"Oh, I'll let you get back," the man continued in his poor voice which almost seemed like a struggle for him. "All I want is the girl."

Katia gripped my arm as I pulled her behind me, and we walked backward as the man approached.

Up close, I could see that half of his head was bald and he was filthy.

"You can't have her! Leave now, o-or—"

"Or what, boy? You'll call the ADS? There isn't a guard around here. She's coming with me, but it seems you'll need to be taught a lesson first."

He lunged for my arm and pulled me aside, then reached for Katia. I jumped on his back and put my arm around his throat. I had never fought anyone in my life, but I felt more strength at that moment than I thought I was capable of having.

He pulled me down to the ground, but I rolled away and sprung back to my feet. He stared at me and held up his fist.

"Okay, boy. You're going to make this painful for yourself." He snarled, then lunged for me. I kicked him in his crotch as hard as I could. For a moment, his gruesome body was lifted by the blow. He buckled over as he held himself, falling to the ground with an agonizing growl. He cussed at me as I took Katia's hand and ran back to the school.

Miss Linda was waiting outside with her hands on her hips. Her brow was furrowed as we approached, perhaps because she noticed the panic in our eyes.

"What happened? Why are you late?"

She rushed us inside, and we told her what had happened.

"It was very brave of you to protect Katia, Zan," Miss Linda said, then turned to face Katia. "Katia, you know better than to stray too far from here. Please don't do it again. You're a lovely girl, and a man like that would not be kind to you. Now, hurry to your rooms and get cleaned up."

We walked through the hall together, but before I broke away to the boy's room, Katia hugged me.

"Thank you, Zan." She kissed my cheek and ran off to the girl's area. I stared after her, my face warming from her kiss. I was beginning to like Katia. Very much.

Over the next year, I noticed myself gaining a lot of strength. I often played soccer with the others, and one day I kicked the ball so hard that it knocked the goalie into the net. He lay on the ground, trying to catch his breath. Everyone looked at me, wondering how I could have kicked it with so much force. I couldn't understand it either.

I also spent time with Katia, talking and dreaming about what it would be like to live anywhere else—especially Xima. Katia had a fantastic smile, and I loved how she would toss her long curly hair behind her head or curl it around her finger. She had a way of looking at me that penetrated right to my soul. I didn't know how to explain it, but I had strange feelings for her, feelings that made me happy every moment I was with her—and even more so when she smiled.

I thought about my parents often, and I wondered why those ADS soldiers—the same ADS soldiers who were supposed to protect us—barged into our home and tried to kill us. I couldn't help but think that the *thing* my father placed in me had something to do with it. He was nervous when he planted it in my arm and warned me to never tell anyone—*but why*?

Miss Linda would stop me occasionally to make sure I was doing well. She would always place her hand on my cheek and smile. I could tell she cared a lot and wanted to protect me, but from what, I still didn't know. ADS soldiers showed up once in a while, and I'd see them talking with Miss Linda. She'd only shake her head in response to their questioning. I didn't know what they were saying, but I suspected they were looking for me.

One day, one of the boys named Danny was goofing around while we were cleaning up for lunch. He jumped into the large, thick metal wash basin we used to get clean. It was mounted to the high, brick wall with windows at the top. He danced in the water while singing some silly song. We all laughed as he splashed everyone.

Within a blink of an eye, the bricks broke loose from the wall and the basin fell over, trapping Danny underneath. He cried out in pain as the bricks piled on top of the basin. All the boys tried to lift the basin off him while I held Danny's hands, ready to pull him out, but it didn't budge. Then I bent down and began to lift the basin and noticed the other boys slowly backing away with their mouths agape.

I pushed it up onto its side as the bricks on top of the basin slid off. Bram pulled Danny out as I turned around to see the other boys standing back and watching me with wide eyes. I lowered the basin to the floor and looked at the other boys, who continued to stare at me.

Bram sent another boy to get help and then faced me. "How did you lift that?" he asked.

"I don't know. I just lifted it."

Bram knelt next to Danny, who cried out in pain as the large cut on his leg continued to bleed. "We were all trying to lift that thing, and we couldn't move it. But you just lifted it so easily, all by yourself."

I looked down at my hands and then at the wash bin. Another brick slid onto the floor. I responded slowly, as I also didn't understand. "I don't know how I did it," I said. "I just did."

Chapter 4

Another year passed, and my friends became more like brothers to me. I also continued to grow closer to Katia. I was beginning to realize what love was, and I knew deep down that I was falling for Katia. She was older, more mature, and more beautiful than ever.

We would walk around during recess, and in the evening we'd sit on the front steps and talk about anything and everything. We laughed about things the other kids did, or how Mr. Adams sometimes didn't wear matching shoes. We talked about the stars, and about Xima, once in a while. We wondered what life might be like there. We would often hold hands, too.

At first, the boys teased me about it, but they stopped after I told one of them that they wouldn't laugh so much if a wash basin fell on them. They all remembered the time I saved Danny, and after that they minded their own business, knowing they might need my help one day. Once in a while the guys would tease me about my strength, but for the most part it wasn't brought up. I noticed my muscles had grown more than the other kids'. My father wasn't a very stocky man, so I didn't know why I was bulking up.

Despite the teasing, I fell in love with Katia's wit, her charm, her grace. Most of all, I fell in love with the way she was so kind to everyone—especially to me. Katia became an important part of my life, and I was beginning to envision our future together.

Thoughts of my parents would occasionally come to mind, particularly when I lay in bed at night, trying to sleep. I tried to push those thoughts away, focusing instead on how happy Katia made me.

I spent time with Katia when I could. Aside from her beauty, I was infatuated with her soft, intoxicating voice, particularly the simple way she said *good morning*. She brightened my spirits every day I spent with her. She was witty, charming and once we got to know each other better, she would throw some sarcasm my way.

The boys would give me crap about hanging out with Katia, saying girls were nothing but trouble. But it was Katia who saved me from the trouble I was in that day when she found me in the woods. I had become very fond of her, and I liked to think she felt the same way about me.

One day, I was walking to recess with Katia when Miss Linda called me into her office and closed the door.

"Zan, do you remember your father giving you anything before he died? Some type of medicine, perhaps?"

My heart surged as I remembered that day when my father put the object in my arm. I rubbed the spot where the device was placed and simply shook my head. "No, Miss Linda. He gave me health shots once in a while, but I didn't know what was in them."

She looked down at the spot on my arm I was rubbing and smiled at me. "Well, I found out a little more about your father. He was working on a secret project with the goal of designing a small device that could be placed in children about your age. Over time, the device would allow the child to develop significant strength and constitution, which would enable them to heal from injuries much more quickly. It was designed to eventually enhance the ADS force, but the prototype he was working on went missing. Rumor has it, the ADS suspected your father took this device and placed it in you. That's likely why he was killed, and it's probably also why they're still looking for you."

My entire body pulsed with my heartbeat. Everything finally made sense; my intuition was correct. More than ever, I recognized how dangerous it would be to talk about what my father had done—even to Miss Linda.

"Sorry, but I don't remember anything like that," I heard myself stutter as my mind reeled from the sudden revelation. "Is that why they want to kill me, too?"

She slid her hands up and down my arms and smiled, comforting me. "I believe they want you and won't stop until they have you." She put her hand on my cheek. "I can see how you're growing, and I heard about the incident with the wash basin. I want you to know you can trust me, and I'll try to protect you as much as I can. But if you do things that make yourself stand out, it might give the ADS a reason to come looking for you here. Do you understand?" I nodded during her pause. "You've been spending a lot of time with Katia. You haven't told her anything, have you?"

I shook my head.

"Good. Even if you trust her, it's important that she doesn't find out about this. If she did know something, they could use her against you."

I nodded, letting the realization of what she was saying sink in. I still couldn't believe that my father had used me as a test subject and hidden the truth about something so dangerous.

Miss Linda opened the door. "Go on back to your room, Zan. Never tell anyone what I just said, and don't do anything that might show your strength. Your life depends on it."

As I walked outside, I thought of that last night in my family's home. It seemed like such a long time ago, but the memory was etched into my mind. My father must have known what the ADS had come for as he told me to run and hide. Why would he take such a risk?

I sensed something approaching me from behind, and I quickly arched to the side as a ball flew by my head.

"Whoa, Zan! That nearly hit your head! Hey, Zan? Zan? Hey, are you in there?"

I looked up to see Bram right in front of me. I heard what he was saying, but it wasn't sinking in. My mind was elsewhere.

I shook my head. "Sorry, I was thinking about something."

He asked again, "How did you know that ball was coming at you? We thought for sure it would hit you in the back of the head."

I shrugged my shoulders, not noticing his question as I continued toward the bedroom.

I sat on my bed and rubbed my arm. The object wasn't noticeable anymore as my muscles had grown around it. But I knew it was there. The ADS was still looking for me, I had no place to go, and I had only Miss Linda to trust.

At times, I imagined myself in a deep trap, unable to get out and simply waiting for the ADS men to hit me over the head and take me as their prize.

The thought of using a knife to dig the object out of my arm came to mind. Maybe if I gave that little black thing to the ADS, they'd leave me alone and I could spend my life with Katia without further trouble. Deep down, I believed my father had experimented on me for a reason. But for what reason? Part of me couldn't help but appreciate my newfound abilities as a gift, rather than a curse.

Chapter 5

It rained for days. Everyone was becoming depressed from having to stay inside for so long. Other than a brief *hi* during meals, I was unable to see Katia because boys and girls were separated while indoors.

Being cooped up in the building made everyone tense and irritable. After our daily lessons, we kicked a ball around in our room until Mr. Adams came in and scolded us for it—as if there was anything breakable in the room.

Some of the boys would wrestle, but I made sure not to participate. I was fearful of my strength and especially of what might happen if I hurt anyone. I reread textbooks on Xima and pondered what life was like there. I read more about Xima's plants and animals as well as the kohls. There was a drawing of one in the book, and I marveled at how similar they were to the horses on Earth. However, not having any pictures of the people who lived there or how they lived was disappointing.

There was a drawing of Xima's first city, Lauri, which reminded me of pictures I'd seen of an old Western movie. The books made it seem like a great place to live and focused on the peaceful lives of all the pioneers who had ventured out into the unknown to build farms.

I remembered other history books that described the expansion in the American West, when settlers traveled in covered wagons to seek a new life in the West. They had wagons full of supplies and enough money to get started. I had neither.

I read that people volunteered to go to Xima, but I figured the trip had to cost someone some money. Did the criminals travel for free? Was there an age requirement? I tried to research as much as I could, but the answers to my many questions weren't available in the books we had.

Imagining the journey like those of the pioneers of the Old West in America made the idea of a fresh start become very attractive to me. *This is where I want to go, and I want to take Katia with me.*

On the first nice, sunny day in what seemed like a long time, Katia and I met up for a walk again. She had a new yellow dress on.

"Do you like my new dress?" she asked when she saw me.

I gazed at how beautiful she looked and how she had grown. I laughed at her twirling her dress, causing the bottom to flare out. Her laugh caused me to laugh more, not because of anything funny, just because her happiness was infectious. Her new dress revealed more of her chest than I'd ever seen, and I fought to look at the white daisy in her hair instead.

She laughed. "It's okay, Zan. You can look at me." I blushed and looked at her chest again and then her eyes. She laughed and took my hand.

"You're much more bashful than you used to be. I'm growing up, you know. We both are." We walked a little more when she asked, "Zan, what do you want to do when you grow up?" Her voice was earnest. It was our first discussion about our futures. I wanted her to be involved in mine, but I didn't want to scare her away.

I tried to think of something simple, perhaps spending life on a small farm somewhere, but we would risk being found by FOG there too—or worse… the ADS.

Many thoughts ran through my mind, but I couldn't put together anything coherent to answer her. What could I do? Work for the ADS like my father? I didn't know any other jobs I could do on Earth where ADS couldn't find me. "I don't really know," I finally replied.

We walked around for a while, talking about the past couple weeks. Then I asked, "What if we ran away to Xima together?"

She stopped and looked at me, grabbing my hand in her excitement. Then she sighed. "It's so far away, and how would we even live there?"

"I'll get a job, and we can build a farm." I held her other hand and looked at her expression to get some kind of read on what she was thinking. I wanted to tell her how I felt about her, how happy she made me, but did she feel the same way? What if I told her how I felt and she got scared? Or worst of all, what if she just wanted to be friends? I looked down to the hem of her dress as she twisted side to side trying to figure out a solution to my internal struggle.

"I love you, Katia. We can make a new start for ourselves… away from all of… *this*."

"Oh, Zan! Do you really think we could?" She smiled up at me. Then her smile widened, her eyes grew brighter. "Did you just say you loved me?" She leaped up , wrapped her arms around my neck, and hugged me ever so tight.

I hugged her back as I felt her long hair against my cheek and draped over my hand. My heart raced faster than it ever had before, hoping she had the same feeling for me.

"I love you, too, Zan," she whispered as she hugged me even tighter. "I would love to go to Xima with you." She pulled her arms from around my neck, then took one of my hands. "Come on. I want to show you something."

We drifted toward the forest, close to where Katia had found me. That day seemed like a long time ago. We were supposed to stay away from that area, but there was a flowering bush Katia wanted to see.

"Have you ever seen such a bush before?" Katia asked.

As we got closer, I was amazed at the beauty of the flowers. It was refreshing to see something so delicate and beautiful in a land surrounded by destruction. The flowers were an attractive burgundy color that stood out among all the green and brown in the area. I got in closer and could smell its sweet scent—far more pleasant than the dust and bland smells I'd endured for the past couple years. It was lovely. I watched as Katia joyfully picked a few flowers from the bush. She looked at me with a smile on her face and blushed for a moment. Then, I saw panic in her eyes.

"Zan, look—"

A blow to my back knocked me onto the ground, hard. I couldn't see my assailant—he was punching me in the head while sitting on my back. "Here's a little payback for kicking my nuts in, kid!" I remembered—he was the man who had wanted to kidnap Katia.

I tried to cover my face as he punched at my cheek when I tried to look up at him, pinning my head against the ground and sitting on me.

I knew I could easily push the man off of me—he was much lighter than the metal tub—but if Katia saw how strong I was, what would she think? What would the man think? He could have connections to the ADS. Leaving Katia would be worse than any bruises, so I pretended to struggle beneath his weight.

"I'm going to make you regret what you did to me," he said close to my ear. "I'm taking your pretty little girl this time!"

"Get off him!" Katia yelled as she pushed the degenerate off me. I rolled over, sprung to my feet faster than I thought possible, and pulled Katia behind me.

"Get away, or you'll get hurt!" I exclaimed while walking backward. Katia was peering over my shoulder, and I could hear the fear in her breathing as she gripped tightly to my shirt.

He laughed. "Oh? Are you gonna kick me in the nuts again?" He pulled out a knife from his waistband. "Perhaps I'll cut your nuts off first, kid—or maybe I'll leave you in pieces for the dogs to eat while I make your girl watch."

He lunged for me. I deflected his arm with one hand and punched him in the chest with all my might. He flew back several feet, landing on his ass.

"Run home, Katia!" I shouted and pushed her away.

Our assailant, who lay between us and the orphanage, jumped on Katia before I could get to him. As he brought the knife down, I grabbed his arm and, without thinking, snapped it over my knee like a stick. I heard it crack as he screamed in pain. He dropped the knife, and Katia took off running toward the orphanage.

"What *are* you?" he moaned as he stood up and walked away, cradling his lame arm. "You're going to pay for this, whatever you are."

A cold dread swept over me. My entire body shuddered as I realized what it would mean if he told the ADS about me. My panic rose, and I realized I couldn't let him leave. I put my arm around his throat from behind and pulled him over to the trees.

"Where the hell are you taking me? Let me go! I'm going to have the ADS all over this place. I heard they were looking for a kid like you." He struggled as I pulled him into the woods. I felt his one good arm trying to pry my grip off his neck as he kicked his feet futilely.

I couldn't let him tell the ADS—they would raid the orphanage just like they did my home and kill everyone. All thoughts disappeared except for one: to kill that man.

I spotted a sharp, splintered stump sticking out of the ground. I picked the man up over my head and stared down at the branch. I didn't think at all about what I was doing. The only thought in my mind was that I couldn't let this man report me to the ADS, and I couldn't give him a chance to hurt Katia ever again.

I slammed him down onto the stump. The narrow piece of tree penetrated through his back and protruded out of his stomach as his red blood soaked into the forest floor.

I stared at him as he lay there motionless and forever silent.

I looked down at my trembling hands.

What did I just do? I've never hurt anyone before.

I ran home as fast as I could. Miss Linda was standing on the front porch with Katia. I stopped running and walked up to them.

"Zan, is that blood on your hands and shirt?" Miss Linda asked. Her voice took on a higher-than-normal pitch as she pointed at the red stains on my shirt.

I slowly looked up at her as I recalled, in detail, how I had hurt the man. I nodded.

"Come with me." We followed her up to the office, where she quickly closed the door behind us. Walking to the back side of her desk, she sat in her chair and stared at the two of us. Miss Linda slowly shook her head, a look of fear showing in her eyes. We walked toward her, and as we looked back and forth at each other, we could think of nothing to say.

"Miss Linda, Zan was just trying to protect me from the man who attacked us," Katia said as she reached out for my hand.

Miss Linda saw us holding hands and slowly shook her head.

"The ADS *will* find out what happened," Miss Linda said gravely. "And when they do, they'll come here. You cannot tell them anything, and if they ask, you don't know anything." She gripped both of our arms tightly. "Do you both understand?" We nodded quickly, with conviction.

She pulled both of us against her and hugged us for a moment. When she let go, she stared into my eyes and then Katia's. She smiled. "Katia, you can go back to your room. And remember: tell no one."

Katia opened the door and, pausing, turned to lock her sad eyes on mine. "Thank you for saving me again, Zan." She closed the door, and I saw her shadow fade away as I looked through the frosted glass.

"What were you thinking out there? I told you not to go too far from the school!" Miss Linda scolded. I glanced up as she grabbed my arms, turning me to face her. She looked disappointed.

Tears welled up in my eyes. The last thing I wanted to do was disappoint Miss Linda, the one person who knew who I was and what was happening to me. "Katia wanted to see the flower bush by the forest. I looked around first to make sure no one was around, but that guy who attacked us before jumped out of nowhere with a knife. He almost stabbed Katia! I had to stop him."

Miss Linda's eyes lit up. "What did you do?"

I looked down at the floor. "I broke his arm. He screamed something about the kid the ADS was looking for, and I panicked."

"And then?" she asked, slowly trying to pry the truth out from me. I looked up to see the raised eyebrow and tilted head my mother would use when she wanted an honest answer. The reality of what I'd done finally sunk in. All my nerve endings pulsated with shock.

"I killed him in the woods." My tears dripped onto the floor. I couldn't look at Miss Linda's face.

She knelt to look up at me.

"You saved Katia, and you did what you had to do. But if that man knew the ADS were looking for you, then others might as well. Even here in the orphanage, people are getting suspicious about your strength. If the ADS come here, I'm afraid they'll find out who you are."

"What do I do?" I asked, remembering that night when they attacked our house and the carnage that followed.

As she looked into my eyes, her mouth hardened into a serious expression.

"I would normally never recommend this to anyone—especially not a fifteen-year-old. But you need to go somewhere far from here, and nowhere on Earth is safe. I might be able to get you on a shuttle to Xima. They would never look for you there. However, I must warn you that I've heard rumors Xima isn't everything we've been led to believe."

My eyes lit up. "I'd love to go there. I've read a lot about it. Perhaps Katia and I could go together."

"No! Katia is too young. You're too young too, but I don't see any other option in your case." She stood up and looked at a document on her desk.

"But that's not fair!" I said. I could feel my temperature rising, my face heating up. "Katia needs to be somewhere safe, too. What if another man tries to take her and I'm not here to save her?"

Miss Linda ignored my protests; her mind was already made up.

"There's a local shuttle scheduled to leave for Xima tomorrow evening. I can make arrangements to have you board as a citizen. You can find a job once you arrive. You'll be in danger, regardless of where you go, but at least no one will know you and the ADS won't be looking for you there. Are you sure you want to take your chances on Xima?"

I saw the concern in her eyes, and I nodded. "Yes, but I know Katia would want to go with me."

She stood up so our eyes were level and smiled. She placed her hand on my cheek. "I know you and Katia have become close, but you need to think of her also. How would you protect her or take care of her there? It would be difficult for you alone. Why don't you write a letter to her? I'll make sure she gets it, and I'll tell her where you went and why. But she can't go with you, Zan. I hope you understand."

She looked through her desk and pulled out some money. "I'll have you driven to the shuttle site tomorrow morning. It's about twenty miles from here, where you've seen the launches. There you'll meet someone named Mule. He'll be a huge man with long black hair and a beard. Tell him I sent you as a citizen. He'll make sure you are given safe passage. Now go to your room, and I'll make the arrangements with Mule. We'll head to the launch site first thing tomorrow."

She hugged me. I wrapped my arms around her, hugging her back. "Always think with your heart *and* your head." She tapped her finger on my temple. "More importantly, your head. Your heart alone might just get you killed. Only use your strength when needed." She opened the door, and I walked back to my room, thinking about what she'd said.

Chapter 6

My blood was boiling. I wanted to punch something. I walked down the hallway and punched at a storage room door with all my might. The door broke off one hinge, and a hole formed in the middle. The image of that man lying in the forest with the tree sticking out of his stomach was burned into my mind. The thought of never seeing Katia made me angry.

I didn't know what to expect on Xima. The sudden changes in my life—being hunted by the ADS, killing a violent kidnapper, and finally expressing my feelings for Katia just to end up losing her—made my head spin. I desperately wanted to take her with me, but I was torn. Miss Linda had made a good point about placing her in danger, but I couldn't leave without seeing her again.

That night, I quietly put what little clothes I had into a small sack and walked downstairs to the first floor, where Katia slept with the other girls. Boys were not allowed in there, but it was late, and I suspected that everyone was asleep. I made my way to the door of the girls' room and slowly peeked inside. The moonlight through the windows dimly lit the room, projecting shadows all over the floors and walls.

Peering inside, I realized the room was identical to the boys' room. I slowly walked inside, hugging the walls behind the beds to stay in the shadows.

I tiptoed by each bed, searching for Katia's familiar face.

In the third bed, I saw her. Crawling on my hands and knees, I crept over the cold concrete floor to Katia's bedside. "Katia," I whispered. She didn't respond, so I tapped her shoulder. "Katia."

Her eyes opened and then lit up when she saw me. I put my finger to my mouth to make sure she remained quiet, then motioned for her to come with me.

She carefully slid out of bed, put her shoes on, and followed me to the darkest corner of the room near the door and the wash basin. There were some tall cabinets against the adjacent wall, but the rest of the room was bare. We knelt on the floor in the corner, and she whispered, "What are you doing here? If you get caught, you'll get in trouble."

"I'm leaving for Xima tomorrow."

"You're what?" Her voice was loud. I quickly placed my hand over her mouth and peered over her head to see if anyone was stirring. Thankfully, no one woke up.

"Shhh!" I hissed, removing my hand. "I killed that man yesterday. I'm a murderer. Miss Linda is making arrangements to send me to Xima before someone here finds out what I did."

"Oh, Zan, no! How—" The concern in her voice caused her volume to become nervously high, and I placed my finger to her mouth. I didn't want anyone waking up, and I didn't want to have to answer her questions. The less she knew about me, the better.

"All you need to know is that I did it to save you, Katia. I–I love you. And care for you so much," I stammered.

Her eyes lit up. She reached out to hug me. "Oh, Zan. I love you, too."

Tears filled my eyes. I never wanted to leave her embrace. When she looked up at me, I leaned down to kiss her.

The alarming sound of a door being kicked open in the hallway stopped our first kiss. A man's voice yelled, "Check every room! I want every boy rounded up."

My heart raced, and I couldn't breathe fast enough. "Oh, no! They're looking for me."

"Who's looking for you?"

I looked at Katia, then at the doorway. Any minute, men would barge in and drag me away. I'd never see her again whether I told her the truth or not. I had nothing to lose. "The ADS," I whispered. "They're looking for me." It felt so good to share my secret with someone else.

"They killed my parents, and now they've come for me. If they catch us together, you'll be in trouble, too." I could hear footsteps approaching the door to the girl's room. Katia pulled a locker away from the wall and told me to get behind it. She went to the sink near the door and turned the water on.

A man wearing military gear and holding a gun barged into the room, jolting everyone awake. He looked around and saw Katia standing by the sink.

Then, scanning the room again, he turned and walked out. "It's the girls' room. On to the next!" he bellowed as he walked down the hallway.

The other girls quickly got out of their beds to figure out what was happening. I stood behind the locker, knowing they'd surely search the room again.

Katia went to the middle of the room, shushing the girls. She whispered, "They're looking for Zan. He saved my life yesterday when a man tried to kill me near the woods. He needs to get away."

"Where is he?" the oldest girl, Maya, whispered.

I stepped out from behind the locker. All the girls gasped as they saw me. Maya scolded, "You can't be in here, Zan."

"I know. I just came here to say goodbye to Katia. I have to get out of here." They were all speechless.

"Check every room thoroughly. He has to be here somewhere!" The same voice barked in the corridor. I stepped back behind the locker. Katia whispered to all the girls, "Please, help me save him."

A man burst through the doors, slamming them loudly against the walls as they swung open. "Is there a boy in here!?"

Maya took charge and replied, "Why would there be a boy in here? We're all girls."

"I need to look the room over." The armed soldier sounded unconvinced. He walked around the back of the room, then back down to the locker where I was hiding. I heard a girl gasp, and another started to cry.

"He's here, isn't he?"

I burst out from my hiding place, and, as the soldier gaped at me, I punched him in the face with all my might. Blood spilled from his mouth as he fell to the floor.

"You knocked him out with one punch? The rumors must be true!" Maya exclaimed.

"Zan, why don't you put his uniform on?" Katia suggested.

"Great idea. Quick! Help me get these off him," I said, starting with his boots.

The girls quickly helped strip him of his uniform. We tied his hands with some shoelaces and used a piece of ripped sheet as a gag. Then we pushed him into a locker, forcing it shut. I quickly donned the uniform, along with his glasses and helmet. No one would be likely to suspect me, as I was already as tall as most men.

I had never fired a gun before. Beyond slinging the weapon around my shoulder to hold it at my waist, I didn't know what I was doing. My only goal was to avoid getting captured.

Maya whispered, "We'll get in trouble if they find that man in the locker."

"After I get away, take him out and untie him," I instructed. "Then tell him that I forced you to do this."

Maya frowned. "Be careful, Zan." All the girls nodded and added whispers of encouragement.

The door burst open. "What's going on?" the ADS agent demanded, sizing up the room suspiciously.

The girls moved away from me, and I said in my deepest voice, "They were scared. I just told them everything was all right. He's not in here." I made a point of not showing too much of my face.

The other militant looked around again. "Well, come with me. We're going to check the basement. All the boys are being interrogated upstairs."

I feared for what would become of my friends. They might get hurt if they didn't give the ADS the answers they wanted. Or tortured if they said too much. I had kept my secrets from them, but I didn't know what to expect anymore.

I followed the armed soldier to the basement. He kicked a door in and quickly investigated the room with the light at the end of his gun. We walked farther into the room, and the moonlight from the upper windows softly illuminated my face.

"There isn't anyone down here," he said, then turned to look at me. "Hey, you're not—"

I punched him in the face so hard that he fell to the ground immediately, but he was still conscious. He started to yell for help, so I pressed my hands over his mouth, harder and harder, until I no longer felt his hot breath on my palm. He was no longer breathing.

What have I done? I just killed an ADS guard militant. But I was only covering his mouth! Was I holding him that tightly? My strength scared me, but I had no time for fear.

I panicked, realizing the other guards would expect him to return shortly. I thought about Miss Linda telling me to think with my head, so I paced back and forth alongside the body and concluded that I needed to get away from the orphanage. My being there would only bring trouble to my friends, Miss Linda, and Katia. I had to escape quickly, and I couldn't wait for Miss Linda to take me to the launch site.

I went back upstairs to Katia's room. Maya tried to block my path. "Why did you come back here?" she asked.

I ignored her and looked to Katia. "I love you, Katia. Will you come with me?"

She jumped from her bed and put her arms around me. "Yes!"

Maya asked, "Where are you going?"

"We're going to—"

I interrupted Katia. "We're going to where my grandparents live. Miss Linda told me they're alive." Katia looked up at me confused, but I simply smiled at her.

She grabbed her coat and put some clothes in a small bag.

"Katia, you can't just leave," Maya pleaded.

Katia looked at their concerned faces. "Can we call this living? When I'm with Zan, I feel alive. I'd rather die trying to create the life I've dreamed of with the man I love than wallow in self-pity here." She walked up to me and placed her arm around my waist.

Maya nodded at me, and the rest of the girls remained silent. I smiled at everyone, then Katia and I left. I peered into the hallway and saw that it was empty. We walked about twenty feet down the hallway and turned to look at the doors leading outside.

Voices and other noises echoed from upstairs, but we didn't see anyone in our way, so we walked quickly to the exit through the glass doors. No one was outside, but there were three vehicles parked near the steps. We quickly went out, down the steps, and walked to one of the vehicles.

I'd never driven a car, but I had seen somebody operate one once, on the compound.

"Quick, get in!" I yelled, taking a knife out of my belt loop and puncturing a hole in the tires of the other two vehicles. I got into the third and stared at the panels. My body was trembling as I tried to recall how I had seen it operated.

I pushed a button on the front panel that said Start.

The lights inside came on. I pushed the lever next to the Start button, which was labeled *Drive*, then forced the pedal to the floor.

The car lurched forward.

"Hey, come back here! Where are you going!?" someone yelled from behind us.

Katia looked back. "Zan! They're outside, pointing guns at us! Hurry!"

I stomped on the pedal, forcing our heads back. We heard gunfire behind us and a loud *bang* as a bullet hit the vehicle, but I focused on staying on the road and driving toward the launch site.

I didn't know how to get there and had never seen the site before, but I knew the general direction based on the fiery trails I frequently saw in the sky.

The headlights illuminated the road in front of us, and I kept driving in the direction we had seen the shuttles launching from. I stopped at a fork in the road. There was a sign—New York Launch Site—with an arrow pointing to the left. I looked at Katia, who shrugged. I squeezed her hand.

I looked at Katia and said, "We could stay on Earth and take the other road, wherever it goes, and always be in danger of being found, or we could take the road that leads to Xima."

"I'll follow you anywhere, Zan," she said. I smiled down at her and decided to follow the arrow to the shuttle site.

Dawn was fast approaching. I saw an old building in a field on the right. Turning the wheel abruptly, I swerved through the grass toward it and maneuvered slowly through the large open doorway. Once inside, I stopped and turned off the car.

"What are we doing here?" Katia asked, as she peered through the window to evaluate the strange building we'd driven into.

"The sun is coming up, and I just wanted a chance to think without anyone seeing us. I'm sure others are looking for us by now." I got out of the car and closed the large door.

The building wasn't very well built. Loose boards ran vertically on the walls, there were cracks everywhere, tall piles of long yellow grass covered the floor, and a strange vehicle with tires as wide as I was tall was parked inside.

Katia got out and looked around. "I think this is an old barn. It's where farmers used to store equipment and livestock."

We looked around to see if there was anything we might be able to use. I opened a drawer to what looked like a large wooden bench. Inside were some old clothes that housed some mice. They jumped out of the drawer when I opened it farther. Katia screeched as they ran her way. I looked up at her with my finger to my lips to remind her that we needed to be quiet.

I took off the ADS uniform and put on the ragged clothes from the drawer. Katia went behind a small wooden wall to get dressed in the clothes she had brought along.

When she walked out to me, I held her hands and said, "I don't want you getting hurt. You can go back and tell them I abducted you if you want." Her eyes got wide, so I added, "It might be for the best."

"What? Are you trying to get rid of me already? I told you I loved you, and I'm going with you. That's final!" I couldn't help but feel the magic from her beautiful face draw me closer to her. I leaned down and kissed her. Some kind of electricity flooded my body from the feeling of her lips on mine. I pulled back slightly to see her lips pursed and her eyes closed. Then she opened her eyes, relaxing her mouth, and looked at me, puzzled.

I looked into her alluring eyes as she smiled and gazed back into mine. I kissed her again, and we pulled ourselves into each other with more intensity. She put her arms around me, and we continued kissing passionately. "Never leave me, Zan. Promise?" she whispered as our lips continued to touch.

I pulled away and smiled down at her, but I couldn't help but feel like I was controlling her fate. She was fifteen years old and still had the same long dark curly hair as when I had met her, but she was also more developed as a woman. I knew she would always attract unwanted attention from men, as she had with the man I'd killed, and I wasn't sure I could always protect her. I was struggling with my selfishness, knowing that keeping her with me was a great risk. *Will this really work? Or am I being greedy?*

The sound of a vehicle in the distance caught our attention. The faint rumble of tires on the road was getting louder. We ran to the wall that faced the road and looked through a crevice between two boards. The sound came from a small bus, travelling to the launch site, no doubt. Miss Linda said the shuttle would be leaving in the evening, but I didn't know what time.

All I knew for sure was that we needed to find a man named Mule.

Once the coast was clear, we walked out of the barn and, sticking to the fields, followed alongside the road. I figured if anyone came by, we could hide in the tall grass and avoid being seen.

We reached the top of a hill where a large lone tree stood, spreading its thick, coarse branches in many directions. We walked up to it and hid behind its trunk. I climbed the tree to get a better look.

The branches went in many directions and were quite strong. It wasn't the kind of tree found on the compound I grew up on.

"What can you see?" Katia asked from below.

I looked down to her and then peered out. I saw many people walking around the launch site as the shuttle sat there on a launch pad. A fence surrounded the entire facility, and the only way in was through the front gate. I recognized the ADS symbol on some of the vehicles inside the fence, but I doubted they would be looking for me there.

I looked back from where we came and couldn't see any vehicles coming for us, but I was sure it wouldn't be long before they did.

I began my descent when a branch broke under my feet. I reached for another, but my hand slipped. I landed on my stomach on a branch just above Katia.

"Are you all right? That was a long fall."

I gripped the branch, pushed myself off and landed on the ground. I seemed to be okay.

I took her hand and looked into her eyes. "Are you ready?"

She nodded, and we started our walk down the hill.

The tall grass tickled our hands as we floated them above the seeds that grew at the tops. I smiled at the prospect of living on a plot of land just like the farm and looking out over my field every day with Katia by my side.

Katia's grip on my hand was very tight. I was nervous too, but I wanted to be confident for her. She trusted me, and I didn't want to let her down. We walked slowly down to the entrance, arriving at the gate, where a guard stood with a small handgun strapped to his side.

He laughed as we walked up to him. "What are a couple of kids doing here all by themselves? You can get hurt playing around here."

"We're looking for a man named Mule," I said.

He immediately straightened and looked at me with narrowed eyes. The guard glanced about, then peered back at me. "Why would you be looking for Mule? He's not the kind of guy you children want to meet, if you know what I mean."

"We were told to find him."

"Go home. This isn't a place to play around in." The man turned, ready to ignore us.

"I'm not playing. We're going to Xima!" I exclaimed.

"Oh, are you now?" He laughed. He stared at us for a few moments, then went into the small shack at the entrance to speak with another guard. He came back out and said in a low voice, "Okay. I'll take you to Mule. But don't say I didn't warn you. He's a very mean man."

We followed the guard through the site. The shuttle looked large up close, almost like a strange box with wings and several large openings. *I can't believe we're actually going to get on the shuttle.* I could sense that Katia was still nervous as she bit her lower lip when she wasn't displaying her façade of a smile. I was quite nervous as well.

"Mule! These kids are looking for you," the gate guard called out to an enormous man hunched over a table.

The man turned around and stepped out from under an awning. He looked like he'd been in many fights; scars covered his face and arms. His hair looked like it was almost completely shaved on one side. It was difficult not to stare at him. Katia's hand was like a vise on mine. She looked to me, looked down at our hands, and then mouthed *sorry* as she relaxed.

"Are you the boy Linda told me about?" he said in a deep and harsh voice—the kind of voice that would scare any child.

I nodded.

"Who's this? She wasn't part of the arrangement." He pointed to Katia, scowling down at her with narrowed eyes. He snapped his gaze to me for an answer.

"This is m-my fiancée," I stuttered. "We're supposed to get married on Xima."

I should have told Katia about a lie like that ahead of time, but I'd thought of it on the spot. I glanced at her, a hint of surprise about our sudden engagement on her face, but she kept quiet.

"Okay, then. Where's the money?"

Katia and I looked at each other. I replied, "I don't know about any money."

He reached down to grab my shirt, lifting me into the air to look me in the eye. I hoped he didn't feel my body trembling in his grasp. "I don't do this shit for free," he grumbled. "I expect to be compensated." He looked down at Katia. "For the both of you."

I quickly replied, "Please! I didn't know about any money, but I'm sure if you call Miss Linda, she'll take care of it." I remembered Miss Linda taking money out of her desk drawer, and I deduced that she had planned to pay when she brought me to the launch site.

He dropped me to the ground, where I stumbled and nearly fell on my ass. Katia reached for my hand as I straightened up. The look on her face told me that we needed to change our plans.

Mule walked back under the awning and picked up a phone. I couldn't hear what he was saying, so I glanced around to find my exit strategy if things didn't work out, but how would I leave with Katia?

An ADS vehicle drove by. I turned my face away to see Mule set the phone down as he talked to some other men. He looked at us and then away again. He picked up a headset near some type of radio. I'd never seen such a thing before. Katia continued to smile, but it didn't hide the fear in her eyes. She trusted me. If things didn't work out, I'd take her somewhere else where we could live. Perhaps an old farm somewhere, providing we could get out of the facility.

I couldn't hear what he was saying, but he turned his head to look at us while he talked and nodded a lot. He set the headset down and walked over to us. "It would seem your Miss Linda was shot last night for harboring a fugitive."

"No!" Katia broke down crying, covering her face with her hands as she tried to hold back tears. I tried to keep from crying, but I soon felt the cool air on the trails made by the tears on my cheeks.

"You wouldn't happen to know anything about this fugitive, would you?" Mule asked, his wary eyes staring me down as though he already knew the answer.

I shook my head. "No, I don't know. We're just a couple of teenagers in love. All we want is to make it to Xima."

He looked at us and placed his hand on his chin, rubbing it as though he was in deep thought. A smile formed on his battle-worn face.

"You know what? Out of the kindness of my heart, I'm going to help you two. If you want to go to Xima, then I can make it happen." He looked around and boisterously said, "Never let it be said that Mule doesn't have a heart."

It seemed like his desire to help us was exaggerated. I wasn't sure I should trust him, but I didn't have any other options. I looked to Katia, who was still grieving the news of Miss Linda's death. I looked back in the direction of the barn. *We could take the car we stole and go somewhere else—but how far would we get before the ADS found us?* We had no choice but to leave Earth—and quickly.

I reached out to shake Mule's hand. "Thank you, sir. Thank you very much."

"It leaves in a few hours, so we need to get you onboard and set up for the long voyage."

He brought us to a man and a woman. "These fine technicians will get you settled into your sleep chamber for the trip. Nothing to worry about; you'll be on Xima in no time."

We followed the technicians to a steel structure with an elevator inside. As we ascended, I looked down at Mule, who remained on the ground. His smile had a hint of sarcasm, as though he was proud of something. Perhaps he was proud of helping us?

He saluted as we went up past a cargo door to another entrance. The view was spectacular—we could see everything above the trees. In the distance, the barn we'd hid in was visible at the center of the field of tall grass.

The thought of running back and just driving somewhere else came to mind one more time before the elevator stopped. But it was too late to turn back. The doors behind us opened, and two large men reached in to aggressively grab our arms.

One of the technicians put her hand up. "No need. They aren't prisoners. These are Mule's passengers." One of the larger men smiled and nudged the other, who also smiled.

As we walked into the next chamber, I overheard one of the large men say, "Damn, that Mule is one lucky bastard."

I looked back but could no longer see them. We turned a corner, then another, and finally, we found ourselves in a large room with what looked like large horizontal tubes mounted to the floor. We walked by, and I could see the face of a person through a glass window on one of them.

"Are we going into one of these tubes?" I asked with a little anxiety in my voice.

The technician nodded. "It's a long voyage, and there isn't enough food or oxygen for everyone. But it's okay. We'll make sure you're comfortable, and when you wake up, you'll have landed on Xima."

We walked up to two empty pods. Katia looked at me, trembling. I couldn't help but feel frightened for both of us.

We hugged each other, and I kissed her. "We'll be together when we get to Xima. I love you, Katia."

She seemed more relaxed. "I love you, too, Zan."

I walked to the next tube and smiled at her. She gave me her most radiant smile as I tried to memorize every part of her beautiful face. Soon, we'd have a life of our own and never be pursued again.

The technician had me take off my clothes and instructed me to put on a loose-fitting gown that tied in the back. I lay on the bed. He put some probes on my head and chest and inserted a needle into my arm. "This is to keep your body alive until you get there. It'll also keep you sleeping, since it's about a three-month journey. Trust me, you'll want to sleep through it."

I looked over at Katia through the glass window. We smiled at each other until my eyes closed.

Part II – Xima

Chapter 7

"Get your ass up!"

Everything was a blur as I was startled by the gruff yelling and my arm being pulled. Pain shot through my body as I hit the floor.

"Remove that needle before it breaks off inside of him. Xerxes will be pissed if you bring him in damaged," another voice called out.

My mind was foggy, and I didn't know what was happening. Something struck the side of my face.

"Wake up, I said!" A sharp pain hit my side as someone kicked me. I struggled to get to my knees.

"Where's Katia?"

Another harsh strike to my face. "Shut your hole. You'll only speak when asked to."

I tried to focus, but I felt like I was submerged underwater and could only see blurry shapes floating around me. Then something was put on my wrists, pulling me out of my haze and grounding me.

"What are you doing? We aren't prisoners. Let me go! Where's Katia?"

But another sharp blow quickly quieted me. "I said shut your mouth!" the gruff voice yelled, spewing a rain of spittle on my face.

Something cold and hard was put around my neck with a loud *click*. I reached up to feel the cold iron and tried to pull at it. Then my body lurched forward as something tugged my neck. *He placed a collar on me! And shackles on my wrists too.*

"What are you doing?" I pleaded. "We're not prisoners." I could finally see better, and I noticed that Katia's pod was already empty. "Where is she? Where's Katia!?" I yelled while struggling and pulling back against the chains.

A long-haired filthy man with shimmering red eyes raised his fist. As it came at my face, I winced.

* * *

My head throbbed, and I tried to use my hand to massage my aching temples as I squinted to see where I was. The rancid blanket I was lying on smelled like death and barely offered protection from the cold stone floor. *Where am I?* I took inventory of my surroundings: the room was small and held nothing but the blanket and a wooden pot propped against the wall. The low ceiling made me claustrophobic as did the lack of fresh air.

I stood up to walk toward the door but was stopped by a tug at my neck. I reached back to feel a long chain securing the iron collar to the wall. The shackles were tight on my wrists, and my head ached. A small window high up on the wall allowed some sunlight to filter through, dimly lighting the room.

My mind raced as I tried to figure out what had happened. The last thing I remembered was seeing Katia as I fell asleep on Earth. Then I awoke to find myself alone and chained to a wall. *What happened to Katia? What's happening to me? This can't be real.*

I cried out as loud as I could, "Where am I? I'm not a prisoner! Where's Katia?"

The sound of doors closing in the distance instilled both hope and fear in me. I didn't know what to expect, but I knew everything was all wrong; we were supposed to be free citizens on Xima.

I sat down against the wall and noticed I still wore the garment the technicians had me put on in the shuttle. I was scared, but I was even more scared for Katia. My mind raced with questions about her safety: *What could have happened to her? She must be terrified. How could I have done this to her?*

I concentrated and tried to use all my strength to break the chains on my shackles. The pain was incredible. A mixture of blood and rust enhanced the rich iron smell as my red life force ran down my arms. I couldn't do anything but sit there and wait for whatever they had planned for me.

There were faint noises—doors opening and closing and some distant voices—but nothing else. I had never felt so lost in my entire life. Even after escaping the ADS raid in that dark tunnel, I hadn't felt as helpless as I did sitting in that cell waiting for whatever my fate would be.

The faint echo of footsteps grew louder.

The sound of a key in the door made my heart flip in my chest, and the room felt a little bit brighter for a second. *This is my chance. Perhaps I can talk to someone and straighten out this mistake.* I heard the key turn, followed by a metallic click before the door swung open. A bulky man with long brown hair and leather armor walked in.

"Stand up, slave!" he exclaimed in a raspy voice.

I watched him walk toward me, followed by a woman. She was old enough to be my grandmother, or perhaps an elderly neighbor. Her hair was long and gray, and she only stood as high as the man's elbow. She was hunched over with a hump in her back, barely able to walk. Her face looked exhausted, worn down. The deep creases reminded me of pictures I'd seen of a rock face that had been weathered by the relentless desert sand.

The man struck at my head. I quickly raised my hands to block the blow, forcing him to strike my steel shackles. His hand bled on the floor.

"Fuck!" he cried out while stepping back to assess his wound.

"Why, you little shit!" he growled, his face red and eyes wide as he reached for the chain between my wrists and pulled me to my feet. He cocked back his fist, and I braced myself.

"Gerd!" another guard yelled from the doorway. "Xerxes said we needed to clean him and clothe him."

"You little fuck! You're lucky Xerxes paid for you or you'd be mud on my boot right now." He stormed off and closed the door.

"Welcome to Xima," the older woman said in a pitying voice which wasn't so welcoming. She set a tub of water next to me. "Let me see that cut." She dipped a rag in some warm water and wiped my head. Pain radiated through my skull as she touched the wound I'd received on the shuttle.

She spoke softly. "I'm sorry you're in this situation. What's your name?" the woman asked as she continued to clean my injury.

I kept my voice low and watched her eyes dart around the room as if searching for spies. "Please, you have to help me," I begged. "Where am I?

And where's Katia?" I reached out to grab her arm, to cling to something for support.

The door quickly swung open. "Don't touch her or you'll be beaten!" one of the guards yelled.

I looked up at the dark man with long greasy hair and the same leather uniform. I let go of her.

"I'm sorry. I mean no harm. I'm confused and don't know why—"

"Stand up. I need to change your clothes." The woman didn't seem to be listening.

I stood up and pleaded silently as she removed my garment. I stood there naked and covered my crotch with my hands. "What are you doing?"

She placed her hand on my arm. "Relax. I have a loincloth for you to wear, and a shirt. Trust me, I'm here to help take care of you and feed you. Think of me like a mother."

I relaxed my hands and thought about food. I hadn't eaten in months, and although the needle they'd had in my arm kept me alive, I was starving. She wrapped some cloth around my waist and under my crotch and tied it off. She pulled a piece of material over my head and tied it at my waist. The tears in my eyes blurred my vision, but I managed to see her saddened look toward me, and it confirmed the fact that my situation was grave.

"I can't help you, but I'll bring your food and keep you clean." She walked out and then returned with a metal plate. On it was what could only be interpreted as food alongside a metal cup of water. "Please, eat. You'll need your strength for what Xerxes plans to do with you."

My eyes lit up. "What's going to happen to me? Who's Xerxes?" I was getting frustrated at her ignoring me. She walked out, the door shut, the lock clicked, and the last sound I heard was her footsteps drifting off into silence. I moved toward the door until my chain was taut.

"Where's Katia?" I cried out again, perhaps not as loud as before. It was more of a helpless plea directed toward no one in particular.

I walked back, and a strange smell made me abruptly stop next to the wall. My food didn't look remotely appetizing, but as I looked down at it, I found that I didn't care. I slowly sat down and pulled the tray closer. Part of me wanted to throw it at the door, but my hunger prevailed.

The food tasted more gray than it looked, and there were both soft and hard chunks that I couldn't identify as plant or animal. Without any taste, I couldn't begin to guess what I was eating. It wasn't even the gel we ate at the shelter. I ate it all and washed down the last of it with water. *What did she mean when she said I'd need my strength? What will Xerxes do with me? What's he done with Katia?*

Confusion and helplessness consumed me. I thought that the whole situation must've been some type of nightmare. Someone had gotten something mixed up—Miss Linda and Mule must have had a miscommunication. Katia and I were supposed to be passengers, not prisoners. *Oh, Katia. What could they have done with you?* I'd promised to protect her, but there I was, in chains.

Chapter 8

The clicking sound at the door woke me. I stood with a growling stomach. The food I'd eaten may have had no taste, but my empty belly hungered for more.

Two large men walked in wearing the same leather outfits as the others.

"What's happening? What are you going to do with me?" I pleaded.

Without saying a word, they unlocked the chain from the wall and pulled me out of the room. We walked down the hallway to another room made of stone.

"This'll be your home until you turn eighteen," one guard said jokingly.

The other guard laughed. "Yeah, and you won't need a room much after that." They put the chain up through a ring on the wall and pulled my head tightly against it. My hands were unshackled, bringing me only a hint of relief.

They turned me around so that my face pressed against the wall as they fastened my wrists to two more wall-mounted rings. I jumped back, struggling to get away.

"No! I'm not a prisoner! Why are you doing this?" I cried out.

I turned my head to get a glimpse of what was happening. Another man had walked into the room. He had long dark hair and was the same size as the other two and wore the same leather armor. As he walked toward me, I could tell he was one of the strongest-looking men I'd ever seen. Without blinking, he put his face close to mine and stared at me with wide, bloodshot eyes.

"What's your name, boy?" he growled.

"Please, sir. My name is Zan. I'm not a prisoner. I came with my girl, Katia. Please, help me."

He laughed, as did the other men behind me. "He said he's not a prisoner." He continued laughing. "You're right. You're not a prisoner. You're a slave. You were sold to me, and I'll use you as I want."

"How? We weren't prisoners when we boarded the shuttle." I couldn't understand what was happening.

"Apparently, your shuttle ride wasn't paid for. So this is how you'll pay your debt." My heart nearly tore out of my chest, and I gasped desperately for air as I remembered Mule asking for payment. I remembered the money in Miss Linda's office that never made it to my hands. Then the man continued. "Do you know how you're going to pay for your passage to this luxurious planet?"

The stone on the wall was beginning to warm from my cheek. I was helpless "I'll pay, I promise! I'll do any work, but please let me and Katia go."

"*My* Katia is doing just fine. She's a house servant for me, but if you don't cooperate, I might just have her serve all of my guards instead. Would you like to have a taste of a young girl like her, men?"

They laughed as one of them yelled. "Yes, Xerxes!"

So this is Xerxes. He's the one who abducted me?

"Please, what do you want me to do? I'll do anything. Just don't hurt her."

His hands gripped my arms, then my shoulders and my back.

"I like a young man who's willing to do anything. I just happen to have some work for you, but you'll have to be prepared first. You have a good build. How old are you?"

"I'm fifteen, almost sixteen."

"Well, we'll have to throw you a birthday party." He and the other men laughed. "Once I toughen you up, you'll be one of my fighters. If you do well, I'll treat you well. The better you do, the better I'll treat you and the girl. If you don't fight well, then I'll have no reason to be so nice to either of you. Understand?"

"Okay. I'll do it—anything! Just don't hurt her."

"See, men? He just volunteered to be one of my fighters. Would you do me the honor of *toughening* him up for me? I have a good feeling about this one."

He walked out the door. One of the men said with surprising sincerity, "Once you stop crying out from the pain, it'll get easier for you." I tried to turn my head to face the other direction to see what they were doing but couldn't look back far enough. I looked in both directions, but I could only see movement behind me.

Crack!

The sound echoed through the room followed by agonizing pain across my back. The pain was so severe that my mouth opened, but I couldn't cry out.

Crack!

My scream was loud and clear after the second strike. Each strike was met with my screams. Tears ran down my face as I pleaded for them to stop. I never knew such pain could exist.

"Stop screaming, or it'll just get worse."

I couldn't help but cry out each time, my eyes flooding with tears as my back was torn to shreds. I lost track of the number of blows I took. I realized the noise was fading, as was my view of the cool rock wall I was pressed against.

A sudden rush of cold woke me. Water was being poured on my face.

"Time to eat." I saw the grandmotherly woman I'd met earlier with a plate of food, and she was accompanied by a guard with a bucket. The woman spoke softly as my mother used to when she wanted to comfort me. My mother. The mere thought of her and my father had caused me pain in the past, but my thoughts were instead of how she had comforted me as the woman did.

"Eat while I clean you." She went back to the door to get a tub of water and knelt next to me. "This might sting a little bit." My body twitched at the cold, wet rag on my back. It stung as though she was cutting my back with knives, and I arched from the pain as I tried to eat.

"They'll continue doing this until you no longer feel pain. Or until you pass out like you did."

"Why are they doing this?" I begged, trying to look into her eyes. She avoided my gaze.

"They want you to be a tough fighter—one who doesn't feel pain in the ring." I stared at her in panic.

"What ring?" I couldn't help but whimper, my tears falling on my plate of food.

"You'll have to fight others in an arena. It's bare hands until you're sixteen, then you use staffs. Once you're eighteen, you fight with real weapons and..." She paused as she continued to clean my back.

"A-and what?"

She washed my back again, and I winced. "Once you turn eighteen, you'll fight to the death."

"Stop talking to him!" a guard yelled from the doorway.

"So, I'll never leave here?" I dropped my food, which seemed like meat of some kind. "I'll be a fighter until I die?" I stared until my eyes blurred, not wanting to believe in the stark reality thrust upon me.

"I'm sorry. My name is Mir. I can only do as I'm told, or I'll be beaten, too." She pushed my plate closer. "Eat. You need to keep your strength up and remember to embrace the pain. It's the only way they'll stop."

"Enough talk! Leave him," a guard yelled. Mir picked up her tub of water turned red from my blood and left the room. The guard locked the door, leaving me alone again.

As I listened to their footsteps fading into the distance, fear mixed with rage ran through my body—I didn't know which was more prevalent. The thought of being used until I died infuriated me, but the thought of never seeing Katia fueled my rage to extreme heights.

I ate the food Mir left and drank the water. I lay down on the blanket spread out on the floor. I preferred to lie on top of the blanket rather than on the cold stone. The air was just cool enough for goosebumps to form on my skin, but it also soothed the burning sensation on my back.

The pain in my back was still there, and each throb conjured up another worry. My thoughts built until my anger became more painful than my wounds. *Did I make the right decision to come here?*

I wondered if I had put Katia in harm's way for my own selfish interests. *Katia… What horrors could she be enduring?* I realized I either needed to adapt or die, and I owed it to Katia to survive.

The sound of the door unlocking woke me from a deep, dreamless sleep. The same guards came in, but this time they shackled me to the wall facing them. They had staffs in their hands instead of the whips they'd used the day before. I didn't say a word as I tried to find my place of comfort. I needed to put my mind somewhere, completely away from the torment and pain.

Whack!

Crack!

The staff struck my chest, and I felt like it broke my ribs. I cried out. I needed to find a distraction.

Whack!

Another strike to the upper part of my legs. The stinging brought tears to my eyes. The guards laughed, seeming to enjoy the torture.

I remembered the expression on Katia's face when I told Mule she was my fiancée. I could never forget the gleeful surprise on her glowing face. I painted a picture of her in my mind… our kiss in the barn… my love for her…

Whack! I winced at the blow, but it wasn't as painful as the others. I kept the view of Katia in my mind through the next several beatings. Her hair, her eyes, the touch of her face…

Whack! I winced again, but after the initial sting, my thoughts absorbed the pain. I'd found a way to channel the agony elsewhere, and I was ready for the next hit.

"Why are you smiling?" One guard put his hand on my face, squeezed my cheeks, then slapped me.

"Why are you smiling?" he asked again, striking my other cheek.

I looked right through him. All I could see was Katia—her curly black hair, her smile, how happy she made me just by being near me, our kiss in the barn again. I embraced the memory, and it was as though I could taste her still.

The guards left, leaving me fastened to the stone wall. I tried to look down at the damage to my body, but I couldn't see because of the chain pulling my neck up. Moments later, the door opened.

"We swear, Xerxes. He feels no pain." I recognized the guard's voice.

"That's impossible. It usually takes weeks to build up that type of resistance."

They walked in and stood before me. I peered down at them as best I could. "Give me that staff," Xerxes barked.

I focused again on Katia as the staff hit my chest. Another strike to my legs. Xerxes slapped my face and grabbed my hair, pulling my head back. "What are you, boy? No one builds up immunity to pain that fast." He growled. "I should cut you open and see what you're made of, but I spent too much ginny for you."

He stood in front of me and stared for a while. I turned my eyes to him with a smile, embracing my minor victory. "Take him down and try again tomorrow with the course floggers. We'll see what he can really take."

When the guards released me, I slumped to the floor. I sat against the wall as Xerxes knelt in front of me. I returned his gaze with steady eyes.

"There may be hope for you yet, boy."

"My name's Zan," I murmured.

He laughed. "Okay, Zan. We'll see what you've really got." He looked up at the guards. "Have Mir feed him twice today. I want him to keep his strength."

"Yes, Xerxes."

The door closed, and I heard their footsteps fade into the distance. I couldn't help but feel like I'd emerged victorious. I rubbed my arm where my father had placed the implant. *Is this little device the real reason for my ability to resist pain?* I remembered what Miss Linda had told me about my father and why he'd been killed. *Why did he do this to me? Why take the risk?*

I lay down on my blanket and stared at the stone wall. My hand glided along the smooth rocks, my fingers running through the rivers of mortar between them. My fingers glided down to a loose stone about a hand's height from the floor. Although loose, it wasn't going to come out. At least not yet. *I expect to spend a lot of time here, so perhaps I'll get it out one day.*

I awoke the next day to Mir bringing a plate of food. The guard stood at the door and waited. Mir whispered, "I heard they're going to test you harder today. Please, try to resist again."

I took some of the meat and whispered back, "Have you seen my friend Katia?"

"Let me see how your wounds are healing." She looked at my back and then my head. "You're healing quickly—much faster than most people do," she said with a slow, curious tone.

"Please, have you seen Katia?" I pleaded again.

"I wish you well today, and make sure you eat everything." She stood and backed away, looking at me as though she wanted to help but couldn't. Her eyes stared down at my plate. The guard took her arm and pulled her out of the room, locking the door behind them.

As I ate the food, I noticed a small piece of cloth with some writing on it: Girl is OK. I looked back up at the door and realized that Mir could've gotten in trouble for giving me the message. *Why would she put herself in danger for me?*

Katia was all right, and suddenly the stone floor felt warmer, the room looked brighter, and I couldn't help but smile. I didn't know how to repay Mir for risking her life to help me.

I swallowed the note with some water. Eating every bit of food, I felt no pain at all. My sole focus became to do as they asked so I could find a way out of the hell I was in.

The next time the guards came for me, they ran a chain through my wrist shackles and up to a ring on the ceiling. They pulled me up until I was hanging in the center of the room, my toes just touching the floor. One guard pulled a looped whip from his belt and another had a small club. They both grinned when one said with an evil laugh, "We're gonna have some fun with you today, Zan. Let's see how tough you really are."

I placed myself in the barn again with Katia, and all I could do was embrace her and long for her kiss as they continued to beat me. I felt the sting of the whip as it cut into my skin, but I only winced. I felt myself cry out in the back of my mind, but I pushed it away and focused on Katia's beauty and how much I wanted to be with her again.

Everything they did to me was in the periphery of my mind. I tried not to pay attention to the pain they were inflicting on me. When I suddenly fell to the floor, I realized they were done and had lowered me. The excruciating pain throughout my body came to life. I moaned, lying in a fetal position.

The guards dragged me back to the wall and fastened my neck chain to the metal ring again. Their footsteps faded as I surveyed the extent of the torment they'd inflicted on me. I had welts and cuts on top of opened scabs all over my body. I cried quietly, not wanting anyone to hear how much pain racked my body.

Moments later, the door opened, and Mir came in with her washtub.

"Oh my." She gasped as she knelt next to me. She washed my cuts and then put cream on my welts. "This is to help with the pain. And to prevent infection."

I stared at her face, waiting for the moment when she looked into my eyes. Once she did, I whispered, "Thank you for your help. I ate every bite."

She smiled proudly, no doubt catching my meaning.

Xerxes came bustling through the door, and we both looked away. He stood over Mir, who was just finishing her work.

"Leave, Mir," he bellowed.

Once she'd left the room, Xerxes knelt in front of me. "Amazing! Your wounds heal so fast, and you resist pain better than anyone I've ever seen." He stared at me for a few moments. "I want him to heal over the next few days. Feed him well, and then teach him to fight."

"Yes, Xerxes," one of the guards replied.

Xerxes stood and continued to stare. "He might be ready sooner than I thought." He walked to the door but paused as if forgetting something.

"Oh, and as for your girl, keep in mind: she's *my* girl. And I'll do with her as I please. Quite a few of my men have taken a fancy to her." He walked back to me and lightly slapped my face, his open mouth showing vile yellow and orange teeth.

"I'd like to keep the girl all to myself—she's the most beautiful house servant I've ever had, and so polite too—but if you disappoint me, boy, I'll have no choice but to share her with every guard on Xima. Understand?"

He slapped my face one more time and laughed.

I was enraged at his threat, but I realized I shouldn't piss him off. Still, I had to ask one thing.

"Katia! How is she? Can I see her?" I asked, crawling forward on my hands and knees. Anticipation filled my soul at the prospect of confirming her well-being.

"Learn to fight well, Zan. I might let you see her one day," he said with a slight laugh as he walked out of the room.

The next few days were empty, save for Mir monitoring my recovery and feeding me. It was the same food every day. I hated eating tasteless cardboard and relished the day I could have that delicious paste at the orphanage. But I knew I had to eat to maintain my strength. I'd do anything to see Katia again.

Chapter 9

I was in the woods again, running from the men who'd killed my family. They were getting closer, and when I turned to look back, they had Katia. She trashed and kicked to break free, but the men were stronger. Just as they were about to throw her in the back of a truck, the sound of a key turning in a lock woke me from my nightmare.

"Time for training, Zan!" *Zan? Oh, that's me.* I was surprised they were using my name instead of "boy."

I stood up as the guards unchained me from the wall. We walked down a couple hallways to a large open room with a circle in the middle. The stench was overpowering, like a mixture of body odor and mildew. The circle consisted of large, mortared stones with sand in the middle. There were benches and chairs everywhere, and then I saw a more decorative table in a corner by a tapestry on the wall. The light came through open wooden windows around the building and along the top of the walls. There were also torches stuck in the walls for nighttime light, I suspected. To the far wall was a rack full of weapons made of a crude metal. One of the staffs had signs of red on it—blood no doubt.

I noticed the stones were bloodied too. One of the guards removed the shackles and the chain from my neck, leaving the iron collar heavy on my shoulders.

"Try to run, and you'll wish you were never born," the guard threatened as he walked out of the room.

Three guards stood around the ring as another man wearing leather pants and no shirt walked into it. "My name is Trev. My job is to teach you how to fight. We'll start with the basics and work our way into weapons when you're ready. How old are you?"

"Almost sixteen," I said, looking around at the guards whose eyes were locked on me.

A hand quickly slapped my face. "Pay attention at all times. I could have just cut your throat while your head was turned. Lesson number one: as soon as you're in the ring, always focus on your opponent. Never get distracted, or you'll be dead."

He reached outside of the ring for a human figure made of fabric stuffed with straw. He walked up to me. "Let's see you punch this dummy as hard as you can."

He held it in front of himself, and I looked at the laughing guards around the ring. I remembered how hard I'd hit the man who had attacked Katia as well as the ADS guard at the orphanage. I looked at the dummy, pulled back my fist, and hit it as hard as I could. Trev flew backward, nearly hitting his head on the stone ring behind him.

The guards' jaws dropped, and mine would have too if I wasn't clenching my teeth so tightly from anger. I looked down at my fist, wondering how much strength I really had, and then I heard Miss Linda's voice in the back of my head reminding me to keep my strength a secret. *Can I trust these men? What could they do to me? The ADS is looking for me back on Earth, not here.*

"Where the hell did that come from?" Trev laughed, standing up again. "I guess I need to brace myself a little better. I didn't expect that."

He positioned himself in a firmer, more supportive position, prepared himself, and held the dummy in front of him. "Okay, hit it again."

I struck it with the same ferocity as before. The dummy slipped from Trev's hands and was forced into his body, pushing him backward, but he didn't lose his footing.

"Wow! Have you fought before or done any training?" he asked.

I shook my head and rubbed my arm, pondering what kind of monster my father had turned me into and whether it would put me in further danger.

* * *

Over the next several weeks, Trev taught me how to attack, defend, and predict my opponent's movements based on their previous moves. I learned quickly, and I noticed my strength had increased since Trev's initial assessment and my dexterity was far better than before. One day, to ward off a kick from

Trev, I managed to lift him several feet off of the ground. The look on his face when he hit the floor was a combination of shock and awe.

I would soon be sixteen, so Trev taught me to fight with a staff. He showed me a fancy display of his ability to wield the weapon by spinning it in his hand, around his back, and throwing it in the air. He was quite confident in his skills and seemed to enjoy showing them off. I remembered when I first came to the ring and he'd told me, "Never get distracted, or you'll be dead." There were many times while he was showing off that I could have attacked him, but I wasn't fast or proficient enough yet. I would remember when the time was right.

Every time I fought one-on-one with Trev, I held back because I believed that one day I'd need to use all of my strength against him. I also wanted to avoid revealing my true capabilities to the guards who oversaw our training. I attempted to learn Trev's techniques, but every time I bested him, he changed his strategy. He was truly a very good fighter, and I learned a lot. But I realized that if I did have to fight him one day, he'd be an unpredictable adversary. I had to be equally unpredictable in order to defeat him.

The concept of becoming more elusive fascinated me, and I daydreamed about how I could use my newfound skill for stealth to sneak away from my cell and find Katia. If I trained hard enough, soon even Trev would be caught off guard by my quick moves.

One day, Trev brought me to the ring along with two other boys who seemed about my age. "These are two of Xerxes's most experienced fighters," he said. "I want you to fight both of them at the same time."

The reality of the situation finally dawned on me. Xerxes had two other boys to fight because it was their main source of entertainment on Xima.

They looked confident but weren't as muscular as me. Then I noticed their backs—scarred and red like mine but much worse. It looked like the wounds had healed and reopened multiple times, and they oozed with pus. *I wonder if they even notice the pain anymore?*

I knew I could deal with a single opponent, but two against one was something I'd never even considered.

"But I've never done that before," I said, grabbing the staff he threw at me.

The two other fighters took their positions across from me, trying to look for an opening in my defense. I tried to keep my eyes on them as they spread out.

"Trev, you never taught me how to do this."

One fighter lunged at me with his staff. I deflected the blow, while the other fighter came down on me, hitting the top of my shoulder. I quickly turned to face him, the first boy swept my feet out from under me, causing me to fall. I wasn't able to concentrate on both of them at the same time—they were everywhere at once.

I stood up and looked at them as they tried to position themselves far from one another so that I couldn't focus on both. One boy swung at me with his weapon, and while I blocked him, the other swept my feet out again with his staff, and I fell into the sand again. I quickly swept his feet out from under him with my leg. Leaping to my feet, I twirled my staff and jabbed the boy who was still standing in the chest so hard he stumbled out of the ring.

The second guy stood up and swung at my face, but I parried his attack. Soon, I noticed he had the same stance and move each time. He'd stare at a spot, pull his elbow back, and lunge at the spot his eyes were locked on. The entire act took no more than a second, but it was enough time for me to prepare.

I purposefully left an opening for him to lunge at me, anticipating his timing. Then I swung my staff around and hit the back of his legs, flipping him backward onto his stomach. I stood on his back with the end of my staff against the back of his neck.

Trev clapped. "Well done. I thought you said you didn't know what you were doing?"

I reached down to help the guy on the ground stand up. As he stood, he tackled my stomach. I fell onto my back, nearly hitting the stones. In one continuous motion, I held his arms, kicked at his stomach, and tossed him behind me over the stone ring and onto the hard floor.

"Excellent! Excellent! As long as your opponent is in the ring and he hasn't given up, you're still in the fight. Never forget that. Either knock him out, make him yield, or toss him out of the ring. When it comes to fighting to the death, you won't have many options."

The other two boys walked up to Trev. He put his arms around their shoulders. "These are my best fighters. I trained them both over the past five years. You'll never fight them in the ring, so consider them your brothers. From now on, you'll train together. The three of you will become the best fighters on Xima."

One of the guards took the staff from my hands and shackled my wrists.

"Why am I still shackled if I'm a brother now?" I said with a grunt, realizing the other boys weren't in chains.

Trev walked up to me and placed his hand on my shoulder. "You have hatred in your system. That hatred can't be trusted. Especially now that you know how to fight." He stared into my eyes, confirming the truth of his statement. "Perhaps once you've been here for a year we might remove the collar." He walked away, and the guards took me back to my stone room.

Mir came in right after me with the same tub of water and a rag. My collar was chained to the wall, but I managed to stand as she removed my loincloth and began washing me. I'd become used to the routine. It was like a mother coming in to take care of her son… who happened to be chained to a wall. As she put my loincloth back on, the guards brought in what looked like a mattress.

"A gift from Xerxes. He wants to make sure you're more comfortable before your fight."

"Fight? What fight?" I looked at Mir for an answer. She shrugged her shoulders.

"You're scheduled for a fight in two days. Rest up, Zan," the guard said in a friendly manner. His tone was almost like what you'd hear from a coach or a teacher, as though my situation was an everyday thing.

They locked the door and walked away. I lay down on my new mattress and was surprised to find it was the softest thing I'd felt for as long as I could remember. They left the other blanket for me, and I grabbed it to cover up against the cool temperatures. I could barely remember the last time I'd lain on an actual mattress with a blanket.

I couldn't help but feel grateful to Xerxes for the gesture, but my disdain for him enslaving me far outweighed the fleeting feeling of appreciation. I had to stay strong and find a way to save Katia and get us both out of the mess we were in.

I continued picking at the mortar holding the loose stone in place. Some light spilled through the crevice, and I knew it was an outside wall. *Light to the outside!* I was exhilarated to have hope, even if it was from looking through a small hole. It was the outside, and freedom seemed inches away—even if it was just wishful thinking. The stone was becoming much looser.

As I continued picking away, one small granule at a time, I kept thinking about Katia. I hoped to see her again soon. *Perhaps Xerxes will let me see her after I win this fight.* The fight… I'd just turned sixteen which meant my first fight would be with staffs. I'd done well against the other boys, but I still had my doubts.

The next day, Mir brought my meal. I whispered, "Please, tell Katia I'll free her one day. Tell her not to give up."

She shook her head. "No, I can't. They're always watching. You'll be punished for saying such things."

"Stop talking in there!" a guard bellowed from the doorway.

Mir turned toward the door and, with an encouraging tone, said, "Good luck in your fight, Zan."

I spent that evening wiggling the stone in the wall in the hopes that one day it would finally come out, allowing me to see the outside world again. It wasn't very large—not nearly big enough a hole for me to escape—but it would be enough to give me some hope that I might see the light of day again. I relished the possibility of escaping my prison, but every strategy I considered would endanger Katia. Unless I had her with me when I left, it wouldn't be worth the risk.

I thought about how much I'd wanted to come to Xima, to see a kohl and the other strange sights the planet had to offer. It was supposed to be our fresh start, but I imagined how, if I did escape with Katia, Xerxes would hunt us down. The fear of defeat brushed my mind periodically, but the hope of eventually getting the stone out of the wall kept my dream of freedom alive.

The door opened abruptly. It was Xerxes. "My boy, Zan! It's your big day today! Trev told me how well you've done and how strong you are. I'm looking forward to more great things from you, boy. Make me proud." His words of encouragement gave me more confidence, but I still needed to know how Katia was doing.

As he turned around and walked toward the door, I said, "Can I see Katia if I win today?"

Xerxes stopped abruptly and turned around to face me with a smile. He looked down at the floor for a moment, maybe thinking about what he wanted to say. He strolled toward me and placed his hand on the back of my neck, which he gripped very tightly.

"Your impudence is trying my patience, boy. Perhaps I'll punish her every time you test me." He slapped my face, leaving a stinging sensation on my cheek. "That's what I'm going to give her when I see her. Just know that it's you who gave it to her. Also, know this: I could simply kill her tomorrow. That's my decision, too. You do well for me, and I'll treat you and your girl well."

He slapped me lightly on my cheek and revealed his atrocious teeth. "Do we understand each other?"

Rage spread through every fiber of my being, but I knew I needed to hide it. Every muscle in my body wanted to lurch forward and strangle him, but it wouldn't end well if I did. I simply nodded. He turned around and walked out. The guards unfastened my chain from the wall and escorted me out of the room.

They took me to the large arena where I'd been practicing. It was full of people yelling about wagers of something called ginny.

"One hundred ginny on Zan," someone shouted.

"Fifty ginny on Gril," many others yelled. I couldn't see the other end of the room because it was packed with heaving bodies. It was the first time I'd seen so many people since arriving on Xima.

The guards removed my shackles as I looked around. I stopped with glee—Katia! But when I looked closer, I saw it was another young slave girl serving drinks. *Maybe she knows how I can find her.* With all the noise and movement, I barely noticed a guard putting a staff in my hand. I habitually grabbed it as the surrounding sounds distracted me from what was about to happen.

"Gril… Zan… fight!" I heard the familiar words being called out just like during my practice with Trev. My mind was still stuck on the commotion all around me. *Where did that girl go?* As I turned to face the center of the ring, a staff hit me square in the abdomen, followed by an elbow to my face. I fell toward the edge of the stone ring, but, catching myself on the stones, I pushed myself up and rolled back toward the middle.

I quickly stood up to see my opponent. He was the same size as me—perhaps a bit thinner. But I saw rage and confidence in his eyes. I glanced at Trev, who stood with a look of disappointment on the other side of the ring. He gestured for me to keep my eyes on my opponent.

In all my training, I was never taught how to deal with the sensory overload of so many people yelling and moving around outside of the ring. After being locked in my small cell with only the sound of my heartbeat for company, the noise made my head spin.

I was filled with confusion, but somewhere in the back of my mind I heard a woman's voice say my name. When I looked in the direction of the voice, I received a blow to the back of my head. I backed away, trying to block out the pain and stare down the combatant. I had to block everything else out and focus exclusively on my adversary.

I dodged multiple jabs Gril threw at me. A double lunge caught me off guard, resulting in a stiff blow to my side. I tried to find a pattern in his routine or some kind of weakness. We clashed with our staffs several times. I swept at his feet, catching one, but he kept his balance. My focus was becoming clearer, and I was soon able to ignore the commotion outside the ring and concentrate solely on taking Gril down.

He was skilled and also unpredictable. He had the ability to deceive me with his eyes by looking one way and then attacking from a different direction. He was a far more challenging adversary than my training brothers, but there had to be something I could do that was just as unpredictable.

I threw my staff to the sand. Gril smirked at me, everyone else gasped, and then the audience's racket was reduced to hushed whispers.

"Pick up your staff, boy!" I heard the familiar gruff voice of Xerxes behind me.

"That was a mistake!" Gril said as he lunged at me, feinting to one side and then swiftly twisting around and swinging his staff at me with lightning speed.

I turned and grabbed his staff with one hand, elbowing him in the face with my other arm. I grabbed the back of his head and reached between his legs, picking him up while he was dazed from the blow. I only needed a fraction of my strength to throw him out of the ring and into the crowd, knocking over several men with Gril's body.

I stepped back and slowly recognized the sound of cheering.

Someone raised my arm. "Winner… Zan!" I looked around and spotted a smile on Xerxes's face.

I walked to the edge of the ring where Trev stood. "That was great, Zan! Good job looking defenseless. I'd love to take credit, but that was all you!" He patted me on the back as the guards put my shackles and chain back on.

Then Xerxes approached me. "Good job, Zan. I knew you'd be a great fighter." He turned to collect his winnings from someone, then cheered while holding his fistful of coins above his head.

On the way to my cell, I asked a guard, "What's a ginny?"

The guard laughed. "It's what you made a lot of for us today. It's money here on Xima."

They took me into my room and chained me to the wall again. Soon, Mir came in with food and her cleaning tub. I grabbed some bread and stood up while she removed my loincloth and cleaned me again. "Congratulations on your win, Zan."

I looked down at her, then at the guard at the door. I looked at the ground and whispered, "Is Katia okay?"

She continued cleaning me while she looked up at the guard. She dried my arms, and while the guard was looking away, she whispered, "The girl's okay."

I smiled as she put a fresh loincloth on me and left. I sat down to finish my food, comforted by the knowledge that she was unharmed. I wanted to see her again so badly I ached. I may have had muscles and quick healing, but the thoughts of her were my true inner strength. When I thought I saw her in the crowd, I wanted to fight everyone in my way to get to her. I just might fight everyone to save her… someday.

Chapter 10

I trained with my fight brothers a few times a week.

They weren't as good as Gril, but even without trying as hard I could still tell that my skills were improving, I was getting much stronger, and my dexterity was improving.

They fought me two-on-one most of the time, and sometimes Trev would fight alongside them, which was challenging. Eventually, I got to a point where I could win against all three of them.

It was exhilarating to know I had such skills, but in the back of my mind I knew Trev wasn't showing me all of his moves. I also was constantly battling distractions. It was difficult, at times, to fight when the thought of Katia came to mind. However, those thoughts quickly faded after a blow to my body. I knew I had to concentrate harder if I wanted to win, especially if I had to fight to the death at some point. Katia was my greatest strength, but sometimes she was also my greatest weakness.

Over the following months, I faced many more opponents. After each fight, I emerged victorious. Whenever I wasn't fighting, training was mandatory.

Because I held back, I had no idea how strong I really was, but neither did Trev. I had a feeling one day I'd meet Trev in a real fight to the death, and I needed him to think I was weaker than I was. He was a good fighter, and all of my contemplations of escape involved having some type of advantage in order to defeat him.

*   *   *

When the guards came in to get me for my next fight, they didn't look as enthusiastic as they had in the past. Over the months I'd spent there, they'd become my biggest supporters—they seemed to have made a lot of ginny by betting on me.

"Is something wrong today, guys?" I asked as they unfastened my chain from the wall and guided me toward the door.

They didn't say a word, and I knew something was wrong. "What's going on?" I asked again, but my words were met with silence.

The guards brought me into the ring where I found myself facing two larger men with pointed staffs. Stricken with panic, I looked to Xerxes, who smiled, then to Trev, whose arms were crossed, his chin resting in his hand. *At least* he *looks concerned.*

I looked to the fight referee and said, "There must be some mistake. This isn't supposed to be a death fight—I'm not old enough."

He looked to Xerxes with a concerned expression but didn't respond. Everyone's strange, silent behavior made me feel like I was going to vomit, but I had to stay strong for Katia.

I was handed a staff without a point as Xerxes raised his hands and yelled for everyone's attention. Silence quickly spread throughout the crowd.

"Today, we have a special treat! Our undefeated Zan will be given a new challenge! He'll fight two surviving death fighters with spears. My money's on Zan. What odds do I have?"

The crowd roared, but all I could hear were my own racing thoughts. *Is he serious? Two death fighters against me? And they have actual weapons! I'm so fucked!* My heart raced so fast that I could've sworn it was going to leap from my chest. The two adversaries just stood near each other with sickening glee. I could see some of the rot on their yellowing and broken teeth.

The room erupted in motion. There was a frenzy of people calling out wagers, and I could hear others shouting that I wasn't old enough, but those comments were quickly hushed. I looked at my two opponents, who stared me down with arrogant smirks. *What am I going to do now?* I tried to evaluate them as best I could but saw nothing that would give me even a hint of an advantage.

The crowd was deafening as I stood inside the ring with my staff in my sweaty hand, searching for a way to escape. I scanned the room to see if Katia might be somewhere even though I knew the chances were slim. If I were to fall, I wanted to at least see her one more time. But I couldn't find her anywhere.

"The wagering is complete!" Xerxes exclaimed. "This isn't a fight to the death, as Zan is not quite eighteen. But if he accidentally falls, I'll take the responsibility."

What the fuck!? Just when I thought I couldn't get any more scared, my entire body froze. I tried to prepare my stance, but I couldn't move. *Is this what it's like to be petrified with terror?*

The ring referee yelled, "Bo… Kent… Zan… fight!"

My heart continued to pound as I tried to keep myself positioned so neither of them could get behind me. My goal was to evaluate them as much as possible in order to find some weakness. But they had survived death fights, so I wasn't expecting them to give away much of their tactics.

Something tells me I was set up to die today. I recalled my last discussion with Xerxes when he said others were interested in Katia. Then I remembered the somber expressions of the silent guards as they brought me to the ring. That's when I knew: *Xerxes bet against me today, and he wants me to lose.*

I stared at the points on my opponents' spears. They would definitely skewer me, given the chance. One of the men lunged at me, but I deflected his attack with my staff. Then both tried to advance on me simultaneously. I blocked their attacks and tried to trip one of them, but he was too quick.

They circled around me, stabbing sporadically with their spears. My heart dropped when I noticed dried blood on the tips. It was difficult to look at both men at the same time because every time I focused on one, the other would attack. One managed to cut my arm when I was too slow to dodge, and the other sliced my leg right after. I was losing blood quickly and needed to do something, or I'd be done for.

One fighter darted to my side, and as I reacted to him, the other ran behind me. I could almost sense his movements as the man in front ran toward me. Without a second thought, I ducked and lay flat on my back, causing the two to collide. The man behind me pierced the one in front with his spear. The audience gasped.

Blood spilled on my face as I lay on the ground under them. While the uninjured man paused after stabbing his partner, I grabbed at his legs and threw him to the ground. I put his arm behind his back, pushing his head into the sand. I could feel the joints in his arm crack from the pressure. I glanced up to Xerxes, who had a gleeful look on his face.

My opponent slapped the ground to admit defeat.

"Stop the fight! Winner… Zan!" the referee called out.

People came in to take the wounded man away, and the other man stood to glare at me, holding his arm, which looked broken. Anger glinted in his eyes.

"I knew you could do it, my boy!" Xerxes bellowed as he walked up to me and patted me on my back.

"They were going to kill me!" I exclaimed.

"That was a possibility, but you proved yourself. I have a reward for your performance today."

He nodded to another guard standing away from the ring. As that guard went into the hallway, others put the shackles back on me and fastened a chain to my collar. The guard came back out, holding Katia's arm.

"Katia!" I yelled. I tried to run toward her, but the guards yanked me back.

"Zan!" she yelled and fell to her knees, crying while the guard gripped her arm.

"Please, let me go to her. Please." The moisture on my cheeks and my blurred vision made me realize I hadn't truly let myself cry for her—for us. I knelt and continued to stare at her like it was the last time I'd ever see her. "Please, Xerxes." I never wanted to grovel before him, but, seeing her alive, I became desperately weak.

Xerxes grabbed my arm and calmly said, "As you can see, she's alive and well. Keep winning fights for me, and she'll stay that way. Cross me, and she'll meet a fate neither of you will like."

"You bastard! If you ever hurt her—"

The slap across my face did nothing but amplify my rage. So did the following punch to my stomach, after which I purposefully fell to my knees to act like I was hurt. A guard pulled up on the chain, forcing me to my feet. Xerxes put his hand on my throat as I stared at Katia.

He whispered in my ear, "Remember who controls the both of you here. I suggest you show a little more respect. Understand?" He slapped my face again and backed away.

I nodded and looked at Katia as the guard pulled her away. "I love you, Zan!" she cried out, and then she was gone

Tears continued to run down my cheeks as the guards pulled me back to my cell. Finally, I knew that Katia was alive and well. *I should be grateful. No—what the hell? I should be livid. We should be free citizens, not slaves!*

As the same guards who always escorted me to and from the arena secured me in my room, I said as firmly as I could through my tears, "If any harm ever comes to Katia, I'll make sure everyone associated with Xerxes is dead."

They turned to face me and laughed. One guard put his hands on my face, pinching my cheeks together, and said, "You got lucky today, kid. The death matches aren't so friendly. Once you're dead, I plan on using my savings to buy that girl of yours and use her as a real man should." He let go of me, laughing, and slapped the other guard on the back. "Ain't that right? Maybe we can both buy her and share."

The chain held me back as I lurched toward them. They continued to laugh as they walked out the door, locking it behind them.

I sat back down on my mattress and smiled at my chance to see her, my Katia. I thought about whether I could fight through all those people in the arena to get to her and the exit. I noticed only the guards were armed with swords, but there were at least a hundred people in the crowd. I didn't know if I could plow through so many and then potentially have to face Trev. I vowed to train more, and with a real sword in my hand, maybe I'd have a chance.

* * *

Xerxes continued to pit better and better fighters against me. Sometimes he'd use two at a time, and sometimes he wouldn't let me have a weapon at all. I actually liked being defenseless better, as I could move quicker and use my opponents' weapons against them.

During one such fight, my opponent wielded a long knife while I had nothing. The referee yelled, "Xerxes! Zan has nothing to fight with against a sword, and he's too young for a death fight!"

Xerxes said to the referee in a stern voice, "That's not a sword; it's a long knife. And, besides, it isn't to the death, so it's legal. Go ahead, ref. Get the fight going." Xerxes held a small bag of coins for the referee to see, to which he smiled and commenced the fight.

I'd never fought someone wielding a knife or a sword before. I knew a knife wouldn't necessarily kill, but it could do a lot of damage. Xerxes didn't seem to care if I was hurt, as I was just property to him. Fortunately for me, I knew I'd heal quickly.

"Tallis… Zan… fight!"

I kept my distance from him as we circled the ring, concentrating on finding each other's weakness. He was smaller than my other opponents, but he had the same tired, disillusioned look in his eyes.

My hands were out while I tried to focus on his entire body, examining his every move. He lunged at me a few times, leaving little nicks on my arms. His hand holding the knife was able to get closer to me without my staff to ward him off. Every time I reached for him, his knife was there to quickly slice at me.

Soon my arms were covered in small cuts, and I was getting mad. Tallis backed away from me and laughed while licking my blood off the edge of his blade. I glanced at Xerxes, who grinned at me. I didn't know if he wanted me to lose or win, but it seemed like the odds were against me.

We continued circling around the ring. Tallis said, "Perhaps the mighty Zan would prefer to simply finish this and put my knife in his belly himself?"

The crowd laughed. My forearms were red as blood from the many cuts ran down my limbs. The air was cooling as it kissed the blood on my legs where I'd also been cut by my opponent's quick jabs.

Each time I tried a maneuver, he was quick to cut me. *Since I can heal quickly, maybe my only option is to allow him to think he has an advantage. But maybe if I drop my guard…*

I stopped moving and put my arms out welcoming him to assail me. There was silence in the crowd as my opponent lunged at me, pushing the blade into the side of my stomach. He looked up at me while his grip remained on the hilt, and the crazy and excited look in his eyes told me his goal had been to kill me all along.

I grabbed his throat with my hand and lifted him in the air. He struggled, trying to break free by hitting my arms with his hands and kicking his feet as his eyes widened with fear. I felt parts of his throat give way and collapse under my grip. He gasped as I walked him over toward Xerxes, then threw him over the ring and into the crowd.

The shouting turned to whispers as someone went to my opponent, who lay with his head to the side.

"Did he pass out?" someone yelled.

"He's dead," the referee said, looking up at Xerxes. More people whispered, and then the whispers grew into even louder shouts than before.

All eyes were on me as I pulled the knife out of my side. I gripped it firmly as I looked up and saw Xerxes. My face hit the sand as guards tackled me, taking the knife from me. My stomach ached from the wound in my belly.

"This was not a death match. You aren't supposed to kill!" Xerxes said as he walked up and stood over my head. He kicked me in my wounded side, and I cried out in pain.

"But he stabbed me! He almost killed me!" I exclaimed, trying to defend my actions.

"It was just a knife. He wouldn't have killed you if you just fought him off. So you got a few cuts. That's no reason to kill someone."

"He stabbed me to kill me!" I exclaimed as the guards struggled to restrain me. I wanted to get up and grab Xerxes's throat, too.

"That's not an excuse. He didn't hit anything vital!" Xerxes screamed at me.

The guards put the shackles on me and lifted me up to face Xerxes. "Show him what happens when he doesn't follow the rules," he said gruffly to the guards. "And I just may reconsider our agreement about your girl."

"No! Xerxes, no! I'm sorry! I didn't know—" I cried out but was quickly pulled out of the arena, back to my room.

A chain ran through the shackles on my wrist, the ring on my collar, to my other wrist, and over a pulley on the ceiling.

My feet quickly left the floor as the guards pulled me up toward the ceiling. My body swayed, and I saw the guards laughing and pulling out their devices of torture—one with a whip, the other with some type of club.

Xerxes burst into the room and looked up at me. "All you had to do today was lose. I had a lot of ginny against you today. And besides losing that, I had to pay for the death of your opponent. Maybe I'll lend your girl to my men to repay me for my losses, huh? Would you like that, boy?" He slapped my face as I struggled to meet his eye.

"Please, no! Please… I didn't know," I said. "I thought I was supposed to win. If you would have told me—"

He smiled and struck me in my face with the back of his hand, and it felt like being hit by a board. I wasn't sure if anything in my face broke, but it was the most painful blow I'd received in a very long time—even more than the bleeding wound in my stomach.

Xerxes gripped my cheeks with his hand.

"Just so there's no question about who does the thinking here, my men are going to show you what happens when you break the rules." He walked toward the door. "He has another fight next week, so don't be *too* hard on him."

Mir came in later to clean me up. She gasped as she saw the bruises and cuts from my beating and the blood that trickled down my body. I didn't even feel the pain as she cleaned me with her cloth and water.

Rage consumed me and kept my mind busy as I devised a way to kill Xerxes and the other guards, then to free Katia. I could see a tear in Mir's eye, although we never exchanged a word, and when she finally picked up her bucket, she whispered, "I'm sorry for what they do to you, Zan." I remained silent, and she walked out.

I liked Mir. She was kind and seemed to care about me. She'd probably be the only one I'd spare when I finally rescued Katia. Perhaps the other slaves, too. My rage overshadowed my ability to think straight, but the one thing that remained clear in my mind was that I'd get my vengeance for what Xerxes had done to me and Katia.

Chapter 11

Being undefeated in the fight ring over so many months should have filled me with pride, but every time I won, I'd look to where I last saw Katia—she was never there. At each fight, I hoped to see her again, but Xerxes wouldn't bring her. I knew it was his way of punishing me.

There were some skilled fighters among my opponents. I would often get hurt—sometimes so badly that I didn't think I'd live—but I was always able to come through. I was surprised at how fast I could heal after a fight. A simple cut would heal in a matter of days. A deeper one was gone in a week. And I grew stronger every day.

I also continued to restrain myself from demonstrating all my strength and dexterity. I used only what I needed to win in fights and displayed even less during my training with Trev. My trainer was always studying me, and I wasn't sure whether he knew I planned to come for him one day.

As I grew older, Trev trained me with a sword and shield. I was going to turn eighteen in a few weeks, and Xerxes wanted to make sure I was trained for the death fights. I'd killed three men in my life and wasn't sure who I was anymore. I remember being afraid to kill that man who had wanted Katia in the woods in what seemed like a lifetime ago, and I'd somehow become this hardened killer who wouldn't think twice about ripping Xerxes's throat out his neck, and I'd smile while he died at my feet.

I'd thought about killing Xerxes and all of his men many times in many different scenarios, but I knew I needed to learn how to use a sword if I was ever going to escape.

Each time we trained, there were several armed guards around the ring, each with his hand on the hilt of his sword. I was told they were there to observe me, but I knew they were really there to make sure I didn't try to run.

Xerxes was taking precautions to ensure he didn't lose the source of his newfound wealth as well as his best house slave.

Something about the way he watched me so carefully told me he knew how strong I really was, and I was beginning to realize it myself. I knew my time in confinement was nearing the end. There were three possible ways I could leave Xerxes: I would either be killed in the fight ring, killed trying to escape, or I'd escape with Katia. One way or another, I knew my time remaining there was short.

The sword training seemed simple at first. We used wooden swords and wooden shields, and I was thankful they were wood because Trev would have stabbed or cut me many times while I learned if they'd been real. I initially used the stances I'd learned with the staff, but the footing was all wrong with a sword. While Trev taught me the flaws in my stance, he knocked me on my ass numerous times, laughing and showing off his moves. He was very good with weapons but also quite arrogant.

He explained how many young fighters fell into the habit of using the staff stances and were unable to change when given a sword. Most found out too late. Trev was always showing off his skill by twirling a staff or going through some demonstration to show how masterful he was with a sword, and I could only watch and quietly study him.

He taught me how to fight with only a shield against a sword in the event that I was ever disarmed. I remembered how I'd defeated the opponent with the knife, but I preferred not to get stabbed by a sword if I could help it, especially during a fight to the death. I had a dream once of getting killed and laying there to see Xerxes giving Katia to his men. I awoke enraged and in a sweat. Often those thoughts distracted me during training.

I didn't think of it often, but I wanted to kill every time I thought of any harm befalling Katia. Then I'd think of her—her smile, her hair, her twirling around in that new dress, her love of the flowering bush. Those thoughts calmed my rage. I just needed to understand how to flip my switch to be the cold-hearted killer when I needed to and the compassionate man Katia would want when we finally got together.

My fighting ability seemed strangely intuitive, and I gave the credit to my ability to think quickly about my opponents' moves and countermoves. I rubbed my arm again, internally thanking my father for the gift. I hoped it would help me escape one day.

Once we began using real swords and shields, the clanging of metal brought real danger to the fight. Trev cut me many times, and I eventually got a nick or two on him. But our sparring often ended with him pinning me to the ground with the tip of his sword at my throat. I learned as much as I could in a short amount of time.

I found that strength wasn't nearly as important with a sword as dexterity and technique. Of course, reading my opponent was still one of the most useful skills.

Trev also taught me how to balance using a sword and shield and how lethal a shield could be when used effectively as a weapon.

Each time I was wounded, I healed within a day or two, and Trev was amazed at how quickly I recovered. I didn't think much of it, as I no longer thought of it as strange, and whenever I did consider it, I'd think of my father and how I knew he was responsible for my new capability.

One day, Mir came in with my food. On the plate was a small piece of cake with three letters carved in the frosting: "HBZ." I looked at Mir and tilted my head. She whispered so the guards wouldn't hear her, "Katia said it was your birthday, so she wanted me to get you this piece of cake."

I failed to fight back the tears, and I gave Mir a hug. I'd withstood countless beatings and near-death experiences without crying, but the piece of cake from Katia told me she still believed in me.

"Now, now. We can't be doing that." She pushed me away. "Happy birthday, Zan."

I stared at the yellow cake with white frosting and those three letters: *HBZ. Happy birthday, Zan.*

I picked up the cake and then set it down. Wanting to save the gift from Katia for later, I ate the rest of my food first, and each small sweet, delicious bite was a reminder that she was still thinking of me.

After several weeks, I was able to fight Trev to a draw. At one point, I had my shield pinned to his throat while his sword was at mine. I was able to match him, but I wanted to beat him. I *had* to beat him if he was the best of Xerxes's fighters.

I studied his many moves and found some that I thought I might use to my advantage. I learned the techniques he taught, but I also used my intuition to predict his moves as best as I could. Focusing on his strategy rather than my offensive moves could make me vulnerable, so I knew I needed to learn a balance.

Meanwhile, back in my cell, I continued to scrape at the mortar around the stone in the wall. The edges of my shackles couldn't fit in the crevices between the stones, so I picked away a little at a time with my fingers.

The little bit of sunlight gave me hope, and I knew I had to do anything I could to escape. So many people had died trying to save me—I owed it to them. Although the details were fading with time, I continued to remember the deaths of my parents and how Miss Linda had given her life to save mine. So many people had risked so much only for me to end up an enslaved fighter, destined to die in a sandpit one day for a wagered sport.

I couldn't comprehend the disparity between what I'd learned on Earth about Xima and what I was seeing around me. Thinking about the cruelty of life on the planet and how primitive the people of Xima had become made me sick to my stomach. I had expected more from the planet, but I was becoming increasingly confident that people like Xerxes were responsible for making Xima the way it was—pure hell.

* * *

Mir came by after a fight. She left my food after she did her standard washing, but I noticed she'd left a spoon just under the edge of the plate. In the past, she'd never given me anything other than a plate and a cup.

My heart raced—the long metal handle was just what I needed to dig deeper into the wall! I listened for footsteps and waited until the sunlight in the high window faded. Then I took the spoon and began digging farther to remove the stone.

I was able to dig much more easily and gouge deeper into the crevice. Eventually, I pushed the spoon in and pried the fist-sized stone out. I wanted to shout for joy at my victory but realized I couldn't. Still, I stood up and jumped up and down in silence, celebrating my little achievement. Then I lay back down and looked through the hole.

It was deep and narrow—just big enough for a rat to crawl through. A stone on the other side seemed to already be missing, which allowed me to see the outside. I pushed my hand through and felt the cool breeze. The sensation brought back memories of playing outside with the other kids on the compound and of Bram and my friends at the orphanage. I saw the stars on the horizon and the tops of some buildings, but the darkness made it difficult to see anything but a few flickering lights. *Perhaps from some type of fire?*

I was able to see the outside world of Xima for the first time since the day I'd arrived, which seemed so very long ago. I wanted to stare out through that hole all night with the cool breeze against my face. The glowing orange to gray lights told me there must have been fires outside. I could hear someone laughing in the distance. I scanned out the hole, my only glimpse of freedom I'd had in my cell, until I fell asleep.

* * *

The lock on the door turned, and I awoke in a panic, hastily pushing the spoon into the hole and putting the stone back in its place. I tried not to look alarmed and sat up as the guards walked in.

"Good news! You, Zan, are the most prized fighter in all of Lauri," one of the guards said. Mir entered behind him with a tray of food.

"Xerxes has arranged your first death fight against two men tomorrow. The odds are not in your favor, as both of these men are excellent fighters. I heard that one of them eats his victims' eyeballs, and the other tries to pull their entrails out before the referee can pull him away. But you're worth the risk. If you win, you'll make all of us a lot of ginny."

I looked up at him, remembering my training in two-on-one fighting. Mir set my tray down as the guard walked out, then she unwrapped my loincloth.

As she washed me, Mir whispered, "Your girl is good, working in the kitchen."

"Have you seen her? Tell her that I'll rescue her."

"Shhh. I'll try. You need to win this fight." She got up to walk away, but I grabbed her arm.

"Stop talking in there!" a guard shouted from the doorway.

She looked up at me in a panic, trying to free her wrist from my grip. "Please, Zan. I'll be beaten if I talk anymore." I looked up to the small window on the door. I could see shadows moving on the other side, and I realized I was hurting her. Having experienced pain for such a long time, the last thing I wanted was for this lady, who had treated me with such kindness, to be hurt. I let go of her hand and allowed her to continue.

Mir stopped at the door, turned, and whispered, "She is to be sold if you die."

I looked at her in horror. The guard walked in and saw the fear on my face. "What did you tell him?" He grabbed her arm and pulled Mir out of the room. "What did you tell him?!"

She cried in the hallway. "I told him 'good luck.' I only said good luck!"

I heard the sound of a merciless beating as she cried out.

"Stop it!" I yelled. "Leave her alone!"

A guard walked in and pushed me against the wall, grabbing my throat.

"What did she tell you?" he demanded. I glanced behind him to make sure the other guard was gone. Then I flexed the muscles in my neck, preventing him from constricting it any farther.

He smiled and showed off blackened teeth. His body reeked of many offensive odors, and I smelled his rotten breath as he whispered, "It would seem there's a lot of demand for your girl. Xerxes is betting on your death tomorrow, and then he's going to auction her off. He plans to make a hefty profit since she's the only virgin on this planet." His breath became even more rancid as his lips parted in a smile.

Then he continued. "It's a good thing I saved up my ginny to buy her but a shame you won't be alive to watch me take her virginity." My anger reached its limit.

I smiled back at him. "You shouldn't threaten Xerxes's prize fighter." I quickly wrapped the chain between my shackles around his neck and pulled him to the floor. In seconds, he was still.

I pushed his body away from my mattress with my feet as the other guard walked in. "What happened!?" he demanded, snarling.

"He attacked me! He said I needed to lose the fight tomorrow, and when I refused, he threatened to kill me. I didn't know what I was doing! When he grabbed my neck, my reactions took over and he fell over."

I was impressed with my ability to kill the guard without hesitation. It hadn't been that long ago that I'd killed my first person out of fear of being found out at the orphanage, but I realized I could also kill just because I needed to—or perhaps because I wanted to.

"He's dead," the guard said. Then he dragged the body through the doorway, locking the door behind him. I sat down to eat my food, content with one of the most gratifying victories I'd experienced since coming to Xima.

* * *

"Did you ask why he killed him?" I heard Xerxes's voice in the hallway as the door was unlocked.

"He said Justin attacked him, Xerxes. I was in the hallway and didn't see what happened."

Xerxes burst in and yelled, "Why did you kill one of my guards?!"

I explained, "He wanted me to lose the fight tomorrow by falling out of the ring."

Xerxes walked up and slapped my face. I wanted to kill him right then. I could have easily wrapped the chain around his neck like I did with the guard. He would have been dead in a second, but I'd still be in chains and Katia would be in jeopardy.

Xerxes stared at me, breathing heavily. "You can take out your aggression tomorrow in the ring. That's also where you'll be punished for your crime." He paced the room and then walked back up to me. His hand quickly latched onto my face, pinching my cheeks together as he stared into my eyes.

He whispered, "You make me a lot of money, but you're no more than property to me. Property I can just throw in the trash if I want. I can find another fighter, and I won't hesitate to sell your girl. Or better yet, I could put her in the middle of the ring and let all of the fighters in Lauri rape the fuck out of her at once while everyone else watches… including you."

I lunged for him, but he jumped backward out of the way, laughing. The edges of the iron ring around my neck cut into my skin as I strained to reach him. "Save that energy, boy. You'll need it tomorrow." He walked out laughing and slammed the door shut.

I yanked the shackles and tried to pull the chain from the wall. Even with my rage and all my might, I couldn't break free. I might have been able to break the chain between my wrists, but it quickly started to cut through my flesh.

I desperately needed to break out, and the next day would finally be the day. But I needed to even the odds somehow. And I knew just how to do it. I had to take out Trev as soon as I killed my opponents, before the other guards could get to me.

Chapter 12

I was already awake when the guards came in.

"Let's go, Zan. It's time for your first death fight." One of the guards snickered, which I didn't think much of.

I hadn't slept much that night. I was busy planning how I would kill my opponents, defeat Trev and Xerxes, and dispose of anyone else who got between me and Katia.

The guards guided me down the hallway toward the fight ring. I'd never been so focused on a task in my life. I could feel the adrenaline racing through my body, and I was more confident than ever. At long last, I would unleash all my strength to free Katia.

We neared the fight ring but continued down the hallway, past the turn we typically took to the arena.

"Where are we going?" I asked. I had a plan, and there was no room for surprises.

The guards kept escorting me. I became agitated and demanded, "Where are we going? I thought I was going to fight." I resisted, but they tugged me along. If I hadn't been wearing the shackles, I would have killed them both.

We approached a door that opened into what looked like a box. I planted my feet to resist going any further.

"What are you doing? I'm supposed to fight!" I exclaimed, fearful I wouldn't be able to carry out my plan. It was a tug of war as I held out, but someone from behind pushed me forward. I tumbled into the wooden structure, and a door with bars slid shut. I quickly stood up and walked to the bars.

"What's going on?!" I yelled, gripping the bars and trying to pull them out of the frame. Xerxes was holding a heavy-looking sack, smiling and looking proud.

"Xerxes, what's going on?" I asked. "I was supposed to fight today." My entire plan to fight my way out seemed to have been disrupted unexpectedly. *But more importantly, what happened to Katia?*

He looked at me and continued to smile. "It seems someone was willing to pay far more for you than I would've made in wagers."

"What do you mean? I want to fight! Let me fight, Xerxes!" I yelled, horrified.

"You can fight with your new owner, for all I care. I don't own you anymore, but I do own your girl." A guard pulled Katia next to Xerxes. Our eyes locked.

"Katia!" I gasped.

"Zan!" She reached for me, but the guard wouldn't let her any closer.

"Perhaps I'll give her to the next ring fighter I buy as a treat." He laughed and walked away, yelling out, "Don't try coming back here, Zan, or the girl dies!"

"No! Xerxes! Don't hurt her! I'll kill you if you harm Katia!" He continued to walk away, laughing as the box I was in lurched away from the building. I tried to rip the bars away again and yelled as loud as I could, "Xerxes! I'll kill you!!"

As I watched the door close, leaving me in the dark, I whispered, "I'll rescue you, Katia."

* * *

I tried to look through some bars on the side of my small prison, my mind throbbing with anxiety and the need to get out. I was in a wheeled cage of some sort, and I watched the faint outline of the building I'd been captive in for a long time get farther and farther away, like waking up from a bad dream.

I ran against the walls to try to break through but only fell to the floor. I needed more room to get enough momentum to get out. Kneeling while holding the bars, I saw the city of Lauri for the first time. I watched as we moved away from my Katia and the only life I'd known since arriving on the godforsaken planet.

Unable to see much through the bars, I scanned the scenery as much as possible. Many buildings were little more than poorly built shacks of wood or stone. They looked like something out of the history lessons I remembered—dwellings dating back centuries to when there was no electricity or running water.

People walked the streets with dirty and ragged clothes. I was amazed to see my first kohl grazing on some grass next to a building. It looked just like the depictions I'd seen in books. I hadn't seen many animals on Earth, as most were raised on exclusive farms, so the kohl left me speechless.

I went to the front of the cart and hit the wall many times.

"Where are you taking me?" I yelled. There was never a response.

I could see Lauri behind us, or something resembling a city, at least. I had mixed concepts of what a city was supposed to look like. The compound I grew up on had nice homes, running water, electricity, and good food, but the areas outside of the compound consisted of only devastated buildings turned to rubble. Even the shelter I stayed at with Katia and Miss Linda wasn't as well kept as homes I'd seen in history books.

There must be some weak point to this wagon, some loose board or bar I could break. I searched every square inch, finally sitting down against the wall to reminisce about Katia—anything to stay hopeful. I remembered how beautiful she looked for those few seconds, how she reached for me again, and how I couldn't do anything to help her. She had placed her trust in me to take care of her, and I'd failed her yet again!

At least I'd been able to see her. I had to rescue her somehow, but I needed to rescue myself first. Anger ran through my veins over my foiled plans. Whoever was driving the cart wouldn't be alive for much longer—I'd kill them and go back to rescue my Katia as soon as I got a chance.

* * *

The entire day went by without a word from my purchaser, who I assumed was driving the cart. *Why was I bought? Why now? Am I going to fight somewhere else on Xima?*

So many questions and thoughts ran through my mind, most of them fueled by anger. Night was closing in, and I got a chill as I sat there only in my loincloth and thin shirt. We had entered a forest of some sort. The trees looked strange—thick vines weaved together to form a canopy overhead. The tree trunks had strange shapes to them like the crooked knuckles of an old person bending upward at odd angles, and tree roots jutted out of the ground and back in again.

Much of the life I'd seen so far on Xima was similar to what I remembered on Earth, yet so much was also different.

The carriage stopped. *Now's my chance! Once he opens this door, I'm taking him out.*

The faint *thump* of feet hitting the ground turned my attention to the side of the carriage. Someone in a wool cape walked alongside the cart with a hood over his head. He was not very tall and didn't look too strong. He wore boots and a sword and carried a blanket. I knew from his size that I could take him once the door opened.

I studied his every move. I held the bars and followed him with my eyes as he walked to the back of the carriage, ready to pounce as soon as he opened it. A blanket was swiftly pushed in between the bars. I strained to get a look at his face but could only see the cloak and a well-made thick leather outfit. It almost looked like the armor Xerxes and his men had worn.

He walked into the forest. "What do you want with me?" I yelled, pulling at the bars and hoping one of them would break loose.

I stood looking at the outline of the trees and other shrubs as night fell. It was quite dark. I heard some footsteps and rustling branches in the darkness, but I couldn't see anything.

He came back with some old branches, looking down so as not to show his face, and started a fire without saying a word to me. I wrapped myself in the blanket and sat on the floor.

Watching his fire come to life, I mumbled, "Why won't you talk to me?" The fire roared, projecting red and orange flecks of light in all directions. "What do you want?" I added.

He took off the hood and looked up at me, smiling. "You look a lot like your father, Zack."

My eyes lit up, and my mouth dropped open at the realization that *he* was a *she* and that she knew my real name. "M-my name is Zan," I stuttered.

"I came a very long way and paid a lot of ginny to get you. I surely hope you're Zack Bates, or I did all of this for nothing."

I didn't know what to say. Somehow, she knew my real identity. I remained speechless as I tried to remember her face from the compound where I grew up—I didn't recognize her. The compound; it was nothing but a foggy memory. I concentrated, and the memory of the ADS coming in the night to kill my parents became clear again, causing my fists to tighten.

"I'm General Tonya Skyler. I was the general overseeing your father's project. The project which, I believe, he gifted to you." I just stared at her and unconsciously slid my hand over the spot where my father injected the little black ball.

General Skyler was a beautiful woman with shoulder-length brown hair, dark eyes, and a very pretty face. I couldn't tell how old she was, but her calming voice threw me off guard. I noticed I was trying to grab my arm again, and I pulled the blanket around me and rocked while sitting on the wooden floor. *Should I say something? But what?*

"I must say, I'm impressed at its effectiveness. It seems to have been everything we had hoped for. I would have liked to see how well you did in the death fights, but I couldn't take the risk of losing you."

"You killed my parents!" I blurted out.

She stood up quickly, anger showing in her face. Then her eyes softened.

"I did not. They weren't supposed to be harmed. We had some ADS members who disobeyed my instructions, and that's why your parents were killed. I suspect those rogue agents received directions from infiltrated FOG leadership within the ADS. It was unfortunate because your father's knowledge and the device were lost with him. Or so we thought. The fact that you got away that night led many to believe your father tested the device on you. The ADS guards who came to your home were directed to kill all three of you, search the house, and, if necessary, cut you open in order to find the device. But it wasn't me who gave that order."

She sat back down and stared into the fire. "I liked your father very much. We were on the verge of turning everything around for the better." She placed more wood on the fire as the flames were becoming more alive.

"About a year ago, we heard stories about this boy who was undefeated in the ring here on Xima. A boy who could take on two fighters at a time.

A boy with incredible strength. The timing of this news corresponded with the findings of our investigation at the orphanage. It couldn't have been a coincidence."

"You killed Miss Linda, too? You bastard!" I jumped up to the bars, gripping them tightly and trying to pull them out of the wood.

She looked up at me and said calmly, "Your Miss Linda is very much alive. After some investigating, we discovered that the man who goes by Mule lied to you and sold you to Xerxes. We didn't find out until he tried to collect the money from Miss Linda. It was Mule's greed that allowed us to find out what had really happened. As punishment, he was sent here to Xima."

"Where is he? I want to kill him!" I was full of rage, and I didn't know which issue enraged me the most. So many hateful emotions consumed my body, making every muscle as tight as a spring ready to explode loose.

"In due time, Zack. He has just arrived and is in the employment of Xerxes."

Her voice was sincere, and it reminded me of Miss Linda and how she'd wanted me to make it to Xima safely. I remembered Miss Linda talking about making arrangements with Mule, but he'd ruined everything. The thought of what Mule did to me and Katia made my face feel hotter than the fire.

I thought about the mess I'd gotten her into, and I knew I alone had to get her out of it. I sat, staring at nothing. The flames of the fire blurred with the tears welling in my eyes.

I wanted to believe Miss Linda was alive. What General Skyler said was plausible, but how could I trust her? She was with the ADS, the group that took everything from me. "What do you want from me?" I whispered, trying to focus on the fire.

She stared into the flames, stirring the coals, and added a few more pieces of wood. I was amazed to see that different pieces of wood created flames of different colors. The greens reminded me of my daunting escape through the forest. The reds, pinks, and oranges were like the lights I saw looking out of that hole in the wall. Then I saw the maroon that reminded me of that bush Katia took me to. How beautiful she looked. I saw the browns and darker colors that reminded me of Xerxes and the guards that put me through hell, the hot coals that I wanted to drag Xerxes over when I got my hands on him. I wanted revenge like no one ever had before.

"The Earth has been in chaos for decades. It was once very prosperous, flourishing with vegetation, wildlife, and people who lived happily. I'm sure you learned much of this in your history classes. Unfortunately, we were reaching a point where more oxygen would be consumed than produced and more carbon dioxide produced than oxygen. Some scientists predicted that life would become unsustainable after a hundred years. Some said a thousand.

"There were some portions of FOG who wanted to create a system to terminate the lives of people who met certain criteria, thereby reducing oxygen consumption for the good of all. They wanted to create an evaluation program to determine if humans should live beyond the age of sixty or sixty-five. These FOG groups also wanted to evaluate babies to determine whether they were worthy to live based on their estimated potential. Those who provided significant contributions to society were allowed to live beyond sixty. Those who had more money also lived longer. The others would be ceremonially executed." She stirred more of the fire, causing sparks to dance upward into the darkness. Their glow floated up and up until they blended with the stars.

"FOG also wanted to slaughter animals in order to reduce carbon dioxide emissions and oxygen consumption. The ADS was formed from a combination of military and police personnel with the goal of fighting FOG militant groups all over the world. FOG wanted a united Earth with a single government that would regulate every being. Terrorist cells formed. Some sacrificed themselves to kill many others with explosives. These suicide bombers blew up entire office buildings in cities such as New York or Chicago, not caring about the innocent people who died. They considered them collateral damage."

I moved as close as I could in my cage to hear what she had to say. I'd never heard a detailed account of that part of history before.

"All the countries agreed that something needed to be done to calm the global panic and halt the destruction, so we pooled our resources into space travel and the occupation of Mars. But, during our exploration, we stumbled upon a wormhole which opened an avenue to this solar system. That was how we found Xima. An agreement was made with FOG that allowed criminals, elderly people, and volunteers to travel to Xima to live. People were allowed to pay for passage and become citizens here, as well, but little did we know those wealthy citizens would ruin our plans for peace with their greed and corruption.

"Each continent built one or two launch sites and began sending people to this planet. They sent engineers, doctors, and many others who were *volunteered* by their governments. No weapons were allowed to be sent. We wanted it to be a planet of peace, and it was agreed the ADS would inspect each shuttle to ensure that weapons were not onboard prior to coming here.

"What we lacked were laws and enforcers to protect the people. Soon, they found the metal ginnium. You may have heard of it referred to as 'ginny' here on Xima. They use it as a currency. It's a metal that melts easily but forms and hardens well. It doesn't exist on Earth, but it's been smuggled back by shuttle crews as an exotic metal to be auctioned off to the wealthy. Since it doesn't form organically on Earth, ginny has a value much greater than platinum."

She paused and turned her head as though she'd heard something. I tried to listen but heard nothing.

"Earth remained in ruins," she continued, "with the exception of compounds like the one you lived in as a child and crumbling cities like where you lived as an orphan. As for Xima, leadership on Earth didn't care much about the people once they left for the new planet. Many believed they were no longer Earth's problem, and whatever happened on Xima was Xima's issue. It opened the door for a lot of corruption, which grew over time. Xerxes grew to be the wealthiest and, of course, the most corrupt of all."

She pushed the wood in the fire, creating sparks that floated toward the treetops. The sparks passing her face made her look more ominous, yet also beautiful. She tossed more wood at the flames, again causing more sparks. I was captivated by what she was telling me, but my mind was swimming in a current of quicksand, captivated with no apparent way to get out.

"Meanwhile, on Earth, the ADS was losing people to greed. Our new recruits were no match for the FOG mercenaries who were paid to eliminate all animal life and reduce human life on Earth even further. We were unable to hold off FOG any longer, and they were bribing our forces to join theirs. Your father was inventing a stimulation device designed to be implanted in young boys and girls which would trigger their growth hormones to make them stronger, their senses more responsive, and their reactions quicker.

Their strength would have given us a chance to bring order back to Earth—and even to Xima.

"Your father was ready to test his implant, but we didn't know who to test it on. We also didn't know what side effects it might have. We began looking for candidates. Then I found out your father took the device home one day. I sent a team to bring him back with the device, but instead they shot him and your mother. It wasn't until later that I found out why."

My gaze was distant as I tried to remember the day he'd placed the little black object in my arm. My thoughts transitioned to that fateful night when my father yelled for me to run and hide, how he told me to tell no one of what he'd put in my arm. Whatever he gave me was important and aligned to what she was telling me.

"Your father left an encrypted message for me before he left with the implant, warning me that the ADS had been infiltrated at the highest leadership level by a FOG spy who wanted to steal the implant. He claimed my superior was a FOG leader in disguise, but I couldn't prove it. I later found out that he met with your father and demanded he turn over the device to him. Your father lied and said it was in a timed safe and wouldn't be available until the morning. He then took the device and, we believe, placed it in you.

"This treasonous ADS officer directed the team to kill you and your family and bring the device back at any cost. When I finally sorted everything out and read your father's message, I realized what he was up to. Then, when I learned that you weren't found at the scene. I searched everywhere for you, but you proved to be more slippery than anyone expected. Fortunately for you—and for me—FOG never found you."

I smiled at her, then frowned again, staring at the fire. I didn't know if I believed what she'd said. It all made sense, but I remembered my father telling me to not trust anyone. She could have been part of the ADS infiltrators who were searching for me.

I looked back up at her. "Why did you come all the way here to Xima, and what do you want with me?"

She stood up and walked toward me. I was uneasy as she approached, staring at me the whole time. It felt as though she was looking into my soul with a nurturing gaze. I sat still, staring back at her and attempting to find truth in her eyes. I tried to avoid the distraction of her beauty—I still couldn't trust her.

She walked up to the bars, inches away from me but not close enough for me to grab her. I asked, "How do I know you're not the part of FOG looking for me?"

She smiled and said, "If I were, you'd be dead already. I'd have cut you up to find the device and then left."

Her words hit me like a wooden board. What she said made sense.

"Zack, I want you to help me bring civility back to Xima and Earth."

My eyes widened, and then I chuckled. "You think the two of us can take on all of the bad people here *and* FOG on Earth?" I shook my head in disbelief.

"Precisely," she said with a confident tone, nodding her head as she walked back to the fire.

She's serious. I pondered the concept and shook my head again. "You're crazy. We'd be killed before we could get through Lauri."

A branch cracked in the distance, and we both looked in the same direction.

"Shhhh." She placed a finger over her mouth and walked toward the front of the carriage.

I'm helpless in this damn cage. Where did she go? I peered into the darkness, but the fire distorted my vision.

Three figures emerged from the shadows. They looked ragged, dirty, and I could tell from their grins that they had a collective tooth-count of maybe six. They held swords and appeared to be ready to fight.

"Where's the other man?" one of them asked in a raspy voice. The others looked around suspiciously, waiting for something.

"Are you looking for me?" Skyler asked as she walked toward the men, stopping about fifteen feet away. She held two short swords in her hands, and she had removed her cloak. The glow of the fire danced on her hardened reddish leather outfit, and she smiled as she tossed her soft dark hair to the side.

"A woman?" one man called out, laughing as he pointed his sword at General Skyler.

"This should be easier than we thought, boys," another man added.

"All we want is your ginny. We know you have some. Give it to us, and you can live," the assailant with the raspy voice said.

Skyler smiled. "I'm sorry, boys. I spent all of my ginny on this slave. I have nothing left for you. Why don't you go home so you can see tomorrow?"

The men looked at each other and laughed. One said, "Then we'll take the slave and kill you… but not before we're done with that gorgeous body of yours. Get her, men!"

Skyler's swords clashed with those of her assailants. I watched her in awe. Although her motions were lightning fast, I could see every detail of her moves. Within seconds, all three of the men were lying on the ground. One remained alive, holding his bleeding chest. I'd never seen anyone strike so fast, nor had I seen someone win a fight when outnumbered three to one.

She kicked the sword away from the one who lived and removed a knife from his belt. Kneeling down beside him, she asked in a soft tone, "Why did you really come all this way? It couldn't be for a few ginny. You knew I didn't have much after buying this slave, so why?"

He spat at her. Skyler pushed the hilt of her sword into his wound. "Does this hurt, or do you like it?" she asked, her voice almost sympathetic. "I don't think you'll bleed out very quickly, so perhaps we can help you with your desire for pain." She pressed her fingers deep into his flesh where he was bleeding badly. I cringed at her barbaric method of interrogation, but I was impressed at how comfortable she was doing it.

The man cried out in agony. "Xerxes! Xerxes sent us to kill you and bring the boy back!"

"Thank you for your honesty. Rest well." Skyler slashed his throat and stood up, as though she'd simply ended a calm discussion.

"I had a feeling Xerxes's scum were behind this," she said, turning to me. "As I'm sure you're now aware, Xerxes is the vilest of humans. You made him a lot of money, and I had a feeling he'd underestimate me because I'm a woman and send his men out to kill me and take you back."

She cleaned her blades on the assassin's clothes and pulled the dead men into the woods. General Skyler didn't look strong, but the way she had effortlessly killed the men and dragged them off as if they were weightless told me she was much more than she appeared to be.

She went to the front of the carriage to get something and brought it to the fire. It was some liquid she heated up in a small metal pot.

"How did you kill them so fast?" I asked. "I've never seen anyone fight so quickly."

She continued to focus on what she was brewing in the pot over the fire, continuously stirring and leaning down to smell it periodically. I remained quiet as I watched her, hoping for an answer. She poured some liquid into a metal cup and gave it to me.

"Drink this. It'll warm you up," she said, also handing me some bread.

I didn't recognize what I was drinking, but it was warm and soothing. When I finished eating the bread, my thoughts returned to the fight. Her skills far exceeded mine and, from what I saw, exceeded Trev's as well. I began to think that she might be able to help me rescue Katia.

"How long have you been in the ADS?" I asked while swirling the liquid in my cup. The drink had an almost immediate calming effect. It was very tasty. A sudden sensation of happiness hit me, and I became very sleepy.

"I've been in the ADS since I was your age. I learned to fight here on Xima."

I was shocked. "You were here and then went back to Earth?"

She nodded while stirring the fire. "Several of us were sent here as boys and girls to learn how to fight so we could be better warriors and leaders for the ADS. We fought in the ring with enslaved fighters like yourself. Once we were proficient, we were sent back to Earth as officers in the ADS."

"You fought in the death fights?" I could hear the surprise in my own voice, unable to believe a girl could've fought to the death in the ring.

She nodded. "I, too, was undefeated, but I don't have anywhere near as much strength, dexterity, or, hopefully, constitution as you have." She stood up and walked toward me. "Your father gave you a great gift. You have the chance to be the greatest warrior who ever lived. You can make a difference by fighting for the greater good. All you need is further training."

Everything became blurry, and I struggled to stay awake. "If you want me to fight with you to save Earth, then why am I in this cage?" I could tell my voice was slurred, but I didn't understand why.

She walked back to the fire. "I gave you a lot of information today, and I want you to digest it. Relax and sleep soundly tonight. We can address your captivity tomorrow." She sat down in front of the fire as I realized there was indeed a ton I had to comprehend. My eyes were forcing themselves closed, and I fought to keep them open.

"Who's the girl?" she asked. "The one you yelled to when we left Xerxes."

The vision of Xerxes holding Katia as we left came back to my memory, reigniting the anger within me. "Her name is Katia. She found me hiding in the woods when I escaped the compound and brought me to Miss Linda. We became friends—close friends. I wanted to come here with her, to live together. But we were abducted when we arrived."

"Well, you need to get her out of your mind, and you need to focus on the task at hand," she said without concern, making me even angrier.

But I wasn't going to put her out of my mind. My thoughts of Katia were the only things keeping me going. She was my top priority, and I was nobody without her. Even *if* I were to do what Skyler had asked, I needed to rescue Katia first.

Chapter 13

The sound of chains sliding from the cage door brought me to my feet in a second. I was expecting a fight but instead saw Skyler unlocking the chains that kept the door locked. I sat up, realizing my mouth was parched, and watched Skyler open the door. She left it open and walked to the fire. I squinted at the morning sun, unaccustomed to such bright light. I closed my eyes and faced its warmth, savoring every ray as it melded on my face with the chill of the morning.

"Come on out if you want," General Skyler called to me as she tended to something on the fire.

I slowly stepped out of the carriage and sat across from her with the blanket wrapped around my shoulders. She placed some food on a metal plate and handed it to me. Once I smelled the aroma, my hunger overwhelmed me. Like a starving wolf with a newborn lamb, I savagely devoured everything as fast as possible. It wasn't anything like the food I was given at Xerxes's. The taste reminded me of the meat my parents had prepared when I was little and living on the compound.

Then I remembered how dizzy I'd felt before falling asleep, and I became more cautious. "What was in that drink you gave me last night?"

Skyler smiled. "It was Barlow Tea, from the Barlow trees here on Xima. Well, from the bark. It makes you relaxed and helps you sleep. It's similar to Valarien root on Earth, but much more potent."

"It worked very well." I smiled and drank the water she placed by my side.

She looked at me while chewing her food. "Do you trust me yet?"

I thought about everything she'd said and realized I didn't have much of a choice but to trust her. Besides, there was no way I'd win a fight against her. I nodded back while staring into the orange and red flames dancing from the fire pit.

"Good, then you'll let me train you to help right the wrongs of Xima and Earth?"

"You'll train me? But you're a woman." I laughed, then quickly remembered how she took out three men at once.

"Did you not see me fight those men last night? I've forgotten more about fighting than you'll ever learn," she said with some irritation in her voice, along with a hint of laughter.

I pondered a little more on how she'd dispatched those men so effortlessly and with a speed I'd never seen before. I wanted to be as good as her. "I apologize for my comment. I didn't mean any disrespect. I'll train, but under one condition: we need to free Katia as soon as the training is complete." I paused, then looked at the ground and added, "I still don't know what I can do to help with everything you're trying to accomplish."

She looked into my eyes with a warming smile. "Don't worry about it. I have thick skin, and I've heard much worse. We'll rescue your girl, but the first thing we'll work on is your self-confidence."

I wiped some of the food from my face and licked my fingers. Part of me knew it didn't matter what Skyler said or promised to do—I'd follow her anywhere if she fed me the best-tasting food I'd had in a long time.

* * *

We traveled for the remainder of the day. Instead of in the cage, I rode on the bench with General Skyler at the front of the cart. I was amazed by our surroundings. I saw more strange trees, bright blue bushes, and a few animals running around, which weren't in any book I'd read. *Katia would love to see these things, and I'll make sure she does.*

Skyler wrapped some long orange leaves around my wrists and ankles to help the wounds from my shackles heal. It was a relief to have those gone.

We seemed to be moving in the direction of a mountain. I never asked where we were going, as it wouldn't have mattered; I was going wherever Skyler took me. We approached a rock wall, which was hundreds of feet high and spread out as far as the eye could see in both directions. Many ledges protruded out from it with large nests of wooded branches resting on them. There was a forest in the opposite direction several hundred yards away.

"What are we doing here?" I asked, gazing at the enormity of the wall and not seeing anything remotely worth stopping for.

She smiled as she steered the kohl a little farther along the rock. As we got closer, a vertical crevice appeared in front of us. Skyler stopped in front of it.

"We're here," she said with a hint of enthusiasm.

I stood up and looked around, seeing nothing but the distant forest and a wasteland in the other direction. I stood and gazed at the sight of a large dog-like creature flying above us. Its wings must have been over ten feet long. It just flew along the rock wall and then toward the forest. As I continued watching it majestically float through the sky, I asked, "What is that thing?"

General Skyler looked up and said, "That is probably one of the most dangerous animals on this planet. It's called a griff."

"A griff?! So it *is* real?" I asked. "Colonel Jenkins was right; it looks just like those figures he carved."

"Colonel Spike Jenkins?" Skyler asked.

"I don't know. He was a retired colonel who lived on our compound and would tell us stories and history lessons. He always referenced something he called the griff, and he told us to always face it or something like that. He helped me escape when the ADS was chasing me."

"It's true. They're usually cautious about attacking a group of people, like we are on this wagon, but a griff will silently swoop down from behind and eat you for lunch if you're by yourself. Colonel Jenkins was attacked by one. It was the first time anyone had ever seen one and lived to tell about it. He was able to fight it off as it lifted him off the ground, but the beast's talons had some type of poison in them that caused him to hallucinate. He never did get better after that. The griff has a nest somewhere around here, and he keeps people from getting too nosy about this hidden location."

She jumped to the ground and said, "We're here" as she barely squeezed through the crevice in the wall. Moments later, the rock moved with a deep, dull sound. I watched in shock as the wall, which looked like it was part of the mountain, began to shift to the side. The portion that moved was perhaps twelve feet tall and ten feet wide and must have weighed several tons.

In the opening she'd created, Skyler pulled and pushed on a lever. She climbed back onto the carriage and guided the kohl into a dark tunnel with light at the other end. Then she climbed off again to close the mountain door.

"How did you do that? That rock's enormous," I said, marveling at how the giant rock face had moved with such ease.

She climbed back onto the carriage and smiled. "Leverage and hydraulics were among the many technologies engineers brought from Earth when the ADS first came here to train."

As we rode through the tunnel, the light at the other end became brighter and brighter until we emerged into a large, colorful clearing. I was overwhelmed by the flourishing trees and plants, and I saw some animals in the distance. The blue flowers embedded in the green and auburn leaves were spectacular. Katia would love the colors of Xima. I thought back to that bush at the orphanage. The bush where I was jumped and killed that man…

There were trees connected together in what formed almost a cave, and some small bright-green birds flew in and out of it. Stone walls surrounded the entire area around us for a mile in every direction. "How can a place like this exist?" I asked.

We continued down a worn, grass-covered path.

"We believe it was once a volcano that, over the course of millions of years, developed life. I'm sure there are other small entrances for animals to get in and out. The ADS found it when they first explored this planet, and they kept it a secret. We were brought here to train many years ago, and it doesn't look like anyone has been here since then."

Our carriage reached a large cabin with tables and wooden practice dummies in front of it. "Here's where you'll complete your training," Skyler said.

I climbed off the carriage. There were birds and wildlife everywhere I looked. I couldn't believe a place so full of life could exist on the planet, but then again, I'd learned very little about Xima while I was imprisoned.

"This is what Earth looked like a few hundred years ago. It's what Earth *could* look like again once we bring peace back to the planet."

We walked into a cabin and saw tables, wash basins, and wooden beds. There was a large firepit centered on a wall, and a stream flowed about a hundred feet behind the cabin.

"Take the tub and fill it with water. There's a well on the side of the cabin. We have a lot of cleaning to do." Skyler ordered me around like my mother would when I needed to clean my room. Strangely enough, something about it put me at ease.

*   *   *

We spent the next few days cleaning the cabin. Skyler inspected the training equipment and instructed me as we ate the last of our food. Once we finished, she handed me a spear similar to the staff I'd fought with, but there was a point at one end, just like the ones the two men had used to fight me some time ago.

My job was to kill an animal for a meal—we wouldn't eat until I did. Skyler showed me the basics of throwing a spear, making sure I had the right stance and grip. She taught me how to smoothly, quickly, and accurately throw the spear at my target.

I practiced on some dummy targets and was proud of how quickly the skill came to me. After I showed I was able to consistently hit my target, Skyler placed her hand on my shoulder and said, "Let's go find some lunch."

We followed the stream and, at a curve to where the water flowed under the rock wall, we spotted an animal the size of a large dog with black and white spots. It was drinking at the stream about two hundred feet away. I assumed my stance as Skyler whispered, "You'll never hit it this far out."

I kept my focus on the animal as it leaned down to eat. It periodically picked its head up to look around—searching for potential threats, I suspected.

"You don't know how strong I really am."

She laughed. "Typical man. Okay, if you insist. Make sure you aim at least twice as high as the animal to compensate for the spear's fall."

I assessed my target and adjusted my aimpoint above it as Skyler had suggested. I took some practice motions to loosen up my throw, concentrated, and threw.

"Holy shit! You got it!" Skyler proudly exclaimed, patting me on the shoulder. It was the second time she'd touched me. That time, I looked into her eyes and saw how beautiful they were. Her enthusiastic smile was euphoric as she rested her hand on my shoulder. I smiled back at her happy glow. She was even more beautiful than I'd initially noticed.

"Okay, time to learn how to clean it," she said, walking toward the fresh kill.

We dragged the carcass back to the cabin where she showed me how to prepare it to eat. Skyler rubbed the meat with salt from a barrel in the cabin so it would last longer.

We got a fire started, put some of the meat on a stick, and roasted it over the fire. It was the most delicious thing I'd ever eaten. We sat by the fire and ate until we were full.

"No average man could have thrown that spear like you did today. When did you notice a change in your strength?" Skyler asked, drinking some water.

I thought back to when my father had given me the implant and remembered how I'd pulled the tub off the boy at the orphanage.

"I don't know. Perhaps a few months after my dad implanted it. I noticed myself getting stronger when I played sports with the other kids in the orphanage."

She looked at me as she chewed her food. "I want you to know that your father was a good man. He was doing something that would have been good for both planets."

We chewed our meat in silence for a few minutes. The memories of my father were nothing more than foggy snapshots. I quietly reminisced about the time I'd spent with him before that fateful night. I wondered why my father had taken the risk of giving such a valuable device to me. *Didn't he realize the danger?*

"Sleep well, Zack. Tomorrow, the training gets harder." We lay down on our wooden beds and went to sleep.

Chapter 14

As we stood outside, Skyler tossed me a wooden sword. She walked around me with her own sword like an opponent would in the fight ring.

"I assume they've taught you how to use a sword by now."

She lunged at me. My instincts prompted me to block her without thinking. She came at me very quickly and from many directions. I was surprised at my ability to block her—I'd never seen anyone move so fast and, frankly, I didn't understand how I could keep up with her attacks. All I could do was defend myself.

She showed me a couple of offensive moves. We practiced slowly at first. Then, when I tried to attack her with the maneuver she'd shown me, she knocked me on my ass. I stood up and asked, "Why did you teach me that if it doesn't work?"

"It would've worked, but I knew you'd use it. You need to learn to be unpredictable. Even if I teach you something, change it up some and keep me guessing."

I tried to use the moves she showed me combined with what Trev taught me. I felt confident for a moment, but then I found myself on the defensive again. Soon I had a wooden sword at my throat.

"You're quite good with your eyes open. Now let's see how good you are with them closed." I squinted at her. She then put a blindfold over my eyes. "Your first new lesson today is on using all of your senses. Your sight doesn't tell you what's behind you. Open your senses of sound and touch, even smell." I felt her cinch the knot on the blindfold and walk away.

"Now, try to avoid being hit."

"How can I do that?" She struck my arm. "Ow! How am I supposed to know where you are or where you're going to hit?"

"Open your ears. Listen for the subtle sound of an object slicing quickly through the air. Listen for the movement of feet, or even the impact of my feet on the ground."

She struck me in the back, then on my arm. I heard her movement in front of me and lunged with the sword. "There you go. You sensed where I was." She hit my arm again and once more on my leg. I was getting frustrated at the unfairness of the exercise.

I listened for her movement and a pause, expecting her to hit my arm again. A soft breeze brushed my face, and I smelled her sweat—tangy and sharp. I smelled the fresh wood on the part of her sword that had chipped after clashing with mine. When the smells got stronger, I knew she was closer.

I raised my sword to block. "Good! Good! Feel where I am, using all your senses. Listen to the sound of my clothing as I move, the grip changing on my hilt. Visualize where I am and how I'm moving in your mind."

The sound of her sword came from my left—blocked—then it came down to my leg—blocked again. "Good! Excellent," She said giving me more encouragement.

Soon, I was able to prevent her from getting behind me. As I concentrated, I could even hear her breathing. I may have been surviving defensively, but how could I attack when she was so fast?

We practiced for an hour before taking a break. I took the blindfold off to look around.

"I never learned this in my fight training."

"That's why I was undefeated in the death fights," she said as she handed me a cup of water.

"Tell me about one of your death fights—one you remember the most."

She sipped some water and pondered for a moment. "I was quite successful in my initial fights. Each one resulted in me killing my opponent. During one fight I was up against one of the other leading death fighters on Xima who was enslaved by one of the elites. He was very quick on his feet and was able to give me a few good cuts before I finally caught him. I pinned him to the ground, and as I was about to force my sword into his chest, I stopped. I looked at him, accepting his fate to die. I realized that wasn't what I was about. It shouldn't have been what any of us were about."

She took another sip of water and continued, "I stood up, and when I offered my hand to help him stand, he tripped me, rolled over to get his sword, and ran toward me in a rage. My instincts kicked in, causing me to trip him and cut his throat."

My mouth opened wide in awe at her story. She took another drink and said, "That's when I realized that we should know how to be the best fighters so we can defend ourselves against FOG, but we need to be above simply killing for sport."

Her story sent shivers down my spine. I considered how if I'd been pitted against someone like her, I would have only wanted to kill. If I had stayed with Xerxes, that would've been all I'd ever become… until I was killed.

As I moved, I was able to hear the water sloshing around in the cup. It was a sound I'd never noticed before. I was puzzled as to why I'd never noticed my surroundings before, then I remembered the ball at the orphanage that was kicked toward my head. At that time, I ducked out of the way without actually seeing the ball. Maybe I'd been using my other senses all along without realizing it until General Skyler brought it to my attention.

For the rest of the day, I trained blindfolded. The challenge was exhilarating, as I strived to attack and defend without the ability to see my opponent. Over the next few days, we continued with new stances, knives, spears, and bare hands. We alternated between regular training and blindfolded practice.

General Skyler was indeed an excellent teacher, but I often caught myself distracted by her beauty. It was hard to think of her as a teacher at those times. I'd look at her as I used to look at Katia. I was able to shake the thoughts out of my mind, but my guilt grew. I was confused as to why I had such feelings for someone other than Katia. General Skyler couldn't have been more than thirty years old—she looked much younger than you would expect from an ADS general.

One afternoon, Skyler had me stand in a clearing. I watched as she walked toward a rack holding several types of weapons. She took a wooden spear and adopted a stance as she lined up to throw it at me. I noticed the tip of the spear had a soft tip, unlike the pointed ones I was used to.

"Try to avoid getting hit by this, and, if you're really good, you'll catch it and defend yourself."

She threw blunt spears at me for a while. My goal was to dodge without moving my feet and, if possible, catch the spears as they came at me. Eventually, I caught one.

"Excellent! Now let's make things more interesting."

She walked to the weapon rack and grabbed a pointed metal spear.

"Whoa, wait! What are you doing?" I protested.

She laughed. "Do you think your enemy will have blunt spears?" Without hesitation, she threw it right at my chest. I turned quickly and grabbed the end of the spear as it flew by. Not letting on how impressed I was with myself, I calmly twirled it around in a stance as if to throw it back at her but waited instead.

She smiled without a flinch and clapped her hands to applaud my success.

"Very good. You're learning faster than anyone I've ever met." I put the spear back in the stand and gazed at the other weapons.

"I had a strange dream last night," I told her as we cleaned up. "I was in a fight, and just as I got to Katia someone shot me with a gun. I heard there are no guns on Xima. Are you sure none have been smuggled here? I can't see us being successful if our opponents have guns."

Skyler replied with a hint of concern. "We've been suspicious of guns getting smuggled here, especially with the smuggling of ginnium back to Earth. However, we've never had a reason to believe there are guns on Xima. You should always be cautious, though, especially with how treacherous Xerxes is."

"When will we actually fight someone?"

"Patience, Zack. Don't be so eager to fight. Embrace all life until it becomes necessary to kill. Wait until it becomes obvious there's no other option. Only fight for a worthy cause."

She walked up to me, placed her hand on my shoulder, and looked into my eyes.

"You'll kill many before you leave this planet. There are evil people on Xima. Earth sent many criminals here, and it's unfortunate that children are raised in a land controlled by a warlord who'd let so many women and children die. But we'll rid Xima of this trash. That's our worthy cause."

That evening, Skyler went for a walk. I decided to go outside to embrace the beauty of our little hideaway. I walked to where I'd killed the animal that we'd eaten many days before and watched the water flow under the rock wall. I followed the stream back up toward the cabin, gazing at the sky. It was brightly lit with thousands of stars that were very clear. It was probably the most majestic night sky I've ever seen.

When I looked back down toward the stream, I realized General Skyler was washing in the water. Her silhouette was like a work of art I couldn't take my eyes off of. She slowly cleaned herself with a rag, and I watched the water stream off her beautiful profile.

I'd never seen a naked woman before, and I couldn't help but study her. She dipped her hair in the water and cleaned it using some type of lather. She was a lovely sight to see. When she pulled her head out of the stream and squeezed the water out of her hair, she looked around, and I darted behind some bushes then snuck back into the cabin so as not to be caught.

She came into the cabin later, fully clothed and with her hair still dripping.

"I needed that. I suggest you clean up, too. You'll feel great," she said gleefully.

I went out back to where she'd been bathing, undressed, and stepped into the water. The water was cool, and with my senses heightened, all I could hear was the sound of the water flowing around me. As I concentrated, I could hear each spot where the water met a rock. The sound was like a whisper of an orchestra all around me. The place was beautiful. It was like a children's movie I saw once that took place in a majestic forest with large brute-like trees but a soft, interwoven canopy. The moonlight beamed to the ground, and the only sound was the water bouncing off the rocks around me. I used the lather Skyler gave me to clean the layers of filth from my skin. As my skin became clean, I had a renewed energy about me.

The stream drifted around me as though I was a boulder in its path. The pressure of the water hitting against my back was almost what I imagined a massage would have felt like.

I stared up at the stars again, thinking about how the events in my life had led me to where I was. I pondered whether it was fate that had brought me there. All I knew for certain was that I wanted to rescue Katia. I knew I'd do anything to ensure her freedom and to hold her in my arms again. But I couldn't help but realize that my feelings for General Skyler were growing as well, and I didn't know what to do about it.

* * *

The next week of training was equally intense. Much of it was redundant, but I was also becoming more confident in my fighting skills. Skyler was a great fighter, and although I'd beaten her in a few sparring exercises, I realized her speed and instincts far exceeded mine. I thought my strength would be enough, but I realized that what Skyler had taught me was far more important.

One morning, I awoke and didn't see Skyler in the cabin. I looked out the window and spotted some movement, so I opened the door.

"Whoa!" I yelled, dodging something that flashed by me and stuck to the door with a *thud.* In a panic, I looked back at the door and saw a hatchet embedded in the wood. I looked back outside, confused. I sensed something else coming and dodged a knife, which also stuck into the door.

"What are you doing?" I yelled.

A masked figure stood in the training area holding a sword. There were other weapons lying around on the ground.

"General Skyler?" I asked. *She must be testing me somehow, but why? What is she up to?*

In a flash, another object came at me. I ducked and ran out to grab a sword from the ground.

"What's going on? What are you doing?"

It had to be Skyler—*who else could find us*—but I wasn't sure with the mask on. *Who else could it be?*

I breathed heavily. Each item thrown at me would have hit me if I didn't dodge. *Would Skyler do something so reckless?*

Suddenly, the assailant ran toward me and swung their sword. As I attempted to block, my leg was cut as I miscalculated where the sword would strike.

I caught a whiff of a familiar scent and noticed the way my opponent held their sword. I knew I was being tested, and I also knew that I needed to win the fight to prove to Skyler I was the man to help her save Earth and Xima.

I focused my thoughts on my surroundings and my assailant. We circled, holding our swords as we tried to find a weakness in the other. The masked figure charged, jumping up and faking me out by falling short. Rolling to my other side, they picked up a spear and threw it at me. I quickly stepped aside, grabbed the spear from flight, spun around, and threw it back. My opponent evaded my attack, and the spear flew past their ear, skidding on the ground.

I smiled at the confidence I had in my actions. I charged forward and, as I went low, I changed my approach and jumped, flipping over my opponent before I landed. Wrapping my arm around my assailant's neck, I pulled them to the ground. That was where my strength came into play, as I was able to pin them down. I placed my sword at their throat and heard Skyler's voice cry, "I yield!"

I got up and smiled, holding my hand out to help her up. I paused. Her expression warned me that the danger hadn't yet passed. I pulled my hand back and pinned her down again with my knee on her chest and my knife to her throat. "Do you give up?"

She laughed. "Yes, I give."

She took her mask off and smiled at me as she sat up. "Excellent intuition. You were right not to trust me. I was going to take advantage of your kindness."

She stood up and walked to me.

"I think you're ready," she said, putting her hand on my shoulder. "How do you feel?"

I looked at her hand, then to her smile. Even with her disheveled hair, she was absolutely stunning. I smiled back and experienced an exhilarating rush throughout my entire being. I was full of adoration for her.

"Like I could take on all of Xima." We laughed as she rubbed my shoulder, which only amplified my longing for her.

I looked around at the weapons on the ground and asked, "What was this all about? Why the mask?"

She reached down to pick up the weapons and replied, "Your assailants can surprise you at any time and from any place. You need to always be prepared or you'll end up dead. I knew you'd know who I was, but the mask probably put some doubt in your mind, didn't it?"

I smiled, realizing she was right. "It did give me some doubt and confusion at first, then I realized you were giving me some type of test. You didn't have to actually cut my leg, though."

She laughed. "Stop being a baby and help me put these weapons back on the rack." I grabbed the spear I'd thrown at her and set it in the weapons rack.

"I have something for you," the general said as she walked into the cabin.

I followed behind, wondering what could be in the cabin that I'd want. *Perhaps she has some more of that drink to celebrate the completion of my training?*

She walked up to her bed, pulled it away, took out her knife, and pried some wallboards loose. I was amazed to see her pull out a sword and a shield. She held them in front of her and appeared to be deep in thought as she stared intently at them. "This was the sword and shield of someone who meant a great deal to me."

"This looks fantastic! How did it get here?"

"We both left our swords and shields in this wall, hoping to come back one day and spend the rest of our lives here. All six of us were given a sword and shield once we completed our training and used them in our death fights."

She walked to me and handed me the sword and shield. It was much lighter than I'd expected. "What's it made of?"

"It's an alloy made from a mixture of ginnium, titanium, and tungsten. When the ginnium was taken to Earth, these were forged to be the strongest and lightest alloy ever created. They were made on Earth and flown here as graduation gifts, of sorts," she replied, and I could tell from her somber tone that the memory of someone close to her was on her mind.

"You are now an empiricist—the most formidable fighter in both worlds," the general said as he placed her hand on my arm.

I looked to her with a grin and nudged her with my shoulder. "One of *the* most formidable fighters you mean?"

She smiled and replied, "No, I think the most formidable. You know everything I know and are much stronger. You're destined for great things, Zack."

I placed my arm in the soft leather sleeves behind the shield and held the sword up to gaze at its beauty.

"Tomorrow, we'll see what type of scum we can find," she said.

I was both nervous and excited. Other than the fighting in the ring, I'd never gone looking for a fight, much less to intentionally kill someone.

Chapter 15

We drove the carriage into the forest and rode on a trail for hours. Skyler knew where some of Xima's worst people could be found and figured everyone would be better off if some of them no longer existed. At first, I didn't think that justified killing people, but she assured me they were arrogant enough to strike first, at which point we'd have no choice but to fight them anyway.

The forests on Xima looked spectacular. There were thick canopies above us and various colored shrubs decorating the forest floor. I noticed the blue bush was prevalent in many shaded areas. There was a cloud formation that looked like a spiral flowing through the sky.

I slapped my neck. "Something bit me."

"It was probably a tikifly. They're small, but their bites really burn."

She wasn't kidding; my neck was soon inflamed. Skyler pulled out more of the leaves she'd put on my wrists and placed them on my neck. They soothed the burn almost immediately.

Besides that fly, I couldn't help but enjoy the views on our journey and appreciate the beauty that Xima had to offer.

As we traveled down a worn trail, I saw a man standing along the path, leaning against a tree and whittling a stick with a knife.

"My, my. What a nice carriage, and what an even nicer piece of ass," he said with a laugh. "Someone riding this carriage should have a nice pouch of ginny, but it'll be a bonus to have a beautiful woman for us to take with it. Wouldn't you say, boys?"

Two men appeared at either side of the trail. We hadn't noticed them because they were in a thicker group of trees. The men gathered in front of us. They were dressed in ragged clothes, two of them wore hats, and they all wore belts with sword and knife sheaths. Their teeth looked brown and broken. After so much time on the planet, I assumed dentistry didn't exist yet on Xima.

"We'll be taking that carriage, your woman, and your ginny, boy. Cooperate, and we'll let you walk back to wherever you came from," another man said in a gruff voice while pointing his sword at Skyler. I breathed heavily, assessing them and our surroundings.

"Or he can watch and learn how a real man takes a woman… hey, men?"

They all laughed, exposing their orange and brown teeth. Filthy from head to toe, they laughed while nodding and slowly walked toward us, drawing their swords.

My heart raced, and I felt anxiety course through my body.

"Let's see what you've got," Skyler whispered to me.

Does she expect me to take them all on at once? Sure, I fought two at a time in the ring, but this is different. Isn't it?

I stepped down from the cart and walked toward the head of the kohl. The men stopped. I was perhaps twenty feet away from them as they stood together. One of them held his sword up on his shoulder, but the others had their weapons at the ready.

The silence was only broken by some birds flying nearby and the kohl's snort.

Skyler blurted out, "I was training my son earlier on how to use a sword and shield. He could use some more practice. I am merely a woman, after all. Perhaps you men might teach him a lesson."

They looked at each other and laughed. "Oh, we'll teach him a lesson, all right. And when we're done with him, we'll teach you some lessons, too." They all laughed at their lustful desire for Skyler.

All four charged me. I quickly pulled out my sword, and as they got close enough, I threw my sword into the face of the one on the right with all my might. It pierced right through his skull. I grabbed his arm as he fell forward and blocked the other three swords with my shield before they could touch me. Placing my foot on the dead man for leverage, I quickly removed my sword and swung it swiftly, taking the arm off the next man as I blocked his attack with my shield.

The other two men backed off to evaluate their situation. I was amazed at how much I'd accomplished so quickly—perhaps seconds—and yet two still remained. I glanced at the blood on my sword and marveled at how well I was able to swing it and the cutting power it had.

Skyler yelled, "I think he was just lucky, men. You won't get this fine ass and ginny if you don't try harder."

I looked up at her, wondering why she was antagonizing them.

The armless man rolled around in agony, holding what was left of his bleeding stump. "Kill him, you idiots!"

They advanced, and I swung at their swords, knocking them to one side. Weaponless, they backed off. One slowly moved behind me as the other stayed in front. I remembered the tactic from one of my fights. I used my peripheral vision to see as much as I could but couldn't see the man behind me. I looked back and forth between the two, then relaxed and thought about my training. My anxiety subsided.

I sensed the change in the breeze as the man behind moved to make his attack. My body twisted quickly, and I severed his head while he had his sword positioned to skewer my back. I stood before the last man.

He looked a little more nervous as he gazed at the other man's head rocking back and forth on the ground. Finding some courage, the man yelled, "I'm going to gut you open, boy, and then I'm going to fuck the woman in her guts!" His eyes were wide, with a hint of yellow and red, and his two teeth showed as he screamed like a madman and charged me.

He swung down at me, holding his sword with two hands. I ducked under his swing and used my shield to block his arms from coming down on me while my other hand pushed my blade into his chest. I yelled, lifting his body off the ground. The tip of my sword came up through his shoulder blades.

As I lowered him, he slid off of my sword and dropped on the ground. Then I walked up to the armless man.

"Who the hell are you?" he demanded, clutching his bleeding stump.

I pushed my sword into his chest and watched him stare into my eyes as he quietly died. For the first time in my life, I sensed confidence and power within me—a power I couldn't quite identify.

"You didn't want to tell him who you were?" Skyler asked.

I wiped the blood from my sword on his clothing just like Skyler had done with the first three assailants in the woods. "What difference would it have made?" I shrugged.

"Good point," Skyler said as she hopped off the carriage and helped drag the bodies into the woods.

We parked on the side of the path and set up a camp right on the trail. Skyler knew others would approach throughout the night, and she was right. I lost count of how many people attacked us. Each time, Skyler made a sarcastic remark to piss them off, and then she sat back to watch me take them on while calmly tending the fire. We made a good team.

I woke sitting with my sword on my lap and realized it was morning. I instinctively gripped the hilt of my sword, letting my shield fall to the ground, and then I relaxed when I didn't sense any threat. Skyler was nowhere to be found and neither were the bodies of the many people I'd killed throughout the night. But the carriage was where we'd left it, so I continued to look around to see where she could have gone.

"General Skyler?" I whispered, wondering what could have happened to her. But before I could panic, she came from around the carriage and walked toward the fire.

"Where were you?" I asked.

"Good morning to you, too. And I like my privacy sometimes. I'm still a woman, don't forget. How are you feeling?"

I shrugged, "Okay, I guess." I examined myself and saw blood on my arms and legs—none of it my own.

"The count I have is twenty-five dead. I dragged them to the woods. The animals will eat well for the next few days."

I paused while staring at the ground where I saw pools of blood all around me. It was like a scene from a horror movie. I couldn't fathom killing so many people, but somehow it was my reality. I stared down at my sword, and I turned it to let the sun glide along its length, revealing an almost pink color from the blood of all those I'd slayed.

"Why don't we go into the camp on the other side of this hill and get you washed up?" Skyler suggested. The way she said it was almost cynical. *Something tells me she has something else in mind…*

We climbed onto the carriage and rode over the hill and down to the camp below. It was a large area, and the path took us to a well in the center of it. There was a large stone building, and trees surrounded the area with makeshift shacks high up in their branches. The large stone building seemed strong, and a stream ran along the backside. Women walked around with some kids in tow, and an elderly man stacked firewood outside of the stone building. Everything looked peaceful other than a stench that grew in strength as we got closer. We soon saw the rotting corpses of dead men in random areas, their bodies decaying and partially eaten by animals. Other corpses hung by their necks from trees, also decaying. The place smelled like sickness and death. *How can anyone live here?*

A man stepped out of the stone house, and others slowly gathered to watch us approach.

"What business do you have here?" the short bald man said with a raspy voice. His beard was split and tied like two ponytails hanging from his chin. He had an eye patch at the center of a long scar that ran from his forehead through the patch and down his cheek. There was no doubt he'd seen a fight or two.

We didn't say a word. I waited for Skyler to speak for us, as I didn't know our plan or why we were there other than to wash ourselves.

When Skyler still didn't respond, I broke the silence. "We just stopped here to clean up," I said as I jumped down from the carriage and walked toward the well.

The bald man asked, "What's all that blood on you? Who have you been fighting?" I was about to tell him we were just hunting when Skyler spoke.

"It's from the twenty-five assholes he killed last night who came from this shithole of a camp," she said. Based on her tone and her laugh, I immediately knew she was trying to start a fight.

About fifteen men drew their swords, and the bald man looked at me with narrowed eyes, slowly removing his sword as well. "Is that right?"

I looked up at Skyler, who winked at me as though she was rooting for me. I knew she was trying to boost my confidence, and I needed it. I never expected to fight against so many.

As all the men slowly approached me, Skyler said, "Why don't we make a deal. You select your best fighter to go against this mere boy, and they'll fight to the death. If my boy wins, we take over the camp. If he loses, you can kill him and take me… and, of course, all of this ginny." She held up a bag that sagged from its weight. *I don't remember seeing that on the carriage.*

I looked up at her in disbelief, certain they would rather murder us than negotiate.

"Why don't we just kill him, take your ginny, and I'll make a necklace with those pretty white teeth for my wife?" the bald man asked, showing off his lack of teeth as he drew closer.

I assessed the men—where they were, their distance from each other, their weapons, and how they held them.

Skyler responded as though she was calmly negotiating the situation. "Well, I was hoping you'd take my offer, but now my boy will have to kill all of you," she said with an overly-dramatic sigh as though she'd given them a chance to save their lives.

They laughed while moving closer to me. I knew what Skyler was trying to do by instilling an attitude in them to make them confident that their numbers guaranteed their victory against me.

One man ran toward me with his sword held high. I ducked while stabbing and cutting a section of meat from his leg as he passed by me. He landed on the ground, perhaps ten feet behind me, crying out in pain while holding his leg.

The others stopped their approach after seeing what I'd done with the first attacker. A large man approached and said, "I'll take this little boy, but I get the girl first." He walked closer toward me, and I noticed he was a giant compared to most men. He must have been nearly seven feet tall and had shoulders too broad to fit through a doorway. He was also bald with only a few teeth, and his sword was very large, as were his arms. If he were to get close enough to touch me with his sword, it would easily lop off a limb. He came closer to me, trying to assess how to attack.

Skyler said, "Those teeth look nasty. Try not to breathe on my boy—he gets really disgusted by bad breath." I found some humor in Skyler's taunting, but the giant didn't. He ran at me with full force, both hands on his sword. I rolled under him and cut one of his Achilles tendons with a very harsh blow. He fell over in agony and howled as he rolled around and cried.

He tried to get back up and realized he couldn't. He lay alongside the other fallen assailant, unable to fight. Then I stood and faced the rest of them.

"I guess you won't be getting me first now, will you?" Skyler laughed at the large man.

The others stared at me with swords in hand. I could tell they were confused about how to attack—and whether they even should. The bald man from the stone house yelled, "Don't just stand there. Kill him!"

On impulse, I grabbed the giant's large sword and dropped the other.

They all rushed me at once. My body automatically reacted, turning on all of my senses at once. I cut, grabbed, punched, tripped, and stabbed at my opponents. An occasional cut on my arm or leg drew some blood but didn't feel like more than a scratch as I continued. With a loud growl, I swung around one more time with all my might as the last man approached, slicing through his waist. His body fell to the ground in two pieces.

"Wow, I've never seen anyone do that before!" Skyler exclaimed. Her excitement threw me off and made me wonder whether she'd have the same reaction to my body being sliced in half. "Thank you for letting me keep my teeth," she said to the bald man, who remained standing at the stone building. *Too cowardly to fight himself, no doubt.*

I looked at the dead and wounded around me. Those who were alive cried out in pain while cursing me. I looked to the bald man at the stone house and another man, who looked to be close to my age, standing near a wall next to the house. Some women were wailing behind trees as they witnessed the carnage.

The bald man looked to the man standing near the wall and yelled, "Kill him!" The man sheathed his sword but didn't move. "I said kill him!" yelled the bald man. I walked up to the bellowing man slowly with my sword pointed at his throat. He ran back into the house, and I could hear noises inside that sounded like objects being moved around.

Skyler, still sitting on the carriage, yelled to the man left standing, "You! What's your name?"

He looked nervous but walked forward with his hands slightly out to his side, letting us know he wasn't going to draw his sword. "My name is Surgy. I've only been here a few months. I was bought from the fight rings to be one of Ingus's guards. Ingus is the leader of this camp, and he's the one who just ran inside."

Skyler yelled, "Ingus, come on out. We want to talk to you." There was no response. Skyler jumped down from the carriage and walked up to Surgy. "How many fighters are here in this camp?"

He replied with a hint of confidence. "I think there are around fifty, but after today, perhaps a handful remain."

I tried kicking in the door to the stone house while Skyler talked with Surgy. I yelled, "Ingus, open the door, or we'll break it down."

The door was very solid and locked tight. I focused on the side that latched and kicked with the flat of my foot—it gave a little. I looked back to Skyler and Surgy, who continued talking, then kicked the door again. It gave a little more as dust fell from the door jam.

"Ingus, you're making this difficult on yourself!" I kicked again as hard as I could, causing the door to burst open and sending wood splinters flying from the door jam. I walked inside with my sword in hand, ready to defend against a surprise attack. The house was a complete mess—food was lying on the table, and a rat ran across the room ahead of me. Ingus was nowhere to be found, so I went upstairs to check the bedrooms, then downstairs again, cautiously looking for him. Either he wasn't inside, or he was hiding somewhere. I stomped on the floor to see if there might be a secret hiding place but didn't notice anything.

When I walked back outside, Skyler was still talking to Surgy. "He's nowhere to be found in there," I told her and looked to Surgy, hoping he might know where the weasel of a man might be hiding.

Surgy walked past me and inside the house, motioning for me to follow. He led me to a shelf in the house and pulled on the side, causing a section of wall to open and reveal a secret area where Ingus was hiding.

"Please, don't kill me. I can help you. I can be of use to you." Ingus groveled as he dropped his sword and held his hands in the air. I motioned him out of his hiding area. He slowly walked out with fear in his eyes, searching for an opportunity to escape, I suspected. I saw him look at a knife on the table.

"You want that knife, don't you?" I said with feigned confidence. "I just killed all your men by myself. What do you think you can do with a knife?"

Skyler sat on the edge of the kitchen table and looked into the hiding place. "Very nice. We may never have found this place on our own." Ingus glared at Surgy.

"What might you have to offer us that would convince us to keep you alive?" I asked.

"I have women here—young girls. I have ginny, and I have mines. I can make you very rich!"

"As I recall, you said I was a slut, or was it a whore, and that I'd be passed around among your men," Skyler said, tilting her head while smiling at Ingus. "You'll have to do better than that."

Then Skyler stood and took out her knife. She placed it to Ingus's throat. "Where is your ginny?" she whispered in a very casual tone. His eyes darted to his hiding spot. Skyler walked inside and found some panels cut into the wall. She pried them open and found many bags of coins lining the shelves. There must have been thousands of coins! "It seems you've been saving for a long time, Ingus. It's a shame the people here live so miserably."

Ingus nodded. "Yes, I have lots of ginny, and I can make you more. I have women also. They can be yours—take them."

I was disgusted at how he treated women and girls like objects that he could give away, just to save himself.

Skyler continued to probe. "Where are your mines?"

"Keep me alive, and I'll work the mines for you. I have men who will work until they die to get all the ginny you want. I'll make you rich," Ingus pleaded, looking back and forth between Skyler and myself.

I thought about how the scumbag kept his camp with dead bodies strewn all over and hanging from trees. I thought of how kids and women struggled to survive while he hoarded so much ginny, keeping everyone else poor. I thought of his eagerness to give women away without hesitation. Every minute I spent thinking about the piece of trash being alive made me angrier.

"Surgy, do you know where these mines are located?" I asked.

He looked at Ingus, then at Skyler. I put my sword up to Surgy's throat—I could barely contain my anger. "I asked you a question. Do you know where these mines are located?" I could see the fear in his eyes as he quickly nodded.

In a flash, I swung my hand around and sliced through Ingus's neck. His head fell to the floor. I watched his body topple, and then I pointed my blade to Surgy. "What do you want in life?"

"I wasn't expecting you to do that so quickly," Skyler muttered while staring at the head settling. He looked to Skyler with wide eyes.

"Don't look at her. I asked you the question."

Surgy changed his gaze to Ingus. "I've been a fighter since I was young. I should have been dead numerous times. Every day I'm alive is a gift for me. I don't know anything else but fighting, but what I want most is to simply enjoy life as a free man."

I stared into his eyes. His apparent sincerity influenced me to lower my sword.

Skyler asked, "What should we do with him, Zack?"

I put my sword into my sheath and looked to him. "I want you to gather everyone who's still alive in this camp in front of this building immediately. Leave the injured where they are for now."

We walked outside and watched Surgy run through the camp, calling everyone to gather. Among the remaining inhabitants were about twenty women, ten children, three elderly men, and Surgy. They all looked frightened, no doubt from seeing the dead or wounded fighters scattered around. I looked to Skyler for help on what to say to them. She said, "This is your show now, Zack. I'm sure you'll do the right thing."

But I was at a loss for words. I looked at all the scared faces and the dirty children with ripped clothes. There was an uncomfortable silence as I heard a few women cry quietly. I tried to understand what they needed. What did they need to hear from me? I walked to the well and pulled up a bucket of water, quenched my thirst with a couple handfuls of water, and splashed some on my face.

I looked around at the bodies lying all over the camp and listened to the groans. I scanned the camp with its poorly built shacks. The one thing I was certain of in that moment was that I didn't know what to do.

The people were shivering and looked terrified, and I needed to do something. So, I walked up to the children whose mothers held them close and said, "I won't hurt any of you." Then I approached one of the women. "Do you have a husband?" She nodded and pointed at one of the men lying on the ground.

I'd killed all those men—some of them husbands and fathers. But they were also killers who had accepted Ingus's orders to kill me. If it hadn't been them, it would have been me.

Skyler put her hand on my shoulder. The look in her eyes told me she knew I was struggling with my guilt. I found solace in her gentle and comforting touch. "You did what you needed to do. Now's your chance to make things right," she whispered in a nurturing tone.

I looked to Surgy. "Who works the mines?"

"There are miners who work them. Typically, the elders. They don't live here. Ingus sends us to collect the ginnium from them."

A few women wept over the fallen men who had once dominated the camp. I stared at the other women and children and realized they were Xima's hope for survival, and with that in mind I spoke. "Surgy is now in charge of this camp. I want all the dead removed. Bury them in a deep grave. Next, clean everything. This building will be a common house for everyone to use for food prep and to treat the sick and wounded." I walked toward Surgy. "What do you do with the ginnium after it's collected?"

"We take it to Lauri where it's turned to coin or smelted for other uses." He paused for a moment. "Specifically, it goes to a man named Xerxes, who manages it from there. He pays the elites with food and wine."

"And who's in charge of Lauri?" I asked.

"There's a mayor, but by title only. Xerxes is in charge of everything, but he uses the mayor as a puppet to speak to the public and take the blame for things that go wrong. The mayor does nothing more than eat and drink all day, which is why he's so fat." I already hated Xerxes for what he did to Katia, but I was even more furious knowing he controlled everything on Xima. *He* was responsible for what had happened here.

"What do you get in return for the ginnium?" I asked.

"We get coins and bring them back to Ingus, who gives us a share for our work."

"You saw how many coins he hoarded. How long will that store last you and the people of this camp so that you can live and improve your homes until we get more people here to help?"

Surgy rubbed his chin, and I could tell he was deep in thought.

"Perhaps a year. We might be able to make it last a little longer, but as you can see, there are very few men left to do any work. The problem isn't so much the coin but the labor and materials. We have no saws to cut trees or other tools, and we have limited knowledge about how to make better housing—just look at the poor quality of the buildings here."

Looking around the camp, I noticed the makeshift housing; some had nothing more than a blanket or cloth for a wall. I smiled at Surgy. "How do people eat or live? Where do they buy supplies? Is there a store?"

Surgy replied, "Almost everything is run by Xerxes. Any supplies from the Earth ships, he takes and sells. We hunt or gather the little food we have from the land."

I said, "I'll see what I can do with getting you more materials to improve everything here. Continue the mining, and use the coin to feed and take care of the people here and at the mine. Maybe use the coin to trade with other camps for more food. Keep the ginnium in a hidden spot near the mine, and tell no one. We'll try to send others here to begin building this camp into another large city."

I could see the glee and hope in many faces, but I also couldn't help but feel guilty for the men I took from them. Skyler walked up to me and said, "Don't feel guilty. Their mourning will fade. What you've given them is far better than the life they had."

I smiled at her, then walked up to Surgy. "I'll trust you with this task. If you betray me, you'll meet the same fate as these men."

Surgy knelt before me and held my hand. "You have my word. I promise to keep peace and prosperity at this camp, and I'll clash swords with anyone who opposes."

As I looked around the camp, I felt a wave of pride course through me. "My name is Zack. I fight for peace on Xima, and I fight for those who want peace."

I walked up to Skyler, who smiled at me. I murmured, "I have no idea what I'm doing. You can help me at any time."

She slapped me on the back and laughed. "You're doing just fine, Zack. Your father would be proud. Surprised, but proud."

I gave a slight chuckle, wondering if my father would have expected me to be in such a situation, then went to clean myself with some water from the stream behind the building. I came back to find Skyler sitting on the carriage. I climbed up and looked at Surgy, nodded to him, and he nodded back. The carriage lurched forward as I watched the people drag the dead bodies away and tend to the wounded.

"Where are we going now?" I asked while staring at a young boy waving to me.

Skyler kept her gaze forward. "I figured we'd clean the roads of trash between here and Lauri." Then she turned her head slightly toward me, and

I saw a smile on her face as she winked. I knew exactly what she meant. My ultimate goal was to get to Katia, but I didn't mind helping clean up a bit if it meant making innocent people safe.

As we moved forward, I reminisced on the boy I'd been when Miss Linda took me in, how she protected me and gave me a home. I thought back at what might have happened if I'd stayed at the orphanage or ran away to another place on Earth. Killing came to me so easily, and I couldn't help but think saving Xima was somehow my designated fate.

Chapter 16

The forest was magical yet ever so strange compared to the nature on Earth. I saw a small mound on the ground that erupted some type of smoke, like a volcano.

"That's an acid geyser," Skyler said. "You want to stay as far away from that as you can. Even the air particles from that thing can burn your skin."

Something that looked like a giant centipede, the size of an anaconda with prey the size of a dog in its mouth, scurried through the underbrush. *That is one bug I definitely don't want to mess with.*

I understood why General Skyler wanted to protect the land by cleansing it of unruly individuals who inflicted pain on the weak, but I couldn't help but wonder why the same thing wasn't done on Earth. *Why had the scientists and leaders back home spent so much money to bring this scourge to such a beautiful planet?*

As we travelled, my skills and confidence continued to increase, but Skyler still had to take out a few men whenever I was up against too many good fighters. She seemed to naturally know when I needed her help, but I also understood why she had me fight alone. She wanted me to build my abilities, and her plan was working.

One small camp we stumbled upon was full of many young women and children. One man managed them as prostitutes for anyone with ginny. Two guards stood in front of some trees, and behind them was a tent where the young ladies must have stayed. I was sickened at the thought of what happened there, but I knew what I had to do to stop it.

A large man walked out of a well-built log building. He said in an unusual accent, "Welcome, guests! We have a good variety of companions here for your choosing. They'll do anything you wish." He clapped his hands, and the girls came running out—many of whom were barely clothed—in front of the two guards.

I walked up to the guards, and they moved their hands to the hilts of their swords, prepared to draw. I smiled at the manager and had two knives in each of the guards' throats, pinning them against the trees, before they could unsheathe their swords.

"Whoa! What are you doing? Those were Xerxes's men. You'll be killed for this!"

I walked up to the manager and, without saying a word, ran my sword up through his gut and out between his shoulder blades.

"I don't think Xerxes will ever know," I said calmly while looking into the bright yellow of his eyes. Then I let him drop to the ground.

The girls huddled together, and Skyler walked up to them to try to calm their crying. "It's all okay. We're here to rescue you. Please, calm down. Who here is the oldest?"

A girl raised her hand—she couldn't have been more than fifteen. Others were as young as maybe nine or ten. *This is the most despicable shit I've seen on this godforsaken planet.*

Skyler walked up to me and whispered, "I don't think we can leave these girls alone, nor can we have them walk to the mining camp by themselves."

"What do you suggest?" I asked.

Skyler replied, "What was happening here was bad, but the girls were safe from the other horrors on this planet. Now, we'll have to take them back to the last camp we liberated a few miles back. The other women and good men we left alive will look out for them."

I saw the fear in the girls' faces as they stood clinging to each other. I had to agree that we couldn't leave them where they were.

Skyler approached the girls and said, "Get all of your belongings. You'll come with us to a new home."

They ran to the tent area and grabbed blankets and some other belongings. Then, all twelve of them climbed into the back of the carriage.

We took them back to the last compound we'd liberated and had the older women there clean them up and find a place for them to live.

Surgy walked up to me, and I could tell he was trying to search for the right thing to say. We were the ones burdening him with the extra girls to care for, so I said, "I understand the extra burden this puts on you, but we'll send help as soon as possible."

"But I don't know if we have enough food." He seemed sincerely concerned.

I looked at the people and realized merely leaving them with ginny wasn't enough. I walked up to the carriage and pulled out a spear. Skyler walked over and asked, "What are you doing?"

"The least we can do is leave them with some food. Want to go hunting with me?" She smiled and grabbed another spear.

As we walked quietly through the forest, I saw another one of those centipedes crawling on the ground and quickly skittering up a tall tree.

Skyler whispered, "You don't want that to get close. It's very poisonous."

"And scary," I whispered back.

In a small clearing, we saw an animal similar to the one I'd killed in the mountains but about twice the size. It was eating grass along a small pond, which was about as far away as the last one, so I was confident I'd get it. I stood back, took my stance, aimed a little high, took a step, and threw.

The spear grazed the animal's back, and it turned and tried to run away. Skyler sprinted forward and threw her spear, hitting its chest, and it fell to the ground.

"Show-off." I looked at her and laughed.

She pushed me. "Go get your spear."

I returned to the animal as Skyler was already cleaning it. With its insides removed, it was much easier to carry back to the camp.

I set my spear in the ground and helped her. She smiled while diligently pulling out guts with her hands and said, "Don't let it get to you. Spear throwing isn't always an exact science. Maybe a gust of wind threw it off." I could see her snickering, and I burst out laughing, causing her to laugh louder as well.

Once cleaned out, we walked to a nearby pond and cleaned the blood from our arms and clothing. When we were clean, we walked back to the animal, and I asked Skyler, "How could anyone use women and children like this?"

"People can be very cruel, but none of this would happen if there weren't paying customers. So don't only look at the men at the camp but also the scum out there paying to use those women and children."

She stopped and reached her arms around me. I was compelled to do the same. I couldn't recall the last time I'd hugged someone other than Katia, and it felt great.

Skyler said, "You're a good man, Zack." She reached up and kissed me, then let go to walk back to the animal.

I touched my mouth, and an almost euphoric sensation and warmth spread through my entire body. I smiled and slowly walked to where Skyler was waiting for me with the animal.

The walk back to camp took perhaps twenty minutes, but the mixed feelings swirling around my head— feelings for Katia, which hadn't left me, and those that were growing for Skyler—made it feel like a lifetime.

Chapter 17

We continued our journey to Lauri, stumbling on a few more camps that had similar problems as the ones we previously visited. Each one had the same bullies, the same women and children, and each visit ended with Xerxes's men dying. I discovered that Xerxes's authority was recognized at every one of them. He seemed to control the entire planet, and I wanted nothing more than to see his face when he saw how I was slowly destroying his little kingdom.

At every camp we liberated, we encouraged those who wanted peace to stay the course, and we encouraged any young man who didn't want to fight back to go to the mining camp and help Surgy turn it into a prosperous city.

We left many camps in the hands of someone who we believed would be a good leader. Each woman and child reminded me of Katia and how much I wanted her in my arms, how much I wanted to kiss her again, and what the despot Xerxes might be doing with her while I was so far away. Rage consumed me every time I thought of him and what he'd done to the planet—a planet that could have been prosperous instead of the depraved wasteland it had become.

After many months of cleansing the countryside, we returned to our volcanic retreat behind the mountain wall. My kill count was high, and it was getting to a point where all I could smell were rotten corpses and blood on my skin and in my clothes regardless of how much I washed. I needed a rest.

I followed Skyler into the cabin where she removed a stone in the fireplace. Inside was a small cavity where she pulled out a dark clay jug. I looked at her inquisitively as she took the cork off and drank its contents.

She closed her eyes and smiled. "After all these years, it still tastes fine." She paused with a smile and stared across the room. "There are a lot of memories in this cabin."

I saw her eyes water. She shook her head and handed the jug to me. I took a drink; the contents burned my throat, and I spit what I could onto the floor. Skyler laughed. "What is that?" I coughed, handing it back to her and trying to wipe the burn from my lips.

"It was something my trainer gave me after my first real battle." She patted me on the back. "My first reaction was the same as yours. The second time's better."

She handed it back to me, and I took another sip. It was sharp on my throat and tongue, yet I was able to choke down a swallow. I couldn't recognize the taste.

"What *is* this stuff?"

"It's distilled food scraps from Xima. There's a man who gathers fruit and vegetable scraps in Lauri and makes this."

"Where do the fruit and vegetables come from?" I asked.

"They used to come frozen from Earth on the shipping runs, but now there's a farm on the other side of Xima that's been developed over the past few decades. It grows healthy crops, but typically only for the elites of Xima. Everyone else gets scraps, or occasionally a shipment of food paste comes in on a shuttle. Those people out in the villages or camps find plants and animals to tend to, and some have small gardens, but there are very few farming tools. Xerxes may sell some abundance of crops to the villages or camps for ginny."

"Doesn't anyone coordinate food shipments from Earth? Why doesn't the leadership of Xima expand their crops or give incentives for others to create farms?" I took another sip of the drink, squinting a little at the burn but able to tolerate it. My head was suddenly feeling foggy.

"Most places are unable to grow large crops because of the lack of tools. Usually, they make do with sticks or chipped stones as they did thousands of years ago on Earth. The forge in Lauri could make tools, but Xerxes controls everything."

Skyler took a long drink from the jug. "All the elites, like Xerxes, simply look out for themselves. They don't care about the rest of the people until their problems start to affect them." She took another drink. "Look at you. He bought you just for sport, and if you had died, he would have just gotten another fighter. That's the way it's been for years, and that's how it'll continue to be unless someone does something about it."

She handed the jug to me, and I took a gulp, realizing how amazing it was. I stared at the jug and marveled at how smooth the liquid was to drink. I found myself staring at the craftsmanship of the jug while swaying side to side. "Skyler, could this planet be more? Could it grow to be better than it is, like Earth was?"

She laughed. "Oh my God. Enough with the 'Skyler' or 'General' already. Call me Tonya. We've been close enough for the past few months to at least be on a first-name basis." She sat on the edge of the wooden table. I could hear a slur in her voice. "It goes down much easier now, doesn't it? Don't drink too much or you'll regret it in the morning. This planet can be everything that Earth was, until greed sets in.

"Xima was planned with good intentions, but when people get power-hungry, the good of society as a whole falls apart. There will always be a need for justice—humans aren't perfect and will always be prone to crime—but the atrocities here on Xima and on Earth should have never been allowed to get this bad."

She took the jug from me as I was about to drink some more and tilted it back herself for another drink. "Let's go clean up by the stream," she slurred, then stood and staggered to the door. I laughed as she flipped me off and also laughed.

My vision was wavy, and I found it difficult to stay balanced as I laughed at Tonya zigzagging outside. I nodded while following her like a disoriented sheep, mindlessly trotting the same path.

We walked behind the cabin, stumbling and bumping into trees while laughing at our lack of balance. When we arrived at the water, Tonya placed her hands on my cheeks, kissed me, and started to strip off my clothes. I laughed when I looked down at my nakedness. "Are you going to put a loincloth on me or something?" I said, remembering Mir's routine with me over the years.

It was a challenge just to stand in place let alone take off her clothes, and I didn't even know where to start. She laughed at my fumbling and took her own clothes off for me. She took my hand, and we stepped into the water and knelt to enjoy the warmth of the sun mixed with the coolness against our bodies. She splashed water at me, laughing, and I did the same to her.

Although my vision was blurry, I couldn't help but stare at her beauty. I thought of Katia, then looked at Tonya again. My heart raced as I simply stared at her naked flesh in awe. I'd never been with a naked woman before, and I was too numb to move or even speak.

She laughed and slowly came up to me, pulling my mouth to hers. Our lips touched, sending shockwaves throughout my body. I thought my heart was going to leap out of my chest. Then her hand reached for my stomach, and she touched me.

I jumped while pushing her back, splashing about. Her furrowed brows and tilted head stared at me, clearly confused. Her beauty was beyond comprehension—she was more striking than I'd ever seen her before. My breathing was fast, and I was experiencing an unrecognizable force within myself that I couldn't understand.

"What's the matter?" she asked, her breathing heavier than normal, and she tilted her head. The concerned look on her face tore me up inside. I gazed at her breathtaking body. I was conflicted—my body desperately wanted to comply, but I had Katia in my heart.

"I-I can't. I'm in love with Katia." Confused, embarrassed, and ashamed, I couldn't face Tonya. Instead, I looked down into the water flowing around us. I was thankful for the babbling sound of the water, as neither of us said a word.

The feeling of Tonya's hand on my cheek was warm. She guided my eyes up to hers. Her warm smile melted me. I realized I wouldn't be able to resist her if she continued. "Katia is one lucky girl," she said with a half-smile. I couldn't help but feel like I'd let her down. Tonya was absolutely beautiful, but I was in love with Katia and would remain loyal to her.

"I want to go to Lauri and free Katia, and I need your help," I pleaded without breaking our gaze.

She took her hand away and slid back into the water, placing her fingers in the stream and watching the water part around her. "That would be very risky. For all we know, she's dead."

But I knew deep in my heart that Katia was still alive, and I needed to rescue her.

"She can't be dead. Xerxes will keep her as a shield in case I come back for him—he knows I'd never risk her getting hurt."

My lust was replaced with conviction as I thought about freeing Katia. With tears in my eyes, I stepped out of the water, grabbed my clothes, and stumbled back into the cabin. I put my pants and shirt back on, and I spotted the jug out of the corner of my eye—the answer to my immediate need. I took a long swig.

"You're going to have a headache in the morning if you keep that up." Tonya came in soon after, wearing her shirt which covered most of her. I couldn't help but notice her shapely legs and that her shirt remained open. I looked away, handing her the jug. She took a long drink, grinned, and said, "Don't be so intimidated by my body. You didn't seem to mind watching me wash in the stream a while back."

I blushed and took the jug out of Tonya's hand, tilting my head back for another drink. "I find you very attractive, and I think I care for, I mean… if…" I shook my feelings for Tonya out of my mind and took another drink. "If you help me rescue Katia and bring her back here safely, I'll do anything you ask of me."

She took the jug back from me, pouring the contents into her open mouth. She squinted as though she was looking into my soul, but if her vision was like mine, she was simply trying to keep me in focus. "You really love this girl, don't you?" she said with a slight slur.

I looked down at the wood in the bench, tracing the scratch marks that went against the grain with my finger. I thought of the time Katia and I had spent together at the shelter and how I took her away. I could picture her expression when I called her my fiancé.

"Yes, I do, and I need to free her." I paused for a moment to think. Then I asked Tonya, "Have you ever been in love?"

She paused to collect her thoughts, slowly nodding. She traced her fingers along the "TS + KD" carved into the top of the table. "My parents were both leaders in the ADS. They were involved in the intelligence field and were killed by FOG when I was twelve. Five others and I others lost our parents in the same week. We lived in a compound similar to the one you grew up in. The ADS decided to train us in a special program to create better leaders and fighters against FOG, so they sent us here. There was one other girl and four boys. We weren't allowed to fraternize or have relations or we'd be punished. Kieren was a boy who was a year older than me. We got along very well. Very, very well."

There was a moment of silence as she stared into the carvings with a reminiscent smile. "Sometimes we went off to enjoy some personal time together. We always got caught, and the punishments started off with simple cleaning. Eventually, our punishments became more brutal, so we staved off personal contact, but our feelings for each other remained.

"When we turned eighteen, we were entered into the death fights. We were far better trained than anyone Xerxes or any of the other elites brought to the ring. We were taught to expel our opponent out of the ring rather than kill them, but sometimes that wasn't possible.

"After six death fights each, we were sent back to Earth to take up leadership roles and to fight FOG. Kieren and I pushed for a way to be together, and we fought well as a team, always watching each other's back. The other four on our team were eventually killed in overwhelming battles. They were given bad information and were sent into fights that were significantly against their odds. We believed the bad information was intentional, but we had no way of knowing for sure.

"Kieren and I were the only two remaining from that original training class. We knew we could never marry, as that was part of our agreement signing on to the program. They wanted us to promise to devote ourselves to leadership roles in the ADS and not focus on relationships or families, but we were still together as much as possible. We couldn't disclose our love for each other, but deep down we knew it was there.

"One day, we were evaluating some alleged FOGn assaults on a city in Virginia. Some locals said FOG militants would come in and take children from their homes. When we arrived at the city center, everything was calm. Kieren noticed it was too calm. We both sensed a trap, and just as he yelled for us to run, we were ambushed by a FOG army. I turned my back to dive behind a car as a flash grenade went off in front of us.

"Blinded, I fell to the ground. I could only hear some other muffled explosions. There was gunfire all around me, but I tried to crawl toward where I remembered the car was. When I could see again, I spotted Kieren on the ground. Our attackers threw shrapnel grenades at us, and he fell on them hoping his vest would protect him and the rest of us. But they blew right through his vest. His last words were, 'I love you, Tonya.'"

Her voice cracked, and she paused for a moment. Tears filled her eyes. "I was pulled away from him as bullets flew by us. I didn't want to leave him. I would have been killed myself had it not been for my troops reminding me to focus."

I could see the tears fall onto her shirt as she caressed the letters in the table. "After, we were able to set up a defense, and I got my bearings. I was more focused than I could have ever imagined, and I set out for revenge. I don't know how many I killed that night, but a record somewhere says it was over a hundred. I wasn't even slightly wounded. I wanted all of them to die, but they eventually retreated.

"Afterward, I was told my actions were too reckless for me to be in the field. The ADS promoted me to general and gave me the task of developing what your father had engineered. He built the first and only prototype of a revolutionary device that would have made Earth a better place. And now, here we are."

"Does that sword and shield belong to Kieren?" I asked.

She nodded. "But now it belongs to you. Take good care of it."

I nodded and pondered the relationship she had with Kieren for a moment. Then I asked, "But you wanted to have sex with me, even though you're not in love with me?" I looked at her with narrowed eyes. I may have been naïve to love and was a virgin, but I was sure two people had to be in love first.

"Oh, young Zack. You have so much to learn about life. Don't confuse momentary sexual desires with love. One is a simple and temporary pleasure; the other is deeper, more emotional, and… far more painful."

I saw a tattoo of what looked like wings on her forearm. I remembered catching glances of it but never thought to ask. "Is there a meaning behind the tattoo on your arm?"

She pulled up her sleeve and stared at it for a moment. "All six of us got this tattoo when we came back to Earth. It symbolized our elite status. We were all immensely proud and hoped to make a positive change in the world."

"Perhaps you can take me to get the same tattoo?" I asked with a grin, trying to give her some hope that we could still make a difference.

"I'll trade you a tattoo for that device," she bartered, focusing on my arm.

"Ha! I don't even know if it's still in there. I haven't felt it for years."

"Oh, it's still in there. If we could make a copy, it could make a difference in our future. But it could also bring unstoppable power to someone with the wrong intentions."

Tonya picked up the jug, put it to her mouth, and realized it was empty. She set the empty jug down on the wood with a *thud*, then stumbled to her bed. "Okay, Mr. Bringer-of-Peace, we'll come up with a strategy tomorrow to rescue your true love. For now, be careful with that sword. I don't want you to cut yourself."

I laughed while trying to stand and fell back down on my ass. My head was still foggy, but I attempted to stagger to my bed only to fall on my face. I could see Tonya lying on her bed, but instead of lusting for her, the image of Katia floated through my head. I could see her as clearly as if she were right in front of me—her dark curly hair, her smooth olive skin, her laugh.

Her laugh was always my weakness. I wanted to see her again so desperately, but I also had to consider that Tonya's instinct could have been right; Xerxes may have done something terrible to her. I wanted to kill him with every part of my being, but all my foggy brain could handle was gazing at Tonya and thinking about how much I'd grown to care for her, too.

Chapter 18

In the morning, I felt like someone who really hated me was beating my head with a mallet—every tiny sound around me sent sharp bolts of pain through my temples, making me nauseous.

I opened my eyes and rolled over to find Tonya drinking water. "How are you feeling, lover boy? Here, have some water." She handed me a cup.

"Did that juice do this? I feel miserable." I groaned while trying to sit up on my bed. I sipped the water and couldn't pour it into my mouth fast enough. I was more parched than I'd ever experienced before. I sat for a moment before standing, then walked to the main table where Tonya had some objects arranged.

Still quite thirsty, I dipped the cup into the bucket of fresh water again. Tonya had an arrangement on the table that she explained was the city Lauri. She discussed the layout with me and showed me which building Xerxes was in. It was the same building I'd spent almost two years in as a chained slave, training and fighting, destined to eventually die in a ring for his pleasure and monetary gain if it hadn't been for Tonya.

She explained that the guards in Lauri were only loyal to Xerxes. "He keeps the mayor in his pocket with food, girls, and ginny," she said. "So, the mayor just does what Xerxes tells him to do. He's become the most powerful person on Xima and has a lot of influence in any type of trade with Earth."

We discussed strategy on how to avoid alerting more guards. We'd need to kill those we came upon as silently as possible and then hide their bodies well before continuing through Xerxes's house to find Katia.

Tonya said, "We'll need to do this at night. I'm sure Katia will be with the other slaves then. He wouldn't have her with him—he's too paranoid. Our goal is to get in quietly, get her, and then get out as fast as we can. Many rooms have iron doors, so if we get caught in one, we won't get out very easily."

I remembered my time in the small cell. The last thing I wanted was to get trapped in one again. What she said made sense, and I was eager to carry out the plan. Excitement coursed through my body. *We're really going to rescue her!* "When do we go?"

She looked at the objects on the table and paused. "We can leave this afternoon. It'll take two days to get there. We'll find some place to hold out while I go into the city and do some reconnaissance. We can get her perhaps two days after that."

I grunted, then asked, "Why do we have to wait so long? You've seen what I can do. I can take them all! I want to get her out of there as soon as possible!" I slammed my hand on the table, exacerbating the pounding in my head.

She put her hand on my shoulder the way she always did. It had become an immediate relaxation drug for me. Her nurturing smile and beautiful eyes penetrated right into my anxious mind, immediately soothing my frustration. "You are indeed very capable against any man, or multiple men, but you can get trapped in a building like that easily. And in close quarters, you'll be a much easier kill for them. Besides, I'm not convinced Xerxes didn't smuggle guns. If he or any of his men have that kind of weaponry, it would make this rescue completely different. Be patient, Zack. We'll get your girl."

During the day, we modified the carriage by removing the bars and building a small hiding place in the floor, where we stored additional weapons such as axes, spears, knives, and swords. Tonya made some healing paste from the plants in the area in case we got injured.

As we approached the wall to leave our sanctuary, Tonya stood up on the carriage and looked back at the cabin. I could tell she was reminiscing, so I didn't interrupt her. I saw a tear form in her eye, then she jumped down and opened the wall to the mountain. I had the kohl pull the carriage through the opening, and Tonya closed the wall again. She didn't say a word as we drove off, but I had a feeling she was looking back at the place that held so many of her memories like it was the last time she'd ever see it.

That evening, we stopped at a camp we'd freed. The people there recognized us right away, and some of them came to welcome us back. I saw clean children and a cheerier disposition among everyone. *The man we left to lead the camp certainly took care of the people with the coin we left him.*

The eldest woman there, who had a ten-year-old child, insisted we stay with her in her small shack for the night. We were grateful and left her with a handful of ginny. The next morning as we were leaving, a small girl ran up to me.

"This is for you, Zack." It felt so strange to hear someone other than Tonya call me by my real name—I'd been my alias Zan for so long, but I was done hiding who I was.

I knelt in front of her as she placed a small piece of cloth in my hand, and I saw it had a smiling blue face on it.

I tried to hold back my tears. "What did you use to make this picture?"

"A berry. Do you like it?" she replied with a proud glow about her. I looked up at her mother, who also looked happy. She mouthed *thank you.*

"It is the nicest thing anyone has ever given me. I like it very much. Thank you."

As I placed it in a small pocket on the belt holding my sheaths, I couldn't help but feel proud of what I'd accomplished so far. I climbed onto the carriage and waved back as we rode off.

In the middle of the day, we came across some men walking in the opposite direction. They stopped to talk while watching us approach. One man took off running back in the direction from where they came. "Get down and handle these men. I'll get that one," Tonya commanded.

I jumped down, not quite knowing what she had in mind. She slapped the reins, causing the kohl to speed away after the fleeing man.

"Who are you?" one man asked me. He was lanky and bald, taller than me, and his grin was full of broken teeth. His hand rested on the hilt of his sword. I looked to the other men, who also looked prepared to fight. Tonya must have thought these men were just like the many others we killed in the past—easy pickings.

I shrugged. "I'm no one. We're just traveling to work out a trade deal in Lauri," I replied while keeping my eyes on all the men.

"Rumor has it some young boy who looks a lot like you was sold by Xerxes and has been killing people in the camps. There's a big reward for him."

I raised my eyebrows and smiled. "I don't really listen to rumors. They tend to be exaggerated."

"Why is your partner chasing one of my men?" he asked, squinting one eye at me and sizing me up. I had a feeling our encounter wasn't going to be peaceful.

"I don't know. She told me to get off and wait for her. Perhaps she fancied him and went to introduce herself, if you know what I mean. She's usually quite determined." I laughed at my humor but didn't see anyone else smile.

The four men spread out, slowly surrounding me. They wore tattered clothing, their faces were dirty, and I could smell their stench from ten feet away.

I remained still, using my senses to determine where each man stood outside of my periphery. I was prepared for anything. I replied, "I heard those same rumors. Some young man with incredible strength taking on many fighters at once." I laughed. "A man like that would probably be able to slice through you four quite easily… if he were to exist, of course." I grinned at the leader, enticing him to pull his sword on me. *I must be picking up Tonya's taunting skills.*

The other three men backed away slightly, no doubt confused about what to do.

"While we're getting acquainted, where are you and your men going?" I asked, gazing down the trail where Tonya went and trying to see if she was on her way back.

"It would seem a mining camp is no longer bringing ginnium to Lauri. Xerxes sent us to find out why. You wouldn't know anything about that, would you?"

My anger grew as they confirmed what Surgy had told me about how Xerxes controlled the camps. I remembered the first camp with Ingus who hoarded all the coin in his secret room like a slimy coward. *These men will no doubt cause trouble for those people and Surgy. I can't afford to let them continue.*

I saw the carriage returning in the distance, and I did a quick scan of my surroundings. The forest stood tall to the right of the road, and there was an open prairie to the left.

"I remember a mining camp like that a while back—very nice people there. A man living in the stone house went by the name of… Hmm, I can't remember his name now, but he was bald and very ugly," I said.

"His name's Ingus. He's my brother, and if the two of you went into his camp, you probably wouldn't have left alive." He laughed, causing the other men to laugh as well.

I placed my finger up to my lips, pretending to ponder. "Ahh yes, that's why I remember him. I killed Ingus *and* all of his men. The man in charge there now is Surgy."

The lead man pulled out his sword, his eyes gleaming. "There's no way you killed everyone. He had almost fifty men, all good fighters."

"Technically, after I killed twenty-five or so on the trail leading to the mining camp, there were much less to contend with, but some could have been hiding once I began killing them." I leaned in and whispered, "Besides, they weren't really that good at fighting. I mean, really, they all fought like little boys who got their first wooden sword." I hoped my cocky smile would fire them up.

"Just so you know," I added, "Ingus died quickly. Well, after I decapitated him, that is. But it did take a while before his head stopped rolling around on the floor. It was almost as though he didn't want to die." I knew my words and my laughter would get him irate enough to attack me.

Sure enough, the bald man came at me, screaming, his eyes inflamed. I pulled out my two short swords, ducked away from his attack, sliced the front of his legs, and then quickly followed through, slashing at his back. He fell over, crying out in pain. He tried to get up and looked at the other men. "Don't just stand there… kill him!"

They gripped the hilts of their swords while looking at each other. All three of them seemed to be in their late twenties. The three standing men seemed to be contemplating their fate. I could tell by their hesitation they preferred not to die by fighting me. *There may be hope for them yet.*

"Ahhhhh!" the bald man yelled as he hobbled toward me again. I effortlessly dodged his charge, slapping his blade to the ground with one of my swords and piercing his lung with the other. He dropped to his knees as I pulled out my sword and kicked him away.

I looked at the others while wiping the dying man's blood from my sword with the back of his shirt. "You three have a choice today. You can die like this man, or you can help us make this planet prosperous and peaceful. The choice is yours, but you have until my partner returns with the head of your friend to make your decision. Otherwise, I'll decide for you."

As the carriage drew closer, Tonya held up the head of the man she'd chased down. The others saw and dropped to their knees. "We wish for peace. Please, let us follow you. We'll do anything."

"You'll all be killed for your betrayal!" Ingus's brother gasped and spit blood while clutching his wounds and glaring at his men.

I walked up to the bellowing leader who was still trying to stand on his cut leg. "What do you know of the girl Katia? Where does she stay in Xerxes's home?"

He struggled to breathe, but managed to get out, "Fuck off! I'm not telling you anything!" He spit blood at me and continued to gasp for air.

I remembered how cold Tonya could get while interrogating someone. Especially someone so disgusting. I pulled out my dagger and said, "Maybe this will distract you from the pain." I stabbed my dagger into his leg wound as deeply as I could. His gut-wrenching scream could probably have been heard for miles.

"I guess I was right," I said with a calm tone and a smile. "Now, as I was asking about Katia—"

"Go to hell! Get him, men. He's just kneeling, for God's sake—kill him!" He tried to scream, but his punctured lung made his words garbled and low.

I cocked my head a little and didn't notice any of them moving. I sensed they didn't want to be part of Xerxes's misdeeds.

I gripped my dagger and twisted it like a corkscrew in the bald man's leg. He screamed out, "I don't know where he keeps his whores!"

I paused for a moment. "There's still hope for this planet, but not while men like you live." I pushed my sword into his throat and kept it there while the gurgling sound of his last breaths were soon met with silence. He fell back to the ground, dead.

Skyler pulled up and threw the head near the man on the ground next to me. "What about these three. Why did you let them live?"

They huddled together. I looked at them and nodded. "Go ahead. Tell her why I'm letting you live, and I suggest you make her believe it or she might kill you herself."

One stammered, "Be-because we want to follow you. W-we want to live peacefully."

Skyler looked at me in disbelief and asked, "And you believe them?"

I walked up to the men and saw the fear in their eyes. They were young and probably forced to work for Xerxes. "I believe them," I said, kneeling in front of the man in the middle. Their eyes pointed down to the dirt. "If I ever have any reason not to, they'll meet a much more painful fate than their friend here. Now, you three take that head and that body into the nearest woods."

They scrambled to their feet to heed my orders.

One of them asked, "Is it true you're going back to rescue the girl?"

I quickly walked up to the man who spoke, adrenaline racing through my veins. "What do you know about that?"

"O-only rumors of when you were sold and how you yelled for her and vowed to get her back."

"Do you know where she is?"

He shook his head. His eyes widened as he started to hyperventilate. "No, no, I've never seen her. I swear!"

I looked at the other two, who also shook their heads.

"You three will continue on to that mining camp and tell Surgy that Zack sent you to help. He's in charge. Don't let me find out sparing you was a mistake."

They nodded, thankful I hadn't killed them, no doubt.

I climbed back onto the carriage. "Ready?" I asked Tonya.

She laughed. "I really think you're getting the hang of this."

The carriage jerked forward. I pictured myself as the leader of planet Xima, bringing peace, encouraging everyone to help each other, and making it a place where Katia and I could live happily. Perhaps I would encourage others from Earth to join us. *And I'd keep that hidden volcano cabin mine and Katia's secret retreat.*

* * *

That night we found a small house near the wall that surrounded the city. A family there allowed us to stay for some ginny, and we paid extra to ensure they wouldn't disclose our whereabouts. It was a very simple house with one bedroom where the parents and both children slept, a small kitchen area with a fire pit, and a living area with some very crude chairs and tables made of wood with what looked like vines woven through it.

When it was dark, Tonya went out to see what we were up against. She didn't want anyone to recognize me, so I stayed behind with the family. They had a boy who was perhaps ten years old. He played with a wooden sword and boasted, "I want to be the best ring fighter in all of Xima one day."

I felt sickened that Earth had let Xima fall to such a primitive state where a young boy strived to be a fighter and would willingly face death before he was old enough to have children. It reminded me of the gladiators in Rome.

"Are you a ring fighter, mister?" he asked, swinging his sword around.

I looked at him, and although I prided myself on being truthful, I didn't want to give him the delusion that ring fighting was a worthy goal. "No, I'm not a ring fighter, but I did learn to fight to protect my family and friends. That's the only reason anyone should fight."

He looked down at his sword, and his smile turned to a frown. "I'm going to be the best ring fighter in all of Xima!" he exclaimed again and walked off, proudly holding his sword in the air.

I couldn't help but feel pity for the young boy. He shouldn't have dreamed of fighting to the death in a ring surrounded by ginny-lusting derelicts. The very thought of what Xima represented repulsed me. What I'd learned about the planet was so far from anything I'd learned back on Earth.

Hours later, Tonya returned and told me that there were minimal guards posted. Our original plan would work just as we'd hoped.

The next day we both walked to town. We wore cloaks to mask our faces, as I was sure I'd be spotted if anyone saw me. From a distance, we walked around Xerxes's house and assessed all the doors and windows as best we could to make our enter and exit strategies.

We walked around town and saw the building where crops were delivered by the farmers to be processed. There were piles of food in the back. and people worked to bundle the food at wooden processing tables. Some were root vegetables, some looked like apples but were all brown. I walked up to a woman working in the building. "Won't this food go bad before it gets sold?"

"What do you mean *sold*? This is all given to the elites. They own the farms," the woman said. Her white hair and missing teeth led me to believe she'd been doing her job for a long time.

"But there's so much here. Won't some of this spoil before it gets to the elites? What happens then?"

She squinted at me and paused, making it clear she was confused by my question. "Are you not from here or something? If it goes bad, we return it to the fields as fertilizer for the next crop. Now, be gone with ya."

"So, no one other than the elites gets to eat this?" I asked, my anger growing by the second at how the elites got everything and left nothing for the poor. I thought back to the camps I'd liberated, where women and children ate what they could find to survive while the elites in the city ate so well that what wasn't eaten was thrown back into the fields. *This is appalling!*

"Be gone with you, or I'll call a guard!"

I stepped away to avoid any further disturbance. As Tonya and I walked through, we saw a ginnium craftsman hard at work, pouring molten ginnium into a mold of what looked like a sword. I saw other tools that looked like a farming hoe, a hammer, and then I saw sets of shackles—the same shackles I'd worn for what seemed like decades while holed up as Xerxes's property. Anger built up within me again. They could have made more farming equipment, shovels, rakes, plows, and done more with the land. Instead, they made shackles for those gladiator games of theirs while so many people went hungry or without shelter.

When we arrived back at the house where we were staying, the door was open. We drew our swords cautiously and walked inside to find the family lying on the floor covered in blood. Mother, father, the girl, and the boy who wanted to be a ring fighter, all lay on the floor with stab wounds. The boy's wooden sword was next to him. We saw the father move slightly and darted to his side. I lifted his head and said, "What happened?"

"Tax collectors. They saw the ginny we had and wanted to know where we got it. It was more than anyone here typically has. We refused to tell them, and..." He placed his hand on the back of my neck, pulling me close to his face. "Please, Zan. Bring peace to Xima." Then he laid his head back, struggling to breathe. His stab wound went through his lung, and he'd been bleeding for a long time.

I leaned back to sit on my heels, surrounded by the family who had risked their lives to take us in. Their only crime was having too much ginny, which we had given them. I looked at Tonya in disbelief. She whispered urgently, "We need to leave here and abandon this rescue mission. Xerxes may know of us already."

"I can't. I won't! I'll go by myself tonight if I have to, but I'm going to free her," I demanded. The tears fell uncontrollably down my cheeks. Staring down at the man, I realized he must have known who I was the whole time and never said a thing to the intruders. *He only wanted to live in peace.*

The father managed to gasp, "They don't know about you." He struggled to breathe and gripped my sleeve tightly. "Please, help me join my family."

I looked up to Tonya, who nodded, and then pulled my knife from my sheath, covered his eyes with my hand, and hesitated. I'd never killed an innocent man before. I looked at his family, dead on the floor, and felt the air cool the tears rolling down my cheeks. I took a deep breath and pushed my blade into his heart. He gasped one more time and then was still.

I continued to stare at the family—the boy who was just playing, the parents who wanted peace. And because they had extra ginny—because of me—they were killed. I looked up at Tonya slowly shaking her head.

"They may be arranging an attack on us right now," she whispered and walked to the window to peer out.

I pointed down. "He said they don't know about us. He died for us. They *all* died for us. We can't abandon this plan now."

"We aren't abandoning it, Zack. We're simply putting it on hold for the greater good. Please, understand that," Tonya pleaded, but I was blinded by my hatred for Xerxes and his men and my desire for vengeance.

I walked over and knelt next to the boy, picked up his toy sword, and placed it in my belt. Wiping tears away from my eyes, I stood and turned around. "Let's go. I want to attack them tonight."

Tonya guided us down some grungy walkways filled with people sitting against the walls. Thoughts of the old Charles Dickens stories that my mother read to me came to mind—the small shacks, each made mostly of wood and stone, the dank smell of sewage in the streets, dirt walkways, and windows that were mostly covered with shutters and no glass. So much more could have been done to improve the quality of life with the help of better tools and engineers.

Some people held out a bowl or cup asking for ginny, and some women revealed their shoulders and legs for a coin or two. Others, who appeared to be suspicious, simply observed us. We had our hoods up, which masked our faces, but it also provided suspicion to those who were likely looking for us.

We entered a large, tattered building, and I had to hold my breath because of the rank odor emanating from it. Tonya led me up some stairs where a burly man sat at a desk. He was older and only had hair on his face, but I could still make out scars on his cheek through his thick beard. He saw us and stood up with his eyes wide.

"Tonya? Is it really you?" he asked slowly, staring at her in disbelief. "Where the hell did you come from? I haven't seen you in years! Baby, this is my old friend, Tonya Skyler!"

A pretty woman, perhaps in her thirties, sat in a worn lounge chair in front of his desk. Her blonde hair looked like she didn't know what a comb was. Her tattered clothes hung loosely on her nearly-exposed breasts. She had one leg over the arm of the chair and waved disinterestedly.

The man walked around his desk and gave Tonya a hug. "Let me look at you." He gazed at her up and down, then glanced at me. The glee on his face told me he was a friend, but I still didn't know if I could trust him. He kept talking to Tonya. "Last I heard, you were a general overseeing new programs with the ADS on Earth. What brought you here? Did something go wrong? Is Tonya Skyler a prisoner now?" He laughed.

"Who's the boy?" he asked, motioning to me with his shoulder.

"Hello, Ian. It's been a long time—perhaps fifteen years?" Tonya seemed like she was trying to recall how long it had been since they last saw each other. "This boy actually brought me to Xima. Ian, I want you to meet Zack. Zack, this is Ian, an old friend. Ian ran our logistics efforts when I was here training and learning to fight."

Then she directed her hand to the girl in the chair filing her nails with some type of stick. "And I see you're still in the *logistics* trade, of sorts," she said, smiling down at the woman sitting in the chair.

Ian's eyes went wide, and he walked around to grab the girl's arm. She cried out.

"Come on, Layla," Ian said. "You need to leave. Go downstairs and clean or something." He pushed her out of the room and closed the door. He looked out a window, and then I saw a look of fear in his eyes.

"Is it true? Is this the boy who's been killing all the people of Xima?" Ian asked Tonya in a whisper.

I grew confused and angry. "Lies! What have you heard?" I walked up to him as Tonya placed her hand up, blocking my approach.

"I think you've been fed bad rumors, my old friend." The floor outside of the door creaked. Tonya ran and opened it. Layla had her ear cupped to the door. Tonya pulled her in, threw her on the floor, and said, "It appears someone was listening."

Layla cowered on the floor. She held up her hands, pleading with us. Her breast fell out of her top, and Tonya scolded her. "Cover yourself, girl! What did you hear?" Tonya pulled out her sword and placed the tip of it at the girl's throat.

I saw Layla looking to Ian for help, but Ian said calmly, "Go ahead and tell her, Layla. Your life seems to depend on it."

She looked back to Tonya. "I-I-I heard the name Zack, how he killed many throughout Xima. Many talk about him as the killer of women and children." She breathed heavier, and fear grew in her eyes. "Xerxes and the other elites in the city said you're killing everyone throughout the lands, and there's a one thousand ginny reward for bringing you in—preferably dead," Layla explained.

I stood in awe, unable to fathom what I'd heard. Staring at the frightened woman, I knelt before her. "How many men have paid for your services? Shitheads who you wish were dead?"

She looked at Ian again, then back to me. "There have been many. Xima has many men like that. It seems only bad people get sent here."

I smiled at her and nodded. "I'd have to agree with you there. What if I told you I only killed the same kind of evil men, and I left the women and children with good men who will take care of them so they can all live in peace?" I paused to let her think for a moment. She looked up at Tonya, who nodded in support of what I'd said.

I asked Layla, "What type of man do you think Xerxes is?" She shook her head, not wanting to answer. "He has my fiancé—a girl I grew up with, a girl who saved my life, a girl who I want more than life itself. I'm trying to save her, and all of these lies are only to stop me."

Her eyes lit up. "Oh, the girl named Katia?"

I quickly lifted Layla by her arms and held her in front of me, her feet barely touching the floor. "What do you know of Katia?"

She looked terrified and began to cry as I held her in place. "You're hurting me. I don't know nothing. I mean, not much. She works in the kitchen during the day, but she's kept with Xerxes at night in case…"

I shook her entire body, hoping she'd drop some answers like nuts from a tree. "In case of what?" Anger raged through me, and I realized I might hurt her if I got any angrier.

She continued to sob. "In case you come back. If you were killed, she was going to be sold in an auction."

I dropped Layla to the floor. She fell onto her back and pulled herself to a chair. "Please, don't kill me."

Tonya asked, "Why would we kill you?"

"I don't know. Because of the rumors? Because they say you're crazy and want to kill everyone on the planet," Layla said with confusion and fear in her voice.

Ian laughed. "Don't worry about her. She won't leave my side, and if she does tell anyone, I'll feed her to my animals down below." Layla looked to him in horror as he smiled at her. "So, what business do you have here? Are you still planning to get that girl from Xerxes?" Ian asked.

Tonya offered a reassuring smile. "For starters, but we're trying to make Xima more of a thriving colony instead of what it is today. We want people of Earth to come here to live peacefully, without the threat of what they'd face if they came now."

"Ha! Good luck with that. As long as the ginny keeps flowing into Xerxes's pocket, he'll remain in power and life will continue as it always has on Xima."

I proudly exclaimed, "Then he should be hurting by now, as we've stopped all of the ginnium from coming here!"

"Ahh, now it makes sense why he wants you dead so badly," Ian said, his hand caressing his beard in thought. "How can I help you, my friend? I do owe you from the time you saved me from a spear headed toward my back."

I saw Tonya smile. "I was hoping you'd remember that. We want to make our way to rescue the girl tonight. Earlier today, Xerxes's tax collectors killed a family who housed us."

Layla cried out, "The whole family?"

I looked her dead in the eyes. "Yes—the father, mother, and their young son and daughter were all killed because they wouldn't tell where they got the ginny we gave them."

"You can stay here until dark, but don't bring the girl back with you. You'll have to take her somewhere else. I'll keep an eye out afterward if… I mean *when* you come back."

Tonya slapped Ian's shoulder. "Thank you, my friend. We wouldn't want you in any more danger."

Ian smiled. "Feel free to rest here, or if you want one of my girls, they're available to you. They're very good at helping to relieve stress." He winked at me.

My mind immediately thought of the young girls we'd freed in the forest, and I grew angry at Ian for putting his girls in a similar situation. "How can you sell them like this? We've killed others who exploited women in the forest."

Ian placed his hand on my shoulder. "I know what you've seen out there, but those women were forced into that life. Xerxes forced them by taking advantage of women and girls whose fathers and husbands had died. I assure you, we have no young girls and all the women here came voluntarily, as they had no other place to go. I provide them with food and shelter until they decide to leave."

He looked to Tonya and continued. "Sure, I might receive a small cut of what they earn, but I make sure they're clean, healthy, and well taken care of while they're here."

I nodded, realizing the difference, and I smiled to show my acceptance of his practice.

Tonya asked, "You wouldn't happen to have any men in your inventory, would you?"

He smiled and walked up to her with a sly look on his face. "You're looking at the only man in my inventory, and I can offer him for a very irresistible fee."

Tonya smiled back, placing her hand on his chest. "Although the offer *is* tempting, I wouldn't want to ruin the friendship we have."

Ian smiled at his failed attempt and motioned to Layla. "Layla's very good at pleasing the ladies also, but perhaps young Zack might like her."

I shook my head. "I'm devoted to Katia, but thank you."

Tonya sighed and looked at Layla, who smiled back at her while twirling her shoulder-length hair around her finger. Then Tonya looked at me and said, "What the hell? I could use a good orgasm, as I haven't had one for so long." I was surprised she'd have sex with a woman, but then I remembered what she'd said at the cabin about temporary fulfilment.

The three of them left the room, allowing me to rest until nightfall. I thought about the city and how run down it was, how Earth seemed to have abandoned the people, and how the leaders on Earth could have provided so much more for the betterment of life on Xima. *Not that Earth is a whole lot better.*

I awoke about an hour later to find Tonya trying to creep into the room, but the squeaking floorboards and creaky door gave her away.

She looked out the window, then lay down on the office table next to where Ian sat and slept.

Chapter 19

We woke abruptly as Ian hastily opened the door and entered the room. I grabbed my sword, ready for more to follow behind him.

"Quick, they're looking in buildings. Spies heard there were two cloaked strangers walking around here," he said.

It was dark, and we would start our mission soon. Placing my hand on Tonya's arm, I suggested slyly, "I've got an idea. Ian, would you mind if we beat you up a little bit?"

Ian looked surprised, but Tonya understood. "My friend, we'd like you to help us with some deception, but it would require you to look as though you were in a fight."

Ian looked at both of us and laughed, understanding what we meant. "Okay, but only you, Tonya. If anyone's going to beat me up, I'd rather it be a friend."

Ian turned his face, closed his eyes, and winced as Tonya's fist struck him in the face. The mountain of a man fell down from one blow. *Damn, she can hit.* He stood back up and laughed, the cut on his cheek bleeding. "Might as well balance me out." He turned his other cheek to Tonya, who hit him again, causing Ian to fall back to the ground.

Ian slowly stood up, checking his jaw to make sure it wasn't broken. "What direction should I send them in?" he asked.

"Tell them we ran off toward the mining camp," Tonya replied.

We looked through a corner in the window upstairs as Ian showed off his acting skills below. He stumbled outside, falling into the building opposite his door. Staggering down the walkway, he ran into two guards. We couldn't hear what they were saying, but he pointed somewhere in the distance and then stumbled into one of the men who helped him back up. The guards ran off.

Ian came back upstairs, laughing as he walked through the door. "It worked; they're more stupid than I thought. I told them a boy named Zan came in looking for girls and then tried to kill everyone. Then I said I fought you off, making you flee to the mining camp."

"You told them you fought me off?" I said, crossing my arms with my eyes narrowed.

Tonya rolled her eyes and laughed. "It worked. Good job, my friend."

Ian continued. "They said they were gathering more men to pursue you. When they leave, it'll be your best chance to get your girl."

Suddenly, Layla burst into the room. "Many men rode off, but they closed the gate."

I looked at Tonya, who seemed concerned.

Ian grinned as though he was about to give us a surprise. "That little gate isn't going to hold you back, is it?" He smirked. We stared at him impatiently, waiting for him to divulge the secret he apparently had.

"I can't take you there, but if you go to the corner of the gate closest to Xerxes's home, you'll find a hidden door. You can't see it unless you're up close. There, you'll see the outline of the door. It's locked from the inside, but if you slide a thin piece of metal up through the crevice, it'll unhook the latch." He walked to a drawer in the back of the room and pulled out a thin piece of metal. "This should do the trick."

He handed it to Tonya, who asked, "When were you going to tell us about this secret door?"

He shrugged his shoulders. "A long time ago, Xerxes liked the ladies to visit him, but he didn't want anyone to see them enter, so he had me sneak them in. I forgot all about it until now. I don't think anyone but Xerxes even knows it's there. He had it built in case he had to escape quickly, but since he's been here, he's never had to use it."

We prepared ourselves and walked downstairs. Ian whispered, "Go down the walkway to the right as you leave. It'll take you to the corner of the gate where you want to be. Good luck, my friend, and good luck, Zan… I mean Zack. I look forward to what you can bring to this miserable planet."

Tonya gave him a hug, thanking him for his help. We put our hoods up and walked out.

The darkness outside created an entirely new city. The wood and stone buildings looked different with street fires dancing on the sides of them. They looked almost haunted as shadows moved with the flames. The fire pits kept enough light in the walkways for us to see our way while also providing warmth for the poor huddled around.

We trekked slowly along the walkway and found ourselves facing the corner of the fence. I couldn't see anything in either direction along the ten-foot structure. We waited a few more moments, then walked swiftly to the fence and hugged tight against it to blend into the darkness. We walked along the wall until we reached where Xerxes's house was located and peered around the corner. Someone with a torch was walking toward us.

We waited at the corner. I watched the light cast by the torch grow brighter on the ground, and when he rounded the corner, I grabbed him, placed my hand on his mouth, and held him while Tonya skewered him with her knife. I kept my hand on his mouth to silence his screams until he was still. Tonya grabbed his fallen torch and pushed it into the ground to douse the flame. I dragged the guard toward the nearest building away from the fence and laid him behind a wooden box.

"Hey, what are you doing? Who's that?" Some man walked around the corner from the building. He wore some type of night gown and was perhaps the one living there. "I'm going to call the guards."

"I can't let you do that," I said as I walked up to the man, put my arm around his neck, and considered my next move. Most of the people on Xima had heard rumors that I was a cold-blooded killer. If I killed that man, those rumors would be validated. Instead, I choked the man until he passed out and then placed him next to the dead guard. *Hopefully, that will give us enough time to get Katia and escape.*

When I returned, Tonya placed the metal piece Ian had given us into a slit in the wall and slid it up. I heard metal hit metal, then the sound of a latch. There was no handle, and the wall was more than ten feet tall, but I was able to put my fingers underneath the door and pull it open enough for Skyler to grab onto the edge. It wasn't a large door, perhaps the width of one person, but it was our only way in.

We walked inside, but before closing the door, we looked around to make sure no one was around. I slowly closed the door and heard the metal latch lock in place. Tonya looked to me and said, "That wasn't exactly quiet."

I replied, "Neither were you with Kayla, or Layla, or whatever her name was."

She laughed. "Jealous?" Then she turned to walk toward the building and whispered, "You had a chance." I stared at her and shook the thought out of my mind. I needed to focus on Katia.

Eventually we reached a door at the building by the gate, but it also didn't have a handle. Tonya gestured to the piece of metal, and we both shrugged our shoulders, hoping it would work again. She tried to slide it into the crevice of the door but couldn't find a latch. I peered around the corner and found a window that was cracked open. It was too high for one person to climb through.

We listened for any signs of movement inside, and then Tonya locked her fingers together for me to step up into the window. I slowly opened the shutters and peered inside at an empty room. It was awkward to climb through, but I finally got in, leaned out the window to Tonya, and pointed to the back door we saw earlier. Tonya nodded and walked to the back of the building.

I looked around and saw several beds in the room, which were nothing more than a mattress, like the one I had in my cell, on some wood with a wool blanket. But strangely, there was no one in the room. Hopefully, they were all out looking for me.

The wooden floors creaked with that long dull creak you would hear when pulling out an old nail from a wooden board. I walked across the room and slowly opened the door. The hallway was empty, but I could still remember passing though it on my way to the fight ring. I walked down the dimly lit passage but couldn't find a way leading to where the back door was located. The walls were made of wooden planks with nothing on them but some old saws and other tools. I tried to feel for another door within the wood, or perhaps a seam to a hidden door, but found nothing. *Where does the door lead to?* When the hallway ended, I knew the next left turn would take me to the fight arena.

I walked a bit farther and saw the open ring. It, too, was empty. I stared at the space where I had fought, where hundreds of people had stood around the ring shouting and placing wagers on my fate in this godforsaken place. The blood on the stones that made up the ring was never washed away. I looked to where I'd seen Katia, then pondered for a moment about how, without Tonya, I would have been here until I died. *Oh, shoot! Tonya!* I quickly refocused on my objective to let Tonya into the building.

I searched the arena, but it was barren except for the sand in the pit, the stone ring, benches, and the spot where Xerxes sat behind a table. I saw a drapery on the wall near his seat, and a feeling in my gut told me to check behind the cloth. *A door!* Xerxes's escape door, no doubt.

I opened it and walked through the darkness until I reached an end, then knocked lightly. I could hear a knock back. It had to be Tonya. I couldn't see anything, not even my hands in front of me, so I slid my hand around the door, trying to find a latch. On top, I touched what felt like a pin, pulled it out of the wood, but the door didn't open. I reached down to the bottom and found another pin, pulled it out, then pushed on the door. There was Tonya.

"Excellent," she whispered with a wide grin as she dragged in a body of what looked like a guard

"Who's your friend?" I asked with a grin.

"Just someone I picked up along the way," she replied with a smile.

I closed the door and placed the bottom pin back into place. Then we walked down the corridor to the fight ring. Tonya asked, "Where would the girl be located?"

"You mean Katia?" I chided. "I don't know. I was on the next floor up. I remember the route to and from this ring but don't know anything else."

We started walking down the hallway to where I remembered Katia standing when I saw her after one of my fights. Tonya and I walked through the halls, which were lit by some oil-burning sconces on the walls.

As we followed the hallway, we heard footsteps approaching. We ducked into a room and prepared to take out the man when he walked by. But the footsteps stopped.

We waited for a sign of movement, but the only sound I could hear was my own heart beating rapidly in my chest.

I realized the door could easily be shut, locking us in if anyone discovered us. *I can't survive being in captivity again. I need to get out of here!*

Then, I had an idea. I whispered, "I'll hold my hands behind my back. Grab me and carry me out like a prisoner."

"Good idea."

Tonya pushed me against the door and turned me to the right, but no one was there. We continued to walk, turned another corner, and came upon some stairs leading up to what looked like an open area.

A voice echoed through the darkness. "What's going on down there?"

Tonya whispered, "There are no female guards here. You need to answer."

"Just a drunk guard stumbling through the halls," I called out.

"Well, throw him in a cell for a few days to sober up," the voice from the top of the stairs yelled.

I peered up the steps but didn't see anyone. We slowly ascended until I spotted a man sitting behind a desk. He had a sheathed sword in front of him and was too close for us to be able to surprise him.

Tonya grabbed me and whispered, "Let's see how far we get with this charade."

As we stumbled up the steps, the guard said, "What are you doing? I told you to put him in a cell."

I tried to act drunk. "I saw Zan in the city earlier and had to tell someone." We stumbled closer as he circled around the front of his desk, eyes glaring and hand resting on the hilt of his sword on the desk. He looked at us, tilting his head inquisitively.

He talked slowly while assessing us. "Yes, we know. We sent men to chase him down. We should have his head by morning. Now, throw this one in a cell immediately or—"

Before he could finish, I jumped up and tackled him to the floor. We both landed with a loud *thud.* Tonya climbed up and placed her hand on the man's mouth as I cut his throat.

Tonya frowned, "This man knew everything there was to know about security. Having him alive would have been invaluable for us to know what to expect when we walk up those steps to Xerxes."

"Yeah, but he also might have given us away. Remember: we were told Katia was always within his reach, so we need the element of surprise."

Tonya placed her hand on my shoulder. "You might be right, but sometimes we need to think logically versus emotionally."

We concluded that Xerxes must be on the next floor judging by the height of the building. The dead man at our feet must have been the leader of Xerxes's guards. We slowly walked up the steps, and as we reached the landing and peeked around the door, we saw a bed and a small blanket on the floor in front, but no one was there.

We crept into the room and looked around. A single candle burned on a nightstand, casting a glimmer of light throughout the room. *Someone has been here recently.* I squinted to see if there was anything hidden in the shadows, which changed as the candle glow danced along the walls.

There were chests along the other stone walls but still no humans. We shrugged at each other, trying to be as quiet as possible while walking through the room. I put my hand on the bed—it was warm, and the blanket was thrown to the side. I nodded to Tonya to let her know the occupant had recently been there.

We walked around the room, and I spied a tapestry on the wall opposite the door through which we'd entered. It looked just like the tapestry covering the hidden door in the fight ring. *Could it be?* I pulled the fine fabric back to reveal another door. As I slowly opened it, a shiny object jabbed through the crevice, and I quickly closed the door. The tip of a sword clanked to the stone floor.

I opened the door again to find Xerxes with a young girl standing in front of him. Her eyes lit up with fear, and she was gagged to keep from crying out. Xerxes held a knife to her throat. "Don't come any closer, or I'll kill her."

Tonya ran to my side. She ripped the tapestry off the wall, allowing us to see inside the doorway with more light. "Oh, good. You found them. Go ahead and kill him so we can get out of here."

"That's not Katia!" I told Tonya. Then I glared at Xerxes. "Where is she, you sick bastard?"

Xerxes pushed the point of his knife further into the girl's neck. I could see the blood form from the slight cut. "I created you. You should be thankful!" Xerxes said. I saw tears forming in the girl's eyes as she whimpered.

"You didn't create me; my father did, and as I see it, you have several options. But only one allows you to live."

"My guards will be here soon, and you'll both be killed."

I smiled without breaking eye contact with him. "You see, that's one of the options where you end up dead. But if you show us where to find Katia, I'll let you live. If you don't tell us, you'll die, and we'll find her ourselves. If you yell for help, you also die. There are so many ways this could go badly for you, but"—I let the disclosed options sink in for a moment—"if you let the girl go right now and show us where you have Katia, I promise I won't touch you. Just give us time to get out of here, and you'll never see us again."

He looked at me, and I could tell he was contemplating his options. "I could just hunt you down after you leave."

I laughed. "You could, but then you *and* your men will die. The choice is completely yours. Give Katia to me, let us leave, and I won't kill you."

"I have your word?" he asked with a shaky voice. I could see the fear on his face. I suspected he was going to take my offer.

"You have my word," I replied.

"Okay, then. Back away. I'm coming out." We moved away from the door, and he walked out with the girl whose eyes appeared to beg us to save her. I struggled to keep from skewering him right there as he passed by me. *Perhaps the girl knows where I can find Katia.*

Xerxes walked her to the other doorway, and we followed at a slight distance. Before I could react, he pushed the girl into the room and ran off. I sprinted to the girl as Tonya ran after Xerxes.

I pulled the gag from around her head, and she hugged me tightly. "Where is Katia?" I demanded while pushing her away and holding her so that she had to look me in the eye.

"I don't know. I haven't seen her all day. There's a rumor that Xerxes sold her. I was moved here to be Xerxes's servant only today."

My entire body tensed. I looked down at my fists and saw my veins on my arms bulge. Every muscle in my body tensed up, and I took a deep breath.

Xerxes.

I sprinted down the steps and stopped when I saw Tonya confronting several guards, two of whom I remembered from the beatings they gave me when I first arrived. Xerxes cowered behind them. Then, a familiar face walked up next to him—Mule, the treacherous scum who'd sold Katia and me to Xerxes. I would have ripped his throat out right then if I could have reached it.

"Looks like he found some leftover guards to protect him." Tonya smiled at me, keeping her sword pointed at them.

Xerxes yelled, "You owe me for making you the fighter you are! Surrender and I'll let you fight for me again. I'll even share my profits with you. That's the best offer I've ever given."

I laughed. "I would've thought you'd be smarter than that, Xerxes. All I wanted was Katia back." As I looked at the two guards from my past, I realized I wanted payback. "I also have some lessons to teach my two professors of pain standing in front of you, and I owe the guy who started all of this my gratitude. We seem to have a reunion here, but I don't anticipate anyone being happy afterward. Tell me where I can find Katia, and you may still be allowed to live, Xerxes."

"You'll both be dead in about two minutes, so it won't even matter that I sold your girl to the ADS and she's about to launch back to Earth."

"Liar!" There would be no holding back. I pulled both of my short swords out and threw one into the face of the guard closest to me.

The blade went right through his head all the way to the hilt. The stone hallway we were in was very confined, and I knew it would be difficult for the men to fight. I dodged two guards, who swiped and stabbed at me, knocking one in the face with the hilt of my other sword and slicing the throat of the next guy. As I pulled my first sword out of the man's skull, a sword skewered the one I'd hit in the face.

Tonya winked at me and smiled, then pulled her sword out of him. "I thought I'd lend a hand this time."

Xerxes ran off, yelling, "Kill them! I want both heads on pikes immediately!"

Tonya and I fought through several other men, and the two who taught me how to withstand pain were the only ones remaining. I didn't see Mule behind them. *Figures. What a lying coward.*

"I have to say," I said to my ex-teachers, "I thought your training techniques were inhumane. But then again, I did learn a lot. I hope you went through the same training." I smirked.

As I stood in front of them, I held a sword in each hand with tips pointed to the floor, leaving myself wide open for an attack. One of the guards said in a raspy voice, "I guess you'll just have to relive some of those lessons now."

As soon as I saw them raise their swords, I thrust my blades into their chins with lightning speed, the tips penetrating through their skulls. They quickly collapsed, and I scowled as I pulled the swords out. *Why did I cheat them of the pain I owed them?*

"Wow, that was faster than I could have ever moved." Tonya patted my shoulder. "Now let's get Xerxes."

We ran down the hall toward the doorway leading outside. We were nearly there when Mule stepped out from the darkness, blocking our escape. He fired his gun at us, and we both dodged the bullets as they ricocheted off the walls in the tight hallway.

Tonya said, "Of course that cowardly bastard would have a fucking gun. We need to shove that thing right up his ass and make him pull the trigger."

Damn, she can be cold, but I have to agree.

Tonya busted into a room, and I followed behind. I stood by the door as she looked at her bleeding leg. When she noticed my look of surprise, she followed my gaze and gasped. She put her hand up to stop me from saying anything. There was a real glass window in the room, which was surprising because I didn't think they had glass on Xima. I hugged the stone wall as I peered around the glass to see Mule on the other side, looking down the hallway while waiting for us to come out. I looked back at Tonya, who was tightening a piece of cloth around her leg. She nodded at me to signal that she was ready.

I backed up into the room until I had aligned myself with Mule's silhouette through the glass, then ran. The glass exploded into pieces as I burst through it. I managed to get to Mule before he could shoot again and tackled him to the ground.

He was much bigger than I was and stronger than I'd anticipated. I hit him once, and he rolled me over and squeezed his arm around my neck. I pulled on his arm, but his choke hold was too tight. I could barely breathe as I tried to pull away from him any way I could. I looked around for Tonya, but she hadn't come out of the room yet. I tried to call for her, but my voice was nothing more than a whisper.

Thinking through my oxygen deprivation, I frantically reached around my belt when I felt the hilt of my knife. I took it out and stabbed blindly behind me, hoping I wouldn't pierce myself. Mule howled in pain as I thrust the knife into his leg, but he kept his grip on me. I was unable to breathe, and I stabbed at the same spot several more times. I twisted the blade, and he finally released me and held his leg, groaning in pain.

I turned to see him trying to limp away as a crowd began to form in the square in the distance. I grabbed Mule by his hair and pushed my dagger into his back, puncturing one of his lungs. He settled to his knees on the ground.

"This is for me," I whispered in his ear.

I took out another dagger and stabbed his other lung. "This is for Katia. And out of the kindness of my heart, I'm going to help you just as you helped us back on Earth." I cut the tendons on his heels so he could never walk again. As I watched him suffer a slow death, I told him, "This is karma, you bastard!"

I let Mule drop to the ground, wheezing and trying to breathe. Tonya came out and walked up behind me.

"Where were you? Fixing your hair before showing yourself to the public?" I snarked.

"I didn't want to interfere with your reunion." She stared down at Mule, who was groaning on the ground, covered in his own blood. I smiled at her as her eyes reconnected with mine.

I couldn't help but love her wit, but my admiration of her was short-lived as I noticed several guards lining up about twenty feet in front of us.

Other people gathered around behind them wearing civilian clothes. We could see Xerxes behind the guards, and next to him I saw Trev, my old teacher.

"There he is. Zan, the murderer of women and children, with his killer whore. They came here with blood on their hands!" Xerxes yelled loud enough for everyone to hear.

There was a great deal of commotion as people started talking while looking at us and shaking their heads at the accusations.

I watched the guards talk to each other, and I could sense hesitancy in their hushed tones and uncomfortable movements. I stood up on a wooden crate near where we exited the building and said, "My name is Zack Bates.

I'm a citizen of Earth, and I came here with my fiancé, Katia. We boarded the shuttle to live here as citizens, and when we awoke, we found ourselves in chains as Xerxes's slaves. That man dying over there sold us illegally to your tyrant of a leader, which is why he was sent here as punishment and why I've killed him. Xerxes beat, tortured, and trained me to fight in the ring for his amusement, keeping my fiancé away from me as his personal slave." Then, I gestured to Tonya. "This is General Tonya Skyler from the ADS on Earth."

"Lies!" Xerxes yelled. "All lies!"

I stepped down and looked at Tonya. She took my place on the box and said, "What he says is true. I'm General Tonya Skyler from the ADS. I came to Xima to find Zack, whose father was my colleague on Earth. Together, Zack and I have cleaned up much of the evil on this planet, leaving it possible for the women, children, and those men who want peace and prosperity on Xima to make it so."

"Lies! They tell nothing but lies!" Xerxes exclaimed as he looked to the elites and guards. More people arrived at the square, adding to the commotion—all well-dressed citizens, who obviously reaped the benefits of Xerxes's reign. "They're both here to overthrow our government—our way of life. They want to kill all of us!"

An obese man hobbled out of a large stone home. "Xerxes, what's happening here?" he called out while slowly making his way toward the square.

His head darted around the crowd like a rat feeding on crumbs on the ground while looking for signs of danger.

"Mayor Brim, we have our killer, Zan, and his whore sidekick. We cannot allow them to live with what they've done," Xerxes replied.

"We can have a trial tomorrow," the mayor said, nodding his head with a wide smile while he searched around, trying to comprehend the enormity of what was happening. The people in the crowd also nodded and continued to whisper to each other.

I stood back up on the box. "Mayor Brim, I'm Zack. I come here in peace and wish to rescue my fiancé, Katia, who Xerxes has kept captive for years. She's about to go back to Earth on the shuttle. How do we stop it from launching?"

The mayor looked confused. He turned to Xerxes, who shook his head. "We cannot stop the shuttle. It departs in thirty minutes."

My anger grew. I realized I didn't have time to argue if I wanted to get to Katia in time, and I was definitely not going to wait a day to stand trial for crimes I didn't commit.

"I don't care when it leaves. I'm telling you I'm going to that shuttle to rescue Katia, and I warn anyone who tries to stop me."

Tonya stood by my side and placed her hand on my shoulder. "I'm sure you've all heard rumors of my friend's abilities. He may not *want* to fight, but I assure you he'll kill anyone who dares to get in his way. Trust me; I've seen him in action."

"Guards, seize these two!" Mayor Brim yelled, but no one moved. The guards stayed in place, staring at each other to see who would move first.

"What is this? I said seize them, or you'll be put in a cell!" the mayor bellowed.

One guard dropped his sword and said as he walked away, "I'd rather sit in a cell than die here today."

The guard walked by Trev, who pierced him with his sword. The guard fell to the ground.

Xerxes yelled, "This is what happens to deserters!"

The men looked at me, and they seemed horrified that their leader would kill them. They were in a hopeless situation—if they attacked me, they would die as well.

Time was running out for me to get to the shuttle, and I knew the guards would attack me from behind if I ran to it. I had to do something—quick.

Finally, I said, "I propose a deal. Your best fighter fights me to the death. If I win, you'll allow us to go free. If you win, I'll be dead, and General Skyler will go back to Earth." I figured that if we were to fight through every guard, I wasn't sure I could face Trev last and survive. If I were to fight him first, though, I might get everyone else to drop their swords. I watched Xerxes and Trev discuss my proposition.

Trev yelled, "I'll fight you!" *Yes, my plan worked.*

"I'll fight this murderer—the one who kills women and children," Trev continued. "And when I kill him, we'll all take turns with his so-called 'general.' Won't we, men?" I could sense hesitancy among the guards. As they looked at each other, I could only hear faint whispers.

"The only ones I've ever killed were murderous bastards who attempted to kill me first. All women and children remained alive and well… except for those who were killed in their villages by Xerxes's tax collectors." With that comment, I noticed the elites talking more frantically among each other and looking at Xerxes. "Perhaps it was you, Trev, who killed that little boy and girl in their home?"

"Taxes must be paid!" Trev answered.

My body tensed with rage, my face became warm, and I noticed my fists clenched—they wanted a target to punch. I thought my entire body might explode. *How could anyone be so cold to kill an innocent family like that?*

The men talked among themselves, and I could see Trev staring me down, trying to get a read on me. I stayed put. He taught me to move randomly, to be unpredictable. I realized that the most unpredictable thing I could do against him was remain still.

Trev said to his men, "If I fall today, I order you to kill both of them!"

I slowly pulled out both of my swords and yelled, "When I kill him today, I want all of you to live in peace and prosperity. You'll need to decide by the time we're done fighting where your allegiance lies." I could hear the men talk among themselves as Trev rushed me.

He raised his sword high, and I knew he would quickly adjust to low. Just as he neared, I blocked low, but he struck at me high. I dodged quickly as he grazed my arm. He was indeed unpredictable and fast. I looked down to see blood leaking from the tear in my cloak. I untied it and threw it to the ground for better agility. I had the advantage—I knew him, how he thought, and how he moved.

I spun around to face his arrogant laughter. "I thought I taught you better than that, boy," he said. "Perhaps you wouldn't have lasted in the ring as long as we thought. It's probably a good thing you die today. I'd hate for you to suffer like you would have in those death matches."

He came at me high again, but I was ready and reached up to block him with one hand. I kept one sword low, which thankfully prevented him from striking my leg. He was far better than when he trained me. Thankfully, I'd withheld what I was really capable of from him. Plus I'd learned even more from Tonya.

We circled each other, looking for weaknesses. "A shame you were never good enough for the death ring. You might have won a few fights before you were killed," Trev said with a grin and calm eyes.

I knew he was just trying to rile me up in the hopes I'd act irrationally, but it wasn't going to work. He thrust at me. I deflected and guarded against his spin as he swung his sword at my arm. I parried and stabbed his leg, penetrating his flesh.

He jumped back and hobbled around, holding his wounded leg and laughing. "Lucky little jab, boy. One day, you might have been a worthy adversary, but now… now you must die." He pulled his sword in half, wielding two sharp blades instead of one. It was a marvelous sword that could be used as one or broken into two—the kind of weapon that could not have been made on Xima.

We clashed swords, and my instincts were the only thing keeping me alive as I attacked and blocked without thinking.

His moves were quick, and he even backed off and put on a little show with his fancy moves, despite his limp. He was no doubt waiting to find my weak spot. Both of his arms wielded swords out to his side, leaving his core open. Even from fifteen feet away, I could tell from his smug look that he had practiced his showmanship. Everyone smiled at his performance. He may have been the best fighter known to Xima, but no one had met me yet.

I kept a look of fear in my eyes, and when he laughed, I threw my sword with all my might at his chest. It moved as fast as a throwing knife and stopped only by the hilt. As Trev fell to his knees, he stared at me and slowly dropped his swords one at a time.

The guards and the people in the square all whispered, probably in disbelief of what had just happened.

I knelt by Trev and grabbed my sword from his body. I held it there and said, "Your arrogance was your weakness." After I pulled the sword out of him, he collapsed. I wiped my blade on his shirt and stared at the guards, who stood there, unsure of what to do next.

Tonya smiled and nodded at me. I acknowledged her, then turned to the twenty or so remaining men.

They looked back at Xerxes and then to me. They seemed to be waiting for someone to say something or give them direction.

"Kill him, you fools!" Xerxes yelled, but no one moved.

"I killed your best fighter. I have killed many men, as you may have heard, but every one was a brutal monster. I truly want peace for everyone. Bring the mayor and Xerxes before me!"

The guards turned and grabbed Xerxes, who yelled for his release. Others grabbed the mayor, who threatened to imprison them. They were both brought before me. Tonya walked up to my side.

"You'll never get away with this. Xerxes, do something! Take care of them!" the mayor exclaimed.

Xerxes replied, "Shut your ignorant mouth, or I'll fucking kill you myself!"

I looked down at the two of them and said, "You saw what I did with Mule and then with Trev. Now the remaining guards have brought you before me, and all you have to say is that I won't get away with this?" I was a little surprised at how naïve the mayor was, but then again, Xerxes probably wouldn't have wanted a pawn who was smart.

I held my sword to the mayor's throat. "I'll ask you again: Can you stop that shuttle from launching?"

Sweat ran down his face, and I could see his heavy breathing as he searched for some nonexistent place to hide. "No, I can't. I don't have any say in that department. It'll launch on time to meet the schedule."

"How far away is the launch site?" I asked the crowd.

Several people replied and pointed toward a tree line in the distance. I could see a large path cut at the edge of the forest.

"Mayor, you have a choice to make. You can choose peace on this planet, or you can choose for the people to live like they have been under Xerxes's rule."

He looked around with all eyes on him. He replied in a panic, "Y-You must answer for your actions."

"Mayor, I don't think you understand the situation you're in. You can either find Xerxes guilty, or you find *me* guilty right now. Someone will die depending on your answer."

He looked around as everyone quietly awaited his decision. Xerxes mumbled, "Don't you stab me in the back, or I'll gut you like a fish right here."

The mayor's eyes darted back and forth, and his breathing rate was fast. I couldn't tell if the sweat on his forehead was from confusion or fear—maybe both. I knew he was under Xerxes's influence, but I also knew he had no idea what he was doing as a mayor.

He looked into the crowd and announced, "I find Zan guilty! Guards, arrest him!"

I stuck my sword through the mayor's throat and pulled it out quickly, letting him drop to the ground. No guards moved, but they continued to whisper among themselves.

"The mayor made the wrong choice. Who's next in charge of Xima?" I asked, looking out to the sea of people watching. No one raised their hand.

"If no one else will lead Xima, then everyone will work the mines and farm the fields! Everyone on this planet will be equals!"

There was some commotion by the elites. Someone walked forward and said, "My name is Rob. I'm the keeper of the coin, and I'm next in line of leadership." He walked up toward where the mayor was lying.

"For a long time, we've lived well here in Lauri, and much of that had to do with Xerxes and the mayor maintaining our fine lifestyle. We heard rumors of what went on outside of the city but turned a blind eye, as Xerxes was very influential." He looked at Xerxes, who scowled at him.

He continued, "It seems you're determined to have Xerxes dead, so why not just kill him?"

I looked into the man's eyes. He appeared sincere. He stood tall and called me out on my intentions regardless of how I might have reacted, which showed bravery. "I'll tell you why I'm not killing him right away. I want to find someone who will stand up to him, someone who will lead these people, and someone who is compassionate to the people. The mayor was not that person. Are you?"

He looked around at his friends, who nodded their heads. Then he looked to the guards, who remained motionless, and said to me, "I accept the responsibility of leading the people of Xima."

Based on his grave expression and his air of humility, I believed I'd made the right decision.

"Now, Mayor Rob, how do you find Xerxes: guilty or innocent?"

Xerxes looked at Rob with his brow furrowed as though he dared the man to cross him. While I gave the new mayor a moment to think, I was caught off guard as Xerxes charged Rob with a knife. But before I could react, a different knife was in Xerxes's chest, and he fell to his knees. I looked back to see a smile on Tonya's face. She winked at me, and I smiled back at her.

I rolled Xerxes over as he mumbled, "You promised you wouldn't kill me."

Tonya walked up to him and said, "I didn't promise anything." Xerxes slumped to the ground, dead.

There was a stack of crates nearby, and I stepped up on them so I could see everyone.

"Xerxes and the mayor were corrupt, and everyone who came to Xima was forced to follow their cruel ways. They sent ginnium back to Earth to barter with other corrupt people there. That's how I was abducted and enslaved.

"But workers in the ginnium mines have been collecting the metal since we rid the nearby camp of Xerxes's scum. The metal will now be used to support the development of cities, farming, housing, and other things the people need. As citizens from Earth continue to arrive in search of a better life, you will expand farms and other means of production needed to support everyone on Xima." I looked around and saw everyone nodding their heads. "I'll return in one year. If corruption still exists then—if people are still killed for sport and crime remains—my punishments will be swift and painful.

"Your new mayor is Rob. Now, who is the current leader of the guards?"

A man from the back walked forward. He unsheathed his sword and knelt before me, placing the tip of his sword to the ground and keeping his hands on the hilt as he bowed. "I'm the current leader. My name is Tull, and I guarantee our swords are yours." The other guards followed suit and knelt.

"Rise, Tull." I looked out to the people and said, "Tull will be the new captain of the guard. He will ensure peace on Xima and will report to the mayor. However, he will not take any orders that would cause harm to others or instill corruption on this planet!"

I whispered, "I'm giving you a chance to make Xima a good place. If you defy me, I'll make an example of you when I return." Tull looked into my eyes and nodded.

"I need to get Katia!" I yelled to Tonya while leaping off the platform and sprinting to the opening in the tree line.

A distant rumble stopped me. The shuttle took off beyond the trees where the people had pointed earlier. My heart sank—I knew Katia was on the ship. I wanted to kill everyone in Xerxes's compound for what had happened to us. The smoke trail left a tower in the sky as the shuttle traveled higher until it was out of sight. My eyes filled with tears.

A gentle and familiar hand was placed on my shoulder. I looked back at Tonya's apologetic eyes. "We'll get her, Zack," she told me.

I looked up at the sky where I'd last seen the shuttle's smoke trail and nodded.

"I *will* come for you, Katia. No matter what."

Part III – Face the FOG

Chapter 20

Every time I looked through that glass, my eyes watered as I saw Tonya lying peacefully in her sleep chamber.] I placed my hand on the cold metal, trying to remember her touch and how comforting it was when she placed her hand on my shoulder. I owed her everything.

Years ago, I thought I had my life planned out for me and Katia, but my plans changed drastically. I was young and naïve when I took Katia away from her home, but what kind of home was it? A shelter with many kids surrounded by rubble from collapsed buildings. Evil men who preyed on young girls. No, that was not a home.

What was once a prosperous society on Earth had become nothing but rubble and food paste to sustain the many lives. That was no way to live… but what I brought her to was even worse.

I reminisced on that first day Tonya rescued me from Xerxes, my reaction when I saw who she was for the first time, her throwing spears at me in training, her charm, wit… her touch. I tried to think back to my first kiss with Katia, how the memory of it got me through the painful fights. It had kept me alive, but the vision had faded away over time.

Not too long ago, I had learned to fight in a ring and was forced to fight to the death against others as entertainment for the elites, who wagered on my survival. But my life had changed, and I was finally headed back to Earth to find Katia.

Having to wait another month was painful. I was impatient and had to keep my mind busy. While Tonya supported laying out new laws for the city, I went back to Surgy to see how he was doing and brought some materials with me.

He was grateful for the building materials and farming tools I brought on a couple wagons. I helped him fix some of the shelters for the women and children, and many of the men who survived were humbled and thankful for breaking them free of Xerxes's servitude.

Helping the various camps get better situated to sustain themselves during that month helped keep my mind occupied, but I still thought of what Tonya had asked of me when we got back to Earth. I knew I would have to help Tonya fight a dangerous Faction I had only heard about while growing up, but I had no idea what to expect from them or how strong they would be.

The past three months of the journey to Earth were a strain on my mind. Other than the pilot, the only other person awake was me. I couldn't risk arriving on Earth and being welcomed as I did on Xima by thugs and chains. I needed my wits, and I needed to keep in shape.

There wasn't much equipment to train with aboard the shuttle, but I made do with some crates and simple exercising to keep myself fit. I also spent time jogging on the mothership as I explored it. The nuclear room was well marked, and the pilot told me not to enter it. Every day I was compelled to go to the shuttle to gaze at Tonya and ponder her vision for me. How had she known I could make peace on Xima? And how did she know I would be key in bringing peace on Earth? Her confidence in me far exceeded my own, but she had changed me for the better and prepared me for whatever we would face next.

I was confident in my skills, but Earth was far more dangerous than Xima. The militaries were larger, and they had guns and more advanced technologies. I would no longer face man-against-man combat, where I had an advantage. The weapons used against me on Earth could kill me in a second, and I knew I had to be cautious, even with my strength and my quick healing.

There were five more days until we arrived on Earth. The mothership pilot would wake the shuttle pilot a day prior. My plan was to wake Tonya two days before to ensure she was alert for whatever—and whoever—greeted our arrival. We both understood that the ADS took Katia to lure me back to Earth so they could get the device in my arm, so we were positive the ADS would know we were passengers on the ship. What we didn't know was what we would find when we landed.

During the long trek, I talked with the pilot to the point where I swore he wanted to push me into space. I couldn't help myself—I was curious about space and the ship.

There was just enough food and water rations for the two of us before we boarded. Tonya wanted to stay awake with me, but that would have required more food, water, and oxygen. Usually, the pilot was the only one who remained outside of a sleep chamber to reduce the amount of supplies carried and, more importantly, to conserve oxygen. People who slept required a lot less oxygen than those who were awake.

I spent the next few days in my normal routine. I skimmed through the shuttle manual again, looking for some areas I may have missed, but after reading it three times, I was convinced I knew every part of the ship. And, dare I say, with some practice, I was confident I could fly it.

Chapter 21

Tonya looked peaceful and beautiful. I stared at her through the glass of her sleep chamber so often that I had every detail of her face memorized. Those moments by the stream and the way we had connected filled me with warmth, and I became confused about who I loved: Tonya or Katia.

When we were two days from Earth, I pressed the sequence of buttons on the head of her chamber, and her recovery process commenced. I watched in anticipation, and within a minute the top of the chamber opened. I quickly removed the tubes from Tonya and waited for her to revive. Moments later, she began to stir and opened her eyes. Her warm smile melted me as her eyes met mine.

"Good morning, sunshine. Time to wake up," I said.

She tried to sit up but struggled. "Just lie there for a few more moments while your body wakes up."

She placed her hand on her forehead, then ran her fingers through her hair. "Ugh, I need to wash my hair. How long before we arrive?"

"Two days, as we planned."

"I see the pilot didn't kick you out into space. I guess you weren't too annoying." She smirked.

I grinned, realizing how well she knew me.

I handed her the glass of water I brought and helped her sit up slowly. She sipped the water at first, then held on with two hands as she tried to drink it faster. I pulled the glass away. "Slow down. You need to adjust back to normal slowly or you'll choke."

Nodding, she looked around at the chamber and shook her head. "I really hate these things. Hopefully this is my last time."

"At least you didn't wake up with two thugs trying to chain you and drag you off somewhere."

She smiled. “This is true.” She tried to stand, holding the edge of the chamber carefully. Her wobbly stance was a far cry from how nimble I’d seen her in the past. Lying still for three months really messed with your body.

“I’m sure you’ll be doing backflips by tomorrow.” I laughed.

She smiled. “I just want to be able to walk for now. I’ve never liked making this journey. It’s a good thing you were worth it.” She laughed and drank some more water.

I pondered what she’d said earlier and asked, “What did you mean when you said you hope this is your last time?”

Tonya was trying to stretch her legs. “Well… if we don’t succeed on Earth, we’ll probably be killed, and if we do succeed, I plan to take on a leadership role to make life better on both Earth and Xima. Either way, I won’t be traveling to Xima again.”

“Is that why you looked back at the cabin for so long when we left the training camp in the mountain?”

She nodded while pulling her arms back, trying to loosen her muscles.

The next day, I helped her get prepared. We exercised together with some of the routines I’d done in the past. As we neared Earth, she was back to her normal self and ready for what lay ahead.

We were strapped into our seats as the shuttle entered Earth’s atmosphere. It was a very rough ride at first, but then the shuttle stabilized and descended to the recovery pad adjacent to the launch pad. I felt like I was falling for a long time, which was probably another reason to stay in a sleep chamber on such a tough trip.

Typical arrival procedures involved a shuttle landing and then unloading its contents. Usually there wasn’t much returning to Earth, as the primary mission was to support Xima, not bring home souvenirs. Then a ground crew would prepare the shuttle for its next mission and move it to the launch site perhaps a hundred yards away, where it would relaunch with cargo for another relay to Xima.

The sudden jolt of touching down confirmed we were safely on Earth again. *But for how long?* It appeared to be morning, as the distant sun peering over the horizon displayed a brilliant orange glow.

I couldn't see any other people from the cockpit window other than what looked like ground crew waiting to take care of the shuttle. Tonya and I put our small packs together. We didn't bring long swords so as to remain inconspicuous, but we ensured our knives were fixed to our belts. The back of the shuttle opened, and as we saw daylight shine through the gap, I caught a glimpse of people outside. Tonya quickly pulled me behind some crates that were strapped to the floor.

"They're ADS," Tonya whispered.

As the door continued to slowly open, we saw several armed ADS guards waiting to enter the shuttle. "There must be over fifty guys out there," Tonya said as she looked around the shuttle for someplace to hide.

We both looked around the shuttle, searching for options, but we had nowhere else to go. There was no way we could get through that many people armed with guns. We'd be captured for sure.

I looked toward the cockpit and remembered something I'd read in the shuttle's manual. There was a small door that led to the radar in the front. *Maybe the radar dome is big enough for us to hide in.*

Before the shuttle door was completely opened, I scrambled to the cockpit, and Tonya followed. The hatch was a flat metal panel next to where the pilot sat. We pulled on some simple latches to unlock the panel, and it opened. We crawled inside, pulling the panel back in place from inside, and remained quiet. I heard faint talking toward the back of the shuttle but couldn't make out anything specific.

Then I heard a deep voice yell, "Where are they? They couldn't have gotten off. Xima radioed us that they were on this shuttle!"

"I don't know where they went; I'm just a pilot." I couldn't blame the pilot for answering—I'd been a pain in his ass for three months. But it was clear I needed to follow up on my future return to Xima to settle a score with some traitors. In that moment, though, we needed to get off the shuttle without getting caught.

The same gruff voice demanded, "I want this shuttle stripped down to scrap if you have to. They must be hiding somewhere. I don't care if you have to take off the wall panels. We aren't leaving here until they're found!"

I could hear the rustling of feet moving around the shuttle. Tonya crawled further down to the radar dome, pushing on the walls to find a weak spot. Our only source of light was the few rays that came through the cracks in the pilot's instrument panel. The structure must have been sealed very well to ensure air didn't escape while in space.

Tonya pulled out her knife and stabbed it into the dome. The tip stuck into the material. She stabbed at it a couple more times, but the pounding noise was so loud that I was sure we'd get caught.

I found a seam near where I was kneeling, which appeared to be where the pieces of the dome were attached. I assumed the seam ran all the way around the nose of the shuttle. With a knife in each hand, I pushed them into the seam, but it only expanded a sliver.

Tonya pushed her knives in next to mine and pried. I tried again, pushing the knives even deeper. We both pulled hard as we started to see daylight through the seam. We looked inside the crack we'd created and saw small holes on either side. Tonya reached in the outer hole and pushed some type of locking pin toward the inside. The seam of the dome separated in that spot, and she found another set of holes and a pin a few feet away, which created a wider crevice but not yet big enough for us to get through.

I stood on one side of the dome and pushed pins in as Tonya had. The crevice on the bottom opened wider. We sat at the widest spot and pushed with our feet and were able to pry it open wide enough to crawl through. The drop to the ground was about ten feet to the concrete landing pad below.

"What's in here?" a nearby voice called out. It sounded like they were in the cockpit. The clanking metal sound told us they had found the small hatch leading to our hiding spot. We looked at each other, turned around, and worked our way down until we dangled by our fingers. Then, we let go and fell to the hard surface. We both rolled out of our fall and stood, then looked back up at the radar dome. Two ADS guards were looking down at us from where we'd just been moments before.

"There they are! They got out. Get them!"

We took off running toward a tree line about two hundred yards away. I looked back and saw a vehicle coming toward us. We fled into the woods, leaping over logs and dodging bushes to get into the concealment of the foliage as soon as possible. We ran approximately fifty yards past the tree line and stopped.

Chapter 21

We both breathed heavily, trying to catch our breath from the sprint away from the shuttle.

Tonya panted. "They'll converge on us within minutes. We need to come up with a strategy. I've never been to this shuttle site before, so your guess is as good as mine, but I estimate others will surround the woods and try to trap us in the middle."

We assessed our surroundings, and I could see some of the guards walking into the woods from where we came. Luckily, we were behind some thick, leafy bushes that concealed us. I looked to Tonya and whispered, "They'll probably think we continued running through the woods. They'd never expect us to come back the way we went in. Let's lure them to us. You distract them, and I'll come around from behind."

Tonya smiled at me and nodded, always ready for a fight. She slowly slipped alongside a large tree root near the trunk. I lay low behind the bush, waiting for them to come by. Two guards approached, and as they got close to Tonya, I slowly moved around the bush so they wouldn't see me.

"Please, don't hurt me. He's crazy!" Tonya cried out with her hands in the air.

"Get up! Where's the other person who was with you?" one of the guards demanded as they both pointed their guns at Tonya.

"I'm right here." I jumped out and tripped the closest guard, forcing his face to the ground while sticking my knife through the eye socket of the other. I quickly came down on the guard trying to get up, grabbed his gun, and pressed it against his throat.

"You won't get away with this!" He gasped while struggling to get free.

The other man held his bleeding eye, screaming until Tonya snapped his neck.

Tonya moved to the guy I had pinned to the ground. "I'm General Skyler. Do you know who I am?"

"Yeah. You're the traitor who fled to Xima to hide!"

Tonya looked at me, then back down at the man who struggled to breathe. "Do you know what I was hiding from?" she asked.

"You stole a classified program and sold it to FOG."

From the way he talked, I could tell the guy was obviously not FOG, but he also seemed to be brainwashed as to who the good guys were. Tonya wasn't the thief—she was the one trying to save both Earth and Xima, wasn't she?

I looked to Tonya, confused at his comment, and then down to the guard. "How many are in your vehicle?"

"Go to hell, you murderer!"

I took my other knife from my belt and placed my hand on his mouth as I stuck the point deep into his shoulder. He attempted to scream out but couldn't. When his panting subsided, I asked again, "How many are in your vehicle?"

Then I saw a knife quickly penetrate his chest. Tonya's hand was on the hilt. I snapped my head to look at her with wide eyes. "I was trying to get information from him!"

"We don't have time, and if he screams, they'll come running. I have a plan. Besides, you stabbed him first." She smirked.

I couldn't help but laugh and replied, "Okay, but for the record, I had everything under control."

She made it a point to make sure I saw her rolling her eyes.

We covered the bodies with leaves, took their uniforms and guns, and walked back to where they'd come from. When we got to where we could see the tree line, I spotted a vehicle just outside of the woods with a guard standing in front of it.

Tonya whispered, "There may be at least one more inside. We need to get close in case they have a radio. We can't afford to let them warn anyone else we're here. You're wearing the clean uniform. Help me walk while I limp and pretend to be wounded. I'll keep my head down so my hat hides that I'm a woman."

We acted out our scheme as we walked out of the woods. Tonya hobbled while I held her up. "Help, they stabbed her!" I cried out, hoping they'd catch the panic in my voice. The vehicle was about fifty feet from the woods, and we stumbled closer when two more guards came out. I yelled again, "Help, she's hurt!"

All three of them walked up to us. One of the men who was inside squinted his eyes and said, "Wait, we didn't have a wom—"

With lightning speed, Tonya stuck a knife up through the chin of one guard, then jumped another. I took on the third, punching him to the ground.

He tried to point his gun at me, and I grabbed the barrel, pulling him closer, then wrapped the sling around his neck and snapped it like a twig. I looked for Tonya to see if she needed my help, but she was already pulling her knife out of the chest of her last foe. *Damn, she's good.*

"Quick! Let's drag them into the woods," Tonya said as though it was just another day on the job.

As we covered them with leaves and branches, Tonya said, "I don't know if you've noticed, but because the gravity is more powerful on Xima, your strength and speed is far greater here on Earth."

I thought for a moment and replied, "Does that make me bullet-proof, too?"

She laughed as we picked up their weapons. "I wouldn't count on it," she said and got into the vehicle.

Tonya was more familiar with the vehicles than I was, so she got into the driver's seat and drove away. We passed another ADS vehicle leaving the launch site, then came up to a gate where several soldiers stood guarding the exit.

I looked to Tonya. Her pursed lips told me she was concerned. She smiled at me and said, "Relax. I'll try to talk our way through this."

I chuckled slightly and replied, "I'd feel more relaxed if I was bullet-proof."

She tried to hold back her laughter but wasn't very successful as I saw her grin.

When we stopped at the gate, the men surrounded the vehicle and tried to peer inside while keeping an eye on where we came from. One guard walked up to the driver's side and motioned for us to lower the window.

"Why aren't you pursuing the escapees, as instructed?" he asked.

Tonya replied, "We were the first ones to find them, but they were armed and wounded us. We're going to see the medic. Let us through."

I assessed the ones on my side of the car. Their guns were lowered, but I had no doubt they could easily get them into firing position before I could throw a punch. Besides, I'd never fired a gun before. But the guards didn't appear to be overly concerned about us—they were more focused on scanning the area.

"I wasn't aware of a woman in our squadron. What's your name, and who's your commanding officer?"

I smiled at the guard next to my door. He didn't return my friendly greeting. I placed my hand on the door handle, preparing to take them all on, when someone yelled from where we came.

"We have wounded! Come and help!"

Tonya pleaded, "Please, I'm wounded too. Let us get some medical attention."

The guards ran off. The one on Tonya's side opened the gate and waved us through. Tonya stepped on the pedal, and we quickly took off.

"Whoa! That was close," Tonya said, glancing at me. "I didn't think we'd get through without a fight.

I stared out the windshield, shaking my head. "I didn't think we'd get past their guns, especially after my fumbling to use the one I took from the guy in the woods. I was unbeatable on Xima with a sword or knife, but knives are no match for bullets."

Tonya quipped, "Hey, I'm pretty fast with a knife!" I looked at her and we both laughed.

I recognized the car from when I lived on the compound—it was electric, and the roof was made of a sun-absorbing material to help power the battery, but we wouldn't have much driving range at night without some type of charging station.

We drove for a long time. Our only view was the ruins of old civilizations in the distance. Devastation was everywhere. I couldn't help but think of how we'd gotten to such a point and what FOG really represented. In their attempt to save the planet, they were literally destroying it. *Or are they even planning to save the planet at all?*

I pondered the concept and asked Tonya, "What are your thoughts about this whole FOG-trying-to-save-the-world shit? How, in actuality, some are only trying to gain power?"

Tonya stared at the road. Her expression was distant, as though she was struggling to find the right answer. "So far, anyone in the ADS who even asked that question ended up dead within a couple of days. It's a belief many have had, but FOG has infiltrated the ADS and, it would appear, is within its top leadership. I wasn't able to trust anyone there to help me, which is another reason I sought you."

I stared at the guns we'd acquired which rested vertically in a rack between the two of us. "Is there more to shooting these things than pulling the trigger?"

Tonya laughed. "Once it's loaded, you put a round in the chamber and turn off the safety. Then, yes, all you need to do is pull the trigger."

I shook my head, not understanding what she'd just said, but hopefully, I'd learn before the real fighting started.

There was only silence for a while except for the dull hum of the wheels rolling down the road. My eyes grew heavy as I stared out into the beautiful sandscape.

"Wake up, Zack," Tonya said while slapping my arm.

When I regained focus, I saw a roadblock ahead with three ADS guards in front of a barrier in the road. Tonya slowed as we approached. "Remain calm, and follow my lead. Many of these guards are young recruits. I'd like to avoid killing them, if we can." I nodded.

As we approached, one guard came to the driver's side, and Tonya rolled down the window. "Where are you coming from?" he asked. The other two guards had their guns raised, but I suspected our uniforms and ADS vehicle didn't give them much cause for concern. I slowly slid my knife from my belt and placed it in my hand to throw if necessary.

"We came from the launch site with important information for the division commander. We're new here, from the East Coast. Where can I find the headquarters?"

"The only place around here is an ADS remote site down the road, where we're assigned. Which commander are you looking for?"

"I'm looking for the division commander. We have some information on the escaped criminals from Xima. Have you seen anything suspicious around here?"

I tried not to show signs of my amusement as I realized how well Tonya was deceiving them.

The guard replied, "Other than you two, we haven't seen anyone for hours. The nearest base from here is about five hours away. It's been cloudy today, so feel free to go down to our outpost and charge your car before you continue on. Hate for your battery to die on the way."

The guards appeared to be much less suspicious and more accepting than the previous ones we'd encountered. "Why don't you plug in at our site, get something to eat, and as soon as you're charged up, you can get going again. Otherwise, you may not make it."

Tonya reached her hand out the window. "Thanks! I appreciate the assistance."

"Sure thing. I'm Knox. Just tell the guys there I sent you to charge your car."

"I'll do that, Knox. Thanks again."

The other two moved the barrier out of the way, letting us through. Tonya turned down the dirt road and followed it toward a large shack-like building in the distance.

When we arrived, I stepped out and met Tonya in front of the car while she plugged it into the charging cord hanging from the building. A guard staggered out of the building.

"Who the hell are you guys? We weren't expecting anyone."

Tonya replied, "We were heading for HQ. Knox recommended coming down here and getting a full charge on the car first."

"That fucking kid! I'll have to teach him another lesson on following orders. No one is permitted to come here. Who's your commanding officer?"

He was an older guard member, obviously seasoned by the number of badges on his uniform, and had perhaps been drinking quite a bit based on his slurred speech and the way he staggered toward us. I noticed him squinting, which told me he wasn't wearing his glasses or was too drunk to see well. Either way, he appeared to be trouble for us.

"I asked you a fucking question! Who's your commanding officer?" He got closer to Tonya, grabbing at her uniform. "What the hell is this?" He examined the blood and the tear in the uniform. He looked up at her, and his eyes got wide as though he'd had a sudden revelation.

The old guard attempted to take off running, but Tonya grabbed him and put him in a headlock. I positioned myself ahead of them in case someone else came out of the building.

"You won't get away with this," he spat. "The ADS is searching the entire Western US for you two."

Tonya struggled to restrain him and replied, "Well, let's make sure we keep this a secret then, hmm?"

She motioned for me to go to the entrance of the building. She followed with the guard struggling in her grip. The man was quite a bit larger than Tonya, but the way she handled him confirmed what she'd said about true strength. After seeing her manhandle the guy, I pitied anyone who dared to get on her bad side.

I walked up the steps, peered through the window, and saw two unarmed guards inside, sitting at a table. I opened the door with the rifle in my hand.

"Come on, Sarge, It's your turn." They looked up to see me and jumped out of their seats, then stared at their rifles against the wall.

"Don't even think about it!" I said, pointing my gun at them.

Tonya and the older guard walked in behind me. I grabbed their weapons from the wall and took the magazines out, adding them to my inventory.

Tonya pushed the drunk guard forward to join his men. "We need some information, guys, and I'm confident you'll give it to us," she said as she pulled out a wooden chair to sit in front of them. I stood about five feet from her with my rifle pointed in their direction.

"We aren't telling you shit! You're both dead as soon as you're found here, and I'm going to put a bullet in your bitchy head myself," the older guard slurred.

Without seeing Tonya move a muscle, I watched a bullet go straight through the sergeant's forehead, causing him to fall to the floor.

Tonya held a handgun at her hip, alternating her aim toward the other two.

"Now, boys, do you think that was any way to talk to a lady?" Tonya asked in a soft voice, her head tilted almost like a mother asking her sons to behave.

I couldn't help but smile as the other two, who appeared to be in their early twenties, shook their heads with fear in their eyes.

"I know you two would never talk to me that way, would you?" They continued to shake their heads. Tonya quickly stood up. "I asked you a question!" she yelled, startling me.

They responded with a stutter, "N-no, ma'am!"

"That's more like it," she said and calmly sat back down in her chair. "Do you two know who I am?"

The two young men looked to each other and then to the dead sergeant on the floor. One of them said, "You're the two people from Xima we heard about on the radio. We were told you're murderers who hijacked your way back to Earth to continue your killing spree. We heard you killed everyone on Xima."

I looked at them in disbelief, slowly shaking my head. Tonya looked up at me and said, "Wow, Zack. I thought you said you only killed the bad guys."

One side of my mouth turned up in a small smile, and I shrugged. I began to wonder if I'd left the right people in charge back there, as it was becoming quite obvious they'd already betrayed us by warning Earth of our arrival, not to mention fabricating lies about us.

She looked back at the two men, tilted her head, and squinted. "If we killed everyone on Xima, who do you suppose made that radio call back to Earth warning you about us?" They looked at each other and shrugged.

"I'm General Tonya Skyler from the ADS. I was involved in a classified project, which involved this man. We went to Xima to clean up the crime, corruption, and scum from the planet and make it a better place to live. Women, children, and men who wanted to live in peace remained alive. But there are many here on Earth who are corrupt, as well." She went on to tell them the whole story of FOG's infiltration, and they seemed to listen to every detail.

Then, I heard gravel crunching as a vehicle pulled up to the building. I saw Tonya put her finger to her mouth to make sure the two men didn't call out for help. I hurried to the door and stood to the side so I would be hidden until someone walked in.

The door opened, and a voice shouted, "What's going on in here? I thought I heard a gunshot." It was Knox.

He entered and saw the situation, but before he could unholster his gun, I pinned him against the wall and lifted him up by his throat. "I wouldn't do that if I were you," I whispered.

He released his hand from the sidearm and raised both arms. I removed his gun and checked him for any other weapons. "Go sit down by your friends."

Knox fell to the floor, stumbled to a chair, and sat by the other guards. "What's happening?"

Tonya replied, "I don't really feel like explaining myself again, so why don't one of you boys tell him. And I recommend you tell him the accurate story." She rocked her handgun back and forth pointed in their direction.

While one of the guards explained everything to Knox, Tonya stood and looked out the window. The sun was just setting, so I doubted she could see anything outside. Still, she seemed curious as she continued to look at the walls and through desk drawers.

Knox asked, "What are you looking for?"

Tonya kept searching but replied, "I'm curious about the purpose of an outpost five hours away from a major base. Why have six guards here to monitor a full-time checkpoint?"

She picked up her foot and put it on the chair between Knox's legs. She leaned in close to him and whispered, "Why is that, Knox? What is this place, and what are you really guarding?"

All three guards looked suspicious and said nothing.

"Hmm, it must be something important, but I don't see anything unusual. Perhaps the sergeant was the only one who knew. I guess I won't need to keep you boys alive after all."

Tonya sat across from them. She smiled at me, then looked to the guards. "Let's play a game. I'll count to three, and whoever doesn't tell me what I want to know will be shot. The others who do tell me will live." They squirmed with their eyes wide, breathing heavily. They looked to each other, then to me and back to Tonya.

"One."

"I'd believe her if I were you, guys. Just look at what happened to the sergeant," I said, still unsure whether Tonya was really going to kill them or not.

"Two."

They looked down at the man on the ground, who seemed to have completely bled out with a pool of blood all around him.

Tonya pointed her gun more accurately at Knox, and I could see her about to say the next number when all three of them began talking at the same time. It was like a flood of information, but we couldn't understand what they were saying as they talked over each other.

"Perhaps I need to shoot two of you so I can understand what you're saying. Knox, you seem like a smart man. I'll reconsider killing the other two if you tell me what I want to know."

Knox looked to them, then focused back on Tonya. "We're a forward-ready reserve post used to store equipment. There's an underground storage facility here that holds mostly vehicles for the ADS to use as needed or to protect the main headquarters down the road."

I grabbed some zip ties from a shelf and threw them to Knox. "Tie the others to their chairs, and for their own safety, they better be secure."

I followed behind him to ensure the guards were tied tightly to the chairs and nodded to Tonya. She walked to the radio and ripped the handset out of the box.

I asked, "What about the other two at the road."

"Hmm, that might be a problem," Tonya said as she looked out the window. "No one's coming at the moment, and if they do come to free their friends, we'll just have to kill them all."

I grabbed Knox by the back of his collar and pushed him toward the door. "Time to show us this storage facility."

Knox led us outside to a small shack. It couldn't have been much larger than an outhouse or toolshed. He typed seven-nine-four-two into a touchpad and opened the door, exposing a stairway that led into darkness. We walked down the steps, and when Knox flipped a switch, lights illuminated an underground warehouse that expanded as far as I could see.

There were hundreds, if not thousands, of vehicles. Some had machine gun turrets on top. Some were vans, trucks, construction equipment, and then there were shelves lining the walls with thousands of ammunition crates.

Tonya walked up to Knox, putting her gun to his head. "This is more than just a storage facility! What the hell is this place?"

His eyes filled with fear again, and his voice quivered. "It's the western launch site. There's one to the east, also. The ADS has been planning to sweep the country and rid it of FOG completely."

She paused, then asked, "You'd need thousands of people to drive these vehicles. Where are they?"

"They're all getting trained at the headquarters down the road. That's why we monitor who drives down there, so no one sees what we're doing."

There was a noise in the distance. I pushed Knox down to the floor and knelt to listen. We saw a vehicle come out of a dark area. It drove toward the sea of other vehicles, and then there was silence.

"What was that?" I whispered, ready to attack anything that came our way.

"It was a delivery. When the manufacturing facility produces a vehicle, the vehicle self-drives through the tunnels to the warehouse and parks."

"There's no one driving these vehicles?"

"No."

"Interesting. Tell me more about these tunnels," Tonya demanded.

"They connect to the two manufacturing plants that make these vehicles. It stretches to one of the munitions plants that make all the ammo, and then it goes to the headquarters and training base."

Tonya grabbed Knox and turned him to face her. "You're telling me this tunnel stretches over two hundred miles to the training facility?"

Knox rapidly nodded.

I watched her ponder that fact before she asked, "How would they get thousands of ADS members here to man these vehicles?"

"There's a conveyor transport on the side of the tunnel. The ADS could send hundreds of drivers a minute through the tunnel."

I could see Tonya's eyes staring toward the tunnel. She looked like she was deep in thought, so I stayed quiet.

"Let's go back up and get the others. I think I have a plan," she said.

We walked back up the steps, and I was the first to open the door and get hit by loud screams.

"It's one of the killers! Fire!"

Bullets exploded all around the door as I rapidly closed it. I could hear loud pinging as the bullets hit the steel exterior, then stopped.

"There must be a dozen or more guards out there," I said to Tonya. My heart nearly jumped through my chest from the surprise. Images of the fateful night when my parents were killed filled my mind as bullets flew by me, and I had to pause to calm my breathing.

Tonya put her gun up to Knox's temple. "Where did they come from?"

"I don't know. Perhaps from a random truck of ADS guards, or maybe the guys at the road said they heard a gunshot. We weren't expecting anyone." He appeared to be sincere as he, too, was trapped in the doorway.

"Is there another way out of here?" Tonya asked.

He shook his head and said, "Only through the warehouse tunnels. But that could trap us for sure if the ADS come in from multiple directions."

Tonya walked up to the door and opened it a crack. "We have your guard, Knox, with us. We simply want to come out and talk," she called out.

"Come on out, and we'll talk," a voice yelled from outside.

Tonya looked at Knox, then at me. "If we use him as a shield and the leadership is FOG, they'll kill him to get at us."

Knox got fidgety and pleaded, "I don't want to die. I'll do anything. I believe you!"

"We don't have a choice," I said, picking up Knox by the back of his collar with one hand. Tonya held her gun over my shoulder, and we slowly walked out the door.

No one on the other side fired. We saw about twelve guards, who had likely arrived in the truck that was parked by the cars. The two guards we had tied up were outside with them.

A young officer wearing a captain insignia yelled, "We know you shot the sergeant inside and that you're the two who killed everyone on Xima and hijacked a shuttle back to Earth. We're here to take you in, dead or alive."

Tonya replied, "I'm General Tonya Skyler of the ADS. I went to Xima to find this man who was part of an ADS experiment to fight FOG. We cleaned up Xima, and all women, children, and men who wanted peace were allowed to live and are now working to improve the planet."

"Lies! We received a report that you killed the mayor and Xerxes, the ones who kept the peace on Xima," the officer stated.

I assessed our situation: many automatic weapons were pointed at us, and we had little to no chance to take them out without getting shot ourselves.

"Shoot them all!" the leader yelled.

One of the guards questioned him. "Sir, are you saying to shoot one of our own?"

"I don't care who dies. We need these two dead!"

Tonya yelled, "He's part of FOG! Why else would he order you to kill one of your own people?"

No one fired a shot. They looked to their leader, then back to us. I could tell they didn't know what to do.

The leader looked down the line of ADS guards with their guns all pointed toward us. "Kill them, or I'll have all of you shot for treason!"

One guard spoke up. "Well, isn't anyone going to take the first shot?"

"No way, man. I think I believe her," another replied.

"Yeah, I think I recognize her."

The ADS guards began to murmur among themselves, and I saw their leader's face turn bright red.

The captain shot Knox and said, "I order you to kill them all!"

Tonya fired a shot and hit the leader in the forehead. He fell instantly, then she yelled, "We can save the man your leader just shot, and I'm telling you the truth. Lower your arms and let me bring him inside so we can patch his wound or he'll die."

They lowered their weapons, but all looked cautious as we walked to the building. Tonya shouted, "Someone get a first aid kit!"

A guard pressed forward. "I'm a medic. Let me take care of him."

Some remained outside, and some followed us inside. Their guns were pointed to the floor, but their fingers were near their triggers, ready to fire if we threatened them, I was sure.

Tonya scanned the room. "Who's next in charge?" she demanded. Her tone would have made any subordinate stand to attention.

A sergeant stepped forward. He didn't look like he was more than thirty years old. "I'm Sergeant Baylor."

Tonya set her gun down on the table. "Sergeant, when I left Earth two years ago, FOG was our main threat. Who is the ADS's enemy now?"

"It's still FOG," he said with some caution in his voice as though he was hesitant to speak.

"Do you know what's underneath this outpost?" she asked.

He remained silent.

"We were just down there. I'm sure you're aware of the thousands of vehicles, weapons, and ammo down there, correct?"

His face remained steady, and he stayed silent. He must have been trained not to give anything away with his facial expressions. It seemed like he was trying too hard from the way he clenched his jaw and stared at Tonya without any emotion.

"I was suspicious of FOG infiltrating the ADS at our highest leadership levels. That's why they wanted to get their hands on this man when he was just a boy, and that's why they want me. Zack is the one who will lead us in cleaning this country of FOG. He and I are the last of the empiricists. We're an elite force trained to fight with ferocity and skilled to help lead the *true* ADS to end the war for good so we can all live in peace again."

The men looked around, whispering among themselves. I heard the word "empiricist" among them. They had obviously heard of the term, but I couldn't tell if that was a good thing.

Sergeant Baylor said, "There were supposedly only a handful of these empiricists, and they're all dead. It was just a pipe dream to inspire everyone and bring hope."

"You don't believe me?" Tonya asked. "Why do you suppose this outpost with so much firepower is so far from the main base and only protected by six guards?"

He didn't answer, but his eyebrows furrowed, indicating his contemplation.

"Why would you have so much firepower in a tunnel that leads directly to where thousands of ADS guards reside in, what I presume is, a fenced compound? How easy would it be for a FOG group to come in, kill the guards here, take down the door, and drive all of those vehicles and weapons to take out all of the ADS on the West Coast?"

The sergeant slowly shook his head. "I trust our leadership has their reasons."

"The only logical explanation for this outpost to be located so far away from the ADS troops is to make it easier for FOG to get to them. Otherwise, why not bring the vehicles closer to where the troops are located? FOG has infiltrated ADS leadership and has planned all of this, and you're too blind to see it." She paused for a moment to let it sink in. "Many ADS leaders are part of FOG, and some are using this common goal in the hopes of a success. They would prevail as supreme leaders of the world, but if not, they would still retain their leadership roles in the ADS. I had such a commander not so long ago."

The sergeant slowly nodded his head as though he accepted what Tonya was telling him.

Tonya walked up to him, placed her hand on his shoulder, and said in her familiar nurturing manner, "Sergeant Baylor, we're on the same side. I can see it in your eyes. We want to rid the world of FOG, and we can start by protecting this site better and getting the troops here to cleanse our country of this cancer."

He nodded.

I heard some movement across the room and quickly threw my knife into a guard, who took a poorly aimed shot at Sergeant Baylor. Two guards quickly grabbed the assailant and disarmed him. The medic went to Baylor, who was only wounded in the shoulder.

"Why the fuck did you shoot me?" Baylor asked his attacker while yelling in pain. He was bleeding through his uniform.

The assailant had a knife in his chest. I walked up to him and said, "I'll take my knife back, if you don't mind."

"Wait!" Tonya exclaimed. She walked up to the assailant. "Why do you want to kill your sergeant?" she asked.

"Go to hell, traitor!" he said, spitting at her.

She smiled and grabbed the knife, twisting it in his chest. He screamed so loudly that I actually felt sorry for him. She said while grinning, "I suggest you be nice to a lady."

"Fuck off!"

"Hmm. I'm sorry, but you seem a little uneven. Let me fix that." She pulled one of her knives out and stabbed the other side of his chest, grinding both knives into his flesh. He screamed louder than any man I'd ever heard. Two other men ran inside only to stop and watch what was happening.

"Um, General Skyler? I believe this is unethical," Sergeant Baylor said as the medic patched his wound.

She didn't give him the courtesy of acknowledging him. "I want everyone here to know that this man and the dead one outside are FOG and are part of a conspiracy to kill off all the true ADS and take over the world. This is an attempt to gain supreme power over America, but also over the world!" she exclaimed.

"This man has a choice," Tonya continued. "He can tell us what we want to know, or he dies. That's how we treat traitors, and every FOG member among us will be treated the same way. Does anyone have any objections?" She stared into the assailant's face, and I scanned the room to see if anyone was going to speak… or try to attack.

No one spoke up; they merely shuffled about and looked at each other. I began to lose my patience. *Stay calm and follow Tonya's lead.*

Then Sergeant Baylor walked up to his assailant. "Is this true? Are you with FOG, and was the captain with FOG also?"

The attacker looked at him and laughed. "The world will be better soon. Your way is destroying our planet. We will liberate it at any cost!"

Baylor took out his sidearm and quickly shot the traitor in the head. The guards holding him jumped back and let the corpse drop to the floor.

Tonya smiled. "Sergeant Baylor, I like how you work."

He put his sidearm away. "So, what do we do now, *General*?"

Tonya placed her hand on his shoulder. "Well, Sarge, do you accept me for who I say I am?"

He looked around the room. He looked to me, then back to Tonya. "I accept it with reservation. If I learn you're lying, I won't hesitate to execute you myself."

She slapped his injured shoulder, smiling. "I accept your terms. Good, now we need to develop a strategy."

We had no idea when FOG would come to the facility to begin their assault, but based on the vast number of vehicles below, it had to be soon, so we had to act fast. We left ten guards at the outpost and in the storage area below to hold off any potential FOG attack for as long as possible.

Tonya, Sergeant Baylor, and I took an electric car and raced down the tunnel as fast as the car would take us. We were on the way to the base to try to start the movement against FOG immediately. As soon as we approached the entrance to the base, we were met by a guard standing beside a steel mesh gate. Our car stopped in front of the gate, and Sergeant Baylor got out and talked to the guard. He got back into the car as the gate opened.

We waved to the guard and drove up a ramp. Cresting out of the tunnel, we found ourselves on the edge of a large courtyard and stopped. There must have been thousands of armed ADS guards in the courtyard marching around in formation. It seemed like some type of parade.

"What's going on?" I asked.

"A new general is taking command. He's from the East," Baylor replied.

"What's his name?" Tonya asked while looking out her window at the disciplined soldiers marching like a line of ants.

"General Strossler."

"Doctor Josh Strossler?" Tonya's head snapped in surprise.

"Um, yeah, I think so. Why? Do you know him?"

Tonya was distant as she stared through the window into the courtyard. "He was my boss on Zack's father's project." Then she turned to face me. "He's the one who directed the ADS to kill your father and take you. He's part of FOG's inside leadership."

I clenched my fists. I wanted to take on the entire faction on my own and finally get the vengeance I deserved. Tonya looked back at me, placed her hand on my leg, and smiled. "We'll get him. I promise."

She always seemed to read my emotions and, more importantly, to bring me comfort when I needed it. I watched out the window at the many ADS members, realizing they were all getting trained to sweep through the country to rid the world of the disastrous plague. And hopefully I could find Katia at last. I'd almost forgotten what she looked like ever since Tonya rescued me and drove me away from Xerxes. I had vowed to find her—and I would—but my feelings for Tonya were strong. Stronger than I ever thought possible.

Baylor drove the car toward the officer's quarters. Several guards and an officer approached and stopped us.

"What's the meaning of this, driving through here during a change-of-command ceremony?" the officer asked.

"We were attacked at outpost three by a small FOG group. I was wounded and forgot about the ceremony." Baylor did some quick thinking, showing his bloody shoulder as they moved aside and let us continue.

We drove to the parking area and walked to the infirmary. The doctor checked Baylor's wound and said the bullet had gone through. The hole was cauterized and bandaged.

I glanced out the window and saw the ceremony had ended and everyone was dispersing, but Strossler was nowhere to be seen.

We walked down a hallway as people returned from outside. Tonya quietly asked Baylor, "Where are we going?"

"To the command center. We need to report what we know."

Tonya grabbed his shoulder, stopping him. "No, we can't do that without knowing we can trust the leadership on our side. We don't know who else might be with FOG. More than likely, Strossler would have brought subordinates and loyal officers with him."

"With all due respect, General, and I'm still not convinced you *are* a general, but what the fuck do you have in mind now that we're here?"

I asked, "Is there a senior officer here who you've known for a long time? Perhaps someone who has hated FOG or has a grudge against them."

Baylor pondered. "I do know someone. Follow me."

We backtracked and went up some stairs, then into what looked like a library. In the back room, an older gentleman sat behind a desk. He studied something and, without looking up, said, "You can make an appointment with my secretary."

"Um, General Clayton?" Baylor asked.

He looked up and tilted his head. "Baylor? Baylor, it is you. It's been a long time. Who are your friends?"

We walked up to him, and Sergeant Baylor said, "They're in need of help—help against FOG."

"Well, then, they're in good company." Clayton walked around the table and shook Baylor's hand, pulling him in for a hug, then shook our hands.

He walked to close the door and locked it, then sat down on a chair in front of a table. "Sit. By all means, sit. How can I be of assistance?"

We sat down, and Tonya asked, "General Clayton, what do you know about FOG?"

He laughed. "What *don't* I know about them? They've been my main mission since I was a young lieutenant."

He told us about fighting FOG when he was young, the many who were killed in bomb blasts, the families who lived on farms and were all killed along with their cattle because of their contribution to global warming. FOG blew up large corporations because they thought they were too rich to care about the poor and not concerned with the innocent people they killed along the way.

The more he talked, the more I was convinced he was the right person to help us.

"Are you the same Clayton who started the empiricist program?" Tonya asked.

He immediately pursed his lips, then squinted at Tonya. He turned to peer at the wall behind me. Then he stood and walked toward the wall, pulling down a photo. He slowly walked back and sat down in his chair, staring at the photo as though he was reliving old memories. He looked up, smiled, and said, "It's been a very long time, Tonya."

My eyes opened wide. I looked to Tonya, who squinted, trying to focus better on Clayton.

Baylor asked, "Do you know this person, sir?"

He handed Tonya the photo. She asked in wide-eyed glee, "Where did you get this? I don't remember you being there. I knew of you only as the one in charge of leading the effort from Earth."

I leaned over to see the photo and saw a group of people about my age at what looked like the training area in the mountain on Xima. There were four boys and two girls upfront and two others in front of the cabin, which I was all too familiar with.

He continued, "I was responsible for the empiricist program. It was my idea to train our young to be the best warriors in the world. They were supposed to come back to Earth after being trained in the way of the empiricists—to use all five senses to fight FOG and bring peace and prosperity back to Earth—but I was overruled, and you six were sent out to battle right away. I was taken off the project and assigned to a remote site in Alaska for a while before I landed in this position. I couldn't stop myself from keeping tabs on each of you and what you were doing."

He took off his glasses and wiped them with a handkerchief, then quickly wiped a tear from his eye before continuing. "My heart sank when I heard all the others were killed, and then when you were promoted to general and assigned to some strength generation program in the East, I was convinced that FOG had infiltrated our senior leadership. I heard rumors you stole the program and fled to Xima, but I knew that couldn't be true. You were too dedicated to our cause to turn on us."

I could see Tonya staring at the photo, her thumb caressing the boy she'd fallen in love with, and her eyes filled with tears.

"Who are you, son?" General Clayton asked me.

"My name is Zack. General Skyler rescued me on Xima."

Tonya sniffled. "This is Zack Bates. His parents were killed—"

"Yes, yes, I know. They were killed for stealing the Hercules prototype."

"General Clayton, Zack *is* the prototype!" Tonya exclaimed.

I looked at the general, who stood and stared at me with wide eyes. "Stand, Zack. Stand for me, boy," he said enthusiastically.

I did as I was told, and he walked around me, feeling my shoulders. "How strong are you, son?"

"I really don't know," I replied. "General Skyler trained me at that mountain cabin in the picture, and we eliminated a lot of the scum on the planet before returning to Earth."

He sat back down in the chair. "So, the rumors are true that you killed many on the planet?" Clayton asked.

Tonya replied, wiping a tear from her cheek. "I trained Zack in the way of the empiricists, just as I was trained, and we cleaned up the villainous activity on the planet. Someone from the ADS on Earth coordinated the kidnapping of Zack's girlfriend and brought her back to Earth. We were met with a large reception party when we landed at the shuttle site but managed to escape."

"Fascinating. Absolutely fascinating," Clayton said as he scanned me from head to toe.

Tonya set the picture on the table in front of her. "General Clayton, we have a very large problem brewing, and we need your help."

"I'll do what I can," he said, looking at me like I was some sort of revolutionary success.

"I believe General Strossler is part of FOG and is responsible for killing Zack's parents. Now he's trying to kill him, too."

Clayton looked down at the picture, nodding. "Yes, yes, I know."

"You know Strossler is FOG? And you're doing nothing?" I asked, beginning to lose my temper.

"I'm an old man now, and FOG is discretely embedded throughout the ADS, but there are only enough of them to make small actions, create instability, or take out a key target on occasion. There aren't enough to simply take over the ADS. They have members in all ranks waiting for orders to attack. I could be killed just for knowing this, as would you all. I fear Strossler will have more follow him eventually."

"We have to do something, dammit!" I exclaimed.

"General Clayton," Tonya said, ignoring my interruption, "are you aware of the underground warehouse facility over two hundred miles away where thousands of vehicles and weapons are staged for battle? There's a tunnel that leads right here!"

He sat back in his chair and pondered, his eyes calculating. "That isn't a good strategy for our troops here to use, but it would be an excellent staging location for an enemy to attack this base."

We all nodded our heads in agreement. Tonya added, "And now a senior leader of FOG is the general in charge of this entire place. Who better to ensure the ADS is dead once and for all?"

I sat in the chair nearest Tonya.

Clayton's eyes widened. "Oh, this is very terrible. There's to be a two-day celebration to welcome Strossler to the headquarters. All weapons have been locked up—to prevent any accidents, or so they said."

I leaned in my seat, deep in thought. "That must be when they'll attack. They're probably about to hit the outpost any moment."

Baylor added, "We need to warn the guards there. Wait here, and I'll return as soon as I check on them." He stood up and walked off.

I asked, "General Clayton, what do you suggest we do?"

"You're in a very precarious situation. General Strossler was brought here to lead the ADS on an assault against FOG, but if his loyalty is to FOG..." He rubbed his chin, staring at his walls full of history. "The problem we have is lack of proof that Strossler is FOG. The only way we can find out for sure is after they attack and he's the last one standing. But then it will be too late." He stood and walked toward a wall with some more old pictures pinned to a corkboard.

"I'm an old man, and I've made some mistakes, but my intentions have always been to free America, and even the world, from these murderers.

Anyone who attempts to kill Strossler will surely be arrested or killed, and I'm not sure who could even get close enough to pull that off." He stood and paced around the room, his hand in his hair trying to concentrate. "As the ADS historian, I can probably get close enough to Strossler, but we must have leadership under him to accept you, Tonya, and what you say."

He picked another picture off the wall and brought it to Tonya. "This is Colonel Todd Krueger. Perhaps you recognize him."

Tonya looked at the picture intently. "I thought he was dead," she said softly, then looked at me. "He was the empiricist program leader. He recruited the six of us and sent us to Xima to train. I saw him when I returned, but then I heard he was assassinated by FOG." She turned to Clayton with a confused look on her face.

"He was leading a highly classified program designed to destroy FOG. When they found out that everyone was trained and ready to fight, FOG leadership among the ADS tried to kill him. They took away everything I had worked to create in the program and sent me out here to be a historian. Their attempt to kill Krueger was a message for me. I just wanted to live out my life in peace after my only hope was taken from me. The reason I'm still alive is because of my valuable knowledge of a vast number of programs."

I saw tears form in his eyes. "Your hopes aren't gone. General Skyler and I are here!" I exclaimed.

He laughed and wiped his eyes. "I love your confidence and enthusiasm, young Zack, but unless we can somehow influence our rightful leadership of these troops and get all of them to that outpost quickly, we may be at a loss."

The silence was deafening. Then, General Clayton stood up with his finger in the air and his eyes moved rapidly. "Colonel Krueger is on this base, but he's only a shell of a man now, running some contracting division. He is well known by his peers, though. If you can sway him to join the cause, I can get at Strossler, and we just might have a chance."

Sergeant Baylor came back into the room. "My men at the outpost are doing okay, but they've seen vehicle traffic in the distance. FOG appears to be doing reconnaissance."

"It won't be long before they assault the outpost. We need to act soon," Tonya said while staring at the picture of Colonel Krueger and General Clayton in their younger years.

Clayton stood up and walked toward the door. "Wait here for a few minutes. Let me check on something. I'll be right back."

I stood and walked around to look at the walls where General Clayton had much of his history pinned, dating from his youth all the way to more recent years. I stared at pictures of him as a young officer with a group of friends after a battle, and their smiles suggested they'd been victorious.

The door opened. Clayton walked in, and another man, perhaps in his fifties, trailed him. Tonya stood up, and the man stopped to stare at her.

"It can't be," he gasped while looking at Tonya with glee and adoration in his eyes. "I haven't seen you in many years. I thought you were dead."

Tonya stood completely still, speechless but with a slight smile. "It's good to see you again, Colonel."

He walked up to her and reached out to give her a hug. "I've heard so many rumors that I couldn't believe—refused to believe."

"Colonel Krueger, this is Zack Bates." Tonya gestured toward me. He reached out to shake my hand and looked back to Tonya.

Krueger went on to ask, "What have you been up to all of these years?" He appeared to be consumed by his reunion with Tonya.

"After my last battle, the ADS promoted me to general."

"Yes, yes, I know. I was very proud of you. I've always been proud of you."

"I oversaw an experimental program to develop a device that would accelerate muscle growth and enhance the senses and constitution in youth to make them better ADS guards."

"Yes, yes, I remember. Project Hercules, wasn't it? Sad that the inventor stole it and the device was never found."

My fists clenched as Tonya glanced at me with a slight smile and continued. "That inventor was Dr. Francis Bates. He was Zack's father."

Krueger's eyebrows furrowed, and he tilted his head to look at me as Tonya explained, "Dr. Bates placed the prototype into Zack when he found out FOG was going to steal it. He told him to run just before Zack's father and mother were gunned down… gunned down on the orders of General Strossler."

I could see Krueger's eyes moving rapidly as he contemplated what Tonya had told him. His eyes searched me thoroughly, then returned to Tonya. "Strossler is FOG?"

We all nodded our heads.

He sat down in a chair. "Oh, this is bad. This is very bad." We gave him a few moments to digest what he'd just learned.

"Colonel Krueger, there's more. We discovered an outpost over two hundred miles away connected to this place by a tunnel with thousands of vehicles and weapons."

"Yes, I know. I coordinated the contracts to have it built. It was part of our plan to sweep through America and rid it of FOG, but if Strossler is the commander now… and if he's FOG…" He began shaking his head and I watched his eyes become empty as fear shadowed his face.

Tonya nodded her head slowly. "You're seeing it now, and we just got word that there are distant recon vehicles near the outpost. It's only a matter of time before everyone here is in a fight for their lives. We were also told that all weapons were to be locked up here during the celebration over the next two days, leaving everyone here defenseless."

"It'll be a slaughter," Krueger mumbled quietly as he placed his face in his hands. "I can't believe I never saw this coming. I knew of the contracts and the plan, but I didn't connect the dots until now. I'm such an idiot!" He slammed his fist on the arm of his chair.

Tonya looked down at him and calmly said, "Zack is the warrior we have always dreamed of. The device his father placed in him enhanced his strength and senses beyond our expectations, and I trained him as an empiricist. All we need is support to take over the leadership of this base and prepare for the battle to end all battles."

"We can't simply walk in and arrest Strossler without evidence. No one will believe us. What do you propose we do?" Krueger asked.

I knew he had a point. *But how do we get the command of the officers? We can't arrest him, and if we kill him, the other officers will kill or arrest us.*

As I contemplated strategies, Clayton went to his desk and began writing. We remained silent, trying to come up with a plan or even an idea of how to tackle our grim situation.

Clayton walked up to Tonya and handed her what looked like a note. After she read it, she looked to him in horror.

"No, you can't do this! We'll come up with another way," she pleaded.

He replied, "This is the only way to make it work, and you, General Skyler, will take command and lead us—I mean *them*—to peace once and for all."

She looked back at the letter and slowly shook her head, then handed it to me without saying a word.

To whom it may concern:

I once had the motivation and drive to bring peace to our world from FOG that destroyed our way of life. I was involved in many battles and dedicated my life toward this goal. A legacy of mine, who was one of the best ADS leaders we ever had, was General Tonya Skyler. She was the most loyal person to the ADS, and to America, I have ever seen.

When I found out about General Strossler's plan to kill her, a friend of mine named Colonel Krueger was nearly killed. General Strossler warned me to stay out of his way or my fate would be the same. I realized then that General Strossler was associated with FOG, and, being too old and tired, I gave up hope to stop him.

When I discovered his plot to raise a FOG army and take over this base, I didn't believe it, but then he took command, and I learned of FOG recon at an armed outpost nearby. I knew then I had to take action. General Strossler would have us destroyed and lead FOG throughout America. I could no longer sit idle.

General Skyler has been brought out of hiding to defend us against FOG. Please let her lead the world to peace and prosperity.

I have served proudly,
General Clayton

"Is this a suicide note?" I asked, handing it back to Tonya.

"I'm the only one who can get close to Strossler, and we need the subordinate leadership to accept Tonya as their new leader. *And* we need to do it quickly. There's no other way," Clayton said, taking the note back from Tonya.

Tonya looked into Clayton's eyes and stared at him the way she might gaze at her own father. "He's right. It's the only way," she said as tears ran down her cheeks.

Clayton looked at his watch. "It's fifteen hundred hours now. I can get into his office at seventeen hundred hours. Sergeant Baylor, I need you to deliver this letter to Vice Commander Mueller in person five minutes before seventeen hundred. Ensure he understands it's urgency—he must read it immediately."

Baylor nodded.

Krueger said, "I'll go to the senior leadership and warn them that militants had been spotted at the outpost and that we need to consider holding off on the celebration. They were planning to lock the arms away this evening."

Tonya nodded and appeared to be deep in thought as she stared at the pictures on the table.

Clayton walked up to Tonya and placed his hands on her arms. "You've become more than I could have ever hoped for when I started the empiricist project. You and Zack are our future. Regardless of how this ends, I'm proud of you. Your parents would be proud of you too."

I could see tears in Tonya's eyes. She had a lot on her shoulders, but the fact that someone was sacrificing their life for our success was a weight I couldn't even imagine.

General Clayton went to his desk and placed his letter in an envelope and wrote Urgent on the outside, then handed it to Sergeant Baylor.

"I have a stop to make first," Clayton said, "and then I'll go visit Strossler. You'll know whether or not I'm successful. I'd like to thank you all for what you've done for our country, and for me, and I wish you the best of luck." He shook our hands and gave Tonya one more hug, looked her in the eyes, and nodded. Tonya nodded back, and he walked out.

Sergeant Baylor broke the silence when he said he'd be in position and wait for a signal. Colonel Krueger said he needed to mention the outpost issue to other leadership members and plant the seed in their minds about a possible attack.

While they went about their tasks, Tonya and I waited until we found out whether Strossler had been killed. We expected someone, hopefully Colonel Mueller, to come and find us after reading the letter.

Tonya explained her strategy to me, which would hopefully get us an advantage over FOG, but our success was predicated on whether we could get to the outpost before anyone else.

Tonya also explained there would likely be more members of FOG within the base who would want to assassinate me, so I needed to watch while she took command. She directed me to use any force necessary to protect her. *That's something I won't need an order to do.*

Our wait wasn't long but agonizing, nevertheless. Seventeen hundred hours approached, and we waited for a sign that Clayton had been successful. Seventeen hundred passed, and we continued to wait.

Suddenly, shockwaves from an explosion shook the entire building. We braced ourselves in our chairs, and the sound dissipated as fast as it came. Tonya and I looked into each other's eyes and nodded, conveying our commitment to the plan and our cause.

We waited in silence for perhaps another thirty minutes. Tonya just stared at the pictures on the table, reminiscing. There was a commotion coming our way, someone was yelling. When we stood up, there was an officer with several armed guards before us.

"Are you General Tonya Skyler?" the officer asked.

She nodded. "I'm General Skyler."

"Come with me, ma'am."

We followed the officer down a hallway with the guards keeping close behind. He led us into an office where we saw Sergeant Baylor. The officer told us to enter the room, and he closed the door behind. He had two guards remain outside his door, and two came inside. The officer stood behind his desk with his clenched fists pressing into the wood. He was quiet and seemed to be contemplating what he wanted to say.

He started out calmly. "I'm Colonel Mueller, the vice commander of this installation. Right now, I have the new commanding general blown up in his office, and I have a letter from our historian who recommended you take command. Will someone please tell me what the fuck is going on and why I shouldn't execute all three of you for treason?"

I asked, "How do we know you aren't FOG?"

Colonel Mueller walked around the desk and pressed his arm against my throat in rage. I twisted him around, and put him in a headlock with his arm behind his back. He yelled, "If I was FOG, you'd be dead by now!"

I released him and realized he was right and I shouldn't have insulted him. He backed away and regained his composure.

"General Skyler, would you please explain what's going on as quickly and concisely as possible?"

I listened to Tonya describe everything we knew so far. Mueller nodded and asked a few questions to clarify what she was saying. She discussed outpost three and what had transpired there. She also informed him of the latest recon we saw out there, and Sergeant Baylor corroborated.

Colonel Mueller ran his hand through his hair. "What you say sounds possible, but it's way too far-fetched to believe without proof."

"Would a decorated general of over thirty years in the ADS have given his life if he didn't believe what I'm telling you?" Tonya asked.

Colonel Mueller paused for a bit, then went behind his desk, dialed a number, and said, "I want to talk to whoever's at outpost three."

We waited. Then he said, "Okay. Try to patch me into their radio." We continued to wait.

Mueller stood up. "What's going on there, Corporal?" His eyes widened as he stared between me and Tonya. All I could hear was the faint voice on the other end. "Hold on as long as you can, Corporal. Help is on the way!"

Mueller set the phone down and stared at his desk. "They're under attack. The corporal said he didn't know how many were outside but estimated thousands. There are two dead guards and three holding out."

"We had half of our squadron stay in the warehouse below ground, well-armed with the larger weapons. There is only one way down that way, but they can't hold out forever," Sergeant Baylor said.

"Good thinking, Sergeant."

Mueller stared at Tonya, then at me. "Sergeant Baylor, sound the call to arms and have all troops form in the parade ground immediately with full battle gear. This is not a drill," he ordered.

I quickly noticed the guard next to me near the door pull out his sidearm, lift it, and point it toward Mueller. I grabbed his arm right as the gun went off. The bones in his arm snapped in half, and I pushed him to the floor. The other guard pointed his gun at me, and as I moved to disarm him as well, Mueller yelled, "Wait! Stand down."

The other guard lowered his gun and backed away. Mueller walked to the man pinned to the floor, knelt, and asked, "Why were you going to shoot me?"

"You'll never succeed! You'll all be killed, and we'll live free of all your toxic filth." Mueller picked up the man's sidearm from the floor and shot the traitor in the head.

He looked up at me. "Will you still challenge my loyalty?" I smiled back at him and shook my head.

"Baylor, call to arms immediately. Guard, ensure he remains safe along the way."

The two of them ran off, and Mueller stood and faced Tonya, saluted her, and said, "Ma'am, I still have my doubts but only because so much has happened so fast. I acknowledge you as commander of this installation and all of its troops."

She smiled at him and saluted back. "Thank you, Colonel. Now, perhaps you can steer me toward where I can get a more fitting uniform?"

A little while later, after Baylor made the call to arms, we stood on the same stage that had just been used for the change-of-command ceremony. Thousands of ADS guards filled the grounds in full battle armor, waiting for instructions on what to do next.

I stood behind Tonya as Colonel Mueller announced the death of General Strossler. He went on to discuss General Clayton's findings about Strossler's loyalty to FOG.

I scanned the thousands of men and women, searching for any kind of a threat. I looked among the senior officers standing on the stage with their hands behind their backs. All wore holstered sidearms, but that didn't seem alarming. The order was a call to arms, so everyone was armed. But if there were FOG members in the room, it would be quite easy for them to take a shot before anyone noticed them raising a gun. I pretended to listen to what was being said, but I was actually trying to ensure no one acted out against Tonya.

Then I heard Mueller exclaim, "I introduce you to our new commander, General Tonya Skyler!"

The troops remained still as Tonya walked up to the podium. I had a sidearm but was not as trained with it as I was with a knife or sword. *Xima was so much easier.* I walked up close behind her and felt uneasy as though something was about to happen. Although I couldn't see anything out of the ordinary, I was still prepared to block any attempt on her life.

Tonya spoke of her history, her accomplishments, her time on Xima, and went on to talk about General Clayton, who gave his life for our interests. I concentrated on using all my senses—scent, sight, and sound—to scan everyone and everything.

I scanned everyone as fast as possible, trying to get a glimpse of everything at once in case anything caught my attention. I could hear the sound of a sling swivel clasp against a gun stock in the formation, someone on the stage adjusting their footing, even Tonya turning a paper of her speech. The smell of the desert air was bland. I concentrated on every little thing that caught my attention to ensure it wasn't a danger.

She continued to talk about outpost three and how FOG was trying to infiltrate the base and kill everyone while all the arms were locked up for Strossler's ceremony.

I heard a nearby *snap* down the line but saw nothing. I got a sense from the change in the room's energy that someone was about to make a move. I breathed heavier but tried to concentrate and scan both the audience and the officers to my side. I subtly reached for my knife and held it firmly in my hand, ready to throw it at any second. Then I heard the rustle of metal hitting flesh—the sound of a gun being pulled out of a holster caught my attention, my instincts kicked in, and I threw my knife toward the sound.

A captain behind us fell to the ground with his hand on his gun. He continued to raise his weapon toward Tonya when another officer stepped on his wrist. There was a lot of commotion, and I looked out to the thousands of troops to scan for more potential risks. They were all armed, and any one of them could easily take a shot at her.

Tonya continued, "FOG is among us and has always been among us, which is why we've never been able to fully beat them. We are at war with an ideology, and we are in a fight for our lives right now. Outpost three is being overrun by thousands of FOG members as we speak. We have a handful of ADS guards protecting our assets, but they need our help. We need to move swiftly, and we need to win, or we'll all be destroyed along with the rest of this planet."

Tonya walked up to the captain who had tried to shoot her. She pulled out her sidearm and shot him in the head. Another officer at the end raised his gun at her. She was too quick and shot him in the forehead too. He fell forward, and she looked at me, tilting her head and giving me a look that suggested I wasn't fast enough.

I smirked back at her and mumbled, "I would have gotten him in time." She smiled back and nodded.

Tonya walked back to the podium and continued as though nothing had happened. "We cannot accept treason. Anyone who attempts to kill or injure any of us will be met with an immediate execution. We cannot take any risks when gaining peace and prosperity in America and the world is on the line." She paused and scanned the troops in front of her.

"Peace and prosperity. Who doesn't want that—the ability to live in harmony, pursue happiness, and make a life you want to live? We need to eradicate those who wish to take this human right from us."

Sergeant Baylor came up onto the stage and whispered to Tonya. She paused and nodded. Then he stepped back by me, and Tonya said, "I was just given word that outpost three may have been overrun, and all of the vehicles and weapons stored there have been taken by FOG militants. All of your weapons were supposed to be locked away for the next few days by order of FOG, which would have been a bloodbath for all of us. We believe the enemy is on their way here, and they'll be coming through that tunnel in about five hours. We need to prepare. Our advantage is their belief that we are unarmed, that we're defenseless. But we'll be ready for them with as much firepower as we can. I'll also ask for a volunteer group to run down to the outpost and attack from behind. I'm confident that this plan will allow us to compress our enemy and destroy them once and for all."

Someone yelled, "Skyler!" Then they all chanted, "Skyler! Skyler! Skyler!"

Tonya stepped back toward me and asked, "How do I stop this?"

I laughed and shrugged. She frowned at me. "You're no help." She then smiled at me and raised her arms. Everyone calmed down.

"We need to prepare. Please understand that you'll be fighting within hours—there's no time to spare. I'll coordinate with your officers, and they'll give you your orders. And when we're successful, we'll take this fight across America and free our entire country!" Everyone cheered. "Then we'll free the rest of the world!" The cheering grew even louder.

She walked back to Colonel Mueller, who was standing behind her. "Thank you, Colonel Mueller. I know how difficult this must have been for you. Bring the officers to the planning room and assign more men to the gate down below. Also, I want you to send troops along the tunnel with a radio that can reach back to us if they spot any movement."

He saluted. "Yes, ma'am!" She saluted back and smiled.

I followed Tonya from the stage and walked back toward the headquarters building. One man jumped through some guards with his rifle pointed toward Tonya, but before I could get to him, an ADS guard took him down. He yelled, "You'll die… you'll all die!"

Tonya took out her sidearm and shot him in the head, holstered it again, and continued to walk. She taught me to be cold and unemotional when fighting to win, but I'd never seen her kill so coldly, and I was proud to be at her side. I followed her as we walked into the building. We entered Clayton's office, closed the door, and she sat down, putting her head in her hands.

"I don't know if I can do this."

I was shocked at her sudden instability after all the confidence she'd shown so far. I watched her break down emotionally, and the only person she had to lean on was me. I'd never seen her appear so weak since I met her.

I walked up to place my hands on her shoulders. "I'm not very experienced in leadership or military discipline, but what I saw was thousands of troops calling out your name. They believe in you, just as I believed in you right after that time you left me to fight fifteen men by myself, or perhaps you don't remember that?"

She laughed. "And you did very well, might I add." She continued laughing. "I would have helped if I thought you needed it, but you handled yourself pretty well."

I rubbed her shoulder. "Exactly, just as you've done today and will continue to do."

Just as she reached up to grab my hand on her shoulder, Mueller came running into the room. "General Skyler, your officers await you in the planning room."

Tonya stood up, and we followed the colonel.

The planning room walls were covered in maps, and there was a large digital map table surrounded by all the officers. We walked up to the head of the table, and the men stopped talking, creating silence in the room.

"Where's Sergeant Baylor?" Tonya asked.

"He's outside. This is the officer's meeting you asked for," Colonel Mueller replied.

"Bring him in here." The door was opened, and Baylor was asked to enter. "Sergeant Baylor, I want you to collect any and all communication devices from every officer in this room. Any one of you who refuses to comply will be arrested and potentially executed."

Baylor grabbed a box and collected everyone's phones and radios as he walked around the room. I scanned and monitored facial expressions to ensure everyone complied with the orders. After everyone did, Tonya went into her plan.

Colonel Krueger said, "General Skyler, you should be aware that there are two plasma tanks in that warehouse. They're the latest in weaponry and have the ability to kill any living thing in its path for over five hundred feet. If these were to get out into the open, they'd be devastating to our effort."

"Do the tanks have a weakness?" I asked.

"The only flaw to its system is its regeneration time, which is approximately five minutes. Our primary objective is to ensure these weapons never leave the warehouse. If they do, we must use all means necessary to take them out. They have an electronic defense shield to deflect smart weapons and manned assaults. The only way one of these tanks can be taken out is by getting to the top of the vehicle and typing the access code into the hatch to open and remove the operators. Or, of course, by another plasma tank striking it at point-blank range."

There was silence, and then Colonel Mueller added, "Those weapon systems, codes, and operating manuals were highly classified. Perhaps we're overestimating FOG's ability to learn how to operate those advanced systems."

Colonel Krueger said, "I was involved in the acquisition of these weapons, and we found the test data at the manufacturing facility was compromised. All data on these weapons was stolen approximately two months ago."

I noticed a captain touch his watch as he stood at the table. He appeared calm and to be listening, but his watch looked unusual. I couldn't hear it tick. I walked up to him and asked, "Captain, may I see your watch?"

He looked to me and smiled. "Excuse me, but we're planning a battle here. I don't have time to show you my watch."

I grabbed his shoulder, pulled him back, and grabbed his arm. He struggled, and I slammed him to the floor, kneeling on his chest as I unfastened his watch. It was very high-tech, and it seemed to have a built-in microphone. Tonya walked over to us, and I handed her the device. She studied it, then looked down to the captain.

"You were recording everything. I suspect you would have transmitted it once you left, as this room is shielded. What do you have to say for yourself?" she asked.

He didn't answer. She dropped the watch onto his chest and shot through it, killing him instantly.

"I will not accept treason. If anyone else has a problem with my policy, they can feel free to voice their concern now." No one replied.

A major asked, "Why don't we blow up the tunnel? We could then attack them from behind."

That's a great idea!

"That's great thinking, major, but we might need that tunnel," Tonya said. She paused for a moment. "Major, I'd like you to set up a detail to rig the tunnel with explosives, but we'll only detonate them if I believe we absolutely need to."

"Yes, ma'am!" he replied.

She continued with her strategy, which involved a defense force at the tunnel's entrance to the base, on the wall of the headquarters, at the manufacturing facilities, and a large team at outpost three, hoping to neutralize the militants from behind. I was assigned to the last team.

The troops for the raid on outpost three staged outside of the fence. There must have been almost a thousand men and women ready to go in armored transports and trucks. With Tonya coordinating the overall campaign from the headquarters, Colonel Mueller volunteered to lead the attack force to the outpost. He took me aside as the last of the troops boarded.

"General Skyler told me of a girl you're looking for, who you traveled back to Earth to find. There was a girl who landed here perhaps a month ago from Xima. General Strossler and some other staff met her at the shuttle. I thought she may have been a relative or someone of importance to them, so I didn't give it much attention at the time."

I grabbed the colonel's arm. "That has to be Katia! Please, do you know where she was taken?"

He replied, "I don't think she's on this base. I'm sorry, but I don't have any more information. If he wanted to avoid you attacking the base, it would make sense to keep her here, but if he knew the real risk was the warehouse, she may be there."

I pondered his logic. *We stumbled onto the warehouse by mistake. Why would they have placed her there? It would make more sense to keep her here.* I looked into Mueller's eyes. "What more do you know, Colonel?"

Colonel Mueller appeared uneasy. I could tell he was hiding something, so I said, "We have zero room for hesitancy or collusion. I want to know exactly what you know, or I'll bring you to General Skyler, who you've seen has even less tolerance than I do."

"Okay, okay. Strossler originally told me about the girl, and we heard of a terrorist on Xima who sought her. I laid out the plan to bring her home so the terrorist would come after her and we could trap him. I sent the troops to the shuttle site and later found that you'd escaped."

I quickly brought my knife up to his throat. "Tell me why I shouldn't kill you right now for not disclosing this sooner." I desperately wanted him to say something that would force my knife through his larynx.

"I don't blame you for being upset, but I didn't know anything other than what Strossler had told me. She was here at the base, but then Strossler had her transported somewhere else. I don't know where."

I could see the truth in his eyes and wanted to drive my knife into him anyway, but we needed every bit of experience if we wanted to win the war. I lowered my knife and sheathed it.

"I should have said something earlier," Mueller continued, rubbing his throat, "but everything happened so fast, and by the time I realized you were the terrorist, or alleged terrorist, General Skyler was about to give her speech. I promise I'm ADS to the core and will die to save our way of life."

"Well, you almost succeeded in part of that promise." I stared at the lineup of trucks against the desert plain ready to deploy. "Do you think she was given to FOG?"

Mueller sighed. "I can only assume so, but we have a mission to accomplish. I'm sorry if this sounds cold, but there are many more lives at stake than your girlfriend."

I snapped my head and glared at him. "Don't tell me what my mission is! I have my own mission, and we'll accomplish both."

Mueller nodded, acknowledging my determination. I looked up on top of the wall and saw Tonya on a veranda. Mueller looked also. She nodded to us. I stared at her for a moment longer, nodded, then we climbed into the trucks to head to outpost three.

Chapter 22

It was noon, and the drive was long. I tried to take a nap, but it turned into several catnaps, as my paranoia kept waking me. The fear that any member of my group could be a FOG mole and kill me in my sleep kept me on edge.

Half of our convoy had fifty caliber machine guns strapped to the roofs of vehicles, and each had shoulder-launched missiles to use as needed by the troops. Everyone also had machine guns, sidearms, and ammo to last for a long fight. Although I had a sidearm, I was much more comfortable with my knives and bare hands. As we drove, I gazed at the desert sand—so barren, yet also so peaceful and serene.

After perhaps five hours, we came over the crest of a hill. I saw light reflecting off of something in the distance. We stopped the convoy and broke out our binoculars to see what was ahead. There seemed to be a recon group in a small truck at the other crest. Most of the convoy remained behind me, and only our first three vehicles could be seen across that distance. We backed up our vehicles and walked forward until we could see the other crest again, keeping low to the ground.

Colonel Mueller came up alongside me. "What do you see?" he asked.

I passed the binoculars to him, and he scanned around as I said, "A small recon group. The outpost is right over that crest. They'll get about five plus minutes' notice of our arrival to prepare for an attack."

"Not a good position for us," he said and handed the binoculars back to me.

"I'll walk there and take them out." I removed my sidearm, keeping only my two knives.

"You're going unarmed?" Mueller raised his voice, and his tone implied that what I'd just said was the most ridiculous thing he'd ever heard.

"I'm not unarmed; I have these." I showed him my knives in my belt and smiled. "It's all I needed on Xima. Besides, I can get closer to them with knives than I can if they see I have a gun."

Mueller motioned for the vehicles to move back a little further, and I began my walk down the road. I felt I had some element of surprise by not wearing the ADS uniform. I was comfortable in some basic military pants and a T-shirt.

As I approached, I saw three men step away from their vehicle and toward me. "Stop! Where did you come from?"

I stumbled closer, trying to look lost and dehydrated. I needed to get near enough to increase the accuracy of my knives. "Please, I need water. I was assaulted by the ADS many miles back and barely got away."

They looked into the distance as I got closer. "I said stop, or I'll shoot!" one of them yelled.

I dropped to my knees and held my arms out. "Please, I'm just asking for some water and maybe someone to tell me where I am."

One of the guards reached into the vehicle and walked toward me with a bottle of water. "Where were you attacked?" he asked while getting closer. The other two remained at a further distance than I would have liked, but I remembered that first animal I'd speared with Tonya and how I just needed to aim a little higher. If I missed and they were to make a radio call to warn their other members, our mission would be jeopardized.

"I was attacked about two miles that way. I was just driving down the road."

As the man got even closer, I attempted to act out a suffering-yet-thankful look on my face. The other two by the vehicle had their guns lowered and didn't seem to be threatened by me. One of them looked in the opposite direction while the man closest handed me a water bottle. I reached up with my knife and shoved it through his throat, not allowing him to scream.

"Thank you so much!" I said, holding him up by my knife.

I saw one of the others look my way, so I pulled out my other knife and quickly threw it at him. In less than a second, I removed my knife from my first kill and threw it into the chest of the third.

I walked up to one of them by the vehicle, who struggled to stay alive. "You are a dead man," he said as I pushed his weapons out of his reach.

I laughed. "It looks like you're closer to that than I am." I looked over the crest of the hill and saw what looked like a sea of ants running around. There were perhaps three thousand or more FOG militants all over the outpost with a line of people formed at the warehouse's entrance. I could see some vehicles driving around the outside of the building. I went down the hill a little toward where I came from and waved for our troops to advance.

I knelt and asked the man as he bled out, "Do you have a young girl with your group?"

"Go to hell!" He spat at me. I saw some blood spray out onto my arm. I pulled my knife from his chest.

"Perhaps this might help you remember." I pushed the knife through his shoulder. He screamed out. "Now, I'll ask again: Where's the girl?"

"Fuck you! She'll be dead before you can get to her." I knew Katia had to be nearby. In the guard shack, maybe.

"What are they going to do with her?" I moved the knife around, ensuring he felt every edge of the blade in his flesh.

He cried out, and I looked back to see the convoy approaching. "I want answers. Where is she?" I placed my other knife into his other shoulder, a technique I'd learned from Tonya.

He screamed again, then finally came clean. "She's bait for some guy named Zack! Some fucking terrorist sap!"

I smiled, pulled my knives out of him, and slit his throat. "Thank you for being so cooperative."

I wiped my knives off on his shirt, sheathed them in my belt, and stood up as the convoy lead arrived.

Mueller and a couple of other officers walked up to me. He asked, "What are we up against?"

I looked at the numbers we had compared to the sea of FOG troops I'd seen over the hill. "We're outnumbered at least three to one," I said as Mueller walked to the crest with his binoculars. He came back down and stared at the ground.

Mueller pondered our situation for a while, then said, "We're definitely outnumbered, but we have a surprise on our side. Additionally, they haven't brought any of the vehicles out of the tunnel yet. We can use this to our advantage also."

He continued with his strategy, and I listened while trying to formulate my own plan to save Katia. If she was down there in the outpost, nothing would stop me from rescuing her.

The first step of our plan was to take the armored all-terrain vehicles down first in a Delta formation to gun down and run over as many FOG soldiers as possible. Our other trucks would follow, unload, and begin their assault. The main objective was to stop people from going down to the warehouse to get more weapons. I was in the first troop vehicle behind the armored vehicles set to take the guard shack.

We came over the hill nearly at full speed. It only took a few seconds before we saw people running frantically near the outpost. I don't know how many of them reached the building in time, but there were too many of them and not enough places for them to hide.

Many tried to seek cover behind the building, some behind a handful of parked vehicles, and the rest ran away. As soon as we were within a few hundred yards, our machine guns rained lead on the outpost, keying on those who were around the building and vehicles. The barrage kicked up spots of sand as smoking dots formed on all the vehicles where FOG members hid.

Our armored trucks advanced toward the camp and began trampling the fleeing enemy, gunning down the rest. The truck I was in stopped near the stationary vehicles, which were riddled with bullet holes. We got out and took our positions. I still wasn't very confident with a gun, but I had my reliable knives with me as I moved around the building.

Gunfire rained around me. I felt a pain on my arm that reminded me of a bee sting I'd gotten when I was five. It was from a bullet, but fortunately, it only grazed me. Other ADS troops moved around the vehicle and fired at those hiding behind it, holding them down while I ran into the building.

Multiple men were in the house. I grabbed the first one I saw, turned him around, and placed my knife into his chest while his colleagues shot holes into his back. When they ran out of ammo, I dropped my human shield and ran at them, easily taking them down. My rage was immeasurable. No one remained standing, and Katia was nowhere to be found. I was furious with myself for not keeping one of them alive to interrogate.

I could hear more gunfire around the building, so I looked out a broken window and saw guns pointed out of the warehouse's entrance. *I need to get down there. They might have Katia there.*

I went out the door and toward the ADS troops who were finishing up with the FOG members by the vehicles. I told them I'd go around back and jump the entrance while they fired at the door.

I ran around the building because if I ran toward the warehouse while the door was open, they would see me and have a perfect shot at me. I waited until I heard firing, then ducked back inside. I ran to the backside of the little shack enclosing the stairwell and waited. When the door opened, I pulled it fully open, catching those hiding by surprise and letting the invading ADS troops shoot them down.

I ducked inside to see if anyone else was there. I slowly crept over the bodies on the steps and down to the bottom of the stairwell where I listened to the many voices echoing in the massive chamber.

Keeping tight against the wall leading down the stairway, I crept down to the final step and peer into the warehouse. Some fellow ADS troops followed me. The sound of other trucks pulling up near the shack told me we had the outpost secured, and we all nodded to each other, signaling it was safe to proceed. Next, we needed to secure the warehouse.

I continued on when someone walked up to the base of the stairs and looked up at us. His startled expression turned to terror as my knife went through his skull. I then held him in place as a shield as I scanned the warehouse.

Vehicles raced down the tunnels, and I saw a bright flash as more vehicles scattered. I tried to focus through the exhaust fumes and saw what looked like a tank pointed right at me. It was one of the plasma tanks I'd learned about, judging by its size. Just as I was about to run toward it, bullets scattered around me.

I jumped back into the stairway and ran up the steps, pushing the others up and out.

At the top, Mueller was setting up a perimeter with his troops. As I reached him, an explosion shook the ground. Our heads snapped in unison to look. The ground opened, and the plasma tank rose from below. It didn't move very fast but managed to level itself on the flat surface and slowly spin in a circle until it stopped to aim the turret toward a large group of forces. It fired a bright beam, creating a large explosion that destroyed the ADS vehicles and all the troops in its path.

"Damn, I didn't think there was another exit. And that was quicker than five minutes!" I exclaimed to Mueller.

"I never got to see the test results that showed how fast it could actually regain enough energy to fire. We need to take that thing out. It'll destroy all of us. If you can get on board, the code to open the hatch should be five-zero-three-six, unless they changed it, but let's hope they didn't get that advanced in their studies. Before it fires, it must concentrate energy. You can hear a tone that increases in volume seconds before it fires. It can't move during this period."

Just as I took off running, Mueller called out, "Oh, and anti-dismount assault defensive system gives off an electric shock that will jolt you from the tank. It must build up energy to operate, but it doesn't take long. You should have time between uses to get the hatch open… if you can stay on it that long."

I nodded and continued to run toward the tank as it slowly turned and drove to the outpost's guard shack. I yelled for everyone to get away, and the turret slowly turned toward me. I ran closer and could hear the high-pitched tone start. It got louder, and I quickly dove away as the blast seared through the air with an ear-piercing sound.

I stood up and saw that nothing had been damaged when the last blast hit the ground, just a small, scorched hold in the ground. I ran up to the side of the tank, found a ladder, and grabbed on. I made it up two steps before I was jolted from the tank. I flew backward and landed on my ass, then clambered to my feet. A tingling sensation ran through my arms, and I realized it was from the electric defense system Mueller warned me about.

All my muscles ached and prickled from the high-powered jolt, but I had to try again.

I looked at the tank, analyzing whether someone had seen me and set off the defense or whether the shock was automatic. I couldn't see any windows, so I jumped on again and, within seconds, was jolted from the tank back into the sand.

Each shock made me dizzy, and my vision was momentarily hazy. My body tingled with muscle spasms that quickly dissipated. I stood up, stretched my arms and legs, and stared at the tank while it aimed its turret toward some troops at the perimeter. The high-pitched tone increased, indicating it was building up energy to fire. A blast of light killed dozens of men instantly. The lucky ones were vaporized, but some were burned severely and rolled on the ground until they became motionless.

"No!" I screamed. Anger consumed me after seeing the innocent men get incinerated. I'd been in hard situations in the past but none like my current predicament. *What I wouldn't give to be against fifty men with swords right now.*

Woosh! I turned back to see a smoke trail from a missile someone had launched toward the tank. It violently veered off and exploded in the sand. I looked around, trying to figure out how to get on the tank, but I was grasping at straws.

I yelled to a group on the other side of the building, "All of you, come out here and shoot at this thing, and when you hear the tone… run!" I ran behind the building, climbed up on an armored vehicle, and then onto the roof. I ran toward the tank, which was about ten feet away—a long leap, even for me. My plan was to jump from the roof and land on top of the tank, hoping the electrical defense was only on its sides.

I moved back, took a breath, and ran toward the tank, leaping for the turret.

I almost flew over the top but gripped the handle of the hatch. Holding on with all my might, I quickly pulled myself on top. My body uncontrollably stiffened like a board as a surge of electricity raced through me. I could barely hold on to the handle, and then the shock stopped. I was dizzy for a few seconds, shook my head to refocus, and tried to catch my breath. I saw the keypad and tapped in the number sequence. The metallic clicking sound within as the hatch unlocked was music to my ears. I grabbed hold of the door, pulled it open, and saw one head near the top look up at me.

I grabbed the soldier by his collar and pulled him out of the hatch, throwing him over the side. I slid down into his place, pulled out my knife, and killed the driver. Then I looked in the back and saw several other troops strapped into seats. They saw me and couldn't get their guns turned around in time before I crawled into the darkness and slit all their throats in what seemed like a couple of seconds.

I climbed out of the hatch and saw Mueller walk up with a few others. I yelled, "Does anyone know how to drive this thing?" I jumped down and walked up to Mueller. "There are about half a dozen dead FOG members in there you might want to clean out first."

He sent some men inside as I scanned around and saw only ADS troops remaining. Thousands of dead lay in the sand. I looked to the building and sulked. After that tip I got from the guards before we attacked, I was confident I'd find Katia.

Mueller sent some men down the ramp where the tank came from with directions to look for a young woman. They cleaned up all the leftover dead FOG militants in the warehouse but didn't find her. I walked into the outpost building to see if there was any sign of Katia, but I couldn't find anything. I pounded on the wall in rage.

Mueller came in the open door and said, "The other tank's missing. I suspect it's moving through the tunnel toward headquarters right now."

My thoughts changed from Katia to Tonya. I couldn't lose both of them. "What's the fastest way back to headquarters?"

Mueller replied, "The fastest way is taking one of these cars, but I can only hope that the defenses are holding off the tank in the tunnel. If they aren't, they're already lost." We looked at each other, both realizing what needed to happen. He said, "I'll leave some troops here to defend the tunnel entrance. You take the rest over land, and we'll sandwich them in the middle."

I placed my hand on Mueller's shoulder and smiled. "Good luck, Colonel."

He placed his hand on my shoulder also and said, "Good luck to you, Zack. We'll find your girl."

I nodded and ran off into the warehouse to find a fast vehicle. There was an armored one near the tunnel entrance. It may not have been the fastest, but something told me that armor would be just as important as speed.

I jumped in and, fortunately, all I had to do was push the Start button to get it going. I'd driven an electric vehicle once before, but that was a long time ago. My instincts told me to place the shifter in drive and step on the pedal, and before I knew it, the truck lurched forward and took off down the tunnel.

Chapter 23

Hours passed as I drove, and my mind was torn between my guilt from putting Katia in harm's way and my loyalty to Tonya, who rescued me and taught me more than I could possibly have imagined. I remembered the time Tonya and I sat naked in the stream and how my gaze never left her during our ride back to Earth. But I also remembered my first kiss with Katia and how happy she made me, and the thought brought tears to my eyes as I realized how much I loved them both.

I hated what had happened to us, but I realized it was selfish of me to only think of Katia when the whole world was in danger. It was my fault for getting her into the situation we were in, but thousands—maybe even millions—of lives were at stake, including Tonya's. I knew I had to stop FOG's assault but was afraid I might be up against more than I could handle. Most of the FOG army may have been destroyed before they reached the end of the tunnel, but I didn't know how many of the survivors I'd have to face once I ran into them.

There were lights ahead in the tunnel. I could see men standing in front of a vehicle, and bullets whizzed past me. I didn't let up on the accelerator and plowed into them, sending flashes and sparks through the dark tunnel. The sound of metal banging on both my vehicle and the walls stopped as I continued driving. I hoped they couldn't get a radio message to anyone in the tunnel and ruin my element of surprise.

There was another roadblock which I ran through again, sending the same flashes through the tunnel. I had no plans to stop until I arrived at the headquarters.

I tried to channel my rage and focus on what I had to do, but I wasn't sure what I would be up against once I reached headquarters. Finally, I saw vehicles stopped in front of me. Troops lined up beside them, and there was a large flash up ahead. *The other plasma tank. It's attacking the headquarters… and Tonya!*

My initial instinct was to ram the vehicles in front of me at full speed and take out as many FOG members as possible, but that would put even more attention on me. I knew I'd be better off if I stopped behind the last truck and tried to sneak in from behind.

I counted approximately twenty vehicles and maybe over a hundred FOG members standing along the conveyor-belt side of the tunnel. Most of them were close to the exit. *We must have gotten to the outpost well before they could get too many vehicles down here.*

I left my car's headlights on, hopefully preventing those in front of me from actually seeing me. I assessed the situation and saw that everyone was looking forward, prepared to advance, no doubt. My gun and knives were in place on my belt. After one deep breath, I stepped out the door.

I made my way toward the troops, trying to take them by surprise. There were so many men on the conveyor side of the tunnel waiting for the signal to run forward. They were too focused on what was in front of them that they didn't notice me slicing through them from behind. The sound from the gun fire ahead and the engines running was so loud that I would have had to make a lot of noise to draw their attention.

One man on a vehicle's machine gun turret saw me and turned to start shooting. I felt a bullet rip through my side, but I was able to ignore the pain. I threw a knife into his chest, causing him to slump over his gun.

Others were alerted to my presence by the shots and tried to turn around. *This just got a little tougher.* I grabbed my gun and fired. As the dead fell one by one, others struggled to turn toward me because they were so tightly lined up in the tunnel. I ran forward, dodging between vehicles whenever I could.

When I ran out of ammo, I picked up another gun and continued to shoot my way forward. Another gunner saw me from a truck toward the front, but my second knife found his chest just like the first man I took out. Bullets bounced off of the walls and vehicles all around me, and one stung my leg as I jumped out of the way behind a truck.

A deep bellowing voice yelled, "You back there! Get him! The rest of you, prepare to advance!"

The complexity of fighting in a dark tunnel appeared to be in my favor. The only people left in the vehicles were the drivers as the remaining troops prepared to advance. The tunnel was large enough for me to move around the vehicles, but the tank nearly filled the entire width of the tunnel where it rested.

Blood was streaming down my leg. I saw a dead guy next to me, so I grabbed my knife to cut off some of his uniform to make a tourniquet and realized I was out of knives. A clanging noise alerted me to someone on the path to my right. I stood up against the truck and grabbed a gun barrel as a bullet flashed by. I disarmed the man, kicked him aside, shot the woman behind him, and then shot him.

I noticed she had a knife in her belt, so I grabbed the knife as more bullets rang out around me. I cut some material off a dead guy behind the truck and wrapped it tightly around the wound on my leg. *I can't afford to bleed out.*

Peering down at the other side of vehicles, I saw soldiers moving between the wall and the line of cars. I fired through the shadows and saw some fall while others ran between the vehicles to hide.

A bullet ricocheted behind me. I ducked down and slowly looked to see a driver in a nearby vehicle standing at his door with his gun aimed at my head. I lay on the ground and shot at his feet. He fell, I shot him again, and he became motionless.

There was a bright flash as the plasma tank shot again, and the tunnel lit up with what seemed to be a microsecond burst of sunlight. I peered around the narrow side of the tunnel and saw the tank driving away with perhaps a hundred FOG members walking behind. I grabbed two guns and sheathed the knife. I surprised a couple more drivers by opening their passenger doors and putting a round in each of their heads.

I popped into crevices between vehicles to shoot at FOG soldiers from behind, hoping those in front wouldn't see me. Some tried to turn to shoot at me, but I took them down right away. My unusual ability to focus and aim seemed to apply not only to knives and fistfights, as my shooting skills were quickly becoming exceptional.

As I slowly worked my way up, bullets stopped me occasionally when I was spotted, and a voice ordered others to get me. I ducked in one spot and popped up elsewhere to shoot again. I felt a sting on my right shoulder, and I looked behind me to see someone had jumped me with a knife. I quickly took out my own knife and slid it up through his chin and into his head. I knelt and tried to remove his knife in my shoulder, but I couldn't reach it. My strength helped me withstand the pain, but having something stuck in my back hindered my movement.

I looked in the truck mirror I was next to and tried to hook the hilt onto the metal mount holding the mirror to ease myself down. It worked; the knife fell to the ground. I moved my arm around, realizing the stab wound was obviously deep as it really hurt, but I shook it off. I couldn't allow pain to influence me after I'd come so far. I picked up the knife and pressed forward, listening to what seemed like a war zone ahead from the sounds of gunfire and screaming. The plasma tank must have already wreaked havoc on the compound. The defensive forces must have retreated into the buildings since the tunnel was clearing out. I had to get up there to help as soon as possible.

There were no longer any FOG members in the tunnel—at least, no one living. They were all in the headquarters parade ground, but I didn't know how many remained. Looking back, I saw hundreds of dead bodies littered throughout the tunnel. Perhaps fifty soldiers had managed to enter the compound. Fifty… plus the damn tank.

I reached the exit of the tunnel and saw a missile get deflected by the tank and hit the side of a building, causing part of the wall to collapse. The tank fired toward the gate. I knew it had to be Mueller's troops out there on the grounds. If they got killed, we'd be doomed.

All the FOG members stood behind the tank, defending themselves from the ADS's guns in the buildings. They must have thought they were protected, but they were exposed to me.

I opened fire on them, taking down several as they fired back at me. I ducked behind the brick entryway of the tunnel as bullets plinked all around me and bounced off walls and vehicles. I heard a slight pause and peeked around to fire some more. They were all in a tiny group behind the tank, making my job a little easier. Fortunately for me, they appeared to lack proper training.

I looked again and saw the door on the back of the tank close. I couldn't believe they'd all fit inside the damn thing. I glanced around and saw no other FOG soldiers. Making a break for it, I sprinted to the tank. A group of FOG popped out from behind a smoldering vehicle, which had probably been hit by the tank earlier. I hadn't expected that. *Perhaps my wounds are impacting my thinking or senses.* My heart stopped for a second and had to get out of their line of fire.

The stinging in my arm was quite painful, as they'd gotten me pretty badly, but I had no time to be concerned with my wounds. I dove around the other side of the tank.

Collecting my thoughts, I realized I was bleeding a lot more. I needed to end the fight, or I wouldn't last much longer. Suddenly, a gun barrel came around the corner of the tank. I grabbed it, twisted it out of my attacker's hands, and drove the stock into his forehead. I shot the next one behind him and ducked down beside the tank again.

I heard the tone as the tank gathered energy. Hoping the sound would distract the dismounted FOG, I ran behind the tank and took out the first person I saw, cutting his throat. I held him as a shield while I used his gun on the others hiding on the other side. I got them all. Next, I needed to stop the tank.

I couldn't find any means of getting on top of the thing like I did with the last one, and I felt noticeably weaker from blood loss. Looking down at the bodies on the ground, I decided to try something different. I lifted the smallest dead FOG soldier and heaved the body on top of the tank. I didn't see a reaction, but it was probably because he wasn't alive.

Hoping they would have triggered the shocking defensive system with the dead guy, I tried to quickly climb the ladder. I was able to get to the top when a painful jolt propelled me back to the ground. My plan had worked, but there seemed to be a delay before they were able to use the defense system again.

I stood up and saw three ADS trucks drive through the open entrance to the headquarters. The tank fired, hitting the third truck and turning it into shredded steel and fire. The other trucks pulled up, and Mueller and several men climbed out. A couple of men tried to climb up the ladder of the tank, but both were jolted off from the defensive system.

Then I had an idea. "Mueller! Drive that truck closer."

Mueller climbed back in and brought the truck near the tank. We only had a few moments as the turret turned toward Tonya's quarters. The tank would destroy a big part of the wall if I didn't stop it. I climbed up onto the truck and stared at the top of the tank.

"Have two more men climb the ladder!" I bellowed as I prepared to jump. Once the men were shocked, I'd have more time.

Two men climbed the ladder, and when I saw them get jolted and fall, I jumped for the tank, scrambling on top and reaching for the hatch code panel. I held the hand grip as hard as I could and typed in the code.

I reached for the last number, and my body stiffened as electricity ran through me, making every muscle spasm. The pain wasn't nearly as bad as the first time. I wasn't sure if it was because my body was getting used to it or whether my loss of blood had dulled my senses. Once the shock was over, I entered the last number and opened the hatch.

Just like last time, there was a man sitting just beneath the hatch. I pulled him out and threw him aside. I climbed into the weapon operator seat and shoved my knife through the ear of the driver next to me.

The yelling behind me, followed by echoing shots and the *ping* of bullets ricocheting, stopped abruptly. Another bullet ricocheted around the inside of the tank, but fortunately, it didn't hit me.

I tried to lean as far back as I could in the weapon operator seat so I could keep out of reach of those in the back. I saw a button on top of the bulkhead labeled Aft Hatch. I pressed it, causing the back door to open. Mueller waited on the other side as FOG members fled.

The sound of gunfire rang out as I tried to collect my thoughts. I looked at my blood-soaked clothes and couldn't tell what blood belonged to me and what was from others. I stumbled out the back of the hatch, holding on to the metal edges to keep from falling. My mind was foggy, but I had to walk out. I had to see whether Tonya was all right.

More trucks poured into the parade grounds, but almost everything was a haze for me. I saw Mueller come over and place his hand on my shoulder. "You did it, you crazy bastard! You did it!" I smiled, feeling my legs start to give.

"Zack! You did it! I knew you could!" I heard a familiar woman's voice.

I looked in the direction of the speaker and saw someone running toward me. I knew it was Tonya, but I could only see a blur. I staggered, trying to walk toward her but had to reach out to lean on the tank, as I was about to fall. I smiled as a sense of euphoria filled my mind and body. I wanted to reach out to her, but then everything went dark.

Chapter 24

The light over my head was more of a dull glow. My vision was blurry, and I couldn't make out anything other than shades of dark and light. I felt a soft grip of my hand and heard a woman's voice whisper, "Zan?"

I looked around frantically. That voice. I knew it but needed to be sure. Everything was coming back into focus. To my side, I saw someone with long dark hair.

"Zan, it's me. Katia."

I reached to place my other hand on hers as tears formed in my eyes.

"Katia?" I shook my head in disbelief. "But how?" I knew what I wanted to ask after all those years apart but was unable to get words out.

"She gripped my hand harder. "Colonel Mueller found me in a locked room under the guard shack after you left the outpost."

I tried to hold back my tears but felt the air cool them as they ran down my face. I stared toward Katia as my vision became clearer. I could see her dark curly hair, and then I made out her face. Her hair was longer, but her smile, her eyes, and her everything looked the same as when I last remembered so many years ago.

I scanned the room and saw a nurse at the foot of my bed. She also had tears in her eyes and said, "I'll be right back."

"I've never given up on finding you, Katia." I sighed, turning my attention back to her.

She began to cry. "I know. General Skyler told me everything."

"I'm so sorry for what you went through. I would never have—"

"Shhh, I know." She ran her hand through my hair. "I know," she said softly. Her smile was soothing, but tears ran down her cheeks.

The nurse walked back into the room, followed by what looked like a doctor, Colonel Mueller, Colonel Krueger, and Tonya. My eyes lit up seeing Tonya again. She walked to the other side of my bed.

I reached up to grab her hand. She smiled down at me and said, "You did it, Zack. You've helped us clean up the West, and we're preparing for our movement east to clean the rest of America, then the rest of the world."

I looked up at my hand holding Tonya's and saw a tattoo on my forearm. It was the same as Tonya's but had a bandage in the middle.

I squinted up at her and was about to ask when she said, "We needed to replicate that device your father created to help us win this fight. As you asked in the cabin, you're now officially an empiricist." I didn't have any words for her. She looked up at Katia, then back to me. "Get some rest… and get reacquainted with Katia." She smiled and walked out of the room.

Mueller moved to the edge of the bed. "You are the most reckless and boldest warrior I've ever met. I would be honored to have you at my side anytime. Get some rest, Zack. There's a big future for you." He slapped my leg and walked off with Krueger, who just smiled and nodded at me.

The doctor came by my side and took my blood pressure while I smiled up at Katia. She was so much more beautiful than when I last saw her. Many years had passed since we first met in the woods when she saved me.

The doctor said, "You're healing well. Much better than I've ever seen. You should be up and moving around within a couple of days." I never took my eyes away from Katia. I never wanted to take my eyes off her face again.

The doctor walked out with the nurse in trail. I looked up to Katia and whispered, "Let's escape, just you and me."

She laughed. "That didn't work out so well the last time we tried it."

I couldn't help but laugh, and then I felt the weight of what had happened wash over me. "I'm so very sorry, Katia."

She leaned down and whispered, "It's been a long time since we did this." She leaned down further and softly kissed my lips. I took in a deep breath as her lips touched mine. I closed my eyes, savoring every moment. She stood up again. "General Skyler told me what you did on Xima, and then what you did here to save Earth." Her eyes teared up again, but I could tell she was trying to hold them back.

I furrowed my brows. "How long have I been out?"

"You passed out in the parade grounds two days ago. General Skyler told me how valuable you are. She told me how she taught you to fight and how many people you fought to bring peace to Xima." Tears rolled down her cheeks and dripped onto the bed.

"What's the matter?" I could see she was troubled.

She placed both hands onto mine. "I know you tried to find me and rescue me, and I'll forever be thankful, but I know you're destined for something much greater. I want you to know that ever since that day at the launch site when you said I was your fiancé, I've loved you, and that love has kept me going all these years. I knew one day you'd find me, and…" She began to cry harder.

"What is it, Katia? I love you, too." Tears poured down my cheeks, sympathetic to her apparent sorrow.

"I know you love me, and that's why this is so hard. She told me that you're the only one who can lead this entire planet to peace, and that's much more important than me." She ran out of the room crying.

"Katia!" I cried out, "Come back!" I tried to get up only to fall back into the bed. I sobbed. The nurse came in, grabbed the tube flowing into my vein, and injected something into it. "Please… please… have her come back," I begged.

"Shhh. Rest now." I stared at her as my vision quickly diminished.

When I awoke, I sat up and removed all the needles and probes from my body. I needed to find Katia. Standing was a challenge, and I reached for the edge of the bed to hold myself up as I walked out of the room. My walking was more like stumbling, and I reached for the wall to hold myself up.

The nurse ran toward me. "Zack, you should stay in bed. You're still healing."

"I need to find Katia. I'll rip this entire place apart to find her!" I yelled, hearing my voice echo through the halls.

I continued to stumble as the nurse talked to someone through the wall phone. The first door I opened was empty, and the next room was empty, too. I yelled, "Katia!"

Tonya walked down the hall, and I reached for her, yelling, "What did you do with her?" She held me up as I was about to fall.

"She's fine. Trust me, Zack. She's safe."

"Where is she? What have you told her?" My emotions rotated between fear, sorrow, and rage.

"I told her the truth, nothing more." I tried not to cry but was choked up with tears. "Come with me, Zack." An orderly came to help me walk with Tonya to some type of room with a global map on the wall. It wasn't the same map room we were in before the battle but one with better technology and more displays. The orderly sat me down and walked out.

"I had Katia sit right where you are while I told her what you've accomplished. I also told her she was your inspiration to stay alive and fight, as you did, in hopes of rescuing her. Then I showed her this map."

Tonya explained to me where the FOG forces were heaviest and how it was growing. She pointed out where we had ADS support and how they were too inexperienced and too few to attack, so we'd been in a weakened defensive position for a long time.

"We'll eventually be overrun again, and everything we've done so far will have been for naught," she said.

I gazed at the map and saw the color differences between the ADS and FOG. I heard what she said, but I wasn't sure what she meant or why Katia was gone.

"What has this got to do with Katia, and what am I supposed to do? I can't fight everyone on this map."

Tonya walked to me and knelt. She placed her hand on my knee. The similar calming effect her touch had on me in the past worked yet again.

"I don't expect you to fight everyone. I want you to *train* everyone to fight better and increase our chances of success. We need you, Zack. Katia realized this also."

"Where did she go? Please, tell me."

"Don't worry—no one will find her. And when we're done cleaning this planet of the cancerous faction, you'll be reunited with her again. Until then, none of us are safe, and they will keep hunting for Katia to get to you. Besides, I need you to focus, Zack. We're all depending on you."

I looked into her compassionate eyes. Her sincerity was calming, but I didn't know if I could trust her. I'd seen both her cold side and compassionate side. *Which side am I seeing now? How do I know I'm not just being used; how do I know I wasn't being used all along?* I had many mixed emotions running through my mind as I looked at Tonya and thought back to everything we'd been through. Tonya had saved me more than once. I had to trust her.

I sighed and nodded. "When and where do we start?"

Chapter 25

Tonya's plan to train the more-experienced ADS fighters in the art of the empiricist seemed like a good strategy. The only question was how many of them would be willing to let me train them?

The top twenty soldiers were selected. After they completed their lessons, they would then each train another twenty. It might take a couple of months, but eventually, we'd have a force to be proud of.

The first day, I walked out to the yard, not knowing what to expect. Tonya wanted to make me a captain, but I didn't want to be in the military or guard or whatever they called themselves. I wanted to be myself, and I fought for myself and what I believed in. Tonya stood on a veranda where she looked down into the courtyard and parade grounds.

I announced, "You are the top twenty guards out of the thousands at this base. You were handpicked to be the first to train to fight better than you could ever imagine. Who among you believes you're the best?"

All twenty walked forward. I smirked and added, "I plan to blindfold the best and see how well they can defend themselves." All but one stepped back, so I walked up to him. "Are you truly the best, or are you just too slow to step back with the others?" I smiled while squinting to see how confident he really was.

"Sir, I'm the best."

"We'll see about that. Confidence is good, but cockiness, on the other hand, will get you killed." I put the blindfold on him. "How well can you see?" I asked.

"I can't see at all, sir."

"Stop with the 'sir' shit. I'm not in the guard. My name's Zack. Here, take this sword." I threw a wooden sword at him. He reached out but missed, and it landed on the ground. I then swung at him with my own sword, hitting him in the arm.

He winced. "Ow! How can I catch my sword if I can't see it?"

I didn't respond. I wanted him to stumble first.

"Don't let that sword sit there. Pick it up!" I demanded.

"I don't know where it went."

I struck him on the arm.

"Ow! I can't see."

"You need to look with your ears, feel with all your senses—your smell. You need to see with everything but your eyes. Did you hear the sword hit the ground?"

"Yes."

"If that's your only weapon, why would you not try to pick it up?"

He paused for a moment, then knelt to find it. He was in the right vicinity and eventually found it. I looked up to Tonya, who smiled down at me and walked back inside.

"Concentrate! Do you hear me moving on the ground?"

"Yes."

I swung my sword swiftly, making figure eights in the air. "Can you hear the swoosh of my sword?"

"Yes."

"Soon, you'll be able to hear my clothes as I move."

I swung at him, and he blocked it. "Good. Very good. Now, stay with me, and listen for where I walk. Your opponent is most likely to strike when you hear them pause." I swung at him, and he blocked again.

"Excellent. Now stand there as I throw a spear at you. I want you to catch it."

He quickly removed his blindfold and stood in a defensive stance while breathing heavily, anticipating a deadly weapon to be thrown at him.

I laughed. "I was kidding… for now. Here, you throw the spear at me."

I handed him a spear, walked about fifty feet away, and put the blindfold on myself. "Now, throw it at me."

I could hear the sound of his feet shuffle mixed with the other's whispers. He took his stance and stepped into his throw. I heard the release from his hand and the sound as the spear flew through the air.

In one swift movement, I turned, caught the spear, and took off my blindfold. They all looked to me in amazement. "I won't expect that of everyone, but I want you to strive for this. This ability will keep you alive. It will allow us to win."

"What about guns and bullets?" one of the other soldiers asked.

I walked up to him. "A bullet is a projectile, right?" He nodded. "Then a spear is a projectile as well, right?"

He nodded. "But a bullet is faster."

"Then *you* need to be faster. I didn't wait for the spear to hit me before I assessed what was happening. I listened to what you were doing until you threw, then I tuned in to the sound of the spear in the air. You won't outmaneuver a bullet, but you can outmaneuver the soldier pointing the gun. How do you think I took out a hundred men in that tunnel? They all had guns, and I only had a few knives."

They pondered the concept.

"I want you to pair off. Take turns with a blindfold, five minutes each. Educate each other. I'll walk around to give pointers."

They complied, and we spent the rest of the day practicing. Some were quick to grasp the concepts I'd taught them. Others weren't catching on as quickly, but their fighting skills showed improvement.

After a few days, they all grasped the concept of the empiricist. They wanted to be blindfolded for the challenge of it. They did hand to hand combat, fought with knives, and became confident in their skills.

Weeks went by, and the training was going well. Most were learning at a rate comparable to myself, although I'd had the benefit of a stimulant in my arm when I was training. I hadn't seen Tonya the whole time except occasionally when I caught her watching from the veranda, or when she went for walks outside. But I knew she was busy, and I had a task to do as well.

One morning, when everyone gathered, a couple of guys talked about a new bodyguard for General Skyler. I asked, "What's all this about a bodyguard for the general?"

One of the guards replied, "Yeah, General Skyler keeps it secretive, but she's been training someone in her quarters at night. Some of my men were directed to put down padding on her floors for the training. She had wooden targets made and put there as well."

I looked up toward the veranda, wondering why she never said anything to me. I could easily help train a bodyguard. Why keep it a secret?

"Zack, I can't believe you don't know anything about her bodyguard, considering how close you are to the general."

"I'm sure I would have found out soon enough," I said, also pondering why I wasn't aware.

Several days went by before I saw Tonya walking along the wall of the base with Colonel Krueger. I walked up to her and asked, "Hi, Tonya. I mean… General Skyler. Can I have a couple minutes?"

Colonel Krueger smiled. "I'll be at the other wall when you're done." He walked off.

"What's up, Zack? I'm sorry I haven't had a chance to see you much lately."

"I heard you were training some bodyguard?" I tried to make my tone more inquisitive than insulted. What I really wanted to say was, *I should have been one of the first people to know of your new protector.*

"You've been doing a great job training the troops, and I needed someone who I can trust near me. I found someone suitable and am training her as I trained you."

"Her?" I snapped, furrowing my brows and tilting my head inquisitively.

"And what's wrong with a *her*? I happen to be a *her*, too, you know."

"I'm sorry, but I just want to make sure whoever's protecting you is the best we can find." I was groveling.

"She's doing great and learning quickly. I have no doubt she'll be able to help protect me if, and when, needed."

I nodded and accepted what she'd said. Then I changed the subject. "What are you doing along the wall with Colonel Krueger?"

She looked toward where he walked ahead and replied, "We're checking the base's defenses. I can't discuss it any further with you, but it's a very impressive system."

I must have looked insulted, and I think I was a little. Why couldn't she tell me something like that?

She saw my expression and placed her hand on my shoulder, but it didn't make me feel any calmer. Smiling, she said, "Don't worry, Zack. You'll be updated about everything, but this is something I can't tell anyone right now. Please understand."

I smiled back at her and nodded. She walked off to the opposite wall where she met up with Colonel Krueger. *I trust Tonya with my life, but why would she keep secrets from me like this?*

I looked up to the veranda and caught a glimpse of someone backing away from view. *Am I being spied on?* I wondered what was going on.

Several weeks later, I walked outside with an assault rifle strapped to my back. I thought I'd have a little fun with the trainees. They were talking in a group as I approached, and some were practicing moves on each other.

I yelled, "Everyone, line up." They looked to me with raised eyebrows, probably wondering why I was carrying a gun.

"Now, everyone turn your backs to me!" I commanded.

"Uh, sir, what's going on?" one of my students asked as everyone else appeared uneasy.

"Some of you questioned how you'll fight against guns. I'm going to show you."

"Is that thing loaded?" another guard asked.

The sound of bullets firing into the air alarmed everyone. They all turned to face me again, stumbling into each other while backing away.

"I want everyone to turn with their backs facing me!" I commanded again.

They looked up to Tonya, who I saw standing on her veranda. As before, her bodyguard backed away and out of my view before I could get a look at her.

Tonya nodded to everyone, and they reluctantly complied. I nodded back to Tonya, assuring her she could trust me.

I yelled while walking parallel to the lineup of guards. "Aggressively fighting against guns is a risk, one in which hesitation can mean death. You must remove your hesitation, which in turn will reduce your adversary's chances of hitting you… or at least reduce the chances of them hitting you *lethally*."

I shot multiple rounds above their heads. They all turned and ducked, and some fell to the ground.

I walked up to Brad, the man who'd claimed to be the best on day one. I lifted him by his shirt, helping him stand. "I thought you were the best?" I smirked.

"I am, but… but it's a *gun*. It's not actual fighting."

I exclaimed loudly, "It's all fighting, only with different weapons!"

"Everyone else, stand to the side. Brad, I want you to turn your back to me, put your blindfold on, and describe where I am and what I'm doing."

He complied and stood with his back to me while the others watched.

I called out, "Okay, how far away am I? Describe what I'm doing."

"You're directly behind me, approximately fifteen feet. You're gripping your gun and now you're moving to my left… now you stopped."

I fired my remaining rounds above his head. He trembled a little, extended his arms, but he remained still. I released my magazine.

He said, "You fired and released your magazine."

I replied, "Good. How long does it take to replace a magazine under duress?"

"If you're good, perhaps a couple of seconds."

"How long does it take to run fifteen feet or throw a knife?"

He turned around, removed his blindfold, and smirked at me as he understood the lesson. "Probably less than a couple of seconds."

I looked to everyone else and said, "When someone is shooting at you, or a gun is pointed at you from a disadvantaged distance, it's very difficult to run at them without getting hit. You must use all of your senses to your advantage, and don't ever hesitate. Use whatever shield you can, including the dead. Pick up a dead person if you need to, and use them as a shield to attack your foe. Many would never expect you to do that and may freeze, especially if your shield is one of their colleagues."

They all nodded at the revelation.

I continued. "War is ugly. There are no winners or losers, only survivors, and to survive, you need to do anything—and I mean *anything*—it takes to take down your enemy. Sometimes, that means you need to be creative and cold."

They continued to nod.

"Now, I want half of you to go to the armory and get a rifle—no need for bullets—and I want you to run through similar drills as Brad and I just did. I also want to see you run through some blindfolded scenarios to enhance your senses. Simulate either throwing knives or attacking, depending on what the situation calls for. Also, never assume that when someone stops shooting, they're out of ammo. Wait for that magazine to drop."

I watched for the next several days as they continued to improve. We set simulations of how they might assault buildings or vehicles, and we formed strategies to defend the wall. I was quite impressed with the skills they'd developed and was confident they'd do well.

A couple of weeks later, I picked a random day, called for everyone's attention, and asked, "Who's ready for the spear?"

They looked to each other. Brad stepped forward.

"Are you sure you're ready for this?" I asked with a cocky grin.

He looked at me with confidence. "I am."

I picked up a spear from the weapons rack next to the lineup of troops. "Okay, get into position."

He stood where I'd stood on the first day of training. I could see him staring at the shiny metal tip of the spear, which I would soon hurl at his chest. He placed the blindfold on and stood waiting.

I could tell he was concentrating with all of his senses by the way he moved his lips, nose, and head. I walked to the weapons rack and replaced the real spear with a practice one that had a rounded end. He turned to face my direction as I moved about. I walked to the other side of the lineup of guards, approximately twenty feet away. His concentration followed me. I took a step and heaved the spear at his chest.

The applause was overwhelming as Brad stood there holding the spear in his hand a moment later. He'd moved to the side just in time to catch the end of it. I looked up and saw Tonya also clapping, and then she quickly stopped. I could see another set of hands clapping behind her but couldn't make out a face. The others looked up to see Tonya's approval and smiled.

I walked up and patted Brad on his shoulder. "Very good," I complimented.

He looked at the tip. "You didn't use a real spear?"

I slapped my hand on his back again and whispered, "I didn't want to lose a good soldier… just in case."

We laughed and walked back to the other men.

Their skills weren't near where mine were when Tonya had me fight for the first time on Xima, but I had learned a lot while fighting for Xerxes, also. No matter how effective his training tactics had been, I vowed to never be as cruel as that tyrant. My students would be strong *and* respected. It was time for them to begin training the others.

Every few weeks, more and more soldiers were trained. Some didn't grasp the concept as easily as others, but we didn't have time to be selective. As long as most could fight well, we were still bettering our odds.

After I trained some more groups of guards, Tonya finally decided I was ready to know some of the bigger plans the ADS was working on. I got to attend intelligence reports which indicated massive numbers of FOG soldiers organizing for something big, though I couldn't help but sense she was holding something back from me.

With our assault vehicles, we were the biggest threat to FOG's cause, and we knew they'd soon mount an attack. We just didn't know when or how big of an attack it would be. We also didn't know if we had any more FOG spies among us. If they were among our officers, it could spell disaster in a battle.

There were many days and evenings when Tonya was nowhere to be found. When she was available, I'd meet with her to give her a report on the training, and she would update me on FOG's movement but wouldn't bring her bodyguard or even discuss her.

FOG was growing, mostly through coercion. They went through small cities and forced everyone to join their way of thinking or else they were killed on the spot. They were nothing more than terrorists and needed to be eradicated. The sooner we could free the planet of them, the sooner I could be with Katia.

I asked Tonya from time to time if she'd heard from Katia or how she was doing, but Tonya always told me she was well protected and doing fine. She also told me how Katia asked about me, too. I knew I was doing the right thing by choosing saving the world over my relationship with Katia, but when everything was over, I wanted to spend the rest of my life with her and put the fighting aside forever.

Sometimes I thought of that hideaway in the mountains where Tonya took me to train on Xima. The thought of living there with Katia often came to mind. I could hunt for our food, grow a large garden, and we'd always have fresh water. It was the most tranquil place I could think of.

Many months passed, and the last of the five thousand guards at the base were trained, or at least as trained as we were going to get them to be. Tonya, Colonel Mueller, and I discussed strategy based on intel reports, but we didn't bring anyone else into our plans until we were ready. We couldn't afford any hidden FOG members giving away our plans.

Our strategy was sound but would depend on many puzzle pieces falling into place at the right time.

Chapter 26

Tonya called the officers into the war room. We stood around the big map table where many markers were digitally plotted to indicate the locations of FOG groups and the ADS. After the treasonous act at our last meeting, I doubted anyone would have a listening device, but Sergeant Baylor and I kept an eye out for those who looked suspicious.

Tonya walked up to the head of the map table. "We've gone through a lot of suffering over the years, and I can't emphasize enough how proud I've been of what we've accomplished over the past few months.

"Now is our chance to win this effort once and for all. You've all spent a lot of time training with Zack. We have the troops and the motivation and skill to take back America, and then the rest of the planet."

I didn't see anyone move. They all looked at Tonya intently, but I saw some eyes follow me as I walked around the room. It was possible that they were purely distracted by my movement, but my goal was to find eyes that might have a hint of mistrust, a hint of a potential spy.

Tonya continued. "There are many remaining assault vehicles in the warehouse at the outpost. My plan is to have forty-five hundred troops go down there and take those vehicles to the south, then sweep across the country to the east."

There wasn't one eyebrow that wasn't raised. They all looked to each other, then down to the map table. It became obvious there was concern among everyone.

One major cleared his throat and asked, "General, with all due respect, this plan will leave only a few hundred troops to defend you and the headquarters."

They all looked to each other with extreme concern—all, that is, but one. One captain just stared at the board, studying it intently and not seeming concerned. I tried not to look at him too much to give him any suspicion.

Colonel Mueller spoke up. "General, if another FOG group like the last one attacks, there's no way you'll be able to defend yourself. No offense, Zack."

I smiled. "None taken."

Tonya and I discussed our strategy at great length and knew it was a risk, but it was a risk worth taking.

"This *is* the plan we will follow. Do you understand, Colonel? Is there anyone else who questions my plan or my authority?"

No one spoke up. Almost all had a look of concern... except for Captain Wade.

"Excellent. Captain Wade, I'd like you to remain with me and lead our defensive forces," Tonya directed.

"Yes, ma'am," he eagerly replied.

She continued, "For the rest of you, have your troops prepared, suited up, and ready to leave in three days for the outpost. They'll travel south immediately to take the city of San Diego first. Get some rest. Dismissed."

As everyone cleared the room, Tonya said, "Colonel Mueller, I'd like you to stay. Sergeant Baylor, could you please go into the hallway and ensure no one comes near that door?"

"Yes, ma'am," Baylor replied and closed the door behind him when he was last to leave.

"General Skyler, this plan has failure written all over it. I must insist—"

"Of course, it does," she said.

Tonya's eyes met mine. "The captain?" I queried.

She nodded. "Yes, I saw, too. That's why I chose him to lead our defense."

"Saw what?" Colonel Mueller asked with his eyes squinted as he shook his head. "What's going on?"

Tonya explained, "We still have FOG spies among us, including our officers. We believe Captain Wade is a Fog spy."

"Then let's arrest him and find out!"

"We don't want to just yet," I replied.

Colonel Mueller's eyes furrowed. His lips pursed in a way that showed he was livid. "Then, with this plan, they'll be free to coordinate an assault on this base while the majority of us are running south." He pondered for a moment. "But we won't be traveling south, will we?" His eyes opened wide in revelation.

Tonya and I both smiled at him. Tonya said, "You'll take those troops down to the outpost and bring all of the vehicles back here, then split them between the tunnel and the road. Stand off a little bit to avoid being detected. I'll have the captain and his men remain to guard the base. When they do come to attack, you can come out in a surprise assault, and we'll annihilate them."

Colonel Mueller nodded and rubbed his chin. "Why wait three days?" he asked.

Tonya replied, "I estimate that if the captain, or one of the other officers, is a spy, they'll get the plan out to FOG leadership quickly so they can come up with a strategy. It will take five days for FOG to consolidate their remaining forces to attack us. That will give you two days to get the vehicles at the outpost and get your asses back here."

"General Clayton was correct; you are the right person for the job." Mueller nodded and smiled.

"Not one of your officers can be told of this strategy until you get to those vehicles. If anyone hesitates to follow your orders, you are authorized to shoot them on the spot. Good luck, Colonel, and hurry back."

He smiled and walked off.

Then Tonya turned to me. "We can't tip off Wade that we know what he's up to, but once FOG does come, I want you to take him out so he doesn't do any further damage."

I nodded and walked off. As I opened the door, I looked back at her and smirked. "I love how your mind works."

Her eyes and smile showed her gratitude. I immediately reminisced on hundreds of images of her eyes and smile that had been burned into my brain.

"I couldn't do this without you, Zack," she said with her nurturing tone.

Chapter 27

When Tonya asked Captain Wade to lead the defensive forces at the headquarters, I could tell he was way too eager to accept. It wasn't so much a look of pride on his face when he agreed but rather an expression more like he'd just won the lottery.

After the meeting, he went through the motions to set up a defensive perimeter at the base, which was no small task, as the base was quite large. He established guard posts where needed, created gun emplacements at ideal locations, and had a good overall strategy. I was beginning to think I may have been mistaken about Wade. I walked around the perimeter to evaluate all the defensive positions, and it appeared Wade had done a great job.

The evening prior to the troop move, Tonya called me into the war room. She lit up her map board on the table and showed me the intel she'd gotten which confirmed FOG did get word of our plans and were consolidating two forces.

One force was staging to the north, and one to the east. There shouldn't have been too many to the south as most of them were killed at the outpost battle. I stood there in awe as I saw the satellite footage and intel reports confirm what looked like the largest gathering of FOG forces we could have expected. It appeared we would be considerably outnumbered.

"What are your thoughts?" Tonya asked while staring at satellite footage as more and more vehicles gathered by the minute in FOG camps.

"My thoughts?" I shook my head with pause, then said, "I think if Mueller doesn't make it back in time with those weapons, we'll lose in a matter of minutes."

"Then let's hope he gets back here with the weapons in time." There was almost a hidden sense of confidence about her. I would have been nervous as hell with what was coming at us. Even with the vehicles and weapons at the outpost, we appeared outnumbered perhaps five to one. If they had any type of advanced weapons, it would be difficult to defend against them.

She asked, "What are your thoughts on Wade?"

I grimaced, then tilted my head and winced. "I have mixed opinions of him."

"Really? How so?"

I thought for a moment. "He initially appeared almost too eager to defend our base, and my intuition told me he was FOG, but he set up a fantastic defensive posture to protect the base. I don't completely trust him, but, for now, he appears to be doing a good job."

Tonya nodded. "That's a relief, but I still don't trust him. Something about him makes me feel uneasy. I'd encourage you to continue keeping an eye on him."

I nodded. "I will, but if we could have another dozen plasma tanks, I'd feel a lot better."

She laughed. "I'll see what I can do."

The morning of the deployment arrived. I stood in the shadows, watching the troops—who were armed with guns, knives, and armored vests—stand at their defensive positions and walk through the compound.

They began marching to the tunnel where they would take the conveyor to the warehouse. The conveyor would start out slow to allow many troops to get on two by two. They would then step to progressively faster belts, which would run at almost twenty miles per hour. Even at that speed, it would take them several hours to get to their destination, then more than five hours to return.

Even though it was a fast means to get so many troops secretly to the outpost, it wouldn't be an easy task to stand there for hours and not get fatigued. I wondered how the personnel would slow down enough at the end, as stepping off a conveyor at twenty miles per hour seemed like it would be a mess. Colonel Krueger explained to me that there were three parallel conveyors toward the end that were slower, and the personnel would alternate getting on as they approached the end.

Colonel Mueller was the last to go into the tunnel. He looked back to Tonya, saluted her, and then nodded to me with a smile before he walked into the darkness.

I spent the rest of the day walking the perimeter ensuring everything was in place and all guards were at their stations. I walked to some of the areas that Tonya had inspected not too long ago but couldn't find anything out of the ordinary. Tall brick walls and brick buildings in front of them. The base was large but heavily fortified. I smiled at the one small patch of grass in front of the headquarters—everything else was brown or gray.

I talked to some of the guards to gauge their morale and confidence in our ability to defend the base. They all seemed to be in high spirits, but then again, they didn't know how many FOG members were coming to fight us. As far as I could tell, everything appeared to be well organized.

We even had that plasma tank in the corner of the courtyard, but I soon found out that no one knew how to use it. It dawned on me that we needed to have every available weapon at our disposal, just in case.

So I went into the vehicle to see how to operate such an advanced piece of firepower. The acidic smell of old blood stung my nose when I opened the hatch, as it had never been cleaned. I looked into a small metal door between the weapons and driver seats where I found an operating manual. I figured I had a little time to study up on how the thing operated, just like I'd done on the shuttle to Earth.

I took the book to my room and studied it thoroughly. It didn't seem that complicated, but I concluded that one person couldn't run the whole thing. I concentrated on what was needed to fire the weapon. It had an advanced fuel cell in it, which powered a small engine. The engine's sole purpose was to keep the vast battery system charged to operate the vehicle.

I soon realized that the majority of the tank was made of battery cells surrounded by armor plating. I began to read about how the plasma beam was created when plasma gas was shaped into a compact toroid. I tried to read what that meant and couldn't comprehend it very well. All I could understand was that it spun at a high rate of speed, and then it was fired out of the barrel also at a high rate of speed and at a temperature so extreme that it disintegrated anything in the main beam, and anything nearby was damaged or burned. *This must be what happens during the time the sound increases before it fires,* I thought.

I read further that the electromagnetic pulse effect could penetrate another plasma tank, but only at point-blank range. *I hope to never get near enough to another one of these things to test this part of its capability.*

I studied further to learn how I could operate the tank on my own. I'd need to start the engine first from the driver's seat to get the generator operative, then move to the weapon's seat, where I'd build up the plasma energy, aim the cannon through a sight window, and push the Fire button to release the blast. It seemed simple enough.

There was a knock at my door. "Zack, it's Sergeant Baylor. General Skyler would like to see you immediately."

I set the manual down and followed Baylor to the war room.

"Zack, it looks like my estimates were off. FOG forces mobilized quicker than I'd expected and began their move toward us already."

I looked down at the satellite map, then at the images she had. There were two large groups approximately three hundred miles away in various vehicles heading right for us. "How long before they arrive?" I asked while staring intently at the vast number of moving red dots on the screen.

She stared down at the map. "I'm afraid it'll be way before Colonel Mueller is able to return."

"We may be wrong about Captain Wade. He has an exceptionally good defense set up—gun emplacements are established, and the men are in place. I couldn't have done it better myself," I told her. She paused for a moment, staring down at the board.

"I hope you're right. I'd hate to use the…" She stopped and I looked at her with my head tilted, waiting for her to finish.

She said with a sigh, "They should be here in about five hours. The soonest Mueller will be back is perhaps eight hours. We need to hold them off at all costs."

She'd never held anything back from me before. I asked, "Was there something else you wanted to say a moment ago?"

She pondered for a moment and smiled at me. "No, it's okay. We need to do everything possible to hold them off until Mueller returns."

I walked to the door, then stopped to look back at her. I was expecting a more concerned expression on her face, but she simply smiled and said, "I need you, Zack."

I smiled at her and left the room. The walls surrounding the base seemed well defended, and the perimeter outside the base was marked with distance references. I talked with the guards, who all appeared to be in great spirits.

The ammo boxes were in position, and the guns were loaded and ready to fire. I periodically watched Captain Wade, who engaged and actively ensured everything was ready. My confidence in him was slowly increasing, and I was thankful my intuitions were wrong about him.

As I walked back down to the tank, I looked inside to see if I remembered what the manual said about operating it.

I sat down in the driver's seat, flipped the power switches, then the Start button. I clapped my hands together in celebration as it started right up with a soft humming noise of the engine.

There was a periscope to look through with something similar to binoculars hanging down near my head. I could see in front of the vehicle and a little bit to the sides. I took hold of two levers and pushed forward. The large machine lurched ahead, nearly throwing me out of the seat, and I realized why there was a five-piece harness for me to wear. I stopped it with the levers back to center. I needed to push the levers slower next time. I eased the levers in opposite directions, and it turned a little one way, then the other.

I kept it running and climbed up to the weapon's seat. There was a Charge button, and when I pressed it I saw the bank of lights go from red, to yellow, and then to green. I looked out the sight window and gripped the large joystick. I turned the turret left and then right. The trigger had a safety guard on it, which I would flip up to access the trigger if I wanted to shoot.

I looked up and saw the electronic defense measure (EDM) switch. I switched that to On and saw another bank of lights rapidly go from red to green. I smiled, realizing how dummy-proof the thing was to operate, but I remembered that, as one person, I'd be limited to either drive or operate the gun—I couldn't do both. The bonus was that the tank was nearly invincible, except from me, of course. I smiled at my cockiness and almost appreciated my father for the risk he'd taken to put that device in my arm.

I turned the turret toward the main gate. I figure if I'd ever needed it, that was the direction I'd want it aimed. After I'd figured most of the features out, I powered it down and climbed out.

Captain Wade was speaking to some guards in the courtyard as I walked through the center of the grounds. I approached him and was enthusiastic by the way he smiled and seemed to be in good spirits. "It looks like everything is set up well, Captain," I said, standing next to him and scanning the walls.

He smiled. "Thanks, Zack. I'm sure we can hold back anything that comes our way." I couldn't help but feel like I'd judged him unfairly.

I walked up to the war room, where Tonya looked at the latest intelligence reports. "They're almost here. I estimate another hour," Tonya said with a little more concern in her voice.

"What's the status of Colonel Mueller?" I asked.

"He checked in and is on his way, but he's still about three hours away. If our defenses don't hold, then he'll be headed into a trap."

"I've walked the perimeter," I told her. Everything looks good. The guards have extra ammo, and the gate's locked."

"I hope you're right, but my instincts tell me there's something odd with Wade," she said.

"I'll keep my eyes on him and oversee the rest of the defenses."

When I walked back to the courtyard, it was nearly sunset, and there was no sign of FOG forces yet. We were at a disadvantage with the darkness behind them as we wouldn't see them coming until they were nearly on top of us. The floodlights that shone into the distance only reached so far.

I walked up onto a wall and watched the sun set on the horizon. It was a majestic orange glow mixing with the pink and orange horizon of the desert. I could actually see the sun sinking and couldn't help but think that it might be my last time to see such a magnificent sight.

I thought of Katia. I understood the bigger picture Tonya had painted, but why did she have to take Katia away, and where was she? I wished I knew whether she was safe. *What I wouldn't do to kiss her one more time before this battle.*

I returned to the guards and told them to keep their eyes open and that FOG should arrive in less than an hour. I could see by their eyes and posture that they were a little more nervous than earlier. I talked to as many as I could, reassuring them as I walked around to check one more time if everything was prepared.

I walked down to the main gate, which consisted of two large steel doors secured by four large steel rods that expanded into slots along the massive walls and between the two doors, locking them together. It was nearly the same as you'd see on a safe or a bank vault door.

The large pins were bright, shiny, and locked into place. Something seemed a little off, though. The lever arm connecting the rods was supposed to be completely horizontal when it was locked, but it appeared to be at an angle. I was no expert with locks and doors, but it looked different than what I'd noticed in the past.

Captain Wade approached. "I think we're ready for them," he said.

"Is the gate locked? I thought that lever arm was supposed to be horizontal when it's locked."

He looked at it quickly, then looked at me. "I never noticed it in any other position before. It looks locked to me," he replied.

I looked at it again and then looked at him. He seemed confident, and the pins did look like they were set into the wall slots.

I smiled at him and walked off to check the armory. We had about thirty minutes before the enemy would be at our door, and I wanted to know as many details of our inventory as possible.

I entered and saw that one green wall, which was supposed to shelve ammunition, was empty. *Distributed to the troops, no doubt.* I looked at the other shelves and saw more boxes of ammo—enough to last a long time. I was a little more relieved to know lack of ammo wasn't going to be a factor in the upcoming battle. I would have felt more comfortable if Mueller returned sooner.

As I walked out of the armory, I spotted something shiny on the floor and stopped. I picked up what looked like a bullet near the door, but it looked strange. The tip of the casing was crimped where there would have been a bullet, and it had a wide green stripe around it. I wasn't too savvy with guns, but the bullet didn't seem right. I went to open another box of ammo, pulled out a magazine, and saw a cartridge with an actual bullet in it. *Why was this one lying here crimped like this?*

I walked out to the gate to find Captain Wade pacing.

I asked, "I found this on the floor in the armory. It looks like a bullet, but I've never seen one like this before."

He had a surprised look and hastily snatched it from my fingers. "It's a practice blank for exercising. It probably fell out of a box one day." He looked at me. "You should probably protect the general. You and her female bodyguard are her last means of defense."

I smiled. "If we get to that point, I don't think two of us alone will be able to save her."

His eyes furrowed as though I was annoying him.

I asked, "I would think you'd want to be up on the wall to coordinate the defense. Wouldn't that be a better vantage point considering they'll be here shortly?"

"I'll be up there soon enough. I'm… just running through my checklist in my head to make sure I got everything. I'll be up there shortly."

He didn't stand as confidently as he once had, and he appeared to be sweating more. I asked, "Are you okay, Captain Wade?"

"Of course I am! It's… it's just a lot of responsibility, and I want to make sure I get it right."

I nodded and glanced at the lock on the gate again, squinting while trying to remember how it had looked in the past.

I walked up onto the wall to one of the guard posts. The two guards stared and pointed their guns north. I squinted but could barely see what looked like a dust storm in the distance.

"They're here! Prepare yourselves!" I yelled.

I looked down to see that Wade hadn't left the main gate. I noticed no one else but Wade was near there. I paused for a moment and considered the bullet I found in the armory, and my inner voice told me to open an ammo can. I reached down to pick up one of the rifle magazines and immediately felt like my heart was about to burst out of my chest. My eyes lit up, and I froze for a half-second, remembering the green wall in the armory. All of the bullets in the magazine were crimped with a green stripe. I stared in horror at the points of defense around the wall, then at the approaching dust cloud.

"Soldier, let me see the magazine in your gun!" I demanded.

The man closest to me pulled it out, and the top bullet was crimped with a green stripe. I called another guard, "Let me see your magazine!" It, too, was a blank round.

My heart raced as I looked down at Wade, then out to the dust cloud coming quickly toward us. I quietly demanded from the guards, "Who assigned you this ammo?"

"Um, it was Captain Wade, sir."

"And you didn't check the bullets before you put the magazine in the gun?" I yelled.

"He handed out the guns with the magazines in them already and said we were locked and loaded," one of them replied.

I looked to the other side of the gate, down below where the controls were, but no one was there. The closest person was Captain Wade.

I looked again at the dust cloud, which was perhaps ten miles away. They'd be at our gate in minutes. "Soldier, I need you to run down to the yard, grab every guard you can, run to the armory, and take real ammo to all of the guard posts! Immediately!"

I ran down to the gate where Captain Wade spotted a guard I'd tasked running to others in the yard. He yelled, "Soldiers, where are you going? Get back to your posts!"

"We were directed to get ammo, sir!"

"Get back to your post! That's an order," Wade bellowed.

The guards stopped and looked at me.

"Captain, you almost had us," I said while staring into his eyes.

He looked at me, and I saw his eyes turn from those of a bellowing commander to a scared, caught rat. Before he could pull his sidearm out of his holster, I had my knife through his chin and up into his skull. As I held him there while his feet twitched, I yelled to the soldiers, "Go get the real ammo and distribute it. Quickly!"

They took off running to the armory as I let Wade's lifeless body fall to the ground. I looked up to see Tonya watching from her veranda—I felt like I'd let her down. Then I looked toward the gate and realized Wade must have sabotaged it somehow.

I yelled, "Does anyone know how to operate the gate?"

A guard ran up to the control panel. "Sir, the key is missing."

I heard one of the guards on the wall cry out, "They're not stopping! A ramming truck is heading for the gate!"

His plan all along was to give the appearance of defending the base when he was actually leaving it undefended so FOG could easily come in and annihilate everyone. He'd accomplished the feat masterfully. I couldn't help but feel like I'd nearly left the base completely defenseless.

I heard the sound of the vehicles approaching. They began firing at the guards on the wall. New ammo was being run up to the walls, but, for now, they couldn't do anything but duck and avoid getting hit. We searched Wade and found the key in his pocket. The guard went to the panel with the key when we heard someone yell out, "They're going to ram the gate!" The sound of a loud engine was quickly getting closer.

"Hurry!" I yelled. The guard nervously put the key in and turned it. The light panel illuminated, and he pushed the Close button. I could see the lever arm turn horizontally when we were startled by the crash at the gate. The rods just took hold into their slots, but the gate looked warped. He tried to extend the pins further, but they wouldn't move. An alert light illuminated the control panel.

He said, "The pins are jammed. Should I open and close them?"

"No, leave them. Good job. Now, get some live ammo and get back to your post."

I could hear the vehicle's engine that had rammed the gate. It was large, from the sound of it. I ran up the nearest stairwell to peer over the wall and saw a truck with a reinforced front end. It was designed to ram through gates, and if it wasn't for our timing, it would have broken right through with ease.

It lurched backward and raced for the gate again. One of the rods gave way from a slot as it slammed into the gate a second time. The door wasn't going to last, but hopefully, it would last long enough for the ammo to get distributed.

Then it came to me: *Rockets!*

"Get a rocket launcher up here!" I yelled.

Several soldiers went to the armory and returned. "The rocket launchers are missing!"

Damn. Wade was far better than we'd thought. He had everything completely set up and had me fooled. I may not have had a lot of military experience, but I was quite proud of my intuition, so I wanted to kick myself for letting Wade trick me like he did.

The guards at the gate finally got live ammo and began firing at the approaching vehicles. The trucks pulled back as they were hit.

I watched the ramming truck run at the gate again, and two more rods broke away. The gate wouldn't last more than another hit or two, then it would be completely exposed for them to enter. *Unless…* I looked at the tank in the yard.

I ran down to the soldiers, who waited to replace a fallen guard position as needed or fight if FOG broke through. I directed them to split up and stand on either side as I was going to bring the tank closer. *Hopefully I have enough time.*

When I reached the tank, I climbed up on top and descended to the driver's seat. I went through the setup steps and pressed the Start button.

"Yes!" I yelled as it roared to life. I heard the faint slam of the truck into the gate again. Being inside the tank reduced a lot of outside sounds, but that metal-on-metal clang was very distinct. I looked through the binoculars and could see the gate was barely holding itself together. One more hit and FOG was going to break through. I climbed up to the weapon's seat and powered everything up. I saw the light indicator was at yellow, nearly to green. *Come on, come on.* I had the trigger guard up and my finger on the trigger, the barrel aimed right at the gate.

Just as the gate burst open, the green light illuminated, and I shot a blast.

The truck exploded brilliantly, then secondary explosions erupted from its back. The entire courtyard lit up. I could see the guards on the wall shooting down at FOG forces, who were no doubt trying to advance, but their large ramming truck blocked the entrance. *That should hold them back for a little while.*

I climbed back down into the driver's seat and pushed the levers forward. The tank jolted, and I slowly moved it toward the main entrance. Through the binoculars, I saw the glow of rockets coming my way. I closed my eyes and heard explosions on either side of me. *I'm still intact.* Then I remembered the missile deflection system in the defense suite.

I got back into the weapon's seat and noticed the weapon power indicator was almost green again. I peered through the sight window and squinted, trying to see through all the smoke outside, but I couldn't see much.

Moments later, two more glowing objects lit up and came racing for me from outside of the base. Their source had to be directly in front of me. I fired blindly into the dark and saw an object explode in the distance.

I opened the hatch, stood, and peeked out of the top to see that the missiles had damaged parts of our buildings. The ADS troops remained on either side of me. There was a pause, and then I thought of Katia. If I didn't survive, I would never see her again, never kiss her again. *Damn it, all I wanted was to be with her and live happily!*

I didn't know how much time had elapsed, but I hoped Colonel Mueller and the rest of the reinforcements would arrive soon.

A bright explosion caught my attention as I stood and looked out of the top of the turret. One of the guard towers on the wall blew up. It was made of cement, and it just disintegrated into falling bricks and mortar. Only another plasma tank could have done something like that, but there were only two made, and I was sitting in one of them. I glanced at the indicator panel and saw the light was yellow. *Come on! I need it green, and I need it fast!*

Finally, my indicators were green, but I wanted to make sure I had a target to shoot at first. I watched the men on the wall look around for a place to hide or an order to tell them to run. They were nervous, and who could blame them? Something with that much firepower would kill them instantly.

Another bright flash illuminated another guard tower on the other side of the gate, and it blew up the same way, raining rock into the compound as though a small volcano had erupted.

There were only two more towers, then we'd lose our advantage of being on the wall. I didn't know how well a plasma tank could stand up to another. I'd read about it in the manual, but getting that close to their plasma tank wasn't something I wanted to do.

I quickly stood and yelled up at the two remaining towers, "Get down from there!"

The men picked up their ammo cases and guns and scurried down the stairs. As one tower vacated, it, too, was blown up. Luckily, the men were safe.

"I want half of you men by the building to take up position in the windows." I looked to my other side and said, "You men, find someplace to shield yourselves and the others behind me!"

We waited, as there was no activity from our attackers. I suspected the FOG leadership was rethinking their strategy once they realized getting into the base wasn't as easy as they had hoped. Their hesitation would work well for us, as Mueller would arrive shortly. At least, he'd better.

The fire of the truck at the gate subsided, and I could see activity behind it in the dark. It looked like trucks were moving to the other side of the wall. Without our guns on the wall to protect us, we were like sitting ducks.

I considered pushing the ramming truck through the gate and sitting there myself, but if I were to get stuck from the debris, the entire base would fall. I couldn't take the risk. I remained perhaps a hundred feet back and kept a defensive posture until Mueller returned.

Through the remaining small flames in the gate came a line of FOG soldiers into the compound.

"Fire!" I yelled as bullets rained down on them from all directions. I fired as well and watched several FOG soldiers in the beam's path light up to their death.

I could see tracer rounds from every angle within the compound as more and more troops tried to get through. Soon there was a pile of bodies blocking the entrance, and then everything stopped. I had an uneasy feeling about the silence, and I could make out a faint sound of an engine outside the gate.

A large blast at the entrance caused what was left of the burning truck to be hurled forward. *Only another plasma tank can do that.* I looked up to see Tonya standing at the veranda with another person next to her, but she moved back suddenly. Her bodyguard, no doubt.

Tonya didn't need to say anything. I knew what was at stake, and I wouldn't let her down. We finally had our chance to eradicate the rest of FOG on the entire East Coast as they came to attack us. Winning the battle would be a huge victory for civility to prosper again.

When my energy level was green, I searched through the smoke for the other plasma tank. Minutes ticked by, and I realized the other tank must have been charging up as well. I needed to get it right after it fired.

Another blast blew the burned ram truck farther into the compound, and an armored vehicle came racing through the wreckage. *Where the hell did they get those? From other bases?*

I lowered myself back into the tank and closed the hatch. *One armored vehicle in my sights and… fire!*

The truck blew up, and the troops poured out the back which was on fire. They ran for their lives.

The other trucks unloaded troops, but our men took them down. I watched as some made their way into the headquarters building… *Tonya!*

I couldn't risk checking on her just yet. I had to focus on securing our win. She seemed to have her bodyguard with her, and her quarters were reinforced.

I turned the turret to the entrance, waiting for another vehicle. A flash burst at me from the darkness. My tank shook, but nothing happened. *What the hell was that? Was it the other tank? Am I defended against it?* I looked at the indicator lights, and everything appeared normal. The gentle hum of the engine told me it still ran.

I remained still, hoping they thought the hit upon me had been successful. More FOG poured in on foot, and the firepower that rained down on them from all angles was intense. Some of the invaders managed to run into the headquarters building, but my focus was on the gate. And my energy level was green again.

The sound of small-arms fire pinged the outside of my hull. A couple more trucks drove through the carnage and into the compound, letting more troops disembark. Some headed toward the armory, but the men had that well defended, and others ran into the headquarters. I fired again, causing one vehicle to explode and many FOG soldiers to flee, screaming and covered in flames.

Those who got through the gate immediately ran into the closest building. I watched through the sight window, glancing at my energy indicator as it turned yellow.

Two glowing rockets came toward me but veered away and exploded nearby. Then it dawned on me that they were testing to see if my tank was still online. Another flash blasted at me, and the tank shook more violently. I looked out the window and could see another plasma tank outside of the base entrance. *It couldn't be the other tank that I'd dealt with outside of the outpost. Where the hell is Mueller?*

A quick surge ran through my veins as I suspected Colonel Mueller may have been the one assaulting us, but he couldn't have come from the northeast.

First Wade and then Mueller. So many thoughts of treason raced through my mind, but the primary thought I needed to focus on was disabling the enemy's tank.

There was a roaring sound of engines behind me, but I could only see what was in front of me through my sight window. I didn't know what to expect next, but then I saw large caliber firepower directed at the trucks entering the compound. *Did the cavalry arrive?*

I saw their plasma tank on the other side of the wall. It was a stare down. I knew how to disable the other tank, but I wasn't going to make the first move or get any closer. Hell, I couldn't make any move from the weapon's seat, anyway.

I dropped into the driver's seat, where there was much more room to move. I reached up and could just touch the trigger on the control stick for the gun, but I couldn't tell where it was aimed. Then I realized if the cannon pointed to the front and was up against the other tank, I wouldn't need to aim.

Slowly pushing the handles forward, I crept closer to the gate. Once the enemy fired on me again, I would push the levers forward and race toward it. I looked into the binoculars and waited for another shot. My visibility was limited to only the tank as the sound of gunfire all around me increased, but I knew I was protected. The high-pitched plinking noises peppering the hull wouldn't break my concentration on my target.

A bright flash lit up my view, and my tank rocked violently. I was temporarily blinded from the flash. When I looked up, I saw the green lights still glowed on the weapons panel. I jammed the levers fully forward and raced toward the other tank before it could recharge.

As I got closer, the other tank began to back away. I couldn't drive and shoot at the same time, so I rammed into its hull and quickly reached up to push the trigger. I brushed it with my fingertips, and there was a loud explosion that shook my tank. After banging my head against the metal panel behind me, I saw the weapon display lights flashing like a Christmas tree, indicating there was a malfunction. The EMP must have damaged my system, too.

I tried to look out of the binoculars, but nothing was visible. I climbed up to the weapons seat, looked out the sight window, and saw the other tank on fire. Men ran out of the back. I peered out the hatch and saw lines of what appeared to be hundreds of trucks. If loaded with troops, there must have been thousands of FOG fighters out there ready to assault our base.

Bullets ricocheted off the tank all around me, and I knew I was trapped. The defense system seemed to be green, so I tried to turn the turret, but it wouldn't budge. I was immobile, but so was the other tank.

The pinging sound of bullets hitting the hull were intimidating, but I figured I'd let them waste their ammo. I shut the top hatch and worked my way through the tank to where I slowly opened the back hatch slightly to get a glimpse back into the compound. I saw many more vehicles coming out of the tunnel—Colonel Mueller had made it. *Now we have a fair fight! Well, at least we can defend ourselves.*

I assessed what we were up against and realized if we came out of the compound through that gate, we'd be torn apart. We needed more firepower out on the grounds. Maybe I could troubleshoot my tank. *Damn, I left the tank manual in my quarters.*

The sound of gunfire began to erupt from the south. *Great, now we're surrounded.*

I tried to look out of the sight window and could see tracer fire coming from the south, but it was toward FOG forces. The reinforcements from the outpost were driving full speed toward the lineup of FOG vehicles, and the gunfire was no longer plinking the side of my tank but instead directed at the ADS troops heading toward them in armored vehicles topped with nice big gun turrets.

I heard a noise behind me and saw our vehicles leaving the compound to join the attack. We had them in a pincer movement maneuver, and I cheered them on from my limited viewpoint when I heard a vehicle pull up behind the tank.

"Zack, are you in there?"

It was Mueller's voice. *Man, am I glad I was wrong about him being a backstabbing FOG spy!*

"Hell yes, I am! You made it just in time!" I cheered.

I pushed the button to further open the rear hatch, but it wasn't working. I peeked out of the upper hatch and saw the two armies engaged. *They won't see me.* I quickly jumped up and leaped to the ground near Mueller's vehicle. The door was open, and I climbed inside.

Mueller said, "They need your skills inside. Many FOG troops are in the headquarters building trying to get the general. She has her bodyguard in there, but they won't be able to hold off for long."

She has her bodyguard, but I don't know if she has anyone with my skills. I can't imagine anyone else protecting her. Hell, they'd just get in her way, I thought to myself.

We drove into the compound as the ADS guards were being shot at near the entrance of the headquarters. We got out, and I assessed what was going on. There were many bodies scattered everywhere, and vehicles were burning all around the grounds. I looked over the headquarters building and realized it was built to resist getting attacked from the outside, but it might only be a matter of time before they got to Tonya from the inside.

Tonya's quarters were on the third floor, and the war room was on the second floor. I didn't know where she was hiding but thought the war room was the most secure location. I looked up at her veranda, where I'd last seen her, when Mueller walked up to me.

"Any ideas on how to get up there?" I asked.

"I just might. Come with me." I followed him as he ran toward a wall under the veranda and a few feet to the right. We reached an air conditioning system. "Let me get some men to help move this," he said while looking around to call on a couple of soldiers running by.

"I got it." I moved between the metal box and the wall and pushed my feet against the box. It broke loose easily, exposing a hole in the wall. I stood and asked, "What's this?"

"This vent goes up the side of the building and all the way to General Skyler's room."

I slapped Mueller on the back and smiled at him.

"Be careful," he said, smiling back. "It's not an easy climb in there. I'll keep trying to push into the building from down here."

I crawled inside, placed my back against one side with my feet against the other, put pressure against the walls, and wiggled my way up the shaft.

When I reached the second floor, I was alongside a vent grate where I could hear people talking. From the sounds of it, they were trying to get into the war room, but it was locked down. I continued my ascent, and my legs burned from the strain of keeping from falling. There was nothing to grab onto if I were to slip. I slowly reached the third floor and peeked out of the grate.

I'd never been to Tonya's quarters, so I wasn't sure what I was looking at. It was a large room that seemed to have tables, and there was a bed in the distance. I didn't see anyone in the room or any signs of movement. Taking out my knife, I pried at the edges of the vent cover to remove it from the wall.

Shadows passed, and I froze in place. Then I heard someone say, "I feel like we should do something instead of just waiting in here."

It's Katia's voice! I slipped a little in my surprise but secured my position so as not to fall.

"Katia. Tonya," I whispered through the vent cover.

"Zack? Where are you?" Katia asked.

"I think he's in here," Tonya said. I saw them walk up to the vent cover. It came off the wall, and they helped me into the room.

"Katia? What…?" I stared at her, utterly speechless. I couldn't figure out what I wanted to say. She stood in front of me with full body armor, knives in her belt, and a sidearm on her leg. She looked entirely different from the woman I remembered, but her black curly hair and smile still melted me.

"Zack, you came for us again!" She reached up to give me a hug.

I hugged Katia and turned to Tonya, raising my hands in confusion.

"What's the status down there?" she asked.

Tonya broke me out of my confusion over Katia being in front of me, armed and ready to fight. "Um… status, right. Mueller's forces are here and engaged with FOG outside the compound. We have a solid defense inside the walls, but there's a large FOG group inside this building."

"Yes, I know. They tried rushing in here soon after the gate gave way. We couldn't get to the war room in time, but we need to get there now—quickly."

"That's what I've been trying to say. Let's go get them then!" Katia exclaimed.

I looked back to Katia. "What's all this? Who *are* you?" I lightly laughed in surprise.

"Tonya told me what your destiny was, and I realized I'd rather die with you than live without you. I asked Tonya to train me, and every day since, she's been instructing me to be an empiricist."

I looked to Tonya with wide eyes. "What could you have taught her to prepare her for this in only a few months?"

"As much as I could. She was quite determined, and she's also a very quick study."

I looked to Katia again. She put her hands on her hips, tilting her head with attitude.

"Besides," Tonya added, "at this point, it doesn't matter. We need to get to that war room."

I considered trying to sneak back down the shaft, but trying to brace myself in there from that hole wouldn't be easy. I asked, "How many do you estimate are outside your door?"

Katia walked to the door. "Why don't we find out?"

I didn't know whether to admire her recklessness or tie her up so she couldn't get hurt. She quickly opened the door, and I had to catch up with her.

I looked down the hall to see perhaps a dozen FOG soldiers who didn't seem to expect the door to open. They quickly gained their bearings, grabbed their guns, and as they were pointed at us, Katia locked the door. Many shots were fired and pinged off the steel.

"What the hell were you thinking?" I asked.

"You wanted to know how many were out there, and the best way is to catch them off guard while standing in the hall waiting for an order. The answer to your question is eight," Katia said.

I couldn't help but stare at her. I knew what she'd said was true, but I wasn't able to accept it. I was still confused at her even being there.

Katia put her ear to the door. "Someone who sounds important wanted to know what was going on. They told the soldiers what happened, and he ordered them to take us alive."

Tonya walked up to us and grinned. "Looks like the advantage is ours, then."

"Ready?" Katia asked.

"For what?" I looked at her with my eyebrows raised. When I'd worked with Tonya, I could almost read her mind, but I had no idea what Katia was thinking.

"I'm going to open the door quickly. You pull the closest guy in, and Tonya and I will close the door again."

I rapidly pondered the idea and, since they had orders to take us alive, I concluded they wouldn't shoot at us. I nodded.

She opened the door, and I reached out to grab a fistful of clothing and pulled in the FOG member. One other snuck in behind before the door could be closed.

As I disarmed my guy, I saw Katia disarm the other, quickly placing her knife in between the man's ribs. He dropped to the floor.

I looked to her with surprise and smiled. She smiled. I couldn't help but laugh. *Maybe she is trained after all.*

She grabbed the doorknob again. "I believe we're down to six. Ready?"

I smiled and nodded. The door opened, but that time they were ready and pushed the door in further. I stabbed the first guy who entered. A woman followed behind, pushing herself in to meet Katia. Her neck met Katia's knife instead. Both fell to the ground as more swarmed into the room, pushing us back.

We got lucky with a few as they stumbled on the dead in the doorway and fell conveniently to the floor where we killed them with ease. We heard the mechanical sound of a gun being adjusted and moved out of the way as bullets sprayed inside. I darted along the side of the doorway, and Katia went behind it. Tonya remained behind Katia.

When the bullets stopped, I assumed they were changing magazines. I leaned out to see that I was right. I took out my knife, and it landed in the eye of the first gun carrier nearest us. Bullets rained into the door again.

"How many are out there?" Tonya asked.

"A few came up the steps down the hall. There are perhaps five now."

Tonya yelled out, "I thought we were to be taken alive! Why are you shooting at us?"

A voice from the hallway replied, "We're only to take *you* alive, General."

"Well, that explains the bullets," Katia said.

"We need to get to the war room," Tonya emphasized.

"What's so important in that war room?" I asked. "You already have all the intelligence you need right here."

She looked concerned and calmly replied, "We just need to get into that war room at all costs before the next wave of FOG forces arrives."

I looked around the room, trying to come up with an idea. I thought about using the table as a shield, but it would be too awkward to carry out the door. I looked to the wall adjacent to the door. "What's on the other side of this wall?" I asked Tonya.

"It's supposed to be my office. I haven't been in there since General Clayton…" She stopped herself.

I put my hand on her shoulder. "It's okay." I saw a white pillar against the wall with what looked like an expensive vase on top. I set the vase on the floor and lifted the pillar. It was quite heavy, even for me. I stood about ten feet away from that wall and said, "I'm going to punch a hole into the wall opposite the office. It should distract them long enough for you to throw a knife at one of them and close the door again."

I rammed the wall as hard as I could, causing the wall to crack. Tonya opened the door as Katia threw her knife.

"It worked!" Katia exclaimed as they closed the door.

I walked back and rammed it again, and the wall split even more, like an egg cracked against a table. Tonya opened the door while Katia was about to throw another knife but then stopped. "They're gone," she said.

I set the pillar down and looked out the door. There was no one there. A good tactic would have been for someone to remain in the hallway. Lucky for us, they weren't very bright.

"Stay here," I said.

I grabbed a sidearm from one of the FOG members lying on the floor and walked down the hallway. I suspected they were in the blown-up office waiting for me to come through the wall. I peered around the doorway and saw them kneeling behind a wooden desk with their guns pointed at the wall I'd hit.

I shot one, two, three, and when I saw the other two guns point toward me, I ducked back into the hallway as they began shooting. I motioned for Katia to come my way as I stood against the wall next to the open doorway.

I waited with my knife in my hand when I saw two FOG soldiers come up the steps. "Hey, you! Stop!" one of them yelled.

I held up my hands, and as one of the FOG men in the room stepped out, I put my knife through his throat and held him as a shield, just as I'd taught my students. His partner came out to jump me when Katia put her knife into his neck. The new arrivals fired at us, but they hit the dead human shield I held, allowing us to duck back into the office.

The door where Clayton had set off the bomb was destroyed so we couldn't close it. I quickly stuck my head out of the doorway, and just as I saw the FOG soldiers standing there, guns pointed in our direction, they fired. *That was too close.* All we could do was wait for them to get closer.

"The general's door is open," we heard from the direction of the stairs. "Quickly, get Colonel Mathews!"

Why didn't Tonya close the door to her quarters? We were trapped with a door that wouldn't close. Reinforcements were on the way, but Tonya was vulnerable. I looked around the room to find something I could use, but all I saw was charred debris. I thought about Colonel Clayton and how he went there to sacrifice himself for our cause. Everything could have gone so wrong had Strossler not been stopped. *What am I thinking? It still could go wrong.*

A voice down the hall said, "Two of them ducked into that room next to the general's quarters."

"This is Colonel Mathews speaking. You have no place to go. Surrender now, and we will allow you to live."

I looked to Katia, who whispered, "I have an idea."

She walked out before I could stop her. "I surrender. I'm alone."

"I saw two of you run into that room," one of the FOG soldiers said.

"We did, but my friend died. You shot him, you bastard." *She's not a very convincing actor.*

"Lie on the floor with your hands behind your head," someone yelled to her.

I was beside myself watching her lie down as she was told. I had no idea how many more were down the hall but knew it wasn't a good idea for Katia to put herself in such a vulnerable position. I considered lying down to fake being dead, but what if they shot me to confirm? I couldn't take the risk.

I heard the squeaks of rubber boots come down the hall. I stood against the narrow wall adjacent to the doorway and opposite the door to hide as best as I could.

"Don't hurt her. Colonel Mathews, I wish to speak with you in my quarters." It was Tonya's voice. *What's she doing?*

I realized I couldn't do anything without Katia being shot. Tonya was up to something, and I had to trust her judgement.

A gun came into the door, and the guy holding it turned and saw me. "Come out of there!" he yelled.

I'd never surrendered in my life and was furious to be in such a pathetic situation. *Where the hell is Mueller and his team?* My only hope was that Tonya had a plan, so I needed to follow along.

I complied and put my arms up. He took my sidearm and the remaining knife in my belt. Another FOG member grabbed Katia's sidearm and picked her up from the floor, pushing her forward.

I pressed my face into the guy holding Katia. "Don't hurt her, you bastard." My head ached after the butt of a gun smacked me in the back of the skull.

"Shut up and move," a man bellowed.

There were four FOG men toting guns and the colonel, who had a pistol in a holster strapped to his leg. We walked into Tonya's quarters, where she stood by the veranda. "General Skyler, I presume?" Colonel Mathews said.

"Colonel Mathews, welcome to our base. I would like to discuss your terms of surrender."

I grinned at how bold she could be, remembering all the past times where she'd made similar taunting remarks, but usually she just watched as I had to fight everyone.

Mathews smiled as the other FOG laughed. "General Skyler, the way I see it, you're currently my prisoner. Perhaps it's you who should be discussing surrender with me?"

Colonel Mathews walked toward her at the veranda as she looked out at the battlefield on the other side of the wall.

"From what I can see, your troops are nearly defeated, Colonel, and soon you will be dead as well, if you don't surrender now."

Colonel Mathews chuckled. "You have perhaps three thousand soldiers remaining. We have all of our forces from the entire eastern part of the country, just beyond our sight on the horizon, ready to clean everything up at my command."

"You're bluffing," Tonya challenged.

Mathews grabbed his radio from his belt. "This is Colonel Mathews. Have the reserve forces turn their headlights on."

Standing a few feet behind Tonya, I could see some lights in the distance. I watched her head scan the horizon and could tell she was in awe at the number of FOG out there. Nevertheless, she held on to her confidence.

Mathews said, "We have over twenty thousand troops lined up out there. We brought everyone from across America here to put an end to your resistance once and for all. You're completely surrounded. Surrender now, and we'll spare you and your people's lives."

Gunfire echoed down the hallway. I remembered Colonel Mueller was still downstairs trying to work his way up. Perhaps having fewer FOG to get through after our encounters would allow him to get to us more easily.

One of the men who kept his gun aimed at me walked out to the hallway. A gunshot echoed, and the man fell to the ground.

"General Skyler, are you all right?" It was Mueller's voice.

"Colonel Mueller, implement Operation Viper!" Tonya called out.

"Yes, ma'am!"

"No operation you could think of or implement will be successful!" Colonel Mathews exclaimed. "It will only cause more deaths for you and your people."

Tonya smirked. "Colonel Mathews, we will never give up. We'll die before we surrender to you, but perhaps you wouldn't mind me watching the demise of my base and people from this view?"

He returned her smirk. "Who am I to deny someone their final wish? And I would agree; this is a great view for you to watch your demise from."

I was aghast at what she'd said and had no idea what she was doing, but I'd learned to trust her with my life, and I knew she was the smartest and most cunning person I'd ever known.

I slowly walked up toward the veranda with my hands on my head.

"Stop there! Don't move," one of the guards said. Colonel Mathews looked to him and nodded that it was okay.

Katia and I walked closer. Just as we got to the veranda, I saw a plasma tank emerge from the tunnel and turn toward the gate. "A third one?" I asked.

"Yes, where did you get *your* tank, Colonel?" Tonya asked.

"I got it from the manufacturing facility just before we came to the base. They took us up on our offer to save them from slaughter. It's a shame you didn't take the same advice," Mathews replied.

We watched the tank move to the gate's entrance, which I knew was well protected with its defensive systems.

Colonel Mathews said, "Even with its defense systems, what good is a single tank when everyone else in this base will be dead, General? Please, surrender and save your peoples' lives."

We saw a flash from the tank followed by a distant explosion among the reserve forces. A truck must have been hit.

Colonel Mathews appeared angered. "I'm sorry it had to come down to this, General Skyler." He pulled out his radio and said, "Implement Operation Cleansing."

"Understood. No survivors?" the other voice asked through the radio.

Mathews looked at me, Katia, then Tonya. "No survivors," he confirmed.

"Copy, no survivors."

"Now General, as it was written in 'The Art of War' you'll see the real FOG of War." Mathews smiled smugly to Tonya.

"Thank you, Colonel," Tonya said.

I saw Tonya grab his radio and throw it into the darkness over the veranda. She pulled out a knife and held it to Mathew's throat. "Put down your guns or he dies."

Mathews laughed. "It's no use, General. You're all dead. They're following my orders as we speak." He nodded to the guards, who set their guns down to the floor.

"Well done, Colonel. Now, why don't you come with me, and we'll show you the art of deception, or perhaps the art of entrapment, either way, I'll show you how this really ends."

Tonya walked by me and looked into my eyes markedly, then to the other guards. I knew what she wanted. As Tonya and Mathews walked out, I grabbed one guard and snapped his neck. Katia punched the one nearest her in the throat, then rapidly hit her with an open hand, forcing the soldier's nose into her skull. They both fell to the floor.

The last remaining guard pulled out a handgun and took a shot at Katia, nicking her arm. In rage, I ran to him, grabbed his throat, and slammed him into the wall so hard that I completely crushed his windpipe with my hand. He, too, fell to the floor, holding his throat and gasping for air.

Katia picked up a sidearm and shot him in the head. "There, no more suffering," she said. I grabbed her arm, pulled her close, and kissed her. I couldn't believe how much more adoration I had for her.

"I didn't think I could love you more than I already did." I kissed her again.

She grinned, "Perhaps we both changed a little over our experiences." She kissed me back, and we left the room.

We walked to the war room, and Katia entered the code to the secured door. Colonel Mueller was seated in front of a computer terminal. *Katia has the code to this room? I don't even have this code.*

Tonya, Mathews, and Colonel Krueger stood in front of the map table, and Sergeant Baylor was in the room with a protective vest and a rifle.

"Where are my men?" Mathews asked.

"They won't be joining us," Katia said while smiling at me. I couldn't help but smile back.

Tonya said, "Colonel Mueller, would you mind showing us the big picture?"

Mueller moved his fingers on a display screen, and the map table opened to reveal a large video that showed the entire area centered on the compound and expanded about a kilometer. I was in awe by the view of all the FOG forces in a red glow driving toward the base. There were a lot of them, and I could even see small red dots inside the compound.

"This is a secret program General Strossler created to protect this compound from any kind of attack," Tonya explained. "I heard of it while I worked for him, but I wasn't sure what it really was until Colonel Krueger confirmed it and showed it to me recently. What you're looking at is a satellite video feed using an infrared camera to see in the dark."

"Regardless of whatever secret program you think you have, we have you outnumbered ten to one. Your screen will just show all of your people dying," Mathews said.

I was a little concerned, watching thousands of small red dots representing FOG forces approaching the compound. The tank was guarding the open gate, but it wouldn't prevent that many forces from running through.

There was a large red flash centered on the plasma tank and then a bright red glow about a half-kilometer away. The forces branched off and split to surround the base as they got nearer.

Another red flash lit up the screen with another explosion. It would take forever for our plasma tank to destroy all the red dots I saw on the display.

We watched in silence as FOG surrounded the base. There were so many; they were layered five rows deep and completely surrounded us. I didn't see any way for us to survive.

Small red flashes flickered on the display from the many vehicles in front of the tank. They were apparently firing at it, but I knew it wouldn't do any good. We saw smaller dots surround the vehicles outside of the gate, and I realized their troops were dismounting from the vehicles.

Tonya nodded to Krueger, then calmly said, "Now, you'll see why I offered to let you surrender earlier, Colonel Mathews. I learned a lot about the defensive system of this base. Strossler anticipated to lead from here for a very long time. He funneled funds to a secret program to take the technology from the plasma tanks and turn it into a defensive system around the base."

I could see concern on Mathews's face as a yellow glow formed around the walls of the compound on the map.

"It's a shame you ordered your troops to allow no survivors. You helped me make the same decision." Tonya nodded to Krueger.

I stared at the display on the table as small red flashes strobed along the walls of the compound, along with red flashes among the FOG forces surrounding the base. The glow surrounding the base grew and grew, almost like a bright red donut. A couple of FOG vehicles tried to leave but were destroyed instantly. I couldn't believe that so many FOG troops were getting killed, but then it dawned on me how things could have been the other way around had General Clayton not sacrificed himself to kill General Strossler. I couldn't imagine what might have happened had he not given his life for our cause.

Katia reached for my hand. I looked at her as I held her hand in return and whispered, "I didn't ask last time, but I will now. Will you marry me?"

"Mmhmm," she whimpered with a small smile on her face and nodded. I saw a tear form in her eye as she glanced up at me. She gripped my hand even tighter as I became consumed with pride.

The plasma guns on the wall stopped flashing on the screen in front of us. There was a red glow surrounding the base, but more red dots outside of it moved slowly.

"Colonel Krueger, is there a problem? Why did the guns stop?" Tonya asked.

"Ma'am, it shows online, but I think the fires from the vehicles are masking the remaining troops from the targeting system."

"Well, it looks like we know one flaw in the system. Send our forces out to open fire on them while they're disoriented."

"Yes, ma'am."

"Colonel Mathews, I'm sure you'd like to reconsider your surrender now, but that time has passed. Sergeant Baylor, would you arrest Colonel Mathews and escort him outside to the courtyard under guard?"

"Yes, ma'am." Sergeant Baylor took out a plastic zip tie from his belt and tied Mathews's hands behind his back, grabbed his arm, and pulled him out of the room.

I asked Tonya, "Why didn't you use this system earlier when we were nearly defeated in the first wave?"

She looked at me and nodded. "I couldn't take the risk. If I'd used this defensive system on that wave, the final wave wouldn't have attacked. I had to take the chance and ensure I got all of them, and it worked. It worked thanks to you, Zack."

I nodded my understanding, but I was still shocked that she'd put us at risk like that. I thought of the lost lives that could have been avoided had she used the system earlier.

"What will you do with Colonel Mathews?" Katia asked.

"He will be executed with the others we round up," Tonya replied.

"Perhaps you might show leniency to those who surrender and want to change?" Katia said. "Some may have been forced to join FOG against their will."

Tonya looked to her, then to me, and walked back to her quarters without saying a word. I wasn't sure if she was upset with Katia's recommendation or whether she'd left to ponder it in privacy, but it was unlike her to leave a question unanswered.

Katia and I walked down to the courtyard and saw the light of dawn brighten the horizon. But then we looked at the death and destruction all around us. It was devastating, with dead bodies and destroyed vehicles everywhere.

"It'll take a long time to clean this mess," Katia said with a somber voice as we scanned the courtyard. Brilliant rays of sun shone in the early morning sky.

We could hear gunfire outside the compound, and soon a few hundred prisoners were guided through the gate with their hands zip-tied behind their backs. They were escorted to the middle of the compound and forced to their knees. The ADS troops surrounded the group and pointed their guns at them.

Tonya walked out onto her veranda. Colonel Mathews was taken to the middle of the compound on the other side of the group. A guard escorted him and placed him against a burned-out truck.

There wasn't a sound other than some secondary explosions in the distance, no doubt from ammo in a truck that was on fire.

Tonya announced, "Colonel Mathews, I called the President of the United States to let him know our status and how you had ordered the death of all the people within this compound. He finds you guilty of treason, and you are to be executed immediately. Do you have any last words?"

"You will all destroy this planet if you go back to your old ways. We were trying to save our world!"

She replied, "If you look at the world today, can you actually say you were saving it?"

He looked away from her.

She nodded to Baylor. "Ready… aim… fire!" Three soldiers shot at Mathews, who slumped to the ground. Fear among all the prisoners was evident from their faces. Like Katia, I didn't necessarily agree with executing all the prisoners.

They were a mix of men and women, some seemed to be in their twenties, probably recruited or indoctrinated young. Some of the men were older. The older men wore uniforms, but most of FOG wore normal street clothes or some combination of camouflage and T-shirt.

I remembered Surgy and the three men on the road to Xima. I recalled seeing hope in their eyes, but Tonya had been hesitant to allow them to live. I'd decided to give them a chance. After what we'd encountered so far on Earth, I wasn't sure I'd made the right decision, but I'd felt it was right at the time.

"For the rest of you: You are among the remaining of a large force who were ordered not to allow any survivors. Some of the ADS believe the same order should be applied to you."

Tonya looked to Katia. I could see a small smile on her face. Katia smiled back at her.

"Who among you wishes to renounce your commitment to FOG and come with us to live again in peace? If you wish to change your loyalties without reservation, stand now."

Many looked at each other. A woman was the first to stand, followed by another woman, and then a man, then many others. Perhaps fifty people stood. We waited a few moments for more, but the rest remained seated—mostly the older men in uniforms.

"You, the one farthest to the right, why do you wish to change?"

The woman looked up to Tonya and said, "Our small city was overwhelmed when I was a teenager ten years ago. Many of our parents were killed, and we were given a chance to join their cause and live, or else die—just like the option you're giving us now."

There was a long pause. What the woman said hit me like a board to the head. *Are we forcing them to change their ideology or else be killed, just like FOG did to them?* I would have liked to think we were freeing them, and I hoped Tonya believed the same.

Tonya replied, "What FOG has done over the decades of fighting has killed many innocent people, destroyed crops, and destroyed animals all because they thought their way was right. What's left is nothing less than death and destruction throughout the world. Perhaps we need to change our ways of living, for to live in fear as many have over the years is not living."

There was a pause again as Tonya looked to me and Katia. She appeared in deep thought.

"Those of you standing. Move toward the wall of that building." She pointed to the building next to Katia and me.

Once they were along the wall behind us, Tonya looked down to those below. "The choice I'm giving you is not the same. The choice I'm giving you is to live freely—not to join another faction, and not to follow me. We want you to have the freedom this country was built on and for all of you to forge your own destinies."

She looked down to the remainder in the courtyard. "The others will be executed for their treason. A special confidant advised me to show compassion for those who deserve it." She smiled at Katia again.

"Sergeant Baylor, escort the traitors out of this base."

"Yes, ma'am!"

Baylor and some of the other troops drove the remaining FOG soldiers up and pushed them to walk out of the gate. There was a long pause, then a couple of random gunshots. Tonya walked back into her quarters, and soon the sober sound of gunfire echoed outside the compound.

Tonya walked out of the archway at the bottom of the building toward those who decided to live. One of the survivors cried out, "You didn't have to kill them!"

Tonya walked up to her. "You're right, I didn't have to, but I needed to. Like a body with cancer, the body might heal over time with slow and steady treatment, but sometimes you need to remove it entirely to ensure the body doesn't die first. What happened has taught us valuable lessons, which we will apply when we rebuild this world, but what FOG did exceeded the essence of humanity. Humanity deserves better than to kill innocent people or eradicate all crops and livestock. We will consider the errors of the past as we build a new future. General Strossler was going to become the leader of the entire world with what he was developing, if he had been successful with his plan."

She walked toward us. "Thank you, Zack and Katia. I owe you my life, and the country owes you its gratitude. The president will be here tomorrow to thank you in person."

I looked to Katia, who smiled and then looked to me.

"What of us?" one of the surrendered asked.

Tonya looked to them, then called out to a guard. "Cut their bindings and let them go free."

Then she looked to them. "You're free: free to stay here, free to leave and go back to what homes you had, or free to go wherever you want. If you decide to stay here, we can provide you shelter and food if you help us clean this mess."

The guard cut zip ties, and the one woman who seemed to represent them said, "Thank you, General Skyler. I, for one, will stay and help until I figure out what to do next."

She nodded and then walked back to the headquarters building. She stopped and looked back to us, motioning for us to follow her. We walked her way and followed to her quarters. ADS troops were dragging bodies through the hallway as they cleaned up from the long night.

We arrived at her quarters, and Tonya asked, "What would you two like to do now?"

I looked to Katia, who smiled back at me. "We'd like to get married," I said.

Tonya smiled. "I thought you might say that. I'd be happy to officiate that myself tomorrow, if you'd like."

I looked to Katia, who held my hand tightly and nodded quickly.

I looked back to Tonya and added, "Yes, that would be incredible."

"Go get some sleep. The others will clean this place. Relax, and we'll see you tomorrow."

Katia walked up and gave Tonya a hug. She let go, and then I went up to hug Tonya too. I could see a tear in her eye as I reached in to embrace her. My eyes were blurred a little from tears as well. I realized I still loved Tonya, but my destiny was with Katia, whom I loved even more.

Chapter 28

I woke to see Katia staring at me. Her face brightened as I smiled at her. "I have never woken to such a beautiful sight in my life," I whispered. My mind was bewildered, almost like everything else had been a dream and my reality came back with her next to me.

"That's the most romantic thing I've ever heard," she said leaning in to softly kiss my lips. Her lips were so soft, and I realized I'd craved her for a long time.

"Let's get up; the president will be here soon," she said.

We cleaned up, got dressed, and walked out to the courtyard. Other than the stains from the dead on the ground, everything looked clean.

A mass grave was dug outside of the base, and all the destroyed vehicles were pushed into a junk heap to be salvaged later. Katia and I looked up at Tonya's veranda to see her standing there. She motioned for us to come up.

We walked into her quarters and saw several men in suits standing in the room. "This is Zack Bates, the one who saved us here and helped on Xima," Tonya said to one of the men. She continued, "And this is Katia, who was also critical in protecting me and saving this base. Zack and Katia, this is President Cooper."

He reached out his hand, and I shook it. "Hello, Mr. President." He shook Katia's hand also.

"Hello to you, Zack and Katia. When General Skyler first came to me for authorization to find you after she told me what happened to your father, I was hesitant, but her intuition paid off. You saved all of us, Zack, and your work here will help shape the future of our world. I couldn't possibly make up for what you've gone through for all of us, but I'll try. What can I do for you?"

I looked to Tonya, who nodded. Then I looked down to Katia, who also smiled at me. I remembered Xima and what it might be like to go back there with Katia by my side—the beauty the planet had to offer and how we could help the people who lived there.

"Sir, I'd like to marry Katia." She held my hand. "And then I'd like for us to go back to Xima. I know a piece of land there where we could live very happily together." I smiled at Tonya, who smiled back.

"Well, as for marriage, I believe General Skyler has the authority to marry you. And regarding Xima, I'd like to offer you the chance for something even grander."

He walked up to me and placed his hand on my shoulder. "Zack, you've proved yourself loyal in many ways both here and on Xima. We could use you to help train and lead our new future on Earth, but I admire your wishes. Xima needs good leadership also, and I'd like you to be the President of Xima. We need someone to bring peace, prosperity, and morality there, and I think you're just the person for the job. We could have you married today and then on a shuttle that leaves from the western launch site tomorrow." He looked to Tonya, who nodded to confirm.

I looked to Tonya, who looked to be waiting for me to accept. I turned my gaze to Katia. She grinned broadly.

"I accept your offer, Mr. President. We would be happy to help shape Xima for the better."

"Excellent! I'll provide you with the declaration papers and orders. In the meantime, I'm only here today, so if it's acceptable to the three of you, I'd enjoy watching you two become husband and wife."

Katia jumped on me, wrapping her arms around my neck. "Yes! Yes! Yes!"

I smiled with tears welling in my eyes. "I think we'd like that very much, Mr. President."

The ADS guards who had fought with us were in the courtyard, as well as those who were previously members of FOG, to witness the wedding. The woman who had told Tonya why she wanted to leave FOG handed Katia the wedding ring from her finger.

"Please, take this ring for your wedding. It was from my husband who was killed by FOG. I believe you helped save many of us, and I want you to know how much we appreciated what you've done."

Katia broke down in tears and pulled the woman in for a hug. "Thank you so very much."

Tonya's ceremony was simple and quick. We said our vows, and we exchanged rings. Colonel Mueller gave his ring to me, and it was my honor to wear it.

When she was finished, her final words were the traditional, "I now pronounce you man and wife. Zack, you may kiss your bride."

Tonya walked up to give each of us a hug. I smiled at Katia while holding her hand. She was elated and had tears running down her cheeks.

"Why don't the two of you celebrate your marriage in the VIP quarters tonight, and I'll see you to the shuttle launch in the morning." We thanked her and quickly made our way to the room to celebrate our union.

We met Tonya the next morning in the courtyard with simple backpacks, each with enough clothes and toiletries to last for the three-month journey back to Xima. I trusted Tonya would ensure sufficient food, water, and oxygen for our trip, as I didn't plan to be in a sleep chamber.

Colonel Mueller pulled up with an armored Humvee. I laughed softly. "An armored vehicle to escort us to the launch site?"

Mueller replied, "It's not for you two. The president appointed General Skyler to four stars, and she's to lead the effort across the rest of the world to eradicate the remaining FOG organizations."

I looked to Tonya. "Wow, congratulations!"

"Thank you, but I couldn't have made it without you, Zack. We've been able to replicate that device your father developed. We're going to develop an army to help with our effort and keep the world peaceful for decades to come."

I looked at where the device was once in my own arm and stared at the tattoo in its place. "Will its effect diminish in me?" I asked.

"Not at all. It was designed to stimulate growth for years past puberty. You should retain everything you've gained, except perhaps your constitution, so don't be too reckless out there."

I laughed. "It shouldn't be as much of a problem without someone antagonizing the adversaries."

We all laughed as we arrived at the site. I stepped out of the vehicle and looked up at the shuttle about to launch.

Colonel Mueller opened the trunk of the vehicle and pulled out a couple of swords. Tonya took them and gave one to each of us. I took mine out and remembered the ones Tonya had pulled out of the wall.

She said, "You may need these before you get to the cabin." I smiled as Katia took hers halfway out to see its beauty in the sunlight.

Tonya continued, "Zack, I want Katia to have my sword and shield which is where we left them. I wish you both success. I'm afraid greed has made Xima unstable again since we've been gone."

I shook Colonel Mueller's hand, and he said, "Live well, Zack. We owe you everything." He gave Katia a hug.

I looked to Tonya, who had tears forming in her eyes. I walked up to give her a hug. She whispered, "I'll always love you, Zack. Continue to make me proud." She stepped back and held Katia in her arms. "I just might come out there to inspect your work, so make sure he does well, Katia."

We laughed as Katia hugged her tightly. "I'll kick his ass if he doesn't," she said, causing all of us to laugh.

There were enough supplies and oxygen onboard for us and the pilot to stay awake during the entire trip to Xima. We exercised and sparred with each other as much as we could, trying to maintain our dexterity on what would otherwise have been a very boring trip.

Part of our cargo consisted of hand tools for farming and seeds to plant crops. There were some additional forging tools to help us make our own tools and equipment on the planet using ginnium.

The trip seemed to take much longer than I remembered. It was even longer for Katia, as she'd been asleep for both of her trips. When we were finally descending to the landing zone, I could see so much more of the planet than what I'd seen while on the ground. It was vast. There were large bodies of water and land yet to explore. The pilot radioed in our arrival once we were within range, and we were strapped in for the turbulent descent.

The shuttle landed with a firm and familiar *thud.* The engines shut down, and the pilot unstrapped himself from his seat. We unstrapped ourselves as well, donned our belts, swords, and slipped our knives into our belt and boot sheaths while the pilot unlocked the large cargo door.

We watched the door open and could hear talking outside. I remembered leaving Rob as mayor to push for peace on Xima, but then again, *someone* had warned ADS I was arriving back to Earth, and that had to have come from Lauri, so I had some reservations.

The door lowered to the docking platform, where we saw twenty men with swords pointed at us. They all looked like the ragged wretches I remembered taking out in the past. I saw Mayor Rob standing behind them. We remained quiet for a moment as I tried to assess what was about to happen.

Mayor Rob yelled, “Arrest them!”

I looked to Katia with a competitive grin. “Ready?”

She smiled back at me while taking out her sword and replied, “Let’s go!”

Made in the USA
Middletown, DE
05 October 2023